The Pactbound Angel

The Soul Mirror Duet, Volume 1

S.J. Brown

Published by S.J. Brown, 2025.

This is a work of fiction. Similarities to real people, places, or events are entirely coincidental.

THE PACTBOUND ANGEL

First edition. September 8, 2025.

Copyright © 2025 S.J. Brown.

ISBN: 979-8999853202

Written by S.J. Brown.

Trigger Warnings

Your mental health is important. Please read the below if you need to, skip if you don't.

- Animal cruelty/abuse
- Domination/submission
- Orgasm denial
- Emotional abuse/manipulation (not by main characters)
- Sexually explicit scenes
- Violence
- PTSD and Anxiety/panic attacks
- *Slight* dismemberment

Table of Contents

To Jenna, the real angel who loved me enough to push, nag, and cajole me into finishing this book. This one's for you, sis.

DULON
LORIL
BALINGUA
EVRAKA
JORNA
ROWIN
FOMONA
LASWA
LAETH
PIDANTAR

FEAWAR
SHAVALAR
PULDONI
GHAU
ELANCIA
CARPATHA
THAEBA
KOPI
THE FEYLANDS
TALOQUA

Prologue

The enraged shriek echoed throughout the massive cavern long after the druid had departed in a flash of green light. A derisive chuckle replied, "Well, at least she's pretty. She has that going for her." Resa hoisted the bloodied great axe onto her shoulder and grinned wolfishly. "I didn't expect her to be such a sore loser."

Max nodded, though his eyes crinkled at the edges in amusement. He put the second fist-sized glowing orb, its radiant golden light casting shadows on the cavern wall, gingerly into his pack. "But we got what we came for, and not without a small amount of trouble for it. At least they'll now be in safe hands."

Resa lifted her head as their priest, a heavily-bearded man wearing dusty robes, called out his report. "All are alive and accounted for, sir."

"Thank you, Rhogar." Max stretched his white wings as he stood, a few feathers ruffled from the brutal fight. "Alive. That's all we could hope for."

Resa sighed. "Wistran better keep their promise, Max. That greedy fey king agreed a little too quickly to house one of those orbs for my liking." She scowled. "You don't think he'll sell it, do you?"

Max huffed a laugh. "No, love. He won't sell it. He'll hoard it like a dragon with a mountain of precious gems. He'll keep it close, if for no other reason than to be known as the one who has it. Besides, Camlynn will have the other. I just hope that'll be enough distance between the two halves of the relic." The protector kissed her on the cheek as he walked past, giving an absent rub to her still-flat belly.

Resa smiled at the gesture. "Good. Much as I like a decent fight, I don't want to have to face her again. We have more important things to do now."

Max stopped and turned to speak over his shoulder. Exhaustion dulled his golden eyes. "She was cowed. We'll never see her again."

Resa ambled up to him and slid her hand into his. "You don't really believe that, do you?" she said quietly.

Max gazed down at her and paused before replying, "No."

A flash of green light preceded the druid's arrival into her small cottage. She stood frozen, shaking from battle fatigue and worse. Even the familiar scent of chamomile, hanging in small bunches from her rafters, failed to calm her.

Her fine robes were dirty and bloodied, her green hair tangled and wild. She ached from bruises and barely-healed wounds, but none of them compared to the burning emptiness in her chest. None of them compared to the rage hanging in her throat like a heavy lump, nearly choking her.

The cheerful chirping of birds outside was the only sound until she hurled her broken staff across the open room into the cold hearth with another harsh, frustrated scream. The staff hit with an unsatisfying clank against the stone of the fireplace and fell to the ground, as dead and useless as her plans now were.

The Twin Spheres were gone. And in the hands of meddling bastards who had no real idea what they held.

She closed her eyes and sucked in a calming breath. Letting it out slowly, she opened her eyes to a new world. A new plan. She just had to be patient and wait for her opportunity.

And, in the meantime, find out where the Twin Spheres were being taken next.

Chapter One

Stories Best Forgotten

"Moral o' the story, fellas. Don't run into a brothel with yer ass on fire. Uhm, beggin' yer pardon, m'lady." The guard across the fire from me held out a hand in my direction.

An almost-smile twitched my lips. There was no point in chiding their rough speech. It wouldn't work anyway. My longsword slid the rest of the way into its scabbard, the whetstone having sharpened it to my satisfaction, and I looked up.

My amusement dwindled when the other guards around the campfire turned my way. Wondering why they were all staring at me, and feeling more than a little self-conscious, I frowned at each of their expectant faces.

In the silence, the soft braying of mules and oxen, the conversations and laughter of other nearby guards, and the crackle of logs splitting seemed to emphasize the quiet of our huddled group. The wind blew the smoke from the fire into my face, causing me to jerk my head with a grimace. *Why does it always seem to follow me?*

"Your turn, celestial. You've never told one," prompted Rorm, the guard standing off to my left side. "A real one, anyway."

Oh.

My preference would've been for him to use my name instead of my heritage, but I wasn't going to make a fuss. Some called me celestial. Few called me Nathalia. Others, m'lady. Hearing them all in one form or another became second nature.

A puff of breath lifted a lock of my hair as I considered what story to tell.

It had become a tradition for guards in our caravan to tell at least one story from their past after we'd cared for the draft animals and eaten our supper. An anecdote. A joke, even. I wasn't much for telling jokes. I didn't remember them well enough to do them justice, and embellishment wasn't possible. Tales I'd written long ago, barely remembered fables penned by a child's hand, were never received well. "Dull with no flavor," one painfully honest guard had said.

Everyone's a critic.

My stories *were* dull and lifeless for a reason I didn't like to think about. Nevertheless, it was the only story that came to mind.

I picked up a heavy stick and poked the fire's logs, unsure what else to do with my hands. The soot from it stained my palm, making me regret picking it up at all. "I was nine and heading to my studies. A carnival had been set up just outside Rowin's walls in Camlynn, and I could see the high tops from our villa's tallest window. I asked my father if we could go, but he forbade it."

A few of the newer guards rolled their eyes, perhaps taking me for some sort of spoiled princess. Maybe they figured this would be a story of the time I broke a nail. Or even dirtied my shoes. I wished it were that kind of story.

The older guards, however, leaned forward to listen.

"My curiosity won out over my obedience. I convinced my sister Raewyn to go to the traveling faire, without our mother and father. We snuck out of our villa, managing to avoid our governess's watchful eye. I paid our entrance fee from my allowance, and we ran in, intent on feasting on fried sweet breads, flossed candy, and whatever else we could get our hands on. We never won any games, but that did not stop us from trying. I spent every coin I had in an attempt to win a stuffed animal for Raewyn."

Deep breath.

"When all our money was gone, our bellies full to the brim with food we were not normally allowed to eat, we decided to go into the Hall of Mirrors. It was the last thing open that was free. We ran around, laughing, watching ourselves get skinnier, older, fatter, taller in the mirrors. But we soon got confused and lost our way. That's when we heard the cackling. It seemed to echo from all sides. Around us, behind us."

I stared into the fire, hoping the heat would dry my eyes and prevent the tears that were threatening to well in them.

"We tried to find the entrance but could not. And, then, we saw her. Her unnaturally green eyes radiated malevolence. The mirrors in the area seemed to multiply her, reflecting the mischief hag in their surfaces. I couldn't tell which reflection was attacking us until it was too late. I hugged my sister to protect her, calm her cries, but it did not matter. We were cornered."

All of the guards were now listening. Attentive. Some part of me appreciated that.

"If you don't know about mischief hags, they take things. Not just prized possessions, but capability. Prowess. Any ability or innate gift, they can steal. Like your sword skill, Rorm. Or your whittling, Maya." My eyes flicked to the guard sitting off to the side, who abruptly stopped carving her block of wood with a frown.

"Created by spiteful druids, they spread misery wherever they go. This particular mischief hag cursed us to ruin. I used to write songs, poetry, everything I could think of. She took it. Never again would I write stories or ballads, she said. Never again would I possess creativity. The stories I've told to you up to now, the dull ones. I wrote those when I was nine years of age. They were some of the last things I wrote." I shook my head. "And my poor sister. She was so lovely. She was cursed with horrible facial scars, which she had to hide behind a half-mask. When we managed to get home, my father was...displeased."

Volcanic, really. Normally a calm man, he roared the night my sister was harmed as my mother tried to comfort her. I'll never forget the look of utter disappointment in his eyes, the gold in them mirroring my own.

I poked the fire again and cleared my burning throat. "It nearly broke me. The one true gift I claimed as my own was gone, and no amount of pleading or wishing would bring it back."

My pause made those around me lean in.

"So, what happened next?" Maya asked, her block of wood forgotten.

My reply was barely louder than a mumble, "I'll not continue. That is the end."

There was no proper way to tell the guards around me the next part, about how I wanted to master something else: my future. It was far too personal. Far too intimate. How if I could not be happy, then I would make another happy. A big part of growing up in the service of Horyn, the God of Protection, was knowing my time would come for me to take up my father's mantle.

Only I didn't want to. Not exactly. My wishes were for what my parents had: a clean, quiet, comfortable existence.

My parents were always affectionate with each other. Always beaming when one looked at the other. They loved deeply and showed it often. An nagging part of me knew that was how I could be happy. So, that became my end goal: to marry someone of my station, have children, and live a nice life.

There was just one problem. A suitable husband was required and, bless them all, no young man in Camlynn fit the bill. Most were either enamored with my unusual coloring, my last name, or my heritage, and not necessarily in that order. None cared to know me. Looking to my parents again for inspiration, realization struck. They met while traveling together. Perhaps I, too, needed to set out to find my future.

The only trouble was that traveling is a dirty, nasty business. Putting aside my disgust, and packing not a small amount of soap, I set out with my parents' blessings.

"You'll find him," said my mother. She unhooked a plain necklace with a smoky gem off her own neck and placed it around mine. "So, you'll have the luck I did."

My father was more pragmatic. "Defend those who cannot defend themselves, and safeguard your virtue, for it is a precious thing."

Meeting all sorts of people from around Laeth, perhaps even some from the Feylands if they had the ability to travel here, would be productive and efficient. I'd find my intended within a few weeks, perhaps a month at the latest. Whoever it was. Because that's what the stories said. You always find who you are meant to. It's an inevitability.

Instead, all I found is that if you are tired enough, a rock will serve as a pillow. Hunger is the best seasoning. There is no pleasure greater than the sudden absence of pain. And traveling is a very lonely business, even when surrounded by people.

Laughter jolted me out of my memories. My thumb brushed the gray stone dangling from my throat before I tucked it back underneath my armor.

"Well! I guess it's my turn again! So, no shit, there I was. Camped out at the entrance of a sapper's tunnel trying to get into the city..." The guard, Elijah, turned to me with a sorrowful face. "Sorry, m'lady. T'was the Siege of Rowin I be talkin' about here. Decades ago, aye, but I remember it like it was yesterday." Elijah stroked his gray beard.

Though Rowin had been rebuilt, buildings in the capital city of Camlynn still bore the scars of that war. Still, there was little point in holding onto a grudge. "I hold no ill will, Master Elijah. It was long ago, as you said."

"Ah, right. Well, all were just beddin' down, like. It got quiet, so quiet. I was on my watch shift and up comes this broodling, walkin' into camp like it was his home. He smiled at me. I could see his long canines and curled horns. Unnerved me, it did! But when he spoke, it was so calming. I listened, despite myself. Told me his name was Ramiren. He snapped his fingers and whoosh! I was elsewhere, in a room with a table, chairs, and wine. Oh, the wine was good. Better than this shite." He took a drink from his wineskin to the sound of an amused audience.

"Anyway, we played cards and talked. He wasn't very good, mind. I beat him almost every hand. But you don't go braggin' to a fellow like that. Elijah Callan ain't no fool. I simply chuckled and asked him to pour more wine in recompense. He laughed and did so. The evening went on. I knew I shoulda been watchin' the camp, but this fellow was such fine company that I didn't want to leave."

Elijah took another hefty swig and wiped his mouth.

"I told him I just wanted to make it out alive, ya know? Make it back home to my missus. He got a serious look on his face and asked what I would give for that. Thinkin' he was joshin' me, I said, 'All the money I had.' He replied, 'the pact is sealed.' I looked at him all dumbfounded, and he asked me to repeat the words. I blubbered 'em, but I said 'em. Then, his eyes just lit up like a lantern. He extended his hand and, bless me, I gave him my gold. I don't know what got into me, but it seemed as natural as breathin'. He told me to stay at the back of the line the next day. He snapped his fingers again, and there I was again. Back in camp. It was still dark out. Everyone still asleep. I even checked the time candle. Not a single nail had dropped since I went into that room, fellas. I swear to ya. When my watch ended, I didn't get a wink o' sleep."

A haunted look passed over Elijah's face. "The next day, the sapper tunnel caved in. Only I made it out." The old guard brought the wineskin back to his mouth but did not drink.

Someone asked if it was fate, or if this Ramiren had caused it.

Elijah shook his head and replied in a mutter, as though he no longer wanted to tell the story. "He dealt fairly with me, that broodling. I went home to my missus."

He downed what was left of his wine.

Three years later, I was once again guarding a wagon train traveling along the outskirts of the Irenian Swamp. Having long gone numb to the routine, my life at least had the predictability I craved. Arrive at a city, find a caravan charter, sign up, travel. Rinse and repeat.

My caravan master called a stop to trade with another caravan headed in the opposite direction, though for what I couldn't tell and it wasn't my business to ask. Their load appeared lighter with a few passengers taking advantage of the warm weather and dry roads.

Staying alert for trouble or an ambush, this road was a popular one for highway bandits looking for a quick bit of coin. My eyes fell on a woman with long auburn hair, wearing the red robes of a Minuen priestess, ambling along the carts. Her back was turned to me as she peeked inside the overloaded wagons. Curiosity mixed with a strange sense of familiarity made me step closer. She straightened and half-turned in my direction, showing a familiar half-mask adorning her face. In shock, I blurted out, "Raewyn?"

The masked woman spun around, and her eyes went wide. "Nat?"

My slack-jawed gaze rested on my sister for the first time in years, since her temple training began. The rare communication I could send often didn't come with a reply, but I chalked that up to my moving around so often. She was here now, though, and that was all that mattered. Raewyn had grown into a full-fledged priestess of Minue, and the Goddess of Love and Beauty had been kind to her. Her porcelain mask still covered her scars, making her look regal. *Always lovely.*

My amazement hushed my words. "What are you doing here, Raewyn?" Taking her soft hands in mine, I spread her arms wide to get a good look at her. What a beautiful woman she grew into. Far more than me, though I admitted my bias. Her hair, so much like our mother's, was artfully curled about her shoulders. Warm brown eyes that could be mistaken for gold in the right light met mine with a hint of impish mischief in them.

She chuckled. "Oh, just traveling from Evraka for the church. I trained some noble girls there. What are you doing here, Nat?" Her lips pursed as she looked over my armor, reaching out with one hand to touch my shield and weapon. She grimaced, rubbing her fingers together when the oil I used to keep my equipment rust-free dirtied them. She wiped her hand on my sleeve, trying to make it seem like an affectionate gesture. "Isn't this beneath you? Guarding caravans?" She removed her other hand from mine and looked behind me at the wagon train.

My tongue clicked in disapproval. I followed her line of sight and turned back to her. "All deserve protection, Raewyn. Remember Father's teachings."

She shrugged, adjusting the red shawl around her shoulders. "If you say so. Me, I remember Mom's teachings. All are deserving of love."

All are deserving of either a kiss to the forehead... or an axe to the face. My mother had been half-joking when she said that, as she kissed my forehead.

My eyebrow raised in challenge while my arms crossed. "Mother never said love."

"Well, maybe not to *you*." She grinned teasingly. She patted my hand like an affectionate grandmother. "You deserve it, Nat. You just need to learn how to give and receive it."

"Love?"

"No. Oral pleasure." Her grin widened, biting her lip at my no-doubt exasperated expression. "Yes. Love. But the aforementioned oral pleasure might do you some good, too."

Though protection was intrinsically an act of self-sacrifice, a kind of love where you put another's worth above your own, what Raewyn meant was different.

But what did I know? Aside from my family, love had only been something I'd read about, never experienced. Putting my shield in a weapon's path for another's benefit, I would argue, was a form of love. And I'd certainly never been *in* love. Infatuations, sure, but never that. Inspiration had never prompted me to give it.

Raewyn departed her caravan to join ours. Her former escort faded into the distance, and we continued toward our ultimate destination of Evraka. After stowing her small pack into a wagon, Raewyn and I caught up. She spoke of Camlynn, of our parents and how they were doing. My four other siblings had reportedly sprouted like weeds in the year I'd last seen them.

I told her of my travels and the difficulties I had faced. She seemed to be half-listening to my accounts of other guards, bandits, and the occasional battle, but in her defense, my tellings sounded more like a registrar report than a story. Soon after, we found ourselves, our caravan, alone on the wide road. It was silent aside from the lull of animals and wagon wheels. It felt like the calm before a storm. I didn't like it.

Something is wrong.

Sidling up to the head wagon, I murmured to Simar, the caravan master, who sat perched up on the wagon's riser, "Look sharp, sir. Something's amiss."

Simar looked over his shoulder and called out, "All hands, look alive!" I took my shield off my back as my sister stood, watching warily.

She shrugged, shaking her head in confusion. "Nat, what's-"

"Best get in a wagon, Raewyn," I whispered while strapping the shield to my left arm. She frowned but did as I told her. After ensuring the tarp to hide Raewyn was secured, my hand gripped the longsword at my side, and I waited.

And waited.

My confidence in my instincts began to waver, when a cry off to my left broke the quiet.

"Now!"

Lifting my shield up under my eyes, my gaze trained on a group of men in crude armor, carrying handaxes, rust-pocked swords, and clubs, rising from the prairie brush lining the road. They charged the caravan through knee-high brown grass with guttural yells no doubt designed to intimidate their targets.

Finally.

The fastest bandit rushed me, yelling, and I raised my shield to block his first blow. It clanked off the metal; the attack countered without effort. Punching forward with my shield, bashing him in the face to stun him, I pulled my longsword from its sheath in a quick backhanded draw, using the momentum to slice across his middle. He screamed in pain and surprise, dropping his club to cover the deep wound with his hands.

Another ran at me as I twirled my sword in my hand to right it. My shield popped up to catch his downward slash. His sword bounced hard as he gave a two-handed swing. My arm felt the bruising impact, going numb for a second. I parried his second attack with my sword, tapping the tip to unbalance him, and stepped in, keen on shortening the distance between us. He stumbled, swinging wildly to stop my advance. Parrying again, this time closer to his hilt, my blade swept his far to the side. He was thrown off-balance again, leaving his back unguarded, and it was my time. I cut across his spine, leaving a deep cut through his thin leather armor. He screeched, arching back violently, and fell to the ground.

A third came for me, and I smiled.

They're attacking me one at a time. Idiots.

This one, too, was quickly felled.

Other bandits engaged with other guards around me. Some guards were having trouble keeping their opponent at bay, making me rush to assist. Stabbing my sword through the back of one as I passed, his club raised high over a tripped guard, the cutthroat gurgled and stumbled away into the grass. I ran to another, blocking a death blow with my shield while the guard next to me took the opportunity and finished the bandit off

Quickly scanning the area showed a few guards unconscious and lying in the dirt, blood seeping out from under them. But the situation appeared to be under control.

A few bandits ran back into the grass, with guards following them in their rout.

I called out, "Raewyn!"

My sister peeked out from under the canvas, coughing from the tarp's dust. She waved her hand in front of her face. "Yeah?"

"Can you heal them? Some might still be alive." I passed my sword to my left hand and walked over to help her out of the wagon.

She nodded and planted her feet on the ground, glancing about. "I can, yes." She headed to the nearest fallen man and began to kneel next to him.

"That's an enemy, Raewyn."

She wobbled, standing back up. "Oh. Well, how can I tell them apart?" She crossed her arms, looking around again.

"Our guards have red bands on their arms." I said, tapping the wide red cloth tied around my right bicep.

"Oh. Clever." She moved to a downed guard and put a hand on his back. Prayers fell from her lips immediately. A moment later, the man opened his eyes and groaned. He rolled over and raised his head, making me sigh in relief.

Tomik's wife won't be made a widow today.

Cleaning my sword on the shirt of a dead bandit, I placed it back in my scabbard.

Raewyn, sitting in a cart as I walked beside her, talked most of the way to Evraka, telling me of her tutoring, the girls she trained, and the mischief she got into while exploring the largest city in Laeth and the center of all trade on the continent. There was a pause after another entirely inappropriate story when Raewyn muttered under her breath like it was a secret, "The traveling Fey Carnival was just opening when I left Evraka. We could go tomorrow night."

My feet stopped cold. Trepidation, and something akin to fear, rippled through me, as did the sudden chill rolling down my spine.

She hopped down from the cart and took my left hand in her two smaller ones. "Oh, come on! It'll be fun, if you remember what that is, and we haven't gone since we were kids, remember?"

"Yes, Raewyn. I remember well. I remember we were caught by that hag, cursed even. Sound familiar? Mischief hag? Ringing any bells?" I stood, rod straight and flabbergasted that she would suggest such a thing could ever be fun.

Raewyn exclaimed, never to be denied, "Exactly! And maybe we'll find out how to get rid of said curse. Hm? Oh, you know you want to, Nat."

My arguments died in order to consider my sister's idea. *Yes, perhaps we could find out how to rid ourselves of the curses. Going to the crime's location might actually be beneficial. If nothing else, perhaps going into the Hall again, seeing it as just a building and nothing more...*

Still, the trepidation remained, as long forgotten memories crept into my mind. The hag's green eyes. My sister's screams, and my bruised fists as I attempted to defend her.

She'll go, with or without me. I would rather she have my protection.

"Very well. I will go with you." I huffed a sigh, resigned as logic overtook reluctance.

Raewyn grinned and twirled as she spoke in a sing-song voice, "And maybe we'll finally get you bedded."

A growling groan left me as my eyes closed, my patience already wearing thin. *Not this again. It's as though I never left.* "Thank you, but I'd rather not."

Her head snapped to me, as though a thought had just come to mind. "You still haven't bedded anyone, right? I can tell. Your spine is still all... upright and stiff." She waved her hand in the air toward me. "And you still don't smile. Definitely a virgin."

Feeling more irritated at her insinuation than her actual words, my face heated. "My spine is not *stiff*. I just have excellent posture, which has absolutely nothing to do with my lack of..." A quick look around ensured no one could overhear us. I went on, whispering harshly, "...sexual partners. And why exactly does it matter if I'm a virgin? I want to be married. I want my husband to be my only lover. Why is that so bad, Raewyn?"

"Because you're missing out on all the fun! Caravans and 'protect the innocent' is all well and good, Nat, but you could be having a full life." She smirked at me, putting hands on her hips. "You know there are more uses for a sword than just in battle."

"Raewyn! I intend to have a full life. When I get *married*."

She blew a raspberry and waved her hand at me again. "As serious as ever, I see."

"And thank the gods for it too, Raewyn. I take my future seriously. Now, get your behind back in the cart. You'll get dirty."

Chapter Two
The Hall of Mirrors

We shuffled past the crowds of people who were heading in the same direction we were. Up ahead, bright lights glowed in pinks, blues, and greens, illuminating the large tents and high-tops of the carnival. The lights moved and hovered above the participants like so many fireflies, causing more than one child to hop up to try to catch one.

There was an assortment of humans here, from far off Balingua near the Pouroe Desert, their bronze skin glistening in the lights. Some were from my own realm of Camlynn, based upon the green dragon insignia on their lapels. Others from here in Gastona, the central country Evraka was situated in, judging by their silk sashes and velvet attire.

But there were also non-humans too. The inquisitive, brawny elves from smog-filled Tirvinir meandered about, effortlessly parting the crowd with their towering presence. There were various fey too, of course.

A large toad, as tall as me, walked along on two legs, carrying a curved cane and bowing with his top hat aloft to every lady he saw. A swamp crone slinked about, with her tell-tale hunched posture and squinted black eyes looking over the assembled.

I didn't see any dwarves, but that was no surprise. Having only met two myself, they didn't like to leave Fomona unguarded, after their original home of Kibel was destroyed.

As we moved into the clearing that housed the entrance gate, there was a dizzying display of jugglers and fire eaters blowing puffs of multi-colored flame out above the heads of screaming, excited children.

Beyond the gates, games, no doubt rigged, dotted the landscape. What looked to be the Hall of Mirrors took up a large plot of land to my far left. It was an inevitable destination, so I noted its location. A haunted house made up the other end to my right. An enormous amphitheater sat in the center, with its bright lights and loud music.

A large human family consisting of two parents herding four squirrelly children jostled me when I had stopped to look at the area. Stating my apologies, and bowing my head, one of the children looked up at me, wide-eyed. She touched the shield covering my back, its steel surface showing a golden four-pointed star, and whispered, "Are you a protector?"

"I am." My smile dimmed when I noticed the child's fingers were covered in chocolate. *At least, I hope it's chocolate.* A series of brown fingerprints now blemished my shield, and I dug into my pouch for a cloth to clean it.

"Wow," she whispered. "I've never met one of you before."

Plucking the cloth from my pouch, I knelt in front of her. "Do you know what a protector is, honey? What we do?"

The girl dipped her head shyly, chewing on her lip. "You help people."

My smile returned at her succinct answer. "Yes. A protector follows Horyn. We are sworn to someone who needs protection." I took my shield off my back and pointed to the four-pointed star.

"Each point of the star stands for one of the four-" I searched for a smaller word than 'tenet' so the child would understand. "...beliefs of a protector. Do you know them?"

When she shook her head, I pointed to the first. "Vigilance. We are always ready."

Then, the second. "Self-sacrifice. We give so others may live."

With the third point, I said, "Patience. We aim for calmness and understanding."

My finger stopped at the final point. "And fortitude. We bear what others cannot."

Protectors often found themselves the bodyguards of the rich and powerful, guardians of the church itself, or, on the rare occasion, adventurers - going where needed and guarding whomever needed guarding. I was the latter, at the moment.

They almost always had a purpose. Someone or something to protect. A charge.

Not yet, but soon.

Wiping down my shield to remove the brown mystery substance, its surface gleaming once more, my hand froze when the girl's brown-covered fingers neared my shield again.

"Come along, Mira." The girl's mother took her hand before she could touch and pulled her away to get into the queue that was now forming at the gate entrance. A nudge from Raewyn drew my attention as I stood. She adjusted her mask and hood as she looked on. A trash receptacle stood off to the side. Knowing better than to toss it from a distance, I simply walked over to throw the dirty cloth away.

Raewyn nudged me again when I returned, harder this time. "We'd better get in line. You're paying."

"And why exactly am I paying for you? Do you not have funds?"

She grinned without looking my way as we joined one of the lines. "I do, but the bigger sister is supposed to take care of the little sister. Besides, you paid last time, remember?"

I sighed, stepping up when the line had cleared ahead of us. "Very well."

It didn't take long before we made it to the booth, though Raewyn was beginning to hop on her toes and grumble about the queue's efficiency. A small green man, with large pointed ears and sharp pointed teeth, hopped up on his stool and spread his arms wide. "Hehe, welcome to the Fey Carnival, misses! Shall that be two tickets?"

I nodded at the little goblin and shelled out some coin. "How much?"

"For adults, five silver per, my dear! One gold coin in total!"

My heavy coin plunked down on the window's sill, and it disappeared, making my sister clap and gasp in delight as she watched.

"Oh, how clever! I need to learn how to do that."

Distracted with closing my coin purse, I hummed absently then replied, "Do what, Raewyn?"

She chirped. "Make money disappear as soon as it's in front of me. It would make gambling so much simpler."

Eyeing my sister, it suddenly made sense to me why I was paying. *I didn't know she gambled.*

The goblin giggled. "Crowns or lapel pins for your tickets?"

"Crowns, please," I answered him while keeping my suspicious gaze on Raewyn. "Am I to understand you aim to pilfer funds before you've won them?"

Raewyn shrugged. "Maybe... oh, our tickets!"

The goblin held out two flowered crowns, one to each of us. They were the same as they had been so many years ago, and my anxiety spiked.

"To signify you have paid, my dears, and here's a program of events! NEXT!"

I plucked the program and the crowns from the teller with a grateful nod, handing one of the flowery pieces to Raewyn as we moved to the side. Raewyn immediately donned hers, adjusting it over her porcelain mask.

"How do I look?" She turned this way and that to give me the best vantage.

"Lovely, Raewyn. As always." It was unnecessary to lie. My sister, despite the scars hidden under her mask, was a striking woman, and the flowers only enhanced her beauty.

She beamed and motioned to me. "Well, put yours on!"

The delicate crown of real flowers sat limp in my hands as I admired the silken petals and woven stems. It was a pretty piece, I admitted to myself. *Maybe I could do this.* Adjusting it over my hair carefully, my sister confirmed it sat well with a cheery smile.

"Beautiful, now let's *go*!"

She grabbed my hand and began to drag me to the nearest game as a child would their parent. The sights and sounds and smells of the carnival hit me fully. Sprites and pixies danced above, tossing tiny globes of the colored lights between them. Though I did not care for the scent of roasting meat, the sweet smell of pastries made my mouth water and my stomach grumble.

Raewyn stopped me in front of a tossing game, one with three blocks in a pyramid set in an open tent with a cloth backdrop.

"No, not these. They're rigged," I said, pointing while shaking my head.

Raewyn groaned and turned toward me. "I know, but the games are half the carnival!"

Sighing for what would probably not be the last time that night, I handed the carnie a silver piece. Enough for three balls. Raewyn squealed, taking up the balls in her small hands and gave a feeble throw. It hit the blocks but only jostled them with none falling.

"Aw, that's a nice throw, lovey. But you still have two more. Give it your best shot!" cried the carnie.

Raewyn grumbled, rolling the two remaining balls in her hands. "What are these blocks made from? Concrete?" She gave another throw. This time it sailed past the blocks to hit the sheet behind them with a dull thud.

She exhaled in exasperation then handed me the last ball. "See if you can, Nat."

Taking the ball from her, I stepped up to the table. "I will try, but throwing is not my strong suit, Raewyn."

Everything has a weakness.

Aiming between the lower two blocks, my arm pulled back and released. The ball careened toward the blocks and then curved to hit the platform holding them. It shook the blocks, but they still did not fall.

"Missed! You missed! I can't believe it!" Raewyn yelled, throwing her hands up. "You did worse than I did!"

A bitter part of me wanted to ask the carnie if the balls were enchanted to curve like that. "I told you. Throwing is not my strong suit."

Raewyn let out a groan, and the carnie stepped up.

"One more silver gets you four balls. Yes, four. I said four. Would you be willing, loveys?"

Raewyn looked at me with childlike hope in her eyes, only to have her hopes dashed when I answered the carnie, "No. We'll find some other game."

"But-but...four!" Raewyn looked back at the game and the carnie, who was now yelling about five balls.

"Come, Raewyn. We'll find something else to do." My eyes shifted again to the area where the Hall of Mirrors sat, as though silently beckoning me to another meeting. Dread clawed my stomach with frosty fingers.

"Like finding you company for the night." Raewyn sidled up beside me, grinning as though the game no longer existed.

Distracted, I turned to her. "Huh?" What she said finally registered, my teeth clenched. "Raewyn..."

"I told you I was going to find you someone. Him? Wait, no, too skinny. You probably want to break his heart, not his body. Ooh, what about him? C'mere, tall, dark, and horny..." She pointed off to our side and rushed in that direction.

"Ho-? What? No!" Panic made me reach out to her, but she had already moved to the side of a man whose back was turned toward me. "Raewyn! Rae-wyn!"

Raewyn tapped the gentleman on the shoulder, and he turned, smiling down at her. "Yes?"

Curses spewed out in a mutter as I stalked to Raewyn's side, intent on dragging her away.

Raewyn giggled. "Hello, sir. M- whoa!"

Gripping her by the arm to drag her away, I tried to produce a convincing laugh, but it came out unnatural and high-pitched. "Sorry! My sister is very drunk! Those Minuen priestesses, right? Never met a drink they didn't like!"

Raewyn cried out, pointing at my torso. "Wait, Nat! You've got dirt on you!"

My grip released her to look down at myself, pressing my hands to my chest. "Wait. What? Where?"

She cackled. My head jerked up at the mocking sound to see her scramble back toward the gentleman again, who was watching as though we were the true entertainment here. Before I could grab her a second time, Raewyn rambled off her monologue. "My sister is badly in need of sexual company for the evening. Perhaps it'll improve her mood. Would you be so kind as to provide it?"

My hands landed on her arm just as my body went numb. "Oh, gods..." I didn't even get a good look at the man. My burning face fell into my right hand. "She... she's drunk. So, so drunk," I muttered, squeaking.

Raewyn's coy smile was audible in her words. "Nat, if you need help getting started, I can show you how."

My suspicions that I must have died at some point in my travels were instantly confirmed, and my soul was sent to the Dark Drop instead of Celestia. I was dead, and this was my punishment for some offense to the gods.

The man's soft laughter pulled me from my morbid thoughts of damnation and eternal torment into the different, but equally painful hell. His anger or umbrage would have been easier to handle.

"I cannot say I would be able to provide that kind of company, but I can at least introduce myself. I am Ramiren, and you are?"

My head slowly lifted. *I know that name. Where do I know that name?*

Before my sister could reply, I blurted out, "You're Ramiren. *The* Ramiren? I've heard of you. I just can't remember how."

Where? Where have I heard that name?

Ramiren's red-irised eyes turned toward me, and he smiled more broadly. "You have? Good things, I hope."

Searching his face in earnest as though the answer lay there, my gaze traveled over his firm jaw, covered in a neatly-trimmed black beard and mustache. His tanned skin was an even shade, and black hair curled and tickled at the nape of his neck.

Oval gold-framed glasses, with lenses the color of blood, sat on his straight nose and emphasized the rubies of his eyes. Small twin black horns curled up from his temples. He wore fine black clothing with red trim, giving himself a wholly duo-toned look, except for the spray of small wildflowers pinned on his lapel that was his 'ticket,' like the flower crowns my sister and I wore. He appeared more scholar than anything, making me even more curious why and where I had heard the name. *I do not associate with many scholars. Or broodlings, for that matter.*

My tutors briefly discussed broodlings in their many lessons regarding the heritages of the known world. While celestials, like myself and Raewyn, were descended from angels, servants of the benevolent Tarindar pantheon, broodlings came from devils, servants of the malevolent Lorindar. And like celestials, broodlings often took on physical characteristics associated with their heritage, which this Ramiren definitely did.

Despite the situation, the tension in my shoulders, normally present, slowly faded. The twisting sensation in my belly that started the moment Raewyn suggested going to this carnival eased considerably. I felt comfortable in his presence. Languid, even.

It was unnerving. *Is that a broodling trait?*

After what must have been an awkward pause, I cleared my throat. "My apologies, Master Ramiren. I am Nathalia Swordhand. And this is my sister, Raewyn."

He inclined his head to each of us in turn with a gentle smile. "Lovely to meet you both." He squinted his eyes. "Hm, Swordhand? I believe I know your father, though it's been a while since I've spoken with him. Maxlian Swordhand, yes? Of Camlynn?"

He's one of my father's associates? What a tiny, tangled web the world is.

"Yep," Raewyn said, popping the P. My teeth ground together at the sound. "That's Dad."

"Please don't pop your consonants, Raewyn."

Her lazy gaze settled on me. "Hm? Oh, too unladylike for you?"

Among other things. "That, and it's irritating to anyone who hears it."

Raewyn rolled her eyes. Ramiren watched us, his amusement returning. "Shall we look around together, then? I aim to meet some clients here to discuss finishing terms, so I may have to step away for a time."

"Clients? What exactly do you do?" Raewyn cut in.

His smile widened. "Pacts, mostly. I broker them for individuals. I facilitate connections, and I am rewarded for my efforts."

We began to walk through the crowded areas of the carnival, looking around at the variety of exotically-dressed people. Fey, humans, and elves alike chatted with each other. Children of all races played together with their small kites and toys. It was harmonious and wonderful to watch. Only there was a dark cloud in the back of my mind about this place. Remembering my childhood, and the night my greatest gift was stolen from me.

My awareness prickled, making me notice Ramiren was looking at me, as though he had just said something and expected a reply. "My apologies, I was far away, what did you say?"

Ramiren replied, "I asked if you and your sister come to this every year?" He looked around. "I've never been myself, but I hear of it often. Truth be told, I've never had the opportunity until today."

Raewyn and I glanced at each other. She frowned while I gave the answer, "We've been once, when we were children. It was not a good time."

Ramiren tilted his head, furrowing his eyebrows. "Why is that? I would have thought a carnival would be a grand time for children."

Should I say anything?

It was something personal and private when I had only just met him. But the comfort I felt lingered, making me finally relent. "Mischief hags."

"Ah." He sighed. "Yes. I've heard of them. They tend to ignore the typical fey rules of fairness and steal what is not theirs. You have encountered one, then? Here?"

My tongue slid along my upper teeth. "We have." My sister touched her porcelain mask. "And she did indeed steal things from us. She cornered us in the Hall of Mirrors, said some incantation, and we were... made lesser."

"I am sorry that happened to you both." Ramiren's gaze bounced between us. "Especially as children just wishing to join in on the fun."

Raewyn, walking on Ramiren's other side, touched his arm to get his attention. "Why do they do that, though? Allow the mischief hag into this?"

Ramiren hummed. "I'm not sure *allow* is accurate. They can disguise themselves, though they are always unable to hide their sickly green eyes. It's also unknown how many there are. Whether there are one or dozens of them is unclear. Some think the mere concept is a myth."

Gods above. Dozens?

"I remember her eyes the most," I said.

It was a white lie. My memory recalled something else even more.

My chest tightened at the memory of the hag. My first failure where placing myself between her and my little sister was not enough. The mischief hag's magic had gone through me to her with no power to stop it.

Ramiren shook his head in disgust. "The mischief hag is a type of fey. In my dealings, I tend to avoid fey. And devils, too. Their words are often double-sided, and you must be quite careful, which I learned in my youth. Even other broodlings, I must be cautious. It's never known how far the apple fell from the tree, as it were. I keep to a more humanoid clientele now. Humans, celestials..." he said, his hand indicating to us, "...elves, dwarves, and occasionally gnomes, when I can pry their attention from gears and gadgetry."

We walked on. Ramiren eventually excused himself to go to his meeting. Raewyn and I played a few more games, winning at nothing. After eating our supper from a vendor, Ramiren somehow found us again just as I'd finished reading through the events program.

"Did you do your deal already? That was fast," Raewyn said, brushing deep-fried cake crumbs from her lap.

"Yes, I did. This one was not particularly complicated, but it did require a meeting in a public place."

"Oh, yeah? What happened?" Raewyn continued.

That's none of our business, sister.

Ramiren seemed to hear my thoughts as he replied, "Apologies, but I cannot disclose. Secrecy was part of the pact."

We cleaned our area and stood as he told the tale of a tricky deal he had to make with an ancient elven sorcerer who wanted to be able to complete his book of self-created spells. It appeared to me that Ramiren did good work in at least securing the elf's goal. I said as much.

"Yes, thank you, but sadly he summoned a devil to help build an appendix to the book. The devil tricked him, to no one's surprise. Immortal beings, though not against the claws of a fiend. I'm told they cannot even be resurrected by the unfathomable effects of fey magic."

The elf reached above his means. Anyone that deals with a devil gets exactly what is coming to them.

Raewyn played a few more games as we watched patiently. When she finally won a small stuffed bear on a ring toss, she jumped up and down while clapping her hands and shrieking. "Yes! Minue's tits! I won!"

"Uh." The carnie's eyes, focused on Raewyn, dipped lower than was appropriate. When I cleared my throat with a hard glare, he broke into a broad, practiced smile, and his eyes lifted. "Yes, you did! Step right up and you can be a winner, too!" The carnie held out the bear to Raewyn, who clutched it to her chest as though it were a valuable keepsake. Her enthusiasm was infectious, making me smile.

Ramiren broke into a wide grin, clapping twice. "Well done, Raewyn. Now, you have a memento for your travels here."

Raewyn giggled and held the bear out to me. "See, Nat? I don't need your throwing *expertise* after all."

Funny.

"No, and thank the gods for it, too. I would not have won you such a token."

Something bumped into me, and a scratchy voice soon followed. "Oh, excuse me, dearie."

The voice caused me to turn, and my body stiffened as though instantly frozen. A shock of unnaturally red hair and a drab purple dress did nothing to distract from her noxious green eyes as she squinted over the crowd.

They're here.

The anxiety that had filled me earlier unfurled in the face of an actual enemy, a living breathing thing that could be defeated. Resolve and training took its place. "Raewyn, Ramiren, walk over and stand behind me."

Ramiren quietly moved behind me. When Raewyn paid me no heed, still preoccupied with her bear, my head snapped toward her as I barked, "Raewyn! Behind me, that's an order!"

She jolted. "What? Yeesh, fine, all right. Calm down." She moved behind me with a scowl.

Securing my shield to my arm then placing my hand on the hilt of my longsword, I stood on my tip-toes to search for the bright red hair in the crowd, and my eyes warily tracked her movements after the search proved fruitful. Ramiren watched calmly. "What did you see?" he asked under his breath, though there was no chance of the foul creature overhearing him.

"That was the mischief hag."

Out of the corner of my eye, Ramiren sharply looked my way. "I see."

Raewyn murmured, "Follow?"

When we all agreed, we did our best to squeeze past a few individuals who stood, oblivious to others, in the middle of the thoroughfare. As though pulled by an invisible string, she darted toward the Hall of Mirrors. *Could she sense someone vulnerable in there now?*

As soon as she disappeared into the Hall of Mirrors, we dashed after her. When we came to the entrance, the feeling of trepidation returned. I swallowed it down as best I could with a dry mouth.

"Come, she has entered."

Raewyn and Ramiren followed me in. Making sure to keep myself between them and whatever might happen, we went through the entrance, and my foreboding nearly choked me. Vivid memories flooded in. I was a child again, crying, screaming at the hideous hag to leave my sister alone. My fists lashed out, but they bounced off her harmlessly. She cackled at my feeble attempt and turned toward me, her voice high-pitched and abrasive. "And you, my dear girl, I see in your mind you are quite the poet. The writer. The songstress. Creation is your joy and it shall be your loss!" She incanted something, gesturing wildly with her long spindly fingers as she did with Raewyn, "I steal from you, your creativity!"

Snapping back to the present, Raewyn looked up at me, concerned.

I shook my head to clear it. "Stay behind me. I can protect you better this time."

Raising my shield to advance through the maze of mirrors, my eyes wandered on their own. It couldn't be helped. Some mirrors made me look shorter. Some made me look taller. Some made me look fatter and some skinnier. Standard trick mirrors. But this was the Fey Carnival, and nothing was mundane. Some made me look younger, the exact age when I last entered this place. Some made me look older, my silver hair turned gray and crow's feet wrinkled at my eyes.

One made me stop in my tracks. My reflection was standing with someone and wrapped in their tight embrace with joyful, happy tears running down my cheeks. My beautiful white dress with gold fey-like embroidery was plain-shaped gown, but its meaning could not be mistaken.

My jaw went slack, trying desperately to concentrate on the face of the one my reflection was shown with, but the mysterious man's face was shadowed. My distraction made me nearly miss my sister calling for me.

"Nat? Nathalia! Listen!" Raewyn tugged on my sleeve. Regaining my composer, my head swiveled up when the cries of someone in distress echoed distantly.

"No!" Taking off toward the sound, my shield bounced off of a trick mirror and shattered it. Moving around it, glass crunching beneath my feet, I dodged into fake alleyways, around blind corners. The shouts were getting louder, and my pace quickened.

Then, a croaking voice rebounded off the mirror-covered walls, "I see in your mind you're quite the tinkerer. Wrenches and gears are your joy and your automaton your life's work. Never again shall you improve him."

A higher-pitched one replied, pleading, "No, please!"

We came to a circular room lined with mirrors. In it, a large automaton, his machinery exposed at the joints, grappled with the thick, snaking vines constricting him. The disguised mischief hag had cornered a small gnome with bright pink hair in pigtails. Goggles sat over the gnome's eyes, enlarging them to an exaggerated degree. She looked like a child, and perhaps she was mistaken for one.

The mischief hag began to incant, "I steal from you, your tools!"

I charged, yelling out a cry to Horyn. As my sword swung down, the mischief hag disappeared, leaving behind nothing but a puff of green smoke and an echoing cackle.

"No!" the gnome wailed, patting herself as if looking for something. She, then, held her hands out. "My tools! You *useless* automaton!" She kicked the brown automaton in the shin with a hollow ding. She yowled then began to hop up and down while holding her injured foot.

The vines around the automaton fell away and disintegrated. He turned toward his owner and let out a soft beep. "YOU DID LESS THAN I DID."

His voice reverberated throughout the chamber, making my ears ring. My hands reached out to her in case she fell. "Are you all right? I'm sorry I could not-"

The gnome put her foot down and wheeled on me, hands on hips. "Well, you *should* be sorry! Fat lotta good you did!"

My eyes fell to my feet. Shame and a deep sense of failure gutted me with yet another innocent being hurt in the same way my sister and I had been. Another person in the wrong place at the wrong time. *Maybe it's not too late, for either of us?* A solution buzzed into my mind, and my chin lifted. "Perhaps we can go to Lord Leviathus and let him know this is happening? I'm sure the carnival owner can help get your tools back."

The gnome's enlarged eyes narrowed on me. "You think so, huh? Well, la-de-da. Who are you, the Queen of Evraka? No one gets a private audience with him without knowing someone."

She's right. And while my name is influential, even in nearby Evraka, this was the Fey Carnival. My signet ring wouldn't get me a foot in the door. So, how do we contact him? Perhaps he keeps open business hours? Or a detailed message?

Suggestion box?

Pulling out the program, my eyes scanned the pamphlet, hoping for a way to contact the carnival owner as I rubbed my mother's luck stone. One event caught my attention.

Found you.

Tapping the plain pendant in gratitude, I asked, "Raewyn, do you remember singing that duet song when we were younger? *Seasons Change?*"

Raewyn looked at me, confused. "Yeah, why?"

"Lord Leviathus presents prizes to the contest winners himself. It says so in the program." Raewyn leaned in to read the indicated paragraph in the pamphlet as my idea took root. "They have a singing contest, which should be starting soon. We could ask him then."

Raewyn smiled. "I'm right there with you, Nat."

Ramiren tilted his head, looking at me. "There are many quality singers who will be participating. Are you up to the challenge?"

My back straightened. "Throwing is not my strong suit, Master Ramiren. But singing is. It's our best chance, I think."

A sneaky noise made me look down at the gnome, who was being smacked on the back by her automaton in an uncomfortable-looking attempt at consolation.

There was another soft beep sound from the automaton. "THERE THERE, GEORGINA. WE WILL MURDER HER, THEN TAKE BACK THE TOOLS." The automaton stopped patting her and put his hand to his side when she pushed him away.

"Yes, yes. Sure." She pinched the bridge of her nose between her fingers. "Gods and gears, today was just not a good day!"

Beep. "WE WILL SQUASH HER INNARDS."

She sighed. "Alright, M.A.L."

Beep. "WE WILL MAKE HER REGRET THE DAY HER FATHER INSERTED HIMSELF INTO HER MOTHER AND SQUIRTED HIS-"

The gnome swerved her head to the automaton. "Don't you dare complete that sentence!"

Beep. "YES, GEORGINA."

My obligation to help her wrestled with the dubious feeling in my gut. She was in the same predicament as my sister and I, but her hostile attitude was difficult to swallow. Not to mention her vulgar, booming automaton.

Ignore it. She needs us.

Addressing the gnome more gently this time, I hoped my words properly conveyed my confidence in our success. "We will get your tools back. My sister and I have also had something stolen from us. Perhaps we can help each other. Georgina, is it?"

The gnome looked up at me with tired eyes. She replied quietly with a slight head bob, "Yes."

"I am Nathalia, a Protector Initiate. This is Raewyn, my sister, a Minuen priestess. And Ramiren, the... uh. Do you have an occupation title, Master Ramiren?"

Ramiren exhaled a soft laugh, "Pactmaker."

"And Ramiren, the pactmaker. Let's get out of this place and register for the singing contest."

Raewyn clapped her hands. "We haven't sung together in a while."

"We haven't, but it will be... fun."

Chapter Three

Seasons Change

As we maneuvered through the considerable crowd to the amphitheater, Ramiren turned his attention to the little gnome at his side. "Georgina, is it?"

Georgina glanced up at him, her legs pumping to keep up with everyone. "Yeah. That's right."

Ramiren's eyes flitted to the automaton walking beside her. "And your automaton is M.A.L.C.O.L.M.?"

Georgina narrowed her gaze at Ramiren. "Yes. What about him?"

Ramiren looked ahead and smiled without pausing his pace. "What does M.A.L.C.O.L.M. stand for? Like most automatons, I imagine it's an acronym and not an actual name?"

Georgina chuckled, tossing a casual look toward M.A.L.C.O.L.M. "Yeah. It stands for Man-like Automated Live Combat Optimized Learning Machine. So, M.A.L.C.O.L.M. for short. When he was made, he was mostly for protection. I've modified him over the years, so he can do a lot more than punch bad guys now."

"Fascinating. I've seen very few automatons with such complexity. You must take a great deal of pride in him."

For the first time, Georgina smiled.

When we arrived, there were swaths of people ambling about, waiting for the performances to begin. It appeared we weren't too late.

Lifting onto my tiptoes to look around over the heads of patrons, I found what I was looking for. "Raewyn and I will head to the side of the stage. I think I see a line. Everyone else, I suppose find a seat."

Georgina huffed and motioned toward the stands. "This had better work. I feel like I'm wasting my time." She and M.A.L.C.O.L.M. climbed into the stands, and Raewyn walked off toward the line of singers now getting even longer, leaving me and Ramiren alone.

We looked at each other, but he spoke first, "I wish you the best of luck, Lady Nathalia."

My head tilted. "Lady? I never introduced myself as such."

He gestured toward me, lifting his hand up and down at me. "Well, if you recall, I know your father, and I doubt Lord Protector Maxlian Swordhand would appreciate it if I didn't give proper respect to his daughter. Also, your posture looks as though it was beaten into you by a curmudgeon governess. You are, most definitely, a lady."

You are not wrong.

A chuckle escaped me, and my hand flew to my mouth.

I'm just nervous. That's all. Nervous energy.

"Thank you for the luck, Master Ramiren. But I carry a luck stone." I took out the smoky-colored gem from under my chain-linked armor.

He raised his eyebrows, looking at it. "A mighty prize, indeed. What exactly does it do?"

My sister yelled from across the crowd, "Nat, come on! We're going to be late signing up. You can bore him later!"

Thanks for the boost of confidence, Raewyn.

My smile felt strained as I responded to Ramiren. "I will accomplish our goal. Trust that."

"I don't doubt it." He returned my smile with a pleasant one of his own and followed Georgina into the stands. My eyes followed him, noting where he finally sat down, and headed to Raewyn's side.

The line of singers moved quickly. A few moments later, a sprite hovered at my eye-level with a tiny notepad in her hands. "Name of group?"

"Duet singers, please. Nathalia and Raewyn Swordhand."

She jotted down my words, finishing with a flourish. "Duet. Swordhand sisters. Got it. Any music you'd like to accompany you?

I replied, "The melody to *Seasons Change*, please."

She wrote again on her notepad, then peeked behind us. "Sure thing. Looks like you're up last."

I looked over my shoulder, seeing no one behind us, and faced Raewyn. "Like always?"

She grinned. "You still have the high notes?"

The one corner of my mouth raised. "If you have the low."

She started to warm up her voice in a rich contralto that always surprised me. *Such a big sound for such a small woman.*

I sang an octave higher. We each adjusted our pitch automatically, looking at each other, and the sound harmonized. The first few songs we practiced with were a little shaky, as we hadn't sung together in so long, but eventually our voices balanced. Like the muscle memory of riding a horse or swinging a sword, you never truly forget how to sing once you've learned it.

It was a long wait to go up, and the anticipation increased the closer it got to our time. Many singers performed, some solo and some as an ensemble. The competition, and our goal, did not hamper my appreciation for their talents. But I felt my confidence rise after the last performance involving a tall woman singing off-key about cupcakes.

The sprite called out, "Swordhand sisters, you're up. Knock 'em dead!"

She fluttered around Raewyn and me, shooing us onto the stage. Climbing up the steps, the bright stage lights floating around us made me squint .

"Ready?" Raewyn whispered to me.

"As I'll ever be."

A soft familiar melody began to drift up from somewhere, filling the entire amphitheater. Two clear notes emerged from each of us, the opening volley to the song. Raewyn and I sang in perfect unison, as though the years had never separated us.

· · · ·

In her silence,
After the violence,
He mourned devotion unsaid.

· · · ·

Drifting away,
He started to pray.
Chained to an anchor of dread.

· · · ·

Seasons change, the moon does too.
But my love remains.

> *Back I will bring you to stand by my side,*
> *Through the wind, the sun, and the rain.*

• • • •

I kept my eyes on the audience, looking around at the faces staring back. The song's mournful, melodic tone never failed to get a reaction when I'd heard it performed. It was an old obscure ballad, one that we had learned as children and often sang together. Raewyn always found it romantic. It always saddened me.

My eyes found Ramiren in the crowd, and his focused attention encouraged me. My song grew bolder, clearer, with his smile. The crowd around him slowly began to blur into indistinct shapes. Thanks to my lack of creativity, there would be no embroidery added to the song. No embellishment. I simply sang it as I remembered it. Not that I'd be able to add anything anyway, with Ramiren smiling at me with his warm, red eyes.

Unable to look away, a distinct flutter filled my belly. Childish crushes and infatuations that everyone experiences growing up. But that flutter sank lower and morphed into a pleasant throbbing.

• • • •

> *His love was gone,*
> *No hope for the dawn,*
> *He knew no way to find her.*

• • • •

> *Little he knew,*
> *The fey they drew,*
> *The magic to raise, then bind her.*

• • • •

> *Seasons change, the moon does too.*
> *But my love remains.*
> *Back I will bring you to stand by my side,*
> *Through the wind, the sun, and the rain.*

· · · ·

Acutely grateful I knew the song so well, my cheeks flooded with heat.

The lights. It's only the lights.

But the feylight gave off no such temperature, only brightness.

· · · ·

A plan devised,
By fam'ly advised,
To beg the monarch fey.

· · · ·

He cried, sir please,
Take coin or keys,
Whatever desire, I'll pay.

· · · ·

Seasons change, the moon does too.
But my love remains.
Back I will bring you to stand by my side,
Through the wind, the sun, and the rain.

· · · ·

The music crescendoed, and our voices with it. I'd never had such accompaniment to my singing.

My skin pebbled from the bracing exhilaration of the moment. Even Ramiren's face blurred along with the crowd. We were nothing more than instruments, plucked by harpists with sure hands and unbridled love for song.

· · · ·

The fey came near,
He felt no fear,
But the terror of failure then.

• • • •

She laid so still,
No breath, until,
Her eyes did open again.

• • • •

Seasons change, the moon does too.
But my love remains.
Back I will bring you to stand by my side,
Through the wind, the sun, and the rain.
'Til the world falls silent once more.

• • • •

When it was over, the last trembling note gone, there was wild applause. Raewyn grabbed my hand to bow together.

"Yes! Well done," yelled the sprite off the stage as we walked over to her. "Now, we're really going to have to get you bedded, Nat!"

When my eyes returned to where Ramiren sat, his seat was empty. The throbbing dissipated to be replaced by a strange irritation. The irritation vanished when Ramiren came through the crowd lightly applauding, with Georgina and her automaton M.A.L.C.O.L.M. behind him. "Very beautiful, ladies. Very beautiful indeed. I can't say I've ever heard that song before."

Georgina grumbled. "Yes, yes, lovely. I hope this was worth it. I'm pretty sure I sat in something sticky." She looked behind her. "M.A.L., do I have anything on my bum?"

A soft beep sounded as M.A.L.C.O.L.M. replied, "YOUR BUM IS NOT STICKY, GEORGINA."

"It's an old favorite of ours," Raewyn said. "Now, Nat, we need to find you someone. Surely, someone in the crowd will-"

I replied curtly, "No, Raewyn. Thank you."

Ramiren chuckled. "She seems very determined."

"You have no idea." Exhaustion suddenly weighed on me.

She needs to stick with training noble girls.

An errant, brazen, wild thought popped into my head. *Perhaps* he *could train me? After all, I'm comfortable around him. Plus, if Father trusts him, then I can, too. But what would I pay him with?*

Rotating slowly, I turned to fully face the broodling. "Master Ramiren, you make deals, yes?"

His ever-present smile increased. "I do, indeed. Pacts, to be precise, if you recall."

My tutors presented very little material on pact magic, the ability to bind two parties together magically for a contract or arrangement. No one really knew where the center of pact thaumaturgy came from or where pactmakers trained, and any attempt to determine them was met with far more questions than answers.

Damn, I had *forgotten.* "Oh, yes, you are a pactmaker. Any kind of pacts?"

He inclined his head. "So long as both parties agree to the terms and no one is harmed or enslaved by the terms, yes."

Explosive cheering from the crowd made us swivel our heads back toward the stage. The corpulent figure toddled across the platform, one hand held up and outwards as he waved to the welcoming crowd. *That must be Lord Leviathus.* His dark gray skin looked waxy, and his large, blocky teeth could be seen from where I stood. Trying to remember the type of fey he was proved difficult. He tapped his cane on the floor of the stage twice, the sound far louder than it should have been.

His booming voice, no doubt magically enhanced like the melody of our accompaniment, rang through the amphitheater, "Ladies, gents, fey of all kinds! We hope you enjoyed the performances here this evening. It is my distinct pleasure to announce the winner, or shall I say, *winners* of the Fey Carnival's Singing Contest!"

Winners? My hope soared.

Whoops, hollers, and claps echoed across. Lord Leviathus laughed, holding his hands out at the crowd to calm them. When the noise died down, Lord Leviathus continued, "And this year's winners are... THE ZACKMAN BROTHERS!"

The crowd rose to its feet, cheering. My jaw went slack, but I began to clap. The four-man group was talented, and it was well won. Still, defeat stung.

"Aw, come on!" Raewyn yelled, throwing up her hands, but she was drowned out by the jubilant audience. "Rigged, like your stupid games!" .

After handing the bouquet of singing wildflowers to the winners, who held it up high in victory, Lord Leviathus began to come our way.

It's now or never.

As he descended the stairs, two-footing each step, he spoke, his voice now a normal volume, "I wanted to congratulate all of you on a job well done, contestants. Especially you, the, I believe, Swordhand sisters? It was a tough call for the judges, I hear." He walked over to us, shaking our hands like a politician begging for support and patting our arms.

Now.

"We have a conundrum. The mischief hag is in the carnival and stealing from others again. This gnome just had her tools stolen. I-" His loud laugh interrupted me.

Lord Leviathus rapped his cane on the ground twice with dull thuds. "An excellent singer, and funny as well!"

"Pardon?" I stepped back, shaking my head in confusion. "This is not a joke, sir. She's here. Now."

He gave me an indulgent smile, his speech dismissive and more than a little condescending, "There's no such thing as mischief hags, miss. Bedtime stories for naughty children who don't clean their rooms."

My shock at his brush-off made me sputter. "But sir! I'm not lying. She's here at your carnival!"

Lord Leviathus' smile disappeared, replaced by a deep scowl. "Now, that's quite enough, miss." He tried to waddle away, but my hard hand on his arm stopped him.

"They're a menace, sir!"

"People are starting to stare, Nat. And I think they're security."

Lord Leviathus removed my hand with a glare. "Keep your hands to yourself, or I will have you removed." He waved off the two burly, tusked fey and shuffled back up the stairs as quickly as he could manage. Jaw dropped and at a loss for words, I watched him depart.

Why is he so ignorant of this? I cannot have been the first person to tell him about the hags.

As Lord Leviathus disappeared from view, a bitter taste filled my mouth.

I failed...again. So much for luck.

"I can help you."

The soft murmur made me spin around to see the woman who had sung about cupcakes. Motifs of vines and brightly colored flowers decorated her robes in fine embroidery. Delicate gold jewelry graced her pointed ears. She held a twisted, gnarled staff in her graceful hands. With her russet coloring and sharp, angular features, she might've been one of the foxlike vulpe fey.

Raewyn replied, "You can? How?" My sister narrowed her eyes. "Who are you?"

The fey woman didn't appear to be offended at Raewyn's accusing tone. She put her hand to her breast. "I am Leraska, and I've encountered them before. I know where the mischief hags reside. In the Feylands. There are three of them. Always three. You could, perhaps, go after them yourselves? Reclaim what they took?"

"And what will we owe you for this information?" Ramiren asked, moving closer to eye the woman.

She lifted her chin. "They are a menace, as she said." She pointed at me and shrugged. "They steal and lie and torment, causing nothing but grief in their wake. They've ruined people, but no one dares to stand against them. Too many are too afraid of what the hag might steal. Their memories. Their abilities. Their most precious possessions. They usually take from children. Less hassle, and they enjoy the fear. But they will not hesitate to take from adults too, if the opportunity presents itself."

"Was something taken from you too, then?"

Leraska's eyes hardened, and her mouth thinned as though trying to keep her emotions in check. "Yes, something was taken from me. Long ago."

My suspicions disappeared as the pain and longing in her words made empathy bloom in my heart. *I can help her, too.*

Leraska exhaled through pursed lips as she sized me up, perhaps wondering if I could handle them. Then, as though my presentation met her expectations, she smiled. "One is in a dilapidated house in the Jorin Swamp, south of Puldoni. It is your Irenian Swamp, south of Evraka. You see, the Feylands are a mirror of this world, merely with different names."

Hearing that about the Feylands and seeing it were two different things, and my lack of desire to travel there meant I'd rarely given it much thought.

My eyes panned around at everyone's faces for a beat before settling back on Leraska's. "And the other two?"

"The second is in a cave east of the Tanta Desert, your Pouroe Desert, just north of the mountain pass there. The third is in a castle built high, in the middle of Carpatha, the capital city of Wistran, in what you know as Camlynn."

My head spun. Keeping these names and places, and their copy in our world, straight would be difficult.

"Do you perhaps have a map, by chance?" I asked, hopeful and nervous. We were not going to get anywhere without a map.

That was when Ramiren interjected with a smile. He looked down at the glowing roll of parchment in front of him I'd been too distracted to notice. Writing materialized on the parchment as he spoke, "Dilapidated house, in the Jorin Swamp, south of Puldoni. Our Irenian Swamp, south of Evraka. That's number one. Number two, is in a cave east of the Tanta Desert, our Pouroe, north of the mountain pass. Third is in Wistran, our Camlynn, in the castle in the capital city of Carpatha."

Leraska replied, eyebrows raised as though impressed, "Yes, all of that is correct."

Holy shit. "You have a gift for memory."

"You have to, in my line of work." The glowing scroll rolled up and disappeared in a puff of purple smoke.

Georgina yawned and scratched her tiny belly. "If nothing else, I can help a little. I've been to the Feylands a few times. Not many places are better than Elancia or Kopi for metalwork and blacksmithing, outside of Tirvinir."

I peered down at the gnome and recalled the large elf I'd seen earlier, wondering how such big beings could work so well alongside such small ones.

How many had accidentally been stepped on?

"Are you coming with us, then, Ramiren? They haven't stolen anything from you. This isn't necessarily your fight." *We could use someone of his skills, not to mention my idea...*

My sharp inhale sounded deafening, so I held the breath.

You want his help. That's all.

He graced me with a one-sided smile, and my stomach knotted. "I am here to assist. I've been to the Feylands before, though perhaps not as often as our tinkerer here, and I believe my presence might be beneficial to you. Besides, I have business there. It should not interfere with this."

The deep breath I'd been holding puffed out in relief. "Thank you." He nodded once at my gratitude.

Leraska went on, "They keep vials of their treasures, those stolen from people, in cupboards. Search there for your name and break the glass. It should give you back what was taken."

"How would my tools fit in a vial?" Georgina questioned, looking skeptical.

Leraska replied, tilting her head down to smile at the gnome, "Those things stolen are often abstract, and rarely physical items. Likely, your ability to use those tools was also stolen. Regardless, your actual tools should be near the cupboard."

Georgina scrunched up her face. "But that's utter nonsense! I know how to *use* tools." She put her hand to her chin. "Though at the moment I cannot seem to recall what a wrench is for..."

"How do you know so much about them?" A warning in the pit of my stomach flourished and would not relent. It seemed too convenient. *What does she gain from this?*

She chuckled and shrugged as though the answer was obvious. "I live in the Feylands. They are well known."

At my side, Raewyn met my eyes and gave a shrug of her own. "I guess," she murmured.

She lowered her staff point-down into the ground and stood straighter. "I am the head caretaker of the Ivory Grove. Go there when you have completed your task, on the eastern Wistran border, and I will be waiting to send you home. Are you ready to depart?"

"This is a lot to memorize," I grumbled. Perhaps she does gain something from their demise, but there was no indication of how. *Or she merely wants to rid the Feylands of evil creatures and cannot do it alone.* "Yes, I am ready. I'll be sure to search for your name in the cupboards."

When everyone else affirmed their own readiness, Leraska smiled. "Then let us begin." A gentle light emanated from the staff she held in her hands, which got brighter and brighter until it exploded.

A sharp, nauseous feeling gripped my belly with the sensation of being thrown violently backwards. The world lurched and tossed me about as though in a maelstrom. I sucked in a breath, and then recognized I couldn't. There was no air. Panic rose in my chest, causing my heart to beat wildly.

And then it ended as soon as it started, only to find myself on the ground choking on weeds and dirt. Rising to my knees, my burning lungs filled in a heaving gasp. Everyone else around me did the same. The tents, sounds, and lights of the Fey Carnival were gone, leaving a prairie of purple grass in its place.

My heartbeat calmed, and the panic faded.

The Feylands.

Up ahead lay a large city, where Evraka would have been if we were still in Laeth. Instead, Leraska had called it Puldoni.

Or was it Dulponi?

We stood with a wobble, coughing, groaning, dusting ourselves off. Mentally ticking off the list to ensure everyone was accounted for, I wasn't surprised to see Leraska was absent. The hope for a guide was pointless, anyway. *Why give us that information if she planned to join us?* We would see her at the Ivory Grove after our mission was completed.

Next to us, a cobbled road cut through the purple grass, leading straight to the city.

"Follow the road, then?" Raewyn said, uncertain.

I marched through the grass to step onto the road, looking both ways. There was no one in sight. Taking off my flowered crown, my ticket, reminded Raewyn and Georgina to take off theirs as well. Ramiren unpinned the spray of flowers from his lapel and dropped it to the ground. Raewyn handed me hers, presumably to keep, after I flung mine into the grass. It was stuffed into my pouch.

She was always sentimental.

We looked around as we made our way along the wide stone path toward the city. The vibrant grass, knee high on either side of the wide path, blew and waved in a gentle breeze. It was dizzying to see an unusual color for one thing when I was used to it being another. The sky in the fading light was a soft red. The purple grass. The green-colored stones of the road. The air smelled faintly of lilacs, though there was no lilac bush in sight.

A hiss made us stop in our tracks as a long jewel-colored snake slithered out. "Greetingssss, travelerssss. You go to Puldoni? The time of the Great Wilderness is nigh. Beware the frog and toad, for they are at war." And it continued to the other side of the path into the grass again.

We all watched it in silence until Raewyn burst into snorting laughter, "That was random!"

Great Wilderness? "And perhaps wise advice? I do not know this place."

Georgina chirped, "Oh, yeah. Frogs and toads have been at each other's throats for a long time. Like a blood feud that probably started over who has the juiciest flies to eat." She leaned down and peered where the snake disappeared. "And I think that was a seer snake." She straightened and snickered. "I bet they didn't make that name up themselves. Can you imagine them saying it? Sssssssseer Sssssssnake. And what if his name was Simon or Sammy? Sssssssammy the Sssssssseer Sssssssnake."

M.A.L.C.O.L.M. beeped. "NONSENSE. A BLOOD FEUD? FROGS AND TOADS DO NOT HAVE OPPOSABLE THUMBS. THEY CANNOT HOLD WEAPONS."

Georgina rolled her eyes. "Maybe they fight with their... paws? Hands? Hm, neither sounds right."

I answered her, "Feet is correct, I believe."

Georgina stared up at me with a challenging look. "How would you know?"

"I've heard of frogs having webbed feet." *Why were we talking about this? We need to move, not ponder something so inconsequential.* Trusting everyone to follow, my feet followed the path to the city. Changing the subject, I spoke again, "If we get into trouble, I hope everyone knows to stay behind me."

"Well, we wouldn't stand in front of you, dummy," Georgina spat.

My left eye twitched. "And M.A.L.C.O.L.M., of course. I assume your automaton knows how to fight?" The large brown machinery next to her had been built with a humanoid's frame, complete with two arms, two legs, a torso, and a head with two glowing yellow orbs for eyes. *How do they function?* Such complex creations began coming out of Tirvinir years ago, a few which I'd had the pleasure to see in person.

"He does!" Georgina said, a mix of pride and excitement as she patted the automaton's flank. "He's very scrappy."

M.A.L.C.O.L.M. beeped. "DID YOU MAKE ME OUT OF SCRAPS?"

"No, silly. You were made from whole parts. I just mean... Oh, never mind." Georgina sighed. "What about you, Ramiren? Are you scrappy?"

Ramiren's mouth twitched in a smile. He put a hand on the hilt of his rapier. "Not nearly as much as your automaton or Lady Nathalia, but I can hold my own. My value lies in exposing and pointing out weaknesses for others to exploit, along with negotiation."

Georgina looked him up and down. "I get it, so that rapier on your side is decorative?"

Ramiren looked down at her briefly as he walked. "No, I know how to use it. I just rarely feel the need to, when often words will cool tempers. But if push comes to shove, yes, I can hold my own."

"What about you, Georgina?" Raewyn asked. "Can you hold your own?"

She frowned. "I have a crossbow in my tool bag, but I built an automaton so I wouldn't *have* to hold my own." Georgina shook her head. "Which means we need to find the mischief hag who took my tools fast. M.A.L.C.O.L.M. gets hit, dinged, even pieces chopped off too often, and he'll become a useless hunk of metal. A paperweight. I need to be able to repair him."

M.A.L.C.O.L.M. beeped. "THAT HURTS MY FEELINGS, GEORGINA."

Georgina replied evenly, "You don't have feelings. You have gears."

The automaton beeped again. "THAT HURTS MY GEARS, GEORGINA."

Making sure to hide my smirk, we continued down the path to the narrow gates of the city. Normally, even at this late hour, a city of this size would have caravans, people coming and going through the gates. Merchants or carriages. Noise. Bustle. Not here. Here, it was quiet aside from the distant clamor of the large fey metropolis.

Two guards, far shorter and even more stout than I, stood sentry in front of a closed gate. As we drew near, one called out, "Who goes there?"

I stopped and called back, "Travelers from Laeth, seeking refuge and rest. May we pass?"

They looked at each other, their faces obscured by helmets, and one nodded, moving to push the gate open. "We want no trouble, hear?"

"Of course not. One question though," I said and moved forward into the city. "Why is it so quiet?"

The guard lifted his helmet visor. His glossy, pitch black skin and friendly black eyes with a small horn between them indicated he was a dyna fey. *With how strong they're supposed to be, I'm not surprised they're used as guards here.* "Oh, this is the King's Gate. Most travelers pass through the Green Gate, since it's wider and can better handle carts and wagons. Might as well let you in here. No point in making Laeth travelers walk all the way around."

"Most kind."

It was near dusk when we entered, and the city was beginning to come alive with stone taverns and rustic inns opening their doors to the merrymakers, drunks, and travelers who had come to spend their coin. Lamplighters rushed about to fill their quota. Street urchins peeked out from behind corners. Carriages rumbled past. Well-dressed merchants rushed around us, their guards in their wake.

"We need to find a place for the evening," I remarked sideways to Raewyn. "Have you ever stayed in Dulponi, Georgina?"

She tilted her head in mock confusion. "What's Dulponi?"

Turning my gaze skyward, a few seconds were spent praying for patience. "Puldoni."

She smirked. "No, I haven't."

My irritated grumble disguised in a rough throat clear, I asked the pactmaker, "Ramiren? Have you?"

"My apologies, Lady Nathalia. I haven't."

A nearby group of male elves were laughing and talking. Moving close enough so I wouldn't have to yell my request, I asked, "Excuse me, could you please tell me a good place to stay for the night?"

One of the elves, a broad-shouldered fellow with tousled blond hair, looked me up and down and grinned in a lascivious manner. "In my bed-"

My muttered reply dripped with petulance. "Nope."

The elves began to rib the rejected man as I went back to my companions. "Let's just walk and find something. There are probably vacant inns along the main avenue."

We followed the street, dodging groups ambling the opposite way, people stumbling out of taverns, and the general ruckus of a vibrant nightlife. I'd visited Evraka many times, usually on a layover in-between caravan trips heading out from the Trading City. The identical layout of Puldoni, however, was eerily similar, with small changes. A toy store I'd once stopped at to buy presents for my twin brothers was a haberdashery here.

A mirror of Laeth, indeed.

The city took on a lively mood. *Is there a holiday or festival being celebrated?* Shops still open kept their doors propped to let in the cooler air, lantern light, and customers drawn in by the savory smells or shiny sights of what the vendors offered. Eventually, we looked up at a blade sign decorated with a large golden star.

"The Forever Inn. This seems as good a place as any." I shrugged, moving to step inside.

"Wait, Nat!" I heard Raewyn yell behind me.

My hand paused on the swinging door. "Yes?"

Raewyn shook her head. "What if they don't want us here? We're not fey."

I answered her immediately, "Then they don't like money." Stepping through the door, we were assaulted by the stomach-churning smell of roasting meat, the yeasty scent of ale, and the din of a roaring crowd all talking over themselves. Though the inn's common room was loud, only half of the tables were taken. Our presence did not seem to arouse any suspicion as we maneuvered to the bar.

"Good evening, sir. We'd all like rooms if you have them available."

The barkeep, a fey with pointed ears and mottled brown and gray hair, looked all of us over with yellow eyes. I saw the same thick hair on his bare forearms, leading to sharp claws at the end of his fingers that tapped on the bartop. *Lupa fey.* "Aye, got rooms for you. How many do you need?"

"Yes, thank you. Four."

The barkeep's yellow eyes lit up as someone behind me hissed a grimace, and I inwardly cursed my mistake.

I said thank you to a fey.

The barkeep eyed me. "Let's just say… your room price is doubled and call it even, aye?"

It was a gracious offer. *I'll have to tamp that down. And fast.*

I grudgingly nodded in agreement.

Raewyn squeezed to my side and raised a hand to interrupt. "I can sing and tell stories for my payment."

The barkeep eyed Raewyn up and down. "Are they good stories and songs? I ain't got time for 'once upon a time, there was a princess, and she lived happily ever after.'"

"No, no, they're good stories. And I have a good voice for singing."

"She does. She's an excellent singer." When we were younger, Raewyn could belt out songs better than I. She sang the songs I wrote, and she never disappointed.

He sighed. "Sure, but only because it's a slow night. Might be you bring in some patrons." He pointed a claw at a nearby table, and we took our seats. A waitress came over, a broad elven woman with a smile and a tray.

"What can I get you all?"

"Wine," Ramiren and I said simultaneously. Ramiren inclined his head to me with a chuckle.

"You appreciate wine, Master Ramiren? I am not surprised."

His chuckle morphed into a grin. "Indeed, good wine is to be savored." He leaned in, as though sharing a secret, "Poor wine is to be chugged."

The waitress winked at Ramiren.

Catching her attention to order was more difficult than it should've been. "Red wine, please. Tawny port, if you have it." The waitress's eyes flickered to me, then back to Ramiren, who asked for the same. Her eyes ran him up and down in a slow perusal, and I quickly became irritated at her disrespect.

Raewyn ordered the same wine as well. Georgina rolled her eyes, muttering, "Fussy wine drinkers," and ordered ale. M.A.L.C.O.L.M. tried to order ale too, but Georgina shook her head, saying something about circuitry. The waitress departed to fulfill the requests.

I finally replied to Ramiren, "Chugged? Or spilled?"

Ramiren lifted a hand to indicate my point. "Or spilled, true. But even poor wine is useful."

"Useful? How?" My back settled into the chair. "Surely, you don't mean to get drunk."

Ramiren let out a barking laugh as he tongued a sharp-looking canine. "I am caught, Lady Nathalia."

Unlike when we first met, his laugh excited me, for some reason. Charmed, I couldn't blame the waitress for wanting to look at him instead of me.

Raewyn clearing her throat made me realize I was staring. I jolted out of my daze. "Hm?" My sister raised an eyebrow at me with a smug smile plastered on her face, causing me to shift uncomfortably in my chair.

Raewyn crossed her arms as she leaned back. "Shall we discuss how we're going to get our stuff back? Particulars? Battle plans? Perhaps, a timely hag-flavored bonfire?"

Flavored? "Slowly but surely," I replied. "We go to these mischief hags one after the other and take them back. Violently, if necessary, yes. Whole beaches of sand began with a single grain. It'll take time, yes, but eventually we will be successful. Through perseverance, we shall prevail."

Raewyn exhaled upwards, puffing the red fringe on her forehead. "What about you, Ramiren? What do you think we should do?"

Ramiren considered before speaking. "I think Lady Nathalia has a point, but perhaps it doesn't have to be so brutal. These mischief hags are dangerous creatures. They will be tough foes to beat."

Raewyn tittered. "Was the bonfire idea too much?"

Ramiren cleared his throat. "What I mean is, maybe these hags can be bartered with. They are fey, and fey love a good deal. It just so happens you have an expert in deals with you."

"I thought you didn't like making deals with fey, Master Ramiren?"

Ramiren replied with a drawn-out sigh, "I don't, but I'd rather oversee a deal than witness a death I can do nothing about. No one enjoys helplessness."

I acknowledged his statement with an emphatic hum. "Certainly, but I'm not sure I feel comfortable making deals with hags, evil creatures that they are. We would leave them to do this to other children or..." I said, looking at Georgina. "...adults."

He conceded my point with a shrug. "Then, the sword will do. But until then, I urge you to give me a chance. We put ourselves at risk as well, starting a fight we might not be able to finish."

Raewyn murmured, "Oh, hello, lovely lady..."

Following her line of sight to a beautiful elven woman sitting with a group of armed fellows, the corners of my mouth twitched when Raewyn's chair scraped the floor as she stood and headed toward the woman with a bright smile on her face. When I turned back around, Ramiren's gaze was trained on me, as though he was studying a curious specimen.

"What? Do I have dirt on me?" I peered down at myself, scrutinizing my clothing and armor.

He hummed before answering. "No. You don't seem much bothered by your sister's proclivities."

My shrug seemed to make him even more interested. "No, I am not. My sister has preferred the company of women since we were young, barely sixteen years old. It's not as though her preferences are something that can be changed, any more than my preferences for men. They just are. As long as she is happy, I am happy."

Ramiren nodded, taking in my words, and brightened when he saw the waitress approaching to place wine glasses and an ale mug on the table. "That's good of you," he said, pulling out a coin pouch. He slid a gold coin toward the waitress, who took it with her fingers brushing his, and it disappeared into her pocket. He didn't seem to notice the touch. Or, at least, he did not acknowledge it.

She grinned at him. "Anything else, love?"

She's not getting either tip she's hoping for. Refusing to acknowledge where that thought came from, I asked the waitress, "Where is a good place to buy rations and other incidentals for the road?"

She finally realized I existed and pointed behind her. "Oh, down the street, there's a grocer. They should have what you need. Mirin's Goods and Grocery."

She's elven. I could thank her.

Part of me didn't want to, but manners won out.

"Thank you. Is anyone else hungry?" When no one said yes, I answered her question to Ramiren. "No, nothing else." She shrugged and departed. "Why is that good of me, Master Ramiren?"

Ramiren paused, as though thinking of his response. He ran a finger down the seam of the wooden table absently. "There are many who do not feel it is right."

The wine swirled in my glass. It smelled like chocolate. Tawny port was sweeter than my usual, but I was in the mood for sweetness. Plus, good wine was good wine. "It hurts none. I do not share her attractions, but she is not me. People who think it is not right are likely incapable of either empathizing or believing someone is able to like something they don't."

Putting the wine glass to my lips to appreciate a sip, I found the tawny port was indeed chocolatey. *Fey-made wine?* "Which *I* don't feel is right. So, see? Everyone becomes disappointed when people can't just leave others alone." My first real smile of the evening creased my face; I felt giddy for some reason.

Is it the wine? Is fey wine dangerous?

I eyed my wine with suspicion.

He returned the smile. "Hear hear." He raised his wine to mine, and the glasses clinked. "Cheers to you, Lady Nathalia. Rapidly becoming the best of us."

A snort burst out of me, but I drank to the toast with a much smaller sip.

Georgina snickered into her ale mug, overhearing our conversation, and muttered under her breath, "The best of us, indeed."

I'll let that slide.

The gnome took a long gulp of her ale and sat the mug down with a loud thunk. "So, Ramiren. You make deals, eh?"

Ramiren turned his smile to the diminutive woman. "I do, Mistress Georgina. Pacts, specifically. I have for some time now."

"And are you good at it?" She raised her eyebrow.

It is rare when men will admit they're not superb at what they do.

To my surprise, instead of answering immediately, Ramiren thought for a few seconds before replying, "I like to think so, yes. I've made many and have never had one broken."

Georgina nodded while he spoke. "I've never met a broodling who wasn't good at what he did." She raised her tankard to him in salute, which Ramiren reciprocated with his own glass.

My attention went back to Raewyn, who was now sitting in the elven woman's lap. *At least her evening is going well.*

But isn't mine going well, too? I suppose we'll see.

"Raewyn! Give us a song!" I yelled over my shoulder, and the patrons all quieted as Raewyn hopped up with a grin and giggle.

She placed a peck of a kiss on the elven woman's cheek and spun to address the common room's inhabitants, "Alright, fey and friend, alike! This one is called *The Dryad's Run.*"

Chapter Four

The First Lesson

"Good night, Nat," my sister said, giggling at the smiling elven woman as Raewyn fumbled for the doorknob. She was so dwarfed by the elven woman, it was almost comical. "Now, c'mere you. Let me show you the first and last rule of living."

"What does that mean?" the elven woman asked as she was pulled gently by the hand into the room.

Raewyn laughed. "Love, dearest. The first and last rule of living is love. Or so Minue says." She closed the door behind them. I couldn't hear anything more, suddenly grateful for the inn's thick walls.

I settled into my room for the evening. The alone time was a rare treat, but it would be cut short very soon. My clothes were dusty and dirty, and I needed to look my best for this.

There was a large metal tub in an attached room. The metal tube pointing down into it, with levers on either side, made me hesitate in going back downstairs to ask the innkeeper for water to be brought up. When I pulled the levers, clear water came out. By the time I figured out the levers indicated temperature, as well as quantity, the tub was filled halfway.

Maybe I should just...

No. I have to go talk to him.

After bathing, and figuring out the drainage system, I pulled a liquidy green silk dress from my pouch that had been packed because it didn't wrinkle, yet it was fine enough for even a host's table.

And it had pockets.

When I slipped it on, the silk was a little tighter than the last time it was worn. My undergarments' edges were outlined through the fabric. *They'll have to go.*

Taking them off, I checked again, noting with satisfaction that the silk finally sat flush and smooth against my skin. It was time.

Locking the door after me and tucking the key in my pocket, I walked down the hall and around the corner, stopping in front of the door I remembered he disappeared behind.

My hand hovered over the wooden planks. *This will all be all right. Grains of sand make a beach. Little steps make a journey.*

A moment after I knocked, the breeze from the door swiftly opening caught my hair.

"Yes?" Ramiren looked surprised. "Oh, Lady Nathalia. What can I do for you?"

Even the comfort I felt in his presence couldn't keep the nervousness at bay. "May we speak, Master Ramiren? I have something to discuss with you."

"Yes, of course." He stepped aside to let me enter, his ever-present and cordial smile on his face.

The comfortable chamber was very similar to my own. The room smelled faintly of lavender due to the ribbon-tied bundles hanging from a few rafters. A large bed with velvet covers commanded most of the room. My slippered feet sank into the plush carpet I stepped onto and then stopped. A low ornate dresser stood in the middle of the left wall, a table with chairs on the right. Artwork hung on hooks, depicting landscapes of the area. A fresh bowl of fruit sat in the corner on a small table.

This inn has not disappointed.

The door closed behind me, and the room grew so dim it was hard to see much of anything. A small pile of papers with tiny writing lay strewn across a small table, making me almost question him about how he could read with so few candles. Then the lesson on broodlings came to mind. *Right, they can see in the dark.*

Ramiren passed me to light a few more candles, likely for my benefit, and then faced me. "Now, you have something to discuss?"

His red-irised eyes, at once alluring and intense, met mine as he waited patiently for me to answer. *This was, at least, not going to be unpleasant.* The corners of my mouth pulled into a half-smile.

Clearing my throat, I answered, "As mentioned earlier, you are a pactmaker, yes?"

Ramiren tilted his head. "I am, yes. Do you wish to form a pact, Lady Nathalia?"

My fingers twisted together in front of me. "Master Ramiren, I recall where I've heard of you. From an acquaintance of yours, who you struck a deal with, of sorts. I think. Elijah Callan?"

Ramiren narrowed his eyes, as though thinking. "The name does sound familiar, yes. I saved his life. What of him?"

My mouth twitched again. "He said you were fair with him when you struck your bargain. You are also handsome, so that should make the task easier."

He raised an eyebrow, but I continued.

"He said you were pleasant company, and that you were discreet. I am counting on that discretion, and your fairness. You see..." I sighed and closed my eyes.

I might as well come out with it.

"I wish to be married. I rather despise what I do, and most of what it entails. But most of all, I hate the uncertainty. I want to be settled. Have a predictable life. And that, Master Ramiren, is where you come in. I want to be happy, yes, but it is paramount for my husband to be happy as well. I have trained as a protector at the Horyn Academy where I scored well. I've also been tutored in music, the arts, history, math and finances, and everything else a gently-bred woman is expected to know. I even know how to cook. Do you know how rare that is for someone of my status?"

He clicked his tongue. "Ah. Not particularly, no."

"Yes, well, I do. It was either that or starve to death on the road."

Ramiren gave me a warm smile that made me pause. "Lady Nathalia?"

"Hm?"

"Take a deep breath, then go on."

A polite way to say I am rambling and to get to the point.

My deep breath helped, but the nails biting into my palms centered me even more. "But once past the bedroom door, I am largely ignorant. It is my last remaining blindspot. My proposal, Master Ramiren, is for you to teach me how to please my future husband."

Ramiren's face was unreadable as his gaze burrowed into mine. Nothing about him changed at my words, and that made my confidence dwindle.

His voice came out low, "Please a man, you say."

My head bobbed rapidly. "Yes. I want it to be a happy marriage. That involves me knowing how to please him, whomever it might be."

His head tilted down as he stared at me over the rim of his glasses. "And... by 'please', you mean sexually."

Is it warm in here?

Though I was appreciative he was understanding, it seemed unnecessary to frame it that way, making me awkwardly clear my throat. "Yes, exactly. I want lessons."

The glowing scroll from earlier appeared near Ramiren and began to record our spoken words. My eyes twitched in its direction before turning my attention back to Ramiren.

He wove his fingers together in front of him, mirroring my pose. "Did your sister suggest this? Did anyone?"

Ah. I understand. "No, she did not, Master Ramiren. No one did. This is my own idea."

He looked up at the ceiling, seeming to weigh my offer. "Pardon my questions, but this is a very unusual request, and frankly, rife with... potential difficulties. Namely control and consent concerns, as well as power imbalances, to be exact. I make it no secret I take consent very seriously; it was why I never trained in enslavement pacts. I *am* able to teach, and you are able to learn, I'm sure. You're a well-mannered, intelligent woman. However, it would be irresponsible of me not to mention those possibilities and ensure you still want to proceed."

Hm. I hadn't considered that. Raewyn never mentioned problems she'd had when training. Perhaps I should have asked her before doing this?

"I understand the possibilities, and I still want to proceed."

His posture relaxed slightly, and a small amount of tension eased in my neck. "And what will you say if your future husband asks how you learned such things?"

My answer was ready, expecting this question at least, "I would say I was trained by the priestesses of Minue."

It was a perfect explanation. The priestesses would sometimes train young noble women, like my sister did, in what was known as bedroom etiquette. Assuming they had both the coin to pay for such instruction and the wherewithal to train at all. Many were squeamish about the prospect and received a few moments of advice from their mothers before adjourning to the wedding chamber.

I had never fully felt comfortable with the priestesses, though, my sister notwithstanding. Those devoted to the Goddess of Love and Beauty seemed somehow far too flowery regarding sexuality and far too raunchy regarding love.

Also, I learned best by doing.

My thoughts snapped back to the present as Ramiren spoke again, "And had you an idea of payment in mind?"

"Oh. Yes." *It'll be worth it. Mother would understand.* My hands moved to the back of my neck to unhook my necklace.

"My luck stone. You asked about it earlier, I recall. It will grant the user some measure of luck as long as it's worn. It did not seem to help with the singing contest, but I suspect Raewyn was correct, and the contest was rigged. I would give it in exchange."

Ramiren took the stone from me, holding it up to his red eyes. He seemed to stare at it for a time, and then his eyes shifted to me. "I saw Lord Leviathus off to the side talking to the Zackman Brothers as everyone was entering the stands, so it's entirely possible." He smiled and went on, "Very well. If you are comfortable with my instruction, even after my caveat, I accept. A few things before we begin."

He lowered the gem, placing it in the palm of his other hand. "The terms of our arrangement are not shackles, and this doesn't work at all if you feel coerced in any way. We may encounter limits while I am instructing, those you are unaware you have, and that I couldn't know about. We can avoid that conflict by making sure that the encounters aren't pushing past your limits. Learning to please is most effective when those boundaries are understood, and no one is harmed. Though this time we will be using this inn's room, subsequent lessons will use a classroom of sorts. It is private and well-protected, but it takes time to create based upon the complexity of what's required."

He moved to the small pouch sitting on the table and opened it, carefully threading the necklace through the opening. Closing it again, he looked back at me. "'No' is a powerful word, Lady Nathalia. Never hesitate to use it, especially with me. You don't need to worry about being tricked or trapped.

I'll hold to both the spirit and letter of the pact, and if you need to stop what we are doing, or renegotiate terms to add conditions, remove them, or redefine, you should have words or phrases in mind to let me know. Please undress."

My back straightened. "Wait, now?"

His voice was gentle, with no judgment detected, "Is this a bad time? You have every right to say no, as I said, and we can begin when you *are* ready."

"It's not that. I just... you surprised me." The confusion passed, to be replaced with nervous energy coursing through me on the way to the dresser. Taking one last look at him, and noting he did not have his back turned, I huffed. *Might as well get this over with.*

After removing my shoes, my gown went up and over my head. Folding my dress, placing it on top of the dresser, I stood before him. My arms and hands stuck to my sides like glue. Grateful for my time at the Academy, the women's barracks had no room for modesty, making my shyness eventually give way. *But Ramiren is not one of my fellow initiates.*

His eyes roamed down my body slowly, though it was unclear if in appreciation or to catalogue. Identifying interest in someone's eyes, especially if they were being overt, was usually not too difficult, but his were hidden behind glasses.

I lifted my chin, hoping it would present the confidence I currently lacked. "I remarked you being handsome would make this easier. It goes both ways, of course. If I am lovely in your eyes, then that will make your task far more pleasant as well." Pausing to get my nervousness under control with another deep breath, I opened my mouth again, my words were thankfully stronger.

It is important he understands this, and it is equally important I convey it with firmness.

"There are just three exceptions I must insist on, Master Ramiren. First, you may do whatever you like, whatever you feel would be beneficial for me to know, and you may instruct me to do anything. I will obey whatever command you give when we are in private, *within reason*. But there's to be no vaginal intercourse. That is something I will do with my future husband only." *One down, two to go.*

"Secondly, no one, not even our traveling companions, can know of this pact. If it is found out accidentally, that is one thing, but we must do our best to keep it between us. Third, this is an exclusive contract. I will not seek outside advice or training, if you'll agree to not have sexual relations with anyone else for its duration. Are those terms acceptable to you?"

Ramiren's smile widened. "Those terms suit me and are well-worded. We may want to revisit the concept of a phrase for boundaries should lessons get intense enough that I'd want one to be certain I don't risk harm with an instruction. The phrase won't be needed immediately, or even in the next lesson. Merely something to keep in mind. If you are amenable, we can begin. The pact is sealed." His eyes flashed from red to a smoldering orange, like a campfire, as he said these last words.

A wave of sudden fear passed through me, making me take a calming, silent breath. "Very well. I am amenable." Extending my hand, palm up in a Camlite handshake, I waited for him to accept my hand.

He waited for a beat, then spoke as though whispering a stage cue, "You need to repeat the words 'the pact is sealed' for it to be finalized."

"Oh. Apologies. The pact is sealed."

The lights in the room intensified with a small roar of individual flames as I repeated the words. It startled me, and my eyes darted around the room. The floating scroll next to Ramiren rolled up and disappeared with a puff of purple smoke. He extended his own hand, placing the palm face down upon mine to complete the handshake. His hand felt rougher than I would have thought, and almost feverish. I wondered what other surprises lay in store.

Gods, why is it so damned warm in here?

His voice took an instructive tone again, and my skin caught fire. "To give pleasure, I need you to understand what it is. If you want to please, we'll want something for you to focus on, and at first, that'll be your own pleasure. We'll be starting from the beginning, and focusing on the physical sensations with the most basic tools for both pleasure and communication: hands and mouth. I want you to focus on what I do and how it makes you feel. Each touch, caress, or lick. Hold the most pleasurable of those feelings in your mind as long as you can, remember them if you're able. You'll find them useful for what comes next."

Listening and watching Ramiren as he talked, so matter-of-factly, my head tilted as I watched his mouth move. His forked tongue flicked between his teeth as he spoke, and a warmth pooled between my legs as my head began to spin. It took me a few seconds to realize he'd finished speaking. "Alright. I will try. Please-" but I was interrupted.

The broodling stepped close, and his extremely warm hands reached out to tentatively caress my bare shoulders. I automatically stiffened and had to force myself to relax in his hands.

"Is this all right?" he asked quietly.

My firm nod was the only confirmation I could manage, not trusting myself to open my mouth.

"First, there are specific areas of the body which are particularly sensitive to touch and elicit arousal. Some are quite obvious, some not. They can vary from person to person, but the most common are here..." His fingertips brushed the shell of my ear with featherlike pressure. My skin broke out in goosebumps.

"Here..." His fingers moved to the sides and back of my neck. My breath hitched with a sharp inhale, and my eyes sealed shut. He'd barely touched me, and I already wanted to burst out of my skin.

"Here..." He moved down to my breasts, grazing the hardening nipples. A sound, not unlike a whimper, left my throat. My face and chest felt like it was burning, but not from embarrassment.

"Here..." His hands reached around to my back, running a gentle touch from my neck to my tailbone. My back bowed as I gasped, pleasure streaking up and down my spine and lighting each vertebrae. I had been touched there before, but not like this. This was not a healer's touch, at least not the kind I was used to.

Fuck!

It was absolute torture that I never wanted to stop. Phantom fingers lingered long after he had moved on to another area, and an unfamiliar ache began to reside in my belly. It was deep, insistent want. I wanted his hands to splay themselves across every inch of me, and I wanted his mouth to follow.

He spoke softly, like he didn't want to intrude on the moment, "I'm going to move lower now. Stop me if it gets to be too much."

At my non-verbal acceptance, his hands traced down my body. "Here…" He reached my inner thighs. The tremble I'd developed wouldn't stop. I felt cold and hot all at once. And so very dizzy.

"And now, for the most obvious area."

His hand rose higher, making me jump when he brushed against my labia. A shaky moan escaped as he explored me with slow fingers. The cold from earlier evaporated, leaving only the heat behind. I wanted his mouth there, too.

But what would he do there?

Mentally, I viciously cursed my lack of creativity.

"Now, I want you to touch yourself and focus on how it feels. It's completely fine and normal if you don't bring yourself to orgasm just yet. This is what practice is for."

"Hm?" Dimly aware of him moving me to the bed, I automatically sat down after the velvet cover hit the back of my knees.

"Lounge back," he instructed. I did so, adjusting the pillows behind my head.

He hovered over me and gently took my wrist to turn my hand, adjusting my fingers over the soft mound between my thighs and pushing them through the damp curls. My face flamed.

The last time I'd touched myself this way, I was fifteen. My governess had walked in on me doing so, and she screamed at me for my vulgarity so loudly everyone in the villa could likely hear my shame. Begging her not to tell my parents, swearing I'd never do it again, barely convinced her. But she's agreed. I kept my word and didn't touch myself again, even though I wanted to. Many many times.

But here… here, it was actively encouraged. Looking into his eyes, expecting admonishment, I saw only patience. No judgment. My fingers flexed in the warm wetness.

Satisfied the assignment was understood, he let go of my wrist, bringing both hands back to my neck as my eyes closed. It felt as though I had been running. He responded by kissing along my forehead, then moving to my ears, sucking and nipping on the lobe before going to my jawline and neck. Each brush of his mouth or teeth spun me higher. Pressure built in my stomach. My chest. And, most especially, between my legs where the pleasant pulsing turned exquisitely intense. I breathed in deeply, feeling like my lungs couldn't get enough air. He wore no cologne, but as his black hair came closer, I detected the faint scent of honey. A wild thought made me wonder if he was from beeswax in his pomade. *He couldn't naturally smell like that, could he?* Whatever the reason, it was a warm aroma, and my muscles loosened.

Letting out a soft moan again, my head turned toward him.

He murmured, "And, finally, here…"

He covered my mouth with a kiss, his tongue sliding over my lips and tongue as I opened for him. If his hands were warm, his mouth was molten. A muffled squeak escaped my throat as I went stiff.

Is this too much? Aren't we supposed to focus on him?

But after a moment, my own questions disintegrated with a low hum against his mouth. My body melted as his chest lowered to mine, noting the lean, hard ridges of his form. His body heat radiated through his clothing, and my chest rose to absorb the warmth. It felt like the coziest blanket.

My unpracticed and fumbling fingertips swirled around a sensitive area that made me shudder. My unpracticed tongue flicked at his, and I perfectly hit the small space between the forks. When he suddenly broke the kiss, I opened my eyes to see him staring down at my face in astonishment.

"Is something wrong? Did I-?"

He shook his head, "No." His eyes on me, he nudged my hand to the side with his own. His fingers circled, finding places I had not, making me suck in a sharp breath.. A pleasant pressure joined the pulsing and began to build.

"I'm going to enter you now. Again, please stop me if it is too much or if you feel uncomfortable. This is meant to be pleasurable, not painful." When his finger entered me, I stiffened again, expecting pain, but none came. The pleasure had dimmed slightly, but not gone away. Now, it was more teasing and tender, but still foreign. Gripping his clothing as a reflex, my breath came in fast gasps. More wetness pooled, easing his movements. Then the pressure spiked without warning, and my head leaned back to let out a long, low moan that rumbled in my chest.

He spoke, saying something no doubt important, but I couldn't hear him. A second finger joined his first, moving them in and out and then curving them in a 'come hither' beckoning motion. The unfamiliar stretch burned, not like fire but scorching all the same. His thumb pushed past my saturated curls, finding a particular spot that sent my head spinning. My arched feet and curling toes rubbed against the soft quilt, causing friction on my inner thighs with his hand. A strained whimper left my lips.

Ramiren positioned himself catlike on the bed at my feet and eased his way up between my thighs, running his hands up my legs to my hips. He parted me and began to lower his mouth. When I lifted my head to look down at him, confusion set in. "I fail to see hoooooooo- oh gods, what are you doing?" When he flicked his tongue straight through the center in a long, languid stroke, I shrieked as the back of my head hit the pillow. Slapping both hands over my traitor mouth, the pressure and warmth combined with the pulsing between my legs where his lips and tongue moved in an intricate pattern only he knew. I had no idea what needed to happen aside from never, ever stopping this. A gentle draft from somewhere ghosted over the gathering sweat on my body, producing a shiver.

Can't take much more..

My hips tried to rise, but his fingers held them down. My watery eyes closed shut.

Need to move.

My thighs contracted, on their own volition, around his temples and the gentle points of his black horns bit into my legs. Somehow, they added to the delicious and new sensations spreading through me. The intense pressure became more and more consuming. Ever building and never stopping.

I felt soft hair in my fingers, vaguely aware my hands had left my mouth without me consciously moving them. It was silky in my hands. A strangled sob escaped from me. My breathing came in harsh pants. My hips pressed into his mouth, rhythmically as the act took over. With my legs shaking and my breathing shallow and high-pitched, I whispered wonderingly, "A-aren't you getting...tired?"

Don't be tired.

He made a noise indicating he was not, and the vibration caused me to writhe. A tightness enveloped me, as though my whole body was poised for something. It was too much. It was all too much.

Don't stop.

I heard a feminine voice, soft but clear, say a word. ***Cordani.***

With no idea what it meant, or where it came from, I didn't care in the slightest.

Ramiren's fingers suddenly sank deeper into my skin. The pattern he traced with his mouth turned frantic as he laved me. When he let out a guttural groan, the pressure tipped. The room spun. The warmth spread to my whole body, and a sharp sensation rose upward and peaked, centered between my thighs until it exploded. I saw stars. My head fell back as I let out a moaning scream that echoed throughout the small room. His licks turned soft and soothing.

After I quieted, still trying to catch my breath, he stood on the side of the bed and looked down at me.

"Are you all right to continue?" He gazed down at me patiently. His chest rose and fell with his deep breaths, as though he was trying to settle himself, though he otherwise seemed self-controlled.

Him now. The whole reason I'm here.

Anticipation flooded me as I nodded.

"I mentioned hands and mouth as our basic tools. We're going to focus on your mastery of using both, at first. I want you to focus on the best, most pleasurable techniques from what we just did as you do this next part."

It was frankly adorable he thought I was coherent enough to pay attention to *technique* while he had his mouth on me.

"Enthusiasm, desire just sort of desperation, is at least as important as technique. It is a common expectation of men, and, I've found especially of noble men, for you to at least appear to want what is happening quite badly. Men are visual creatures. If they see you are enjoying yourself, it will only encourage their own desire. However, I will be honest with you. Many do not care what pleasure you derive from this, but I hope in your case you are paired with one who does. Does that make sense?"

I wanted to laugh. *Women talk, Ramiren.* "Mm-hmm."

He began to undress and folded his clothing to place them beside my gown on the dresser. I watched as his body was revealed to me, piece by piece, noting the tightly muscled, lean figure he was until he stood naked in front of me. My gaze went down, down, and thankfully my face didn't heat. *Don't be rude.* My eyes met his to see he was definitely amused.

Wait. Appear *to want it?*

"But is it all right if I do actually want it? Whatever it is? You said *appear to.*"

He pursed his lips, as though trying to hold in a broad smile. "Of course, that's all right. I wouldn't have it any other way. You can tell me if you do want it, or keep that secret for yourself, as you desire. I want you, as we start, to kneel in front of me on the floor. Grip the base of my cock with one hand. Avoid using your teeth at all times. You'll start slowly at first, your lips and tongue on the tip and moving down the shaft, while you pull from the base in the direction opposite from the base with your hand. We'll move to the bed if we need to, but you can play some by increasing the pull to a caress as my cock becomes slick while you flutter your tongue. I'll let you set the pace, but it should build in speed and intensity. Don't hold back any sighs or moans while you're doing this. Allow me to show you."

The lump in my throat almost choked me. *My tutors never talked like this.*

He sat down on the edge of the bed and beckoned me to scoot toward him. He took my right hand, folding all fingers down except for my index. He looked at me, over the rim of his glasses, before closing his eyes as his lips wrapped around the tip of my finger. I stared at him, caught, as I felt his tongue glide over the underside of my finger, and then flicked forward. A gentle sucking sensation accompanied his licks, and my finger slid farther into his mouth until he reached the top of my palm.

The finger came out again, and then back in. I felt no teeth or anything sharp, just a pleasant, warm wetness. I watched his jaw undulate with his tongue's motions. I tried to pay close attention to what he was doing, the speed, the depth, and his tongue flicks, but my vision became hazy as he continued. The warmth between my legs renewed, and I shifted on the bed as my breathing picked up. Then my finger exited his mouth with a soft pop.

"Your turn." He grabbed a pillow from behind me and stood back up, moving a few steps away. He tossed the pillow to the floor in front of him and gave me an encouraging smile, extending a hand to me.

With a deep breath to steady myself, I rolled off the bed. Taking his hand, he helped lower me to kneel in front of him. My fingers wrapped gently around his cock. It felt almost silky, and the heat from his skin was incredible, as though he were feverish. My mouth inched closer. Taking one last look up at his reassuring face, my eyes closed just as I enveloped his cock with my lips.

My tongue flicked to facilitate a swallow. When he groaned, I licked again to see if that's what caused his reaction. My experiment was successful and rewarded with another groan. I moved my tongue over the tip, then lowered my mouth down his shaft. My mouth filled with saliva, and I began to gag. He must have noticed, because he whispered, "Breathe through your nose and relax your throat. It will help."

Leaning back to remove him from my mouth while lowering my hand, I took another deep breath. He brushed his fingers on my throat and under my chin, almost like a massage. "You're doing very well. Remember the sensations you experienced on the bed."

Memories of his mouth taking my finger, sliding in and out with gentle suction, were clear in my mind. Determined to try again, the flat of my tongue slipped over the crest at the base of his tip. The ridge of it felt satisfying against my tongue. Raising my hand to his cock again and encircling it with my fingers, the tips overlapped around him but just barely. Gentle at first but with a rhythmic squeeze, I used my thumb to travel up and down a vein I had found.

Hard and soft at the same time.

He murmured, "Yes. Like that. Good."

My lips slipped over the rest of his cock that my hand didn't cover, sucking, licking, and nuzzling with my tongue that same crest as before. I pressed my thighs together when the greedy pulsing returned in earnest. A hiss made me peek up at him.

He stared down at me, his jaw slack with his elongated canines showing. Though unable to hear it, his rapid breathing caused his chest to undulate. It wasn't the verbal response I craved, but it ignited me to try harder. I desperately wanted those groans. My spurred enthusiasm made my pace quicken. A vibrating moan escaped me without thinking.

He gave a quick, breathless instruction, "Use your tongue more,"

Immediately, my tongue flickered along the underside of his cock, and he let out a huffed breath. "Just like that. Good girl."

The heat flared into a raging furnace but no idea as to why.

I blinked.

I could feel wetness running down my inner thighs.

And I blinked again.

When I leaned back, his cock sliding from my mouth, he violently shuddered. "Did you just call me a good girl?"

He seemed composed when he replied, "I did, yes."

"Oh. Is that normal?"

My expectation was he would be exasperated or angry, and my expectation was wrong.

Instead, he gifted me another smile.

"Very good, Lady Nathalia. Never be afraid to ask questions. The answer is that some enjoy praise. That phrase, in particular, can be very effective. Did you like it?"

Fuck yes. "Yes."

His smile widened as his hands went into my hair, messing the strands. "You were truthful." He gripped my hair in a tight hold, and my lungs filled full. Leaning down, his breath brushed my lips as he whispered, "Good girl."

I was wrong. I died and went to Celestia instead.

He straightened, and my lips wrapped around him again, working my tongue in flicks and wiggles. His breathing quickly became audible, speeding up and deepening. Each harsh breath sent me spiraling, each puff of air a reward. Something within me knew this was important, and I sucked gently while my hand ran up and down the shaft of his cock. The intense throbbing turned torturous, and I groaned in frustration.

He tried to mutter something with a strained wheeze, but I couldn't make it out. When hot liquid pumped into my mouth, the taste of salted caramel coated my tongue. I squealed in surprise and almost pulled back, but the taste kept me there to get as much as he would give me. I gulped him down until his breathing calmed. My head lifted to look up at him, out of breath myself.

"You have good instincts," he said, regaining his regular rate of breathing by the third word. "I have an idea of what we can focus on with future lessons using these first tools and techniques." His gaze turned serious. "I want to make sure you know what that feels like, to hold that feeling in your mind for next time. Ideally, it would be on your mind from time to time in the moments between this time and the next. Here, please stand."

My shaky legs tripped over the pillow under me, and he kicked it aside before wrapping his arms around me in an embrace. Not expecting a hug, of all things, I lifted my hands to wrap around his bare waist and pressed myself into him. The comfort I'd felt around him earlier came back doubled. Skin to skin, with his pyretic body next to mine, the instinct to curl into his lap like a cat was almost overwhelming. Settling for merely a lean into him, I felt him smile against my shoulder before he released me.

"You did well, Lady Nathalia."

One last look at him was all I allowed myself before getting my gown from the dresser. There was quiet between us, as we dressed. Fidgeting with my dress, I pretended to inspect it because I didn't know what else to do. My thoughts were jumbled, speeding from one memory to another. His hands. My lack of control. His tongue. That desperate need. His smile. The taste in my mouth. His cock...

After what seemed like forever, the silence made me speak. "Any lessons on how to talk afterwards? Or is it awkward because we do not know each other that well?" I bunched up my dress to slip it over my head before smoothing the silk on my waist and hips. "Not to suggest you are cold, Master Ramiren. You are a far warmer figure that I could have hoped for. Both emotionally and... physically."

He put his arms into his shirt sleeves, then placed the garment over his head. "I think figuring that out will come naturally as we get to know one another. I don't think there's a lesson that can account for every possible combination of people. If there was, I suspect someone would be giving those lessons and making a king's ransom in the process. The only certain way to dispel any discomfort and awkwardness is practice. I'll be available for more of that as often as you need."

"When will I be able to undress you myself? Or is that later? I think I'd like to learn that sometime. If we start out with my pleasure, I believe you are depriving me."

Wait. Am I actually flirting?

Ramiren looked surprised, but he sounded pleased. "If you'd like, you can undress me yourself as part of our next lesson."

I lifted and freed my hair from the back of my dress. With no doubt I looked unkempt, my hands ran through my hair in a feeble attempt to tame it. Fitting my feet into my shoes, I finally replied, "I thank you for your availability and dedication to helping me. Speaking of which, what precisely are you getting out of this?” *Besides a necklace. Besides any pleasure he may derive from it.*

At his head tilt, I clarified. “I suppose I’m asking, why help me? Why agree to this pact at all?"

“Ah.” He nodded in sudden understanding. “In addition to the price you agreed to for the pact, I get pleasure out of this as well. It is equally important that I keep how it feels in mind to be sure that I know how to give it.” He stared at me before speaking, clearly enunciating his words as though he wanted this point to sink in. “Enjoying both the process and the moment-to-moment experience is not only okay, it is normal and natural. For both of us."

Magically-imbued jewelry and a refresher class, as expected. What the hell else did you expect him to say, you nitwit?

My gaze fell. "I understand." My hand went to the doorknob but did not turn it. "I can memorize almost any song I wish, and have, so I am quite familiar with poetry and the poets' attempts to capture what happens in the bedroom." I looked back at him over my shoulder, feeling both elated and disappointed somehow. "Woefully inaccurate, I'm sorry to report." Finally twisting the knob, it opened.

Behind me, I heard the frown when he spoke, “I see.”

Chapter Five
The Offer of a Secret

Breakfast the next morning consisted of fruit, pastries, poached eggs, and some kind of gray sausage I did my best to avoid. Raewyn was notably absent, and no one had seen her since last night. My concern about her welfare made me knock loudly on her door, which earned me a fit of yelling to let her sleep.

"So, what are we doing today?" Georgina asked before stuffing a colored pastry into her mouth.

M.A.L.C.O.L.M. beeped. "RECOVER THAT WHICH WAS STOLEN. KILL THOSE WHO STAND IN OUR WAY."

His volume didn't reverberate here as it had in the Hall of Mirrors, but my glance around the common room confirmed elves and fey of all sorts gave us a side-eye. "Can't you lower the voice on him?"

Georgina shook her head, looking down at her plate. "Nope. Not without my tools and know-how. His voice box must have gotten damaged in the fight with the mischief hag."

M.A.L.C.O.L.M. beeped again. "CONFIRMED. MY VOLUME LEVEL IS LOCKED TO THE SCREAM SETTING."

Georgina patted her automaton's leg as he stood over her.

"What exactly is the purpose of a scream setting?"

Georgina looked me up and down. "Ever been in a Tirvinir factory?"

When I shook my head, she explained further, "Well, they can be pretty loud. If the automatons need to talk, you need to be able to hear them." She went back to finishing her food.

Dismissed, my eyes found Ramiren while Georgina was preoccupied. Racking my brain for something to talk about, I came up with asking how he slept.

He put his utensils down, weaving his fingers together with his elbows on the table as he gave me his full attention. "Very well, thank you. Yourself?"

My mouth twitched into a smile. "Same. Best I've slept in a long time." I paused. "My bed was quite comfortable. It's far better than the hard ground."

"Agreed. My work often has me sleeping in unfamiliar, but usually acceptable, accommodations. I take it yours does not?"

"Not really, no. At the Horyn Academy, we had barracks. Rope beds and such. When traveling, I sleep on a bedroll. I rarely stopped for the night in cities, so I haven't had a proper bed in a long time. Last night was... quite nice."

His eyes softened as he peered over the rim of his glasses. "I hope it was."

My gaze met his, and the sides of my mouth twitched again. *More than nice.*

"Oooh, boy. Pastries!"

I shifted on the bench when Raewyn loudly traipsed down the stairs to our table. "Raewyn. Sleep well?"

"Like the dead, and I'm still waking up. Exhausting day, but the ending was pleasant. Boy, can she scream. Nat, we need to have Mom and Dad install whatever these fey water pipes are in the villa." She took up a plate from the stack and began to fill it with fruit and tarts.

Beep. "I CAN SCREAM TOO."

Raewyn jumped with a shriek, nearly dropping her loaded plate. "Minue's tits, you scared me." She poked Georgina in the shoulder. "Can't you lower his sound or something?"

Georgina rubbed her forehead.

Ramiren's attention went back to his plate as he finished eating. The moment was lost; so I did the same. Having collapsed into my bed after getting back to my room, little thought had been given to the encounter last night. My green dress actually wrinkled when I slept in it.

But from the moment it woke up, my brain refused to do anything but remind me.

Did I go too far?

With cold clarity, the truthful response to my own question wasn't a *yes*, but a wish to do even more. More of his deft hands, more of his tongue, more of *him*. My impossible thoughts jumbled as my fork pushed purple strawberries around my plate. There was no way anything further could have been done. *What else is there to do? And what was with that voice? Cordani? What did that mean? Did I hallucinate?*

I risked a side glance at Ramiren, who was putting his cleaned plate on the dirty stack. *What more does he have planned for me?*

That question would have answers soon enough. Until then, patience was a virtue. A thrill of excitement waved through me at his plans, but I stamped it down.

This was for learning, not for pleasure.

"Two pounds of olives, three pounds of seasoned almonds, a satchel of dried fruit, apricots if you have them, a half-wheel of hard cheese, five pounds of oats, five pounds of rice, two pounds of mixed dehydrated vegetables... and if it's almost entirely carrots, I *will* come back to have words with you. Five pounds of dried lentils or beans, a pound of salt, a sealed jar of honey, and, of course, five skins of Evrakan white, Pouroen red, or Laethi fruit wine. Along with travel rations, please. No meat. Four weeks' worth for one person." I ticked off the list on my fingers as the fey man behind the counter wrote a hurried list on a scrap of paper.

The grocer, Mirin, a sciur fey with a twitchy nose and striated gray and brown hair, paused his writing. "No meat at all?"

"Correct. None. That should be, by my math, two gold pieces even."

He kept scribbling on the paper as his eyebrows raised. "Yes, miss. That's correct. Anything else?"

What els-

Oh!

"Do you have a map of the Feylands?"

Mirin shifted his weight. "Yes, miss. But they are expensive. All Feylands maps are magical, you see. Because the Feylands mirror Laeth, any time a building is raised in Laeth, it's raised here. Which means anytime a city or village is founded, it is founded here. The maps need to update themselves, or they'll be useless eventually." He frowned. "Though for some reason, most natural features don't change."

I have so many questions.

What would happen if someone was standing at the spot where a city or building suddenly appeared? And at what point was a building considered done, or a city officially founded? And, indeed, why did the Feylands mirror Laeth at all?

Though it was food, and not information, that brought me to this store, my curiosity was undeniably piqued. *Ignorance never solves anything.* "What if something is built here? Is it also built in Laeth?"

His pencil paused. "Oh. No. It only goes one way." He went back to writing.

"What happens if there's a house here, but another gets built in Laeth?"

He grimaced deeply and lowered the paper and pencil in his hands. "Uh. Goodbye, Feylands house, though with that trade agreement a few decades ago between Laeth and the Feylands, I don't think it happens nearly as often as it used to. But that's why there are a lot of remote villages here. Fewer chances of that happening."

What a horrible situation.

"Do you know why the Feylands mirror Laeth?"

Another grimace from him. *Is this a touchy subject here?*

"You'd need to ask someone smarter than me, miss. I don't actually know."

Just drop it, then. I don't want to make the man uncomfortable.

"Then the map should do nicely." A 'thank you' nearly tumbled out again, making me push down years and years of ingrained manners, but the encounter with the innkeeper last night quickly reminded me to not indicate gratitude to a fey. It makes you beholden to them, as though they've done you a favor, and you will owe them.

What's to stop someone from just leaving the Feylands to avoid the fey's obligation? Is there some kind of obligation debt collection agency keeping track? Something about the innate magic of this place? My room price would have been reasonable if I hadn't thanked him.

Still, it was a cheap lesson.

Mirin disappeared through a side door to the stocking room to fulfill my order.

A bell dinged over the front door. The noise reflexively caught my attention, and Raewyn grinned at me and bounded over. "Nat, buying us food for the road?"

"Buying a map for the group and food for myself, actually. Not us. I leave everyone to determine the best rations for themselves."

Raewyn pouted and looked around the racks of items for sale. She picked up a strange metal object, possibly a kitchen implement or perhaps a medical device. I wasn't sure, and neither was she, based upon her scrunched face.

"I never got used to road rations, not like you, Nat. How could you live off them?" She made a grimace as Mirin came back with a cartful of tins, sacks, and canisters. He began to dole out the food into cloth bags after weighing them on a scale. Raewyn came over to see what I had purchased and raised her eyebrows. "Almonds? Olives? Those aren't rations. Has your sense of taste finally improved?"

"It never left, Raewyn. Th-" I grunted, just barely stopping myself from telling her what, or who, it was for. She would have many, *many* questions. And like a pup with a juicy bone, she would gnaw me down to the marrow to get answers.

Facing Mirin, I asked, "How much do I owe you?"

"Two gold pieces for the food, miss. And one hundred for the map." He winced, his nervous nose twitching. "I understand if you don't want it."

Without a word, gold coins were plucked from my larger money pouch to rest on the counter. Mirin's eyes widened the more gold I placed down, until one-hundred-and-two coins sat in small, neat stacks. I placed the sacks and bags into the small pouch at my side, watching them disappear into the opening.

A gift from a particularly grateful caravan leader who was still breathing because of my shield, the pouch was far larger on the inside than outside, making it much easier to carry all my gear. It was a good day when my bulky, heavy pack was replaced. Raewyn watched me, eyeing the pouch.

"Really? You got an Extended Pouch? You have all the fun. Can you carry a tent in there for me?"

It was important to me for Raewyn to be comfortable. *There should be enough room. Who knows what manner of weather we'll encounter here in the Feylands?*

She clapped her hands together with my nod in agreement. "Thank you! And my pack. And a bedroll, too, please. And maybe a cot."

The pouch could hold a great deal, but it was closer to capacity than I preferred. "It can hold whatever you require."

"Yay! I'll get rations, then." She stepped up to the counter, and the fey grocer turned to her.

"You are in need of food as well, miss?" he said, taking out another scrap of paper.

"Yes, I'd like everything my sister just purchased." She rolled her head back to smile at me. "My food will fit too, right?"

With another sigh, I searched for the coin pouch I just had in my hand. "You might want to alter the order. I didn't get any meat."

"You still don't eat critters, eh?"

With an absent shake of my head as a reply, distracted with pulling out coins, she leaned in and bit my hand. Hard.

I recoiled with a shriek, more in surprise than pain, then brought my hand close to my face to make sure she didn't break the skin. "Raewyn! Are you *feral?* What the-"

She deadpanned blithely, "What? You eat like a rabbit. I like to eat rabbit. Seemed logical to me."

Don't laugh. It'll only encourage her.

But pursing my lips, clenching my jaw, and biting my tongue couldn't stop the laugh from coming out.

In-between chuckles, I stuttered and rubbed my watery eyes with my unbitten hand, "You are a gods-damned brat."

The landscape changed quickly, from miles of blowing purple grass to wetlands. It was another two days before the scenery changed again to full-on swamp. Thankfully, Georgina had survival capabilities built into the automaton. He managed to find drier ground so our feet wouldn't get sucked under. I grumbled about the cleaning my greaves would require, keeping my unladylike cursing to thoughts only.

To pass the time, Georgina told a few snippets she'd heard regarding Jorin Swamp. To my surprise, as she'd mentioned keeping to cities, she delved into a story about a special bog mine within the swamp that produced some of the strongest iron known.

"I'd heard that the fey don't like iron. Is that true?" I barely avoided falling into a deceptively deep puddle that everyone else had somehow managed to ignore.

"They don't like cold iron, specifically." At my confused look, she explained. "Cold iron is iron that's alloyed with silver, but it's not common. It's hard to get the ratio of iron to silver right. If you're off, it's either a soft hunk of metal that's good for nothing or not real cold iron. We won't find cold iron here in the Feylands. For obvious reasons."

She's quite pleasant when she talks about her work.

In fact, everyone was pleasant, even Raewyn. We all seemed to take the situation in stride. Literally, as we had no transportation or horses, though Georgina had to sit on top of M.A.L.C.O.L.M.'s shoulders to keep out of the water and muck.. Eventually, we developed a strategic marching order. The automaton led the way, with me taking up the rear in case we were attacked from behind. Raewyn walked behind M.A.L.C.O.L.M. to avail herself of the least traversed path possible, which meant Ramiren was directly ahead of me for the entire time we were traveling.

My time was spent looking out for dangers, at least that was my intention. But then Ramiren's dark hair would come into view, and I'd remember how soft it felt. In my hands, between my thighs, against my skin. Then my thoughts flitted rapidly between everything we did. A few times, Raewyn smirked over her shoulder and accused me of daydreaming. I conceded the point and tried to go back to watching the grayish-green landscape that had the pleasant scent of petrichor rather than the sulfurous smell I was used to with swamps.

But then Ramiren would look back at me with his red eyes, and the process would start all over again. My Academy instructors would call it dereliction of duty. I called it inevitable.

His words, hands, and tongue had made sure of that.

On the third day at dusk, we made camp, this time on a small rocky hill that overlooked the mire of the swamp.

As everyone was setting up their bedding for the evening, I decided it was time again. Grateful of my years of practice on maneuvering an acceptable tent bath with bowls of campfire-warmed water, soap and clean clothing felt like a luxury from the grime of the day.

It took a full year to figure out a system. That first year was extraordinarily unpleasant, to me and everyone who had the misfortune of standing downwind.

Ramiren was exiting his enormous tent as I waved to him.

Earlier, I'd watched, fascinated, as he took a tiny tent out of his pouch, noting he too carried an Extended Pouch. Miniature in size, it looked like it belonged in a little girl's ornate dollhouse. When he set the tent on the ground of our clearing and uttered a strange set of syllables, the tent enlarged, bigger than some small houses. Ramiren entered the new structure with a pleased grin. Desperately wanting to know where he got it, I went back to set up my old, mundane tent.

Even Georgina had shelter and bedding, which were somehow folded in or out of M.A.L.C.O.L.M.'s ribcage with the push of a covered red circle near his neck.

Shooting a look over my shoulder, suddenly wishing my large, but threadbare tent had been replaced before leaving the fey city, I motioned to it with my hand. "Evening, Master Ramiren. I'd like to invite you for a light supper and discussion, if you'd be agreeable."

"I would. And thank you for the offering." Ramiren noticed my green-eyed perusal of his tent and smiled. "A gift from a client. I've only used it a handful of times, but here it will be wildly convenient." Peeking inside the open tent flaps, my gaze ran over a desk, two plush chairs, a chest and...

My envy nearly felled me.

Is that a feather bed?

With a small bow, I led him to my tent, walking side by side. The tent flaps were tied back to reveal a squat folding table covered in the fresher items I'd purchased in Dulponi.

Puldoni?

Donpu-

Whatever. I'll get it eventually.

Motioning toward a sitting pillow on one side of the table, I sat down on the other. "Please. Join me. I admit, I'm being a bit presumptive, but I thought this would be a good opportunity to get to know each other a little better. Again, if you are agreeable."

Ramiren looked over the table as he sat, his eyebrows raised. "I appreciate the gesture, and I would be agreeable to that. There may be questions that I cannot answer, but I'd be happy to share what I can."

"Let's start with, I suppose, the obvious one." After pouring from a wineskin into one of the ceramic goblets on the table, I began, "Where are you from?"

He took the goblet from me and raised it in thanks. "I'm not actually certain where I was born. My family was always on the move, all across Laeth. We would stay in a town for a few days or weeks, circle back to previous haunts within a year, or never." He turned wistful. "I remember the big cities the most. Evraka, Loril in Tivandir, Balingua next to the Pouroe Desert, Rowin in Camlynn, even the former capital city of Pidantar in Kibel. I'd call all of them, any of them, home, I suppose."

Leaning back with my own goblet, I took a sip, the tart fruit of the blackberry wine spreading over my tongue. "I hope I don't ask a question that is painful or too invasive. That, I wanted to say, is certainly not my aim here." I raised my wine to indicate it was his turn.

He thought for some time after popping an almond into his mouth. "Not painful. Pidantar is lost to the orcs, but the dwarves have a new home now in Fomona. I find that where people are from reveals less than what they want or need. This would be a harder question for me to answer, if you asked it in return, so I understand if you do not wish to answer a question that I might not. What I am curious about is, if there was one thing you wanted to do right now, more than anything, what would it be?" He looked at me over his goblet as he took a drink.

My eyes turned downcast, and my back straightened.

Interesting question, Ramiren. Should I fib?

I thought about just enjoying the meal, but his question spiked instant arousal. Anticipation. Desire. Want. When it hit during my song at the carnival, this need was foreign. Now, after so many days of being around him, it seemed almost normal.

Is this something I'm meant to learn? To recognize and be comfortable with it?

Lying would gain me nothing, I decided, and it might tarnish what we were trying to accomplish. My thumb rubbed on the side of my goblet, and the rough hand-thrown texture of the ceramic scratched the pad. "There are many things I want to do. Surface desires, you know. Eat and talk with you. Then, there are deeper ones. Ones that would require us to use that place of yours, that you mentioned before."

My eyes lifted to meet his as I went on, "If I were to ask the question back to you, I'd be pleased if talking or a lesson was your choice. You are a witty and brilliant conversationalist with an... actual personality." *Unlike the men from my kingdom.* "But I also recall your promise to me last time."

Ramiren put his goblet down and requested for me to do the same. "That would be something in line with what I planned for our next lesson, a core part of the theme, actually." He lifted his hand and snapped his fingers.

A blink later, my eyes opened to see we were somewhere else. It was a bedroom, exactly like the room Ramiren stayed in at The Forever Inn, with every detail accounted for, from the velvet cushions to the fruit on the table.

His classroom.

Well, almost every detail. The artwork on the walls at the inn had shown landscapes. Here, they showed men and women in various positions together. Some acts were known to me, based upon our first lesson. Some not.

I asked in a hushed tone, "Where are we, exactly?"

"A safe place to facilitate pacts. It changes, with each pact, based upon what is needed. You need not worry about anything here. Not even time. When we return, after our lesson, it will be at the exact moment we left."

As Elijah had said. How clever.

There was comfort in the familiarity of the space, and I said so. He shot me a pleased grin before continuing. "We're going to focus on a few things. One, what you desire. You may remove my clothing. Last time, you mentioned you felt deprived by our focusing on your pleasure initially, so you will decide the agenda. I want to see what you retained, though I have a new oral technique for you to try. Previously, we focused on the use of your hands and mouth. This time, I want you to concentrate on specifically using your tongue. From small circles around the tip to up and down the entire shaft. When I am completely in your mouth, flutter your tongue as often as you remember, even as you bob down and then back up. I also encourage creativity with your mouth and hands, while maintaining an emphasis on use of your tongue."

A pang in my chest hurt enough for me to wince. My eyes dropped to my feet. *Encourage all you like, it won't work.*

He must have noticed the look on my face because he stepped forward, lifting my chin with his hand. Concern warmed his eyes. "What's wrong? Do you not wish to do this tonight?" He must have taken my expression for one of reluctance, because he emphasized his next words, "Never be afraid to say no, Nathalia. I will always hear and respect it."

I'd never told him what was stolen from me.

My fingertips touched his wrist, trying to be reassuring. "It's not that. I want to. Very much, but... I can't be creative. That's what the mischief hags took. I can mimic when shown how, but that's it."

Concern quickly morphed into horror, then changed to understanding. "Oh." He gave my chin a gentle squeeze, then dropped his hand. "My deepest apologies."

He paused to consider his next words, then swallowed. "Do not worry. Remember, I am here to help you achieve what you desire, not judge you for any lack or inability. I will say I was impressed with what you did during our last lesson. Expand upon that. Please excuse me for a moment." He stepped past me, through a thin door I hadn't noticed before. I heard splashing water and surmised he was cleaning himself up.

With a cleansing breath, I went to admire the paintings.

I'd never seen such artwork before. They were simultaneously educational and erotic, with tangled limbs and ecstatic faces. There was one in particular that made me lean in to study, with the woman lying reversed on the man's chest. Her knees rested on either side of his head while she…

A gentle tap on my shoulder jolted me from my stupor. Glancing over my shoulder, an amused-looking Ramiren stood with his arms crossed. "I called, but you didn't answer." His eyes flicked to the painting I was preoccupied with, and he smiled. "Shall we continue?"

I cleared my throat, feeling awkward. After lifting my hands and sliding the now unbuttoned jacket from his shoulders, I began to fold it. Ramiren took it from me, tossing it to the ground off to the side. He seemed entertained at my startled expression.

But it'll wrinkle.

Frowning at the jacket, now lying in a misshapen heap, my confusion prompted me to ask. "Am I supposed to throw them?"

"If this is done right, you won't care about your clothing. In fact, you might find you hate clothing."

What a ridiculous notion.

Resuming, I was grateful for the fact most of my clothing consisted of just loose shirts, tunics, and trousers when traveling. *At least I know how to take those clothes off.* My hands went to the sides of his waist, then untucked and slid the shirt up over his head, careful of his glasses.

He threw the shirt, too.

My touch went where I wanted, and he never stopped me from exploring. His hot skin wasn't rough, exactly. For some reason, sturdy and rugged came to mind, like supple leather. *Another broodling trait, perhaps?* He wasn't a great deal taller than I was, maybe three inches from my nearly six foot frame, so I could reach everything. My hands passed his shoulders, which relaxed under my palms. Running the fingers down his chest to his stomach, a grin creased my face when the muscle under my hand twitched.

Lifting to my toes to kiss and lick his neck, curious what he tasted like, I scented honey again. It overrode my tastebuds.

"Do you use some sort of beeswax pomade in your hair? You smell like honey."

If he was surprised by my random question, he did not show it. "You have a sensitive nose. I do, yes."

Well, that solves that mystery.

Unlacing his ties, my hands hooked into the band of his trousers. Sliding them down just enough, I followed their descent, taking one look up at him before wrapping my lips around the tip of his cock.

Pressing my tongue into him, and remembering his instructions, it circled his cock to find that ridge again. An ache began to develop between my thighs, spreading from there to my lower belly, when my hand lifted to grip him at the base. *Was I giving him as much pleasure as he had given me?*

Excitement at the prospect made a moan rumble in my throat.

He responded in kind, and I could feel the awareness of his eyes as he watched me. Recalling what he had done against my finger, I continued with shallow circles, then flicked my tongue. I made sure to relax my throat, as he'd suggested last time, and swallowed his cock halfway.

His soft voice floated down to me. "Undo your laces and touch yourself, Nathalia. Your pleasure is equally important here."

I did as bidden, my fingers immediately finding the wetness I'd already suspected was there. The blistering sensation of standing far too close to a fire, but entirely without discomfort, ran roughshod over me, causing a low humming that was somewhere between a moan and hard breathing.

My fingers fumbled over sensitive flesh until they found an area that spiked the building pressure. Neediness, for his pleasure as well as my own, made me lower my mouth over his cock, and my gag reflex triggered. An unexpected touch to my throat, followed by a gentle massage, reminded me. Forcing my throat to relax, the gagging disappeared.

"Excellent..." he whispered. The praise heated me and demanded I respond.

All. Give me all of it.

My tongue glided over that throbbing vein underneath. I closed my eyes, relaxing completely, and briefly took him, all of him, into my throat to see if I could. I was gifted with a groan and more praise. My entrance clenched in a hard throb, and I dipped my fingers in to relieve the ache. It nearly finished me.

I lifted my eyes to watch his face as he closed his eyes. His breath quickened. "Yes. Just like that. Now wiggle your..."

Anticipating the instruction, I quickly plunged all the way down, and then back up again with a fluttering tongue. His entire body stiffened, and he didn't complete the phrase.

That disembodied voice spoke again, almost breaking my rhythm. **Cordani.**

Where is that coming from?

My hand on his cock began to follow the bobbing movements of my mouth, my saliva coating the shaft. His hand shot to my wrist and gripped it. Though he didn't stop my strokes, it still felt like I was restrained by him. The vibration from my groan that followed must have pushed him over the edge, as immediately after a harsh noise escaped his own lips. The taste of salted caramel once again flooded my mouth.

After I released him from my mouth and hand, he composed himself while my breathing slowed. Looking down at me, then at the wrist he still held, he peeled his fingers from it. I hadn't realized he'd begin to squeeze until his grip suddenly lightened.

"You've become skilled in... a very short period of time and are ahead of where I thought we'd be. We may have other technique sessions, but practice what you did today. You can master it and will be exceptional in that area. We may focus more on themes in the future, like 'desire' for this one."

Standing with his help, I smiled as he talked. "I'm sure those lessons will be... exceptionally pleasant. Like this was."

Exceptionally pleasant? You're hopeless.

Say something else! Anything else, like how he's all I think about. How his hands on me makes me feel. How his tongue-

He chuckled. "I agree. As they say, practice makes perfect, but passion is priceless."

Should I ask him about the voice?

The question was dismissed immediately.

Oh. Sure. "Ramiren, I am hearing voices. Are you harboring people here to watch me pleasure you and then mutter a word at me or am I hallucinating?"

That would definitely not sound insane.

Besides, part of the pact is secrecy. It's not only a matter of if he wouldn't, but he couldn't.

Instead, I just smiled at him, as though grateful for his comment and nothing was amiss. "Shall we finish supper?"

"No, it's your turn," he said simply.

My eyebrows went to my hairline. "Why?" My question came out weak and wispy. Of course, I wanted him to pleasure me in return. *But I am here to learn.*

Ramiren smiled down at me, as he ran a hand through my hair. "Remember what I said? In order to give pleasure, you must understand what it is. Your pleasure truly is just as important as mine."

My scalp tingled where he touched. The caress felt intimate, soothing, though no doubt it was merely to get hair out of my face. "Oh, um, you make a good point. Yes, please continue."

Yes, Nathalia. Well done. Not awkward at all.

He undressed me, as I had done to him, though he folded my clothing and set them to the side with each piece removed. Anticipation quickly led to impatience, and his comment about hating clothing now made sense. He guided me to the bed with a gentle hand on my lower back and asked me to lie back. I obeyed, and he followed to my side, propping his head up with his arm bent at the elbow. His other hand grazed between my breasts and down my belly in a slow meander, as though we had all the time in the world.

Which, here, I suppose we do.

He whispered, "Hands or mouth this time?"

"Hands, please." Much as I wanted his mouth on me, I wanted to look at him. To watch him. See his red eyes on me when I found that peak again.

I was also self-conscious regarding my hurried tent bath.

He swirled his fingertips between my thighs just as they parted for him. "Use your fingertips where it feels best, above where my hand is now." He then plunged his fingers into my...

What was it the women in the barracks called the entire area between their legs? My mind buzzed with thought. *Oh, right. Pussy.* I remembered how brazen they were with it. But here, it somehow felt appropriate. Then he curved his fingers, and the memories floated away on the wind. My fingers sank into swollen and sensitive flesh, this time with my dominant right hand, and the difference was remarkable. The pressure mounted immediately, curling from my pussy, to my lower stomach, and even into my chest. Pulsing caused my walls to clench against his fingers, and I bit my lip hard to not release sooner than I wanted.

No, this I want to savor.

My hips rose and rolled of their own accord as my fingers found a small bit of flesh that practically sizzled when touched.

Is that important?

Cursing my tutors' lack of focus on the specifics of female-specific anatomy, I rubbed there. The familiar feelings of building heat made me let out an impatient groan. There would be no stopping or savoring this. Rolling my hips against the two hands pleasuring me, my breath quickened to match his pace with his fingers.

As he developed a distinct rhythm, he leaned in to brush his lips along my ear, nipping down to my neck. A strained moan parted my lips as I turned my head to look at him. Our eyes met, gold pleading to red for mercy. He flicked his tongue over his lips, and I tracked the movement. I wanted to request a kiss, even going so far as to lean in for it, but the shift tipped my pleasure without warning. My eyes slammed shut as a keening scream emptied my lungs. My hips buckled hard against his hand as instinct tried to squeeze every bit of ecstasy it could.

In my haze, I heard that word again. **Cordani.**

He stayed by me, pressing against my body long after my release. He lowered his head to the pillow next to mine, his free hand splayed across my stomach. Unsure of what I was allowed to do, I chewed on my bottom lip.

There was a beat of silence before he said, "We don't have to keep a careful distance while we're here, Nathalia. There is inevitably something about what we're doing that lets us know one another in a way many people never will." There was genuine warmth in his tone, making me relax.

The intense need to hold him, to be close as he had said, overwhelmed me until I could no longer deny it. I whispered, "Then I hope this is allowed." Rolling to face him, I wrapped my arms around him in an embrace.

He immediately chuckled softly. "Of course, this is allowed." His hand moved from my stomach to around my back, returning the embrace.

Contentment settled in me, and I whispered, "If we are to get to know each other, I'll tell you something secret." This had never been admitted to anyone else before, but the need to share, to be close, was too much to bear. I wanted him to know me. The real me.

With a hard swallow, I continued, "Sometimes, it feels as though I've been sabotaged. Somehow, I'm both privileged and unprepared for the life I would eventually lead." My irritation always rose when this thought came to mind. I even heard it in my voice. "Innocence and ignorance protect nothing except those who kept them innocent and ignorant."

His fingertips ran lazy circles across my skin as he thought of a response. "I won't claim any special insight on the subject of innocence, so my input might not come from expertise, but I happen to be a great listener in any case." His small smile was crooked, with a hint of mischief.

My shoulders relaxed as I exhaled. "I will not burden you with all of my troubles. They may not be trifling to you, and you may be a great listener, but I still feel self-conscious. Perhaps next time, I'll give you another secret. Perhaps that can be my gift to you. Or my curse to you, depending." My smile curved into a grin that nearly cracked my face.

"If you like, I will keep them, and be honored by your trust in the offering. A secret is no small thing."

Leaning in, with the intention to kiss his mouth, my lips changed course at the last second to press against his cheek instead. "Secrets are assassins. They kill when you least expect them." I rolled off the bed and began the task of redressing.

He stood as well, and my eyes caught his occasionally flicking toward me as he gathered his own clothing. Eventually, he sighed, "Nathalia, there is nothing wrong with asking for what you want, so long as you can accept an answer of no and voicing your desires does not hurt anyone. I urge you to think about that. We'll be talking more about that next time, maybe over the next few lessons."

I wasn't sure what to say to that, so my response was a simple nod.

He finished dressing a moment after I did, and when he put the last item of clothing back on, he snapped his fingers. We were at once back in the tent, before the low table. Without missing a single beat, he took a long drink of his wine.

Picking up my own wine, as well as an olive, the salty brine of the fruit burst on my tongue. "I believe it is my turn to ask a question." I put the lip of the goblet to my mouth, thinking. "If there is one thing about yourself you would change, what would it be?"

Chapter Six
Wixin and the Bunyip

The next morning, the soft light of dawn illuminated the beige walls of my tent, waking me. Stretching in my bedroll, the smile I went to sleep with returned in full force. *Another successful lesson.* Besides the knowledge gained from these encounters, the lessons themselves were also... enjoyable, for multiple reasons.

Snorting at the lackluster description, I tried to conjure a better adjective but stopped before any came to mind. Enjoyable was all I'd allow myself.

It seemed my skills were improving under his tutelage. Something told me, based upon his reactions, that I was getting better. While getting cleaned up and dressed, my thoughts went over everything last night, especially the supper. His refusal to answer the question regarding what he would change about himself didn't surprise me. In fact, when he said *no* abruptly, we both burst into laughter.

We went back and forth, asking and answering various other questions while drinking wine and eating far too many olives. Some Ramiren also refused to answer, but he was gentler those few times he did. It was a good conversation, one that'll be cherished long after our pact has concluded.

Pact concluded. Fulfilled. Done and over with.

The thought threw ice water on my good mood, though I was excited at the prospect. It would mean my lessons were successful, and I had, potentially, found someone to settle down with. But it would also mean there would never be another. *Will my future husband make the intimate times we spent together this... interesting?*

Or is maddening the right word?

My doubt answered me, though it was certainly a heartfelt wish. Having heard tales of women married off to certain men and the things they had to endure, my stubborn refusal to accept just anyone meant my choice would be difficult but necessary. Since my intention was to swear the protector's oath to my husband, my life depended on finding someone who would treasure me and the children we would have and who would allow me to do my duty and protect them without feeling emasculated or overstepped.

Who won't hurt me.

I donned my gambeson and armor, the heavy mail links clinking as it molded to my frame. After my sword was belted on, and everything placed back into my Extended Pouch, I stepped outside to take down the tent. Everyone else was stretching, waking up, moving around to get their own gear put away. My eyes met Ramiren's, and he smiled, calling out with a lifted hand, "Good morning, Lady Nathalia."

"Good morning, Master Ramiren," I replied, my expression hopefully betraying nothing. It was a tiny moment, merely a standard greeting to start the day, but the elation at seeing him again was almost palpable.

But you just saw him last night. You see him every day.

Yes, and I am elated every day.

"Admit it, we're lost!" Georgina grumbled at me from atop M.A.L.C.O.L.M.

Her grumpy tone was unhelpful, but adding my own frustrations to the mix would not help matters either. "Perhaps we are. We are looking for a mischief hag in the middle of the swamp. The map I acquired does not have Mischief Hag's Hut marked on it, so we are doing the best we can." The map in my hands showed we were indeed lost, by my reckoning, but I wasn't about to confirm it and cause panic. Or, more likely, insults and whining.

"Perhaps we can ask for directions?" Raewyn chirped with a dubious look on her face.

"From who, Raewyn? I don't see an inn anywhere around, do you?" Georgina's questions steadily increased in volume, almost to the point of yelling. "Who, *pray tell*, do we stop and ask directions from, huh?"

Beep. "WHAT ABOUT THAT WEIRD PUPPY OVER THERE LOOKING AT US?" M.A.L.C.O.L.M. pointed behind us.

We all snapped our heads in the direction M.A.L.C.O.L.M. was looking. Indeed, there was a dog-like creature, sitting in the water, looking our way. It did not look hostile, merely curious as it tilted its head back and forth. It hopped out of the water, shook the excess off itself, and approached slowly. The creature was much longer and skinnier than any dog I'd ever seen, though not unhealthily so. It sat down on its haunches.

"Visitors to the Ol' Jorin Swamp? My my, what curiosities you have brought forth into our home!"

Its odd speech sent alarm bells ringing. Putting the map away to leave room in my hands for a weapon and shield should they be needed, I stepped forward to get a better look at this being and to put myself between it and my companions. "Who are you talking to?"

It lifted its pointed snout into the air and inhaled deeply. It resumed stalking toward us. "My my, it asks questions too. It wants to know you. It wants to see you too. I can tell. My my."

The alarm bells got louder. *Nope, I don't like this.* Schooling my face to not betray my thoughts, I unhooked my shield from my back, trying to look like I was adjusting it. "We're looking for a mischief hag's home. It should be in the area. Do you know where it is?"

The dog creature's eyes widened, and it snarled. "It wants to hurt you! I will kill it instead!"

My shield was brought to bear just in time for the creature to pounce and bounce off it. The impact made me stumble. It was then that Ramiren yelled, "Stop!"

The dog creature turned his attention to Ramiren, and my blood went cold. It snarled again, but Ramiren simply smiled at it.

"We are not here to hurt or kill your mistress, if indeed the mischief hag is your mistress. We wish to treat with her. You, I think, are a bunyip. You can scent someone's intentions. You can see she has no weapon in hand, merely a defensive shield. We are not here to harm. We are here to bargain."

The creature growled, then sniffed the air again. "My my, it tells true. It wants to bargain, yes, but that one wants to hurt," it said, indicating me with a toss of its head.

My shield lowered as I sighed. "Your mistress did a great injustice to me and mine. It would make sense I'd want to hurt her, but intent does not equal action. If we are able to bargain, then I will not attack."

The creature scented the air a third time, then panted. "It tells true, too! Come, this way then!"

"Hey, slow down!" Georgina yelled from atop M.A.L.C.O.L.M.'s shoulders. For once, there was a need to concur with Georgina. The bunyip was traveling at a breakneck speed through the maze of the swamp, leaping over bog and pool, making it difficult for us to follow.

Every so often, it looked back, its canine face inscrutable. "My my, it needs to hurry! My mistress does not like to wait!" Then it continued at the same pace. Ramiren looked back at me and frowned unhappily.

He was out of breath from running, but his words were understandable. "Wait? That would mean she has been, somehow, alerted to our presence." He nearly tripped over a small log hidden by moss but managed to right himself before falling. "I am not sure if this is a good or bad thing."

Thankfully not as winded as him or Raewyn, who was wheezing loudly, I replied, "Perhaps it may work in our favor. Harder to bargain with her if she's caught by surprise. This way, we're expected guests and not intruders."

Ramiren's eyes lit up at me. "Well played, Lady Nathalia. You are almost certainly correct."

My mood lifted at the praise, a small thrill climbing my spine and buzzing my head.

It was just a small compliment. Calm down.

It was similar to when he had complimented and praised me during our... lesson. They were simple phrases, though who knew just how much meaning was behind them.

The bunyip ran up a hill and yelled, its voice echoing through the swamp, "Not long now! My my, not long at all!" It sat down on the wet grass and waited for us. I expected to see the mischief hag's hut on the other side. But when we came to the top of the hill, there was nothing but more swamp. Raewyn stopped and leaned down with her hands on her knees, too out of breath to speak.

I scowled, looking in every direction, "Where is it? Where is her home?"

The bunyip bounded forward. "It will see soon!"

There was a dull roar and movement in the water off to my right. Without thinking, I set my feet, raising my shield to just under my eyes. My longsword left its scabbard in a smooth pull as foreboding settled in my gut, putting me on edge. "Raewyn, Ramiren, Georgina. Get behind me. Now," I said firmly. "Something comes."

All did as bidden. Ramiren unsheathed his blade, too. "So, we've been led into a trap."

The bunyip paced around excitedly. When he was fifty feet away, he started laughing, which sounded more like crude hacking. "Meet Wixin!"

A dark blue shape emerged from the water, enormous and strange, that blended perfectly into the muddy, brackish water surrounding us. It was, by my quick estimation, roughly twenty feet long, from nose to tail. Rough leathery skin covered its form, bumpy and lizard-like. Its long snout opened just enough to show rows of razor-sharp teeth. It gave a low, rumbling laugh.

"Meat," the creature growled and crawled closer, flicking his tail back and forth.

A blue talking alligator. Interesting.

"So, did he say 'meat' as in for eating, or 'meet' as in 'hi, it's nice to meet you.'" Raewyn, having finally regained her breath, waved a hand at Wixin. "What's the word for those, Nat?"

I registered, suddenly, that we had not seen any living creatures in the swamp. Until the bunyip. Until this Wixin.

I guess he ate them all.

"Homophones. And I suspect the former, Raewyn." My shield moved to the side as my longsword thrust forward. The tip of the longsword struck his snout but did not pierce.

It lunged, faster than should have been thought possible for a creature of its size. I bore my shield down to block it, but I was not fast enough. It grabbed my leg in its jaws and heaved backwards, throwing my balance. Landing hard on my back with a whoosh, the air forcefully exited my lungs. My hand struck the ground hard, and the longsword within it fell from my grasp.

I reached for the sword's grip when the alligator began to drag me back to the water, my weapon quickly out of reach. Georgina hopped off of M.A.L.C.O.L.M.'s shoulders as she yelled, "M.A.L.! Attack!"

Beep. "FINALLY! KILL MODE!"

The automaton's lighted eyes turned from a gentle yellow to bright red. It gave an echoing scream and descended upon the alligator.

Beep. "DIE, BIG LIZARD!"

Hovering over the alligator, whose crushing maw was beginning to bend and kink my plate greaves in its mighty jaws, M.A.L.C.O.L.M. punched down on its head. The alligator let me go and howled in pain, shaking its head as though to clear it. M.A.L.C.O.L.M. continued to hammer his fists into the alligator's skull, keeping Wixin occupied.

Crawling to my longsword just as Raewyn was running toward me, her hand extended with prayer already on her lips for healing.

Ramiren spotted an opportunity, jabbing his rapier into the alligator's left eye. It recoiled with a screech. Ramiren backed away, looking at me, and calmly yet forcefully asked, "Are you injured?"

I picked up my longsword and stood, putting a test weight on the leg the alligator had grabbed. *Definitely injured.* Stifling a pained grunt, I limped back over to the alligator, doing my best to dodge Raewyn's hands. "I'm fine!"

"You're not! You're limping!" Raewyn argued, pointed at my leg.

My answering growl made me sound a bit more like the alligator than I wanted to admit. "Heal me *later*, Raewyn!"

Then Ramiren called out, "There's a section behind his skull. A crack in his bone plates!"

Yes, a joint between sections of his bone armor...good eyes, Ramiren. Raising my longsword above the preoccupied alligator, above its neck where Ramiren had indicated, I jammed the swordpoint downward with a silent plea to Horyn. My prayer was answered as my weapon sliced straight through this time. The alligator gurgled and jerked.

Beep. "PERISH!"

M.A.L.C.O.L.M. swung down with his other mechanical fist, just above where my sword was. I twisted as his fist landed, and a sickening crunch followed. The alligator shuddered and finally laid still.

Pulling my longsword from the creature, I stumbled to the driest spot available. Raewyn began to pray again, calling upon Minue to repair my damaged leg. I plopped down onto the ground as she did so, inspecting my injury. *There will be no repairing the greaves without an armorsmith.* Gingerly removing it by unbuckling the straps around my calf, I winced more at the sight than the pain.

The twisted greave had cut into my leg, causing several deep lacerations. *I'm lucky it didn't bite my leg off.* Someone knelt next to me. Expecting it to be Raewyn, but instead, it was Ramiren. He looked at my leg, watching blood pooled and dripped onto the ground, then back to my face. He said nothing for a long beat, as though he was inspecting me. "You were not fine."

My hand did little to staunch the wound, but Raewyn finally stepped forward, placing gentle hands on my shoulder as I shrugged and tried to respond casually. "I *was* fine. I barely felt it."

You are such a liar.

The bleeding stopped, and the cuts closed under my hand. Raewyn's work.

His tone was soft, not chiding, but instructive. "You should be more truthful if you are injured. Raewyn's intervention may be needed in the Feylands *during* a fight, not at the end."

His tone made warmth glow in my lower belly, and lower, while his words made me flustered. *I had to finish the fight. There was no time.*

Patting my sister's hand that still rested on my shoulder, I thanked her. She gave my shoulder a squeeze before she let go and straightened. "You're welcome, and he's right, you know. You need to be honest with me if you're hurt."

Surrounded and ashamed, there was no path forward but to agree. "Yes, very well. I will not avoid you again, Raewyn. My apologies."

I stood and put some test weight on my leg. It felt sound enough to walk, if a bit achy. "Does anyone see the bunyip?"

Georgina, after inspecting M.A.L.C.O.L.M. for dents, piped up. "He ran off. Probably to tell the hag that he got us killed with an overgrown gecko."

We need a way to track him. "Can anyone track?"

Georgina smiled proudly. "M.A.L. can!" She reached into his ribcage from underneath. There was a soft click when she pulled a tiny lever. M.A.L.C.O.L.M.'s eyes went to a soft yellow again.

Beep. "TRACKING COMMENCING. STATE YOUR TARGET."

Georgina said, clearly enunciating the word, "Bunyip."

Beep. "AFFIRMATIVE." The automaton looked down, then around the area, and began to walk steadily in one direction.

"We'd best follow. He won't stop until he finds it." Georgina clapped her tiny hands in glee.

I spoke low and slow, "Now, about the location of your mistress's home."

The bunyip shrank from my raised sword. We had cornered it in a small rocky alcove, and as it looked around, it saw no way to escape.

It whined. "My my, I am sorry! Perhaps a deal can be made."

Ramiren stepped forward. "A deal, it is. Your life for the location of the mischief hag's home. Do we have an accord?"

The bunyip began to bob its head. "Yes yes, my my. An accord."

Ramiren extended his hand, which made the bunyip recoil. "The pact is sealed."

The bunyip paused, then extended its paw to the pactmaker.

Ramiren commanded sharply, "Repeat the words, bunyip."

The bunyip blurted, "The pact is sealed!" Its face twisted with confusion. "My my, but why? Is this needed? Necessary?"

"It protects you and us, bunyip. A pact sealed is a pact protected. Dangerous consequences can happen if it is broken."

My gaze bounced between the pactmaker and his newest pactee, wondering what these consequences might be. *Ask him about it later.*

The bunyip nodded vigorously. "My my, I understand. My life for the location of my lady's hut." It turned and pointed its body. "Due east from here, maybe five miles, in the middle of a woody clearing."

Ramiren showed his sharp canines in a threatening smile. "Now, was that so hard?"

The bunyip whined, its tail tucked and ears back.

Chapter Seven
A Whispered Calling

A few hours later, we decided to stop and make camp. We'd need to be fresh and rested before confronting the first mischief hag. *Who knows what she can do?*

Everyone was busy preparing dinner and arguing about what to make. I offered my supplies, as no one else besides myself and Raewyn had gotten anything besides basic rations. Though the dried goods had been purchased for my own use, I didn't have the heart to deny anyone after seeing Georgina nibbling on nothing but a stale cracker our first night outside of the city. A hot meal was a needed comfort, which everyone agreed on. What they did *not* agree on, however, was whether to make lentils or oats.

Raewyn sputtered. "Oats are for breakfast, Georgina. You can't make oatmeal for supper! It's not natural!"

Georgina crossed her arms. "Oh yeah? Says who?"

Raewyn threw up her hands. "Everyone!"

A whisper brushed against my ear. ***"Could you come to my tent, please? I'd like your opinion on something."***

Spinning my head to each side and behind, and seeing he wasn't near, confusion set in. Raewyn and Georgina were too busy arguing to hear it or pay me any heed. It was definitely Ramiren whispering, but I didn't know how.

Can he throw whispers?

Closing my eyes with a smile, I opened them again to stand. "Excuse me, everyone."

His tent barely fit in the area Ramiren had placed it, taking over much of their available space. I did not begrudge it, though, even if mine was stuffed into some ragged brush. *He needs his comfort, too.* Tapping my hand on the tent, the canvas felt much warmer than the ambient temperature should've allowed.

Large. Comfortable. And now apparently heated. *He really didn't need my luck stone.*

"Ramiren? It's Nathalia."

When he called out to enter, I ducked through the opening.

He had many pieces of his typical outfits hung out, strung across a line, and there were various cleaning implements spread about. He was standing in soft, black linen underclothes with a small brush in his hand. "I never got the hang of not having access to a launderer, but on the road, we must make do." He surveyed the clothing, smiling proudly. "What do you think?"

I gaped at him.

Laundry? You asked me to come look at laundry?

The anticipatory fluttering in my belly snuffed out like a candle, even if the disappointment felt silly. *He needs my advice. He is my friend first. Not everything has to be about lessons.*

I stepped forward and inspected the clothing thoroughly. After picking a few pieces of lint off a jacket and running my hand down the front of a shirt a few times to unwrinkle it, I moved back. "I think you did a remarkable job, especially given the circumstances. You seem to have used the correct bottle for the correct material." Accessing the jackets, I pointed at a red and black one, the one he had worn at the carnival. "This one looks best on you. It brings out your striking eyes and hair."

"Thank you for the compliment, and I agree. That is one of the few items of clothing that I've had for a long time, almost thirty-six years. Nearly every other piece I own is new. I don't think I'll be able to cast that jacket aside as long as it lasts, which should be my lifetime with magical assistance."

Wait. Thirty-six? The light of realization hit me full in the face. *That would mean...*

I asked, suddenly breathless, "And how old are you, exactly? If you don't mind my asking."

"I don't mind in the slightest. I am sixty years old, though the date I will become sixty-one... isn't completely clear. I've settled on a favorite date, instead."

Shifting my weight from one foot to the other, I placed my hands behind my back so he wouldn't see me fidget. "You don't look a day over twenty-eight. Must be your broodling blood. And what is your favorite birthday? I do enjoy spoiling my friends, especially on special days."

He ran a hand through his hair and gestured to a small desk with a calendar on its surface, where a specific day in the very near future was circled in gold ink. "My blood, and spending most of my years where there is always access to a laundry doesn't hurt, either."

After noting the day on the calendar, a laugh bubbled out of me. "No, no, it does not." When there was a slight lull in the conversation, I remembered there was a very important question to ask. *Now is as good a time as any.* "About earlier. With the bunyip. You said there would be consequences if the pact was broken. What are those consequences?"

He raised his eyebrows. "That was not a true pact. No material payment was given in exchange for it. I was bluffing the bunyip."

"Oh. Yes, but... what if ours is broken? It is a true pact, right?"

He bowed his head in agreement. "Yes, it is a true pact." He tilted his head with narrowed eyes. "You don't know the consequences of a broken pact?"

When I shook my head, his mouth thinned. "Well. The answer is, I don't know. You can't know. The pact magic I wield, that I trained for, is quite non-specific as to the consequences of a broken one, if indeed there is one at all. And I've never had a pact broken, so I can't even describe my own personal experiences. Keep in mind, I say broken, not dissolved. We are both within our rights to dissolve it at any time. But if the stipulations of the pact are somehow breached, there are potential ramifications. It's different for everyone. Random consequences, by design. That's part of its power, the fear of breaking a pact and what might happen. I've heard of people being flayed by an invisible blade, people showered with mountains of rose petals for the rest of their lives, blinded..."

"Flayed? Rose petals? Why did you not warn me?"

He gave a reassuring smile with a one-shoulder shrug. "It won't come up. Secrecy is my specialty, so no one will learn of our pact. I'll not take your virginity. You won't seek outside influence, and I'll not bed anyone else." His eyes dimmed when he saw how unimpressed I was about his casual attitude. "My apologies. You initiated the pact, so I thought you knew. I shouldn't have assumed. That was my mistake."

I did not like it at all, nor the uncertainty. But he said he had no idea of the consequences, and he thought I didn't approach him blindly. My trust in that, at least, was solid. *We'd better not break the pact then.* "Not that I'm not enjoying talking with you, but is your laundry really the reason you called me in here?"

The light in his eyes returned. "It actually was. If you had tips on improving anything, I was eager to hear them, as you have always kept yourself in a manner a cut above those who live on the road." He paused for a moment. "I also will periodically give you an excuse to slip away for discretion's sake, while getting conversation or advice I genuinely want if you were not in need of an excuse to retire somewhere private."

With the previous moment's awkwardness forgotten, I couldn't help but preen. "Thank you for the compliment. I have a method, but it's not easy to bathe in my tent, which is why I insisted on stopping near the strangely clear spring this morning. I pride myself on my presentation, and I am grateful you noticed."

He chuckled. "You know, bathing in that strangely clear spring in the middle of a swamp in the Feylands with a mischief hag nearby was likely not the wisest course of action."

Returning his chuckle with my own, I replied, "And nothing happened, except Raewyn jumping in afterwards when I came out unscathed." My chuckle faded. "Discretion's sake, indeed. Ensuring the pact is not broken is, now more than ever, paramount. I can't say I wish to be flayed, let alone showered by rose petals for eternity. What an odd punishment."

"I'm glad we have a place where prying eyes cannot compromise or even discover what you desire, where someone cannot look in on us by chance or design. I am ready and willing, whenever you require, and will continue to present opportunities where you can ask for lessons more often than you'll need those opportunities."

My eyes flitted to his mouth and need flared in me again. Sudden and potent. *I guess the candle wasn't snuffled completely.* "Then would it be inconvenient for you to provide a lesson now?"

He placed the brush down. "Not at all, I chose this time because it would be convenient for us both. We can depart now, if you wish."

"Yes, please."

He snapped his fingers and, a second later, we were back in the softly lit bedroom. Without instruction, I began to remove my clothing. Half-way through, only a shirt, stockings, and undergarments left, I whispered, "Would you help me, please?"

"Of course. You're already on topic." He began to untie the lacings at the top of my shirt, a strange smile on his face. He smiled so often, there had to be different meanings behind each one. Resolving to figure it out, he lifted the shirt above my head, which he folded and set aside.

Next, came my stockings. His palms smoothly traveled up each leg in turn, brushing my undergarments with teasing fingers before running his hands together down my thighs, removing the stockings one at a time. Finally, when only my undergarments remained, he looked up at me from his crouched position. "What was the difference between how we arrived here last time, and how we did this time?"

The answer popped immediately into my mind. "You asked for my consent first," I said aloud.

He gave a proud nod, and his smile widened. "Yes. Permission is what we're talking about, coupled with the theme of desire, to tie into the last lesson we had. This time, we're going to explore asking for things we want, if that's all right?"

I said, in Celestial, "***But there are so many things I could ask for.***"

He lifted his chin at my foreign words, but he did not ask for a translation.

When I spoke again, it was in Common, "I think that would be a good lesson. I cannot please without first making sure what I am doing *would* please."

He flicked his tongue to wet his lips. My gaze caught the movement immediately. "You will ask me for each thing you want next and wait for an answer. Permission passes back and forth this way. Be specific and try to avoid metaphors. Talk about specific actions done to specific body parts, with them, or both. To avoid feeling like you are giving orders, I recommend the use of please, and when that is not enough, the questions can move from request to plea." He finally slid my undergarments down, then stood.

The sheer want in me bubbled out. It no longer made me feel self-conscious, because here, with him, it was safe to voice my desires. *I'm not here to judge you*, he had said. And I trusted that.

Specific actions to specific parts?

Sure.

"I want to suck your cock. Please. I want to feel that vein pulse against my tongue. I want to feel you expand in my mouth. May I, please?"

My educated guess was that my sudden audacity caused the amusement, or something akin to it, to spark in his eyes. "Of course. You can start by taking off my clothing, and then I want you to keep the same techniques with hand, lips, and tongue that you demonstrated with so much proficiency last time. You know the technique now. You can always return to starting with your lips on the tip and sliding all the way down to the base and back up, while fluttering your tongue. You'll continue to ask at each stage."

Feeling like I just passed a test, my hands slid along his sides to lift his dark undershirt over his head, again cognizant of his glasses, and tossed it aside. Moving to his short breeches next, they went next.

He stood naked before me, and my eyes traveled up and down. He was already erect, the tip glistening. *Gods, he is beautiful.* "I would like for you to sit, please."

He nodded and sat in the nearby chair. Following, then kneeling in front of him, I leaned in to lick up the pearly moisture at his tip. Again, salted caramel landed on my tongue. The need to play, to reward him for tasting so good, made me raise my right hand to cover his shaft with my fingers.

He murmured, "A new technique for you to try. Cup the balls underneath gently and lift a little, please. Some..." He grunted when I put my left hand where he requested but continued to instruct, "...some like this, some do not. Something to keep in mind for..." He blew out a slow breath when I delicately lifted it.

He shifted in the chair and grunted quietly, "Use your right on yourself, not me, please."

My right hand moved down between my legs. I was becoming more proficient, more comfortable, at finding the areas that elicited the most reaction, both in him and myself. I let out a low groan as my fingertips sank into the wetness he always seemed to wring from me.

As I relentlessly hunted for his reactions with my lips, hand, and wiggling tongue, the need for his hands on me, in some form, prompted me to ask. "I'd like for you to put your hands on me. The back of my head, please." He obliged, gliding his fingers into my loose hair and pushed down on my head gently. The feeling of being caught by him, again, flared need in me.

Searching fingers circled the bit of sensitive flesh I'd found earlier, and my pussy answered with an empty, aching clench. When my tongue flicked along the vein I wanted, Ramiren sharply inhaled. When my left hand massaged his balls, his hands twitched and gripped in my hair.

He murmured, "Good. You're... doing so well..." The words trailed off, making me steal a glance at him. His eyes were half-lidded, the irises almost black. His chest rose and fell silently, but rapidly.

Is he trying to hide his reactions?

Pulling back, I removed my mouth and hand from him. "I'd like for you to get on the bed, please."

He hesitated, then removed his fingers from my hair with a husky reply, "Of course."

Ramiren reclined on the bed, and I followed. My hand hovered over his chest, and when I asked permission to touch, he grinned with a nod, as though pleased I got there on my own. My fingers brushed his chest, gliding over his lean frame with exploring hands. My eyes went to his face and saw he was watching me again. His glasses were perched on the end of his nose as he peered over the rims.

I moved my hand to his stomach, circling each divot I could find, while paying attention to other tells, other signs of body language. His abdominal muscles twitched under my hand. His breathing had deepened again. His gaze heated, almost imperceptibly. Almost.

So he is trying to hide what I'm doing to him. Let him keep his secrets. I already know.

The fact he was trying to conceal his arousal, and failing, did more to me than if he was open about it. A competition mixed with pleasure instantly became my new favorite contest.

I let myself grin as my hand moved lower, tracing lines down his hips and thighs. When my fingers went past his cock, he sucked in a deep breath. His hands were fisted. Even his right leg shook. It filled me with smug satisfaction.

I am pleasing him.

Cordani.

That voice again! Is he doing this?

I dismissed the thought immediately.

No. I know what his whispered voice sounds like now. This is something, or someone, else. Perhaps it's a quirk of this place?

There was no point in dwelling on it. Though the origin of the voice was still a mystery to me, I had become accustomed to it.

I asked to return to sucking his cock. He swallowed hard. "...And what do we say?" There was no reproach in the question. Merely a low intonation.

An unbidden smirk curled my lips. "Please."

He nodded once, and I leaned forward to resume. I teased him with my tongue, drawing slow circles over the tip before moving down. Propping myself up with one hand, I used the other on myself. Each flick of my tongue reminded me of his own tongue laving me. Each brush of my fingers recalled his hands gripping my hair. A low moan rumbled out of me.

He murmured, his voice taking an odd tone I hadn't heard before, "Say you want me to cum in your mouth."

My stomach tensed, and the throbbing in my pussy made me dip my fingers into my entrance to ease the needy ache. I curled my fingers as he had before, and the ache got worse.

Yes. "I want that, please."

Something shifted in his eyes. He breathed out and sat up to reach for my hair in a firm grip. Despite the sharp tug on my hair, it didn't hurt. Quite the opposite. The sting boiled me. He pulled me closer until his face was inches from mine to emphasize his words roughly, "Say it. Say you want a mouthful of cum, Nathalia." This close to him, I could see his pupils dilated until they enveloped the entire iris. The red was gone except for a thin ring. The unmistakable heat in them made me want to give whatever he asked for.

I marveled, realizing just how close he was to breaking.

My eyes didn't stray from his intense gaze. "Give me a mouthful of cum. Please." I closed my eyes and went back to licking with more vigor, this time using my hand around his shaft. I gripped firmly and pressed down while my mouth sucked and hollowed, moving in the opposite direction of my hand. His hands continued to fist my hair and did not ease.

His breathing got faster and rougher as I increased in speed and intensity. He let out another breath and whispered, "Now?"

My answer was muffled, but the vibrations were the tipping point. I tasted salted caramel against my tongue as he let out a gasp, then another gasp, then a loud, tortured groan. His hands, still tangled in my hair, guided me while his release went on even a little longer than in our previous sessions, and he laughed just a little when I did not stop.

I laughed with him as his cock popped out of my mouth. "Apologies. Your taste is... Do all men's releases taste like dessert?" I wiped the side of my mouth with my thumb and stretched out next to him.

He quirked an eyebrow. "Dessert?"

"Yes, you taste like something my family's cook used to make."

His other eyebrow raised. "Oh." He cleared his throat. "No. That is not usual. Most men taste bitter and salty."

I hummed in disappointment.

He rested a hand on my hip and squeezed the flesh there. "Shall we take care of you now? "

With a nod, my hands lowered to the soft curls between my thighs. Though the pulsing had lessened, the moment I touched my pussy again, it came back to life.

"What would you like me to do, and what do we say?"

"Caress my breasts..."

He spoke when I trailed off, "Caress my breasts, what?"

"Caress my breasts, please. And..." I breathed in as his fingers moved over my breasts and the peaked nipples softly, barely noticeable. He pinched them, certainly not enough to hurt, and I groaned. Sharp tendrils wrapped around my chest and snaked down to between my thighs, enhancing what my fingers were already doing.

"And what?"

I breathed out. He wouldn't move until I finished my request. "And lower, please. Use your fingers on..." My words kept getting caught in my throat. I wanted to say them, but something kept me from it.

"On what?"

Oh, to hell with it.

I looked at him with half-lidded eyes and said, "On my pussy." I gasped as he entered me with two fingers, with his thumb out and pressing on an area just above that made my head spin. He moved them in and out in response to my reaction to angle, intensity, and speed. He stopped and pulled his hand back when I requested that he stop, the "please" firmly in place now.

I wanted to see *his* creativity. *His* desires. "I want you, next, to do something that you'd like to do to me, please."

He furrowed his eyebrows, as though analyzing my request, and then nodded to himself. He moved to between my legs, lied down, and parted me to lick, tasting me. I sighed and leaned back fully, groaning. Only, this time, the feeling of building toward something wasn't there. It was pleasurable beyond measure, but... I felt something was missing. I was confused. *I don't need a release. I need him.* Part of me wondered what that meant.

Aren't those the same thing? Shouldn't I want a release?

I considered that they might not always be necessary.

Sometimes you just need something else.

And right then, I needed his arms around me.

"Stop. I'd like for you to lie beside me, please." When he did so, I embraced him. After a beat of him lying stiff, I grinned. "Please return the embrace."

He laughed under his breath. "Good. Now, tell me what you need." He pulled me closer, his arms encircling me tightly, but not suffocatingly so.

I buried my face into his neck and sighed. I should be frustrated, but I wasn't. "I just need this, nothing else."

"Really?" It was both an honest question and an expression of surprise. His jaw jumped. "Only if that's what you *truly* want, Nathalia. I'm more than willing, but if you'd rather not, I won't put my pride before your needs."

I nodded against him, the movement causing me to nuzzle his neck, and replied, "Really."

He held me and continued to hold me even when I told him that he could stop when he wished to. He ran his hand along my spine, making me groan and arch my back. "Careful. Might change my mind." I smiled at him, breaking the embrace and moving to get dressed again.

He, too, got up. "Very good. I'm even more pleased with a lesson where a mistake is made, noticed, and corrected, over one where no mistakes are made at all. It is so hard to tell in the latter case whether or not it is a coincidence, or if something was learned."

I watched him get dressed as well. Pondering, I walked over to him. Standing a hair's breadth away, looking up, I said, "Permission to kiss you, please?" When he gave it, a slight change to his smile, I got up on my tip-toes to give him a soft kiss. Afterwards, I whispered, "As promised, I have another secret for you." I paused before continuing, "What I said in Celestial, at the beginning of this lesson, was there are many things I could ask for."

I heard myself and felt somewhat embarrassed.

Well, that sounded a lot better in my head.

I turned toward the door. Behind me, I heard a quiet question, "Do you want to go back now?"

I nodded and stepped forward, and when my foot touched the ground, it was outside his tent once more. The whisper that only I could hear returned, ***"Until next time..."***

I squinted and hunched down, moving aside the damp, dead flora that was blocking my line of sight. Up ahead was a small, rickety cottage in the middle of a clearing.

Finally. We made it.

Slowly drawing my longsword out of its scabbard, the glint of the metal dim in the fading light, I looked back at my companions. Georgina bounced on her toes next to M.A.L.C.O.L.M. Raewyn fidgeted. Only Ramiren appeared calm and collected. I envied his demeanor. On the outside, we both appeared equally calm, but inside...

Inside, I was a mix of emotions, with fear and trepidation being the most prevalent.

Was this the hag that stole from me and Raewyn or Georgina or Leraska? Would I soon be getting my creativity back?

It hardly seemed possible after all these years.

My doubt regarding the hag making a deal with us, which Ramiren was pushing for, meant I had to be ready to pounce before she could attack either one of us. Regardless if Ramiren wanted an accord or not, my role was to ensure safety. Then my fear melted away when Ramiren turned his reassuring smile toward me, though the trepidation remained.

"Shall we, then?" Ramiren said, stepping through the brush. I quickly stood and matched his speed.

"Yes, though I urge everyone to be on their guard. This is not a being to be trifled with," I warned.

"Yes, we know she's dangerous, dummy!" Georgina exclaimed, marching behind with M.A.L.C.O.L.M in her wake. She shook her head, almost in disgust.

Though my initial reaction was irritation, something struck me about the surly gnome. She was more grumpy than usual today, and it became worse as we got closer to the hag's home. *She's afraid and has trouble showing it. That's all.* My pity for Georgina replaced my annoyance.

Raewyn piped up, "So, the plan is we try to deal with her? And if she won't deal, then squish? Hopefully a bonfire?"

"Yes. Are you ready, Ramiren?" I said, turning to the broodling at my side.

He gave a confident nod. "Yes, I'm ready."

We approached the cabin with caution. I kept my head on a swivel, looking around for danger, but there was none to be found.

Strange. You'd think her home would be well-protected.

We climbed the stairs leading to the porch, the rotting wood underneath our feet increasingly groaning, squeaking, and straining with our weight.

The gnome held out a hand to her large automaton. "Best stay back off the porch, M.A.L. You might break through the boards."

Beep. "YES, GEORGINA." M.A.L.C.O.L.M. stopped just shy of the first step, alert for the next command.

As I raised my hand to knock on the pitted, wooden door, a series of scrawling words began to form on the door's surface. I read them aloud.

"'Blessed be those who know me. Cursed be those who scorn me. Righteous be those who honor me. This, the first rule and the last, is eternal.' A riddle, then?"

Raewyn's eyes lit up. "Oh, the first rule and the last. That's a Minuen saying. The answer is 'love.'"

At her word, the portal swung open with a creak, followed by a squeaky whine, hitting the wall next to the door. Inside was a lit hearth, a few tables littered with bottles and ingredients of all kinds, an unmade bed, and another door on the far wall. But no hag.

We carefully stepped forward as one, looking around. Thankfully, M.A.L.C.O.L.M. did not break through the boards when instructed to walk across the porch and into the main room.

Raewyn browsed off to the side and leaned down to peer at the bottles on the table. She unstoppered a few to sniff at the contents. "Hm, some interesting stuff in here." She began to put the bottles in a pouch when I shook my head.

"Stop. Now, Raewyn." I commanded in a whisper.

Raewyn pouted, a bottle paused halfway in the pouch. "But why?"

"Because we're meant to make a deal with her for the things she stole. Stealing from her would only anger her and make my job much more difficult," Ramiren said calmly.

Raewyn huffed a sigh, moodily putting the bottles back on the table one at a time. "Oh sure, fine. But if we gotta kill her, I'm coming back for these."

My sigh echoed Raewyn's, but for another reason.

Standing in front of the second door, I raised my hand again to knock. Again, words appeared on the wood, almost burned into it. This time, Ramiren read the words aloud.

"'That which opens is difficult to close. And that which closes is impossible to open.'" Ramiren frowned, looking perplexed. "I know this one, for elves are immortal, unless killed by violence. And they can never be raised again, even using fey magic. The answer is 'the eyes of an elf'."

Again, the door swung open.

Georgina eyed Ramiren in astonishment. "How in the Dark Drop did you get that, pactmaker?"

Ramiren chuckled, looking at the little gnome next to him. "I have cleverness in me, tinkerer."

Behind the door was a set of uneven, decaying stairs, twisting down into the dark. My shield raised automatically, and I waited, expecting something to jump out. But nothing did. Confused, I looked back at everyone. "Why these children's riddles? Where is the hag?"

"I suspect she is either testing us or merely having a bit of fun at our expense." Ramiren shrugged and leaned forward. He peered into the dark. Behind me, a bright light suddenly glowed. Georgina lifted her arm, holding up the strangest torch I had ever seen. The end of the stick flickered and danced as though aflame, though no smoke curled off of it, and no heat radiated from it. Georgina smiled smugly.

"And you certainly have cleverness, too, Mistress Georgina. Shall we?" Ramiren said, extending his hand into the dark. I walked forward first, slowly making my way down the stairs and praying that these stairs held our weight. Ramiren followed behind, with Raewyn, Georgina, and finally M.A.L.C.O.L.M. in his wake.

The stairs seemed endless. Though they looked treacherous, and loudly squeaked when my foot landed on every step, they held firm. I was almost dizzy by the time we reached the bottom. With the light source from Georgina, we saw a long hallway leading to yet another closed door. I murmured, "Another door, another riddle."

Walking to it, I expected to see words when raising my hand. When they appeared, I read them aloud, not even thinking of their meaning.

"Look up."

My eyes shot up just enough time to see a massive barbed spike above my head. When it dropped, spearing down, I tipped backwards to dodge. It pierced in the dirt where I'd just been standing. Here was a half-second pause before it raised again, resetting itself into the ceiling.

Ramiren managed to catch me, though only just, from hitting my behind on the ground. He smiled down at me as my head tilted back to look at him. I was surprised, given his lean frame, that he was able to do that.

He is much stronger than he looks.

My mouth wanted to smile back. It twitched in protest, but I simply stood, embarrassed at missing such an obvious trap. "My apologies, Master Ramiren. Thank you."

He replied smoothly, "Some lessons are easier to learn than others, and far more pleasant."

My face warmed, and I turned back toward the trap and the offending door before anyone else could see.

Ramiren called out, "Does anyone know how to deal with traps?"

"Thaaaat would be me." Georgina toddled forward. "I might not be able to use my tools, but I can certainly tell you what mechanism goes where." She looked up at the hole where the spike was set, careful to remain away from its path.

She hummed in thought. "The mechanism is in the walls, or on the other side of the door, which means someone will need to trigger it while another waits with a sharp blade to cut the rope. Or... M.A.L. I can't remember. Did I remove the scissors from you?

Beep. "YOU DID NOT, GEORGINA. I CAN STILL SCISSOR."

Raewyn snorted in laughter.

Ignoring Raewyn, I volunteered to activate it. No one protested. Everyone else stood back while M.A.L.C.O.L.M. and I took our places, I under the spike and M.A.L.C.O.L.M. to the side. Large scissors folded out from his forearms and extended forward, ready and waiting.

My hands rubbed together. "Let's see. I approached the door, raised my hand to knock. Words appeared..."

Sure enough, the words that had been there before appeared again, this time brighter.

"I looked up." My head tilted back as I spoke. A second before the spike plummeted, there was an audible, soft unlatching sound that I had missed the first time.

Now.

I jumped back as the spike came down hard. As it landed, M.A.L.C.O.L.M. extended his arms and snipped the rope attached to the upper portion of the spike. I heard a hitch, presumably to bring the spike back up. The rope disappeared, but the spike stayed put.

I smiled at M.A.L.C.O.L.M. "Well done."

The automaton snipped his scissors in the air a few times in apparent excitement. Beep. "I SCISSORED."

This time, Raewyn laughed fully while receiving a glare from Georgina.

"Yes, well done, both of you," Ramiren said. He fixated on the door and squinted. "And more writing is appearing." The rest of us faced the door simultaneously.

Instead of 'look up,' other words scrawled over the door, as though written by some invisible hand.

"Give those without creativity a riddle? It'd be unfair, I must confess. So, what are you, little girl? Give the question a mighty guess," I recited slowly.

My nostrils flared as my face flamed. Gritting my teeth, I answered, "Above all else, I am a protector. Also, your meter is off, hag."

At my words, the door swung open into a large cavern, brightly lit with torches, candles, and lanterns. The air smelled musty, earthy, like mushrooms. Despite the lit lanterns and my armor, the dampness and chill of the stone chamber washed over me, causing me to shiver.

A wizened and hunched creature tinkered at a table, her back toward us, pouring bottles of something into bottles of something else. She murmured to herself, but whether it was magical incantations or simply muttering, I could not tell.

"We're here," I called out.

The creature turned. Her facial features were bulbous and exaggerated, covered in warts of all sizes. Her acid eyes settled on me and recognition crossed her hideous face. "Oh, yes! Hello! Come in! Come in! I've been waiting for you." She cackled, a familiar sound that set my teeth on edge. I stepped into the cavern, the others following closely behind.

"Now, my sweets. What is it that you want? You made it through my clever riddles. My clever traps. Surely, you are clever, too! What do you want from dear old Anoira, hm?"

I doubt that's her real name. I've heard fey are often finicky about their names.

Ramiren replied to her, "We have come to strike a deal with you, Anoira. You have something of ours that should be returned. A stolen thing that belongs to one of us."

"Ahhh, yes. I see. You wish to reclaim. Very well. What would you give in return?"

"Your life?" Raewyn muttered derisively. Both Ramiren and I turned back to glare at Raewyn, who did not shrink under our gaze. She shrugged, looking unbothered.

The hag cackled again. "My life, you say? Oh, but what do I feel it is worth, hm? Equal to the restoration of a beautiful face? Tools and the knowledge to use them? Oh, perhaps not all that. Perhaps something else, eh? Something more substantial. One of *your* lives, maybe?" She grinned, ragged and rotted teeth showing.

"We come in good faith, mistress." Ramiren stepped forward, though his hand moved to rest on the hilt of his rapier. He knew what was about to happen. I spared a second to mentally applaud his instincts before he continued, "We wish for a return of things stolen. Perhaps you can..."

The hag frowned. "Good faith? You come to my home, break in, and expect fair play? Oh, no." She tsked in disappointment.

Ramiren replied with impatience, "The doors opened automatically. The riddles and traps were so easy as to practically be an invitation. Simple and strangely specific to us. In fact, I recall talking about an elf at the carnival."

"Oh, shit! And I said that Minuen phrase in the riddle to Chadra at The Forever Inn," Raewyn added.

It was no surprise I hadn't remembered that, too. *Especially given my mental state at the time.*

"Indeed," Ramiren said, without turning from the hag. "You've been watching us. Scrying. For quite a while now."

The hag laughed and clapped as though pleased. "Indeed, I have! Some *very* interesting happenings. Strange things surround you, Ramiren. And you, Nathalia. Blips. Flashes of fire and then nothing. Mmm. I wonder what that is..."

My blood ran cold. My heart dropped into my stomach.

My first lesson and the pact's discussion had not been in the protected bedroom.

It was at the inn.

Has she seen? Did she know? And, more importantly, would she tell?

Before the hag could continue, Ramiren drew his rapier as simmering anger twisted his handsome features. "No deal. And no more talk."

Chapter Nine

A Vial of Whistles

The hag lifted into the air, hovering just a few inches above the ground. She giggled with delight, pointing a finger at Ramiren. "The pactmaker doesn't want to talk anymore? Fine by me!" A black light appeared at the end of the hag's finger and shot out at Ramiren, who ducked down just in time. The black bolt continued past him, hitting a surprised Georgina directly in the chest. She toppled and landed on her back, sliding a good foot or two from the force of the attack.

The hag howled in laughter. "Got one!"

Beep. "GEORGINA! ARE YOU BROKEN?"

Georgina groaned out a command as Raewyn ran over to her, "M.A.L.! Kill mode!"

Beep. "AFFIRMATIVE."

The automaton's eyes turned red, and he charged the same moment Ramiren and I did, my longsword and shield held high. The hag grinned as electricity danced along her fingers before loosening onto M.A.L.C.O.L.M. The automaton stopped in his tracks, arcs of lightning sizzling around him. He shuddered and a soft beep followed.

"RECALIBRATING. RECALIBRATING. RECALIBRATING..."

"No!" Georgina screamed, "Damn it, not now!"

Ramiren arrived a half second before I did, lunging at the hag. It was a sloppy maneuver. Easily dodged. I wondered if him being in a fight was a good idea.

As the hag moved out of the way, almost mockingly, her flank was left wide open. The thoughts of him not being in the fight vanished.

I took the opportunity and stepped forward, giving a backhanded slash with my longsword. It cut deep. Deep enough for the cackles to turn into wails.

"Ow! How dare you!" A red glow illuminated her hands as her acid-green eyes turned to me. I didn't want to find out what it meant.

Evidently, neither did Ramiren. He feinted again, and I chopped down at the same time, leaving no room for the hag to move with her back to the table. She tried to levitate even higher to get out of the way, but that only pushed her into my blade. My sword sliced into the hag's neck. She gurgled, holding her throat as the red glow dimmed, and dropped to the ground in a heap.

Running to check on our tinkerer, with a side glance toward her automaton, I came to Georgina's side. Raewyn sat hunched over a downed Georgina, peering at the wound. The spell to her chest had left a gnarly mark, blackened and bloody, which had barely begun to heal with Raewyn's ministrations. Raewyn wiggled her fingers at Georgina. "Now, say pretty please with a cherry on top."

Before I could chide her pettiness, Ramiren sighed in exhaustion. "Raewyn..."

Georgina shrieked, "Pretty fucking please with your long-lost cherry on top!"

Raewyn grinned and prayed to Minue. The black-sooted hole in Georgina's upper chest lightened and disappeared, leaving healthy skin behind.

M.A.L.C.O.L.M. shuddered again, and he looked around, as though confused.

Beep. "IS IT OVER ALREADY?"

"Yes, it's over." I walked back to nudge the dead mischief hag with the toe of my boot, her hissing blood the same color as her green eyes that had been shut forever. "She'll never trouble another again." After leaning down to clean my sword on her skirt, I sheathed it.

Raewyn's voice was tinged with confusion. "What was she saying about you and Ramiren? Flashes of flame and all that?"

My heart went into my throat. Ramiren replied without a hint of panic, "No doubt attempting to sow discord and cause hesitation. You shouldn't trouble yourself over it, Raewyn."

"But...you confirmed it. You said she had been scrying." Raewyn narrowed her eyes, and the lump in my throat choked me.

Ramiren, bless him, replied again, "I confirmed the origin of the riddles, that's all."

"Oh, right. Well..." Raewyn shrugged, appearing placated. "...never mind then."

The lump in my throat disappeared, leaving an ache in its place.

Thank you, Ramiren.

We searched through the vials in the large cupboard, reading the names on small tags attached to each one. I started picking up random vials, smashing them on the ground after reading their names to see if it was mine or Raewyn's. We did not see any tools near the cupboard, which made Georgina groan.

"Not my hag!" She grumbled, heading back out of the cavern.

M.A.L.C.O.L.M. beeped. "CAN I STAY AND SMASH THINGS?"

Georgina waved a hand over her shoulder, not bothering to turn around as she walked. "To your metal heart's content, M.A.L."

Beep. "WEE!"

I read the tag on the vial in my right hand, "Vassily Horngodder." Smashing the glass at my feet, my confidence rose when the purple glow contained in the vial released. Vassily now had whatever was stolen from them.

Raewyn called out, "Jamira Tipple... you're welcome!" *Smash.*

Beep. "I CAN'T READ." *Smash.*

I picked up another from the cupboard and turned the tag over. "Ramiren O... wait, what?" Staring down at the vial in my hands, a faint golden glow emanating from the crystal-clear glass, I looked up at an approaching Ramiren. "You never said something was stolen from you."

He smiled pleasantly, a contrast with his words. "You assumed and did not ask. May I have the vial, please?"

I handed it over wordlessly, and Ramiren hesitated for a moment before smashing it on the ground. The golden glow flowed upwards like mist and then disappeared.

"What was stolen from you?" I asked quietly.

Ramiren pursed his lips together and blew, whistling a perfect, high-pitched note. He seemed satisfied and finally looked at me. "The ability to whistle. This exact mischief hag, it seems, was the one who took it from me. I thank you for helping me to retrieve it."

"But you've never before been to the Fey Carnival. You said so."

He inclined his head in acknowledgement. "Correct, I had never been there before. Merely in the wrong place at the wrong time in the Feylands."

I didn't ask, but why not say anything? What does he have to lose?

My scowl deepened. "And what else are you not telling me?"

He arched a black eyebrow. "Many things, but nothing that will harm you, I swear it."

My eyes narrowed with suspicion.

He tilted his head, and his smile diminished but did not disappear. "I've never lied to you. Nor have I kept anything from you that might be dangerous. My secrets are my own, Nathalia. I keep them because secrets are powerful, remember?"

I paused and whispered, "There are some things that shouldn't be secrets, Ramiren."

He replied, just as softly, "And there are some that should always be."

Georgina frowned. "Pretty please?"

Raewyn shook her head, shrugging. "I'm not being difficult this time, I swear. I can't heal him. He's an automaton. He's not a living being, Georgina."

Georgina cursed. "Well, then, what good are you?"

Raewyn rolled her eyes. "You know, Georgina, your attitude will get you in trouble one of these days."

Georgina's exaggerated eyes narrowed at my priestess sister. "But not today, Raewyn." She inspected M.A.L.C.O.L.M. with a glance. "Will you be all right?"

M.A.L.C.O.L.M. beeped. "YES, GEORGINA. I WILL BE FINE. I LOST MY NUTS."

Raewyn snickered, making Georgina go red. The tinkerer did her best to ignore her. "You lost nuts and bolts. You didn't 'lose your nuts.'"

Beep. "I DON'T UNDERSTAND. ISN'T THAT THE SAME THING?"

The gnome put her fists on her hips. "No."

Beep. "NUTS ARE NUTS, GEORGINA. AND I LOST THEM."

Georgina frowned. "And bolts. It's an important distinction."

Beep. "MY NUTS ARE ON THE FLOOR."

Georgina gritted her teeth. "And bolts, M.A.L.C.O.L.M."

Beep. "MY NUTS ARE BROKEN."

Raewyn couldn't hold it in any longer and started to belly laugh. Doubled over, she held her stomach with both hands. "Oh! Oh, I'm going to pee myself."

Georgina huffed. "Stop it, Raewyn. You know what he means."

Raewyn wiped her eyes as she giggled. "Ow, my nuts!"

I watched the proceedings silently. *This kind of conflict can only lead to resentment.* "Raewyn, please stop."

Raewyn's giggles subsided, but she still looked amused. "Oh, you old biddy. I was just having a bit of fun."

"At another's expense. We still have two more mischief hags to get to with a long way to get there. We cannot have this the entire way. I mean it, Raewyn."

She smirked at me. "Then, tell M.A.L.C.O.L.M. to keep his nuts close by. Can't just have them, you know, *dangling* there for me to grab."

"Raewyn!"

She let out another laugh and walked off. Ramiren smiled when my helpless gaze turned to him.

Ramiren said, "A little levity is not unwelcome sometimes. And we did just have a nasty encounter. Perhaps give your sister some grace."

I sighed, conceding the point. "Georgina, I apologize for my sister."

Georgina frowned as she began to search for and pick up the aforementioned nuts... and bolts. "I can see why it would be funny, but I don't like it. More of these fights, and M.A.L.C.O.L.M. may become non-functional."

Her sadness was understandable. M.A.L.C.O.L.M was her life's work. To see it destroyed piece-by-piece while you could do nothing had to be difficult.

Glancing at Ramiren again, remembering earlier, I wondered if our friendship would be chipped away piece-by-piece because of his secrets.

Why had he kept something important from me, from us? He knew one of the mischief hags had his vial, his ability to whistle. Why didn't he say anything? Why keep quiet about it?

With a resigned exhale, I concluded his secrets were his business. I was not privy to his entire life and believed him when he said he wouldn't put me in danger. Still, the knowledge that he was keeping things from me when I'd been so open with him stung. My desire to know everything about him was the real reason for my reaction. The fact that he didn't want to was like a thorn in my side: ever-present and frustrating.

Be patient. I haven't earned the privilege of knowing everything yet. Perhaps I will in time.

We set out, after consulting the map and Ramiren's notes, to leave the swamp with a northbound heading. We managed to retrace our steps through the mire, finally making it onto dry land just south of Puldoni. We met up with the now crowded eastern road and headed toward the Tanta Desert.

After an hour, dodging wagons, carts, and cranky drovers, Raewyn's whining began. "Why do we have to walk everywhere? Can't we get horses?"

"No, Raewyn. We're just fine traveling on foot. Besides, the horses here aren't like the horses back home." I motioned to one of the six-legged feyhorses nearby. His master was trying to pull him forward with the reins, but the animal wouldn't budge. After giving a mighty heave, the feyhorse moved just enough for his master to fall on his rear in the dirt. The feyhorse sauntered past with a stuttering wheeze .

Is it laughing?

One had almost trampled us when leaving Puldoni. I blamed the rider, idiot fey that he was, but that did not stop me from noticing the feyhorse almost bit Ramiren when he passed us.

Raewyn clicked her tongue unhappily. "But maybe we could try?"

"Perhaps we can try after we leave the Tanta Desert. We might have to go into the mountains there. That's no place for a horse, no matter how many legs it has."

Raewyn grumbled, and Georgina shook her head from her perch on M.A.L.C.O.L.M.'s shoulder. "Quit your bellyaching. It's annoying me."

"Easy for you to say, Georgina. You're not walking," Raewyn replied bitterly.

I took the excuse to talk to him that I'd been given. "Ramiren, how are you holding up?"

Ramiren looked back at me and smiled as though we had never argued. The nervous knot in my belly tightened. "I am just fine. My boots are comfortable, thank Jessina."

Jessina, the Goddess of Law. And, by extension, contracts. It made sense that the Arbiter of the Gods would be his patroness. Deals and contracts were often stamped with her sigil in an attempt to curry her favor in the bargain. But it was odd that he would thank her at that moment. I asked him why.

Ramiren chuckled. "Old habit. I tend to thank her whenever my life goes according to plan."

I raised an eyebrow. "Does your life often go according to plan?"

He looked back at me again with a grin. "Often."

My other eyebrow went up. "Often?"

He faced forward again. "Yes, the pieces often fall where they should. If they don't, and rarely they don't, I can always adjust."

"Would you two keep it down? I can't hear my own misery," Raewyn hissed in pain as she stepped on a large pebble. "Why me? Why did you allow me to do this, Nat? How do you live like this?"

I hesitated before speaking, to make sure my tone was even and patient, "We'll get you better shoes in the next town, Raewyn."

"And maybe a piece of fabric to stuff in her mouth." Georgina smirked from her perch.

"Uncalled for, Georgina." *It was a little called for.*

Beep. "YES, UNCALLED FOR, GEORGINA."

Georgina casually propped her elbow on the top of the automaton's head. "When I get my tools back, M.A.L.C.O.L.M., I'm turning off your voice box."

Beep. "THEN WHO WILL TALK TO YOU, GEORGINA?"

My hand hid a smirk as Georgina smacked the automaton on the forehead.

The journey toward the Tanta Desert was blessedly uneventful, except for the occasional mutter from Raewyn, subsequent mocking from Georgina, and the obstinate feyhorses that caused more than one traffic interruption. The quiet gave me ample opportunity to think while enjoying the lush floral landscape containing every rainbow color. There were no orange trees in the meadow of vibrant red, purple, and white flowers, but I definitely smelled oranges. The strange scent only added to my confusion.

Though I had concluded that I had nowhere near earned his deepest thoughts and secrets, the question remained. *Could I trust him?*

The thought made my head and heart hurt.

A crystal clear butterfly fluttered past, a yellow light on its backend blinking rhythmically, like fireflies back home. My eyes followed its path, admiring the way the sunlight hit its iridescent wings, until a passing fey with eight eyes and eight legs jumped up and caught it in mid-air. The butterfly was swallowed before he hit the ground.

Arachne fey.

I made a face and went back to what I apparently did best: overthinking everything.

Having freely shared my own secrets, without asking for his, he was also right. None of us ever asked if the hags stole from him, including me. If his secrets were wanted, I should have asked for them instead of throwing a tantrum that he wasn't a mind reader. Unmet expectations were the root of all disagreements. That was one lesson Ramiren didn't have to teach me.

It wasn't the secrets that I wanted. I wanted to know him, yes. But it was the trust he'd have in disclosing them that I desired.

With a loud sigh, which caused everyone to look my way, I rubbed my eyes. "Tired. Apologies."

Ramiren's gaze stayed on me a little longer than everyone else's. His red eyes bored into me, as though trying to suss out my thoughts. I met his look for a second before focusing on the landscape again. He looked almost disappointed in me, and that stung the most. *I'll talk to him about it this evening, once we reach Ghau.*

Making a mental note to purchase as much water as my already burdened pouch could hold for the journey through the Tanta Desert, my thoughts turned to what would need replacing in my dwindling food supply.

Raewyn tripped, barely catching herself, and wailed in anguish. "This damned road!"

And new boots for Raewyn. My patience is wearing as thin as the soles of her shoes.

Raewyn flexed her feet forward and back, admiring the soft leather of her boots. "So comfortable. They even put sheepskin on the bottom!"

I sat across from her at a long table in the Soggy Rooster Inn, which Raewyn saw the sign for and emphatically insisted we stay there, though she refused to tell me why. My tired arms propped up my tired head, watching her gaze lovingly at her new purchase. Or, rather, my new purchase for her. After getting my greaves repaired, she'd been promptly pulled into a leatherworking shop for proper traveling footwear. She argued, begging for silk slippers. I had to talk her into something a bit more practical.

"They should ensure your comfort and be very protective," I replied, nursing a glass of Dulon white. It was delicious, though expensive, given it had to be transported from Laeth.

I need to get a small wineskin of this before I leave Ghau.

"Like you, Nat." Raewyn grinned at me.

I closed my eyes for a brief moment and bit my lips to keep from smirking. "Sure. Like me."

To my side, Ramiren sat drinking his own wine. He had been quiet, obviously mulling something over. A sharp pain went through my chest at the random idea he was considering ending our pact over our disagreement.

Why is this so damned messy?

I rubbed my eyes. *Be realistic. You two are being intimate. It's only natural to develop certain feelings. Perhaps, it'd be best if you ended it before you develop inconvenient ones...*

"No!" I shrieked, aloud.

Everyone turned to me, even a few patrons sitting near our table looked over. My face burned, and my hand flew to cover my mouth.

"I... apologies." I tried to swallow my embarrassment, which stuck like a lump in my throat. Raewyn furrowed her eyebrows at me, then shrugged as though she had not a care in the world and went back to looking at her new boots.

Georgina snickered and muttered mockingly, "No!"

Beep. "YES!"

Georgina looked at M.A.L.C.O.L.M., and grinned. "No!"

Beep. "YES!"

I slowly rubbed my forehead. *A headache is definitely forming.*

"No!"

Beep. "NO!"

"Yes!"

A soft beep followed a strange grinding sound that seemed to be M.A.L.C.O.L.M.'s laughter. "I TRICKED YOU, GEORGINA. I MADE YOU SAY SOMETHING YOU DID NOT INTEND."

Georgina shook her head and started going over the finer points of verbal manipulation to M.A.L.C.O.L.M.

Taking the mockery with as much dignity as I could muster, a soft whisper cut through the noise, "Are you all right?"

"Hm?" His question sunk in. "Oh. Yes, I am fine. Just thinking."

"About what, if I may ask?"

Oh, so you can learn all you wish to know of me, but I cannot learn the same?

The bitter thought startled me, and I pushed it down deep. *Oh. Sure. Because miscommunication solves everything, doesn't it? He asked. You never did. He is only curious, perhaps even wishes to help me. Now, for the love of Horyn, stop acting like a child.*

I replied low, whispering so no one else could hear, "I was thinking of our pact. That's all."

A concerned look crossed his eyes, but his smile persisted. "Oh?"

"Yes. Just going over it in my head."

He studied me, his facial expression not changing. "And? What did you come up with that made you exclaim so suddenly?"

My face burned hotter. "It's not important." I briefly contemplated telling him but didn't want to get into something I wasn't prepared to fully explain.

Then a thought occurred to me. "Why did you never tell us that the mischief hag had your ability to whistle?"

His smile faded. "I told you. You did not ask."

My head tilted downward. "But when I do ask, you avoid the question."

Ramiren spoke, as though the reply was obvious, "As is my right. Remember, I said you can request anything if you can stand hearing *no* as a reply. You're asking the wrong question, Nathalia. Ask the right one."

My teeth gritted painfully in frustration as I slouched into my chair, the back of my head hitting the wooden backing.

But what's the right ques-

Oh.

"Would you have avoided the question had I asked if one of the hags stole something from you?"

His smile returned, as though pleased. He swirled his wine glass and watched the liquid agitate. "No, I would not have. I simply make it a habit of not sharing information about myself."

You can't know if you don't ask. "Why?"

Ramiren sighed, his shoulders rising and falling with his deep breath, and set his glass down. He leaned forward with his clasped hands on the table. "Nathalia... I know what I am. I am a broodling with more than a little resemblance toward my ancestors. I use that to my advantage in making pacts. If people fear me, my kind, it makes them more pliable to terms and less likely to try to trick me or someone I am dealing on behalf of. The less they know of me, the better. Sometimes an assumption can be the difference between death and a mutually beneficial pact." He gave me a hard look that immediately softened. "Does that help you?"

I stared at him, jaw dropped. *Finally. Something.* "Why share that information with me, then? Now?"

"Because you do not fear me, at least no longer. I do trust you, despite my hesitation to share. And I hope, despite the lack of information I provide, you trust me." He tipped his head downward, looking at me over the rims of his glasses.

"You trust me because I keep nothing from you."

He replied without lifting his head, "I trust you because of who you are, Nathalia. Not because of what you can give me, even information."

It felt as though he was making a firm point. I decided to make a point of my own. "Trust is earned, Ramiren. It is not something that comes without a price paid, in some form or another. Everything has a price."

"That, I think, we can both agree on," he murmured as he took a drink of wine.

The knot in my belly returned. *When the time came, would I be willing to pay?*

I firmly put to rest the idea of ending the lessons, ending the pact.

What harm could it do now? I've already paid that *price.*

Chapter Ten
Hummingbird

We decided to take an extra day in Ghau to rest and recuperate. Raewyn wanted to explore, and she dragged me along with her. Probably because I had more money than she did. I bought the waterskins and refilled dry food and rations, this time for the whole party, a pragmatic purchase that bored my sister until I asked if she found starvation or dehydration boring.

She, blessedly, shut up.

We went to various shops. She found a crimson silk cloak that I insisted she get, and I pushed the coin into the vendor's hands. I remarked that the silk would help with the heat of the desert, but, really, I just thought it looked beautiful on her.

Ghau was not nearly as big as Puldoni was, but it had its charms. Besides the bright yellow paint covering the front of most homes and shops, there was a city square-wide fountain, feylights dancing under the waves and coloring them in brilliant hues. It was a place of both relaxation and play. Old and young alike ran about, chasing the cascading showers spraying in random spurts across the entire square. I asked Georgina about it during supper, who informed me the water was cleansed and recycled in a special reservoir under the city.

"In fact, that's where the city gets its name. Ghau in the old fey language means 'water,'" she said in-between bites of some kind of spicy dish that had Raewyn going for said water. "The reservoir is really something. No rust. No mustiness. Nothing. It's pristine."

The rest of supper was restful and pleasant. Even Raewyn and Georgina got along. Ramiren threw me a smile that I had no problems translating, for once.

I raised an eyebrow. *Lesson?*

He nodded once.

I leaned back in alarm. *Oh fuck, can he hear thoughts?*

His smirk neither confirmed nor denied my suspicions.

Later that night, I found myself in the secret bedroom with Ramiren looking around to see if anything had changed but very little had. There was a small chest on the table against the right wall. Velvet cushions now occupied the chairs. I touched the soft bed cover, ran my hand through a silken scarf hanging from the ceiling, and then finally turned to look at him to speak.

"Last time, we talked about permission. Is this session where you ask permission from me? Or are we extending my own lesson from last time?" Approaching him carefully, my bare feet sinking into plush rugs on the floor, I lifted my hand to touch him, but didn't. Instead, my gaze went to his, hoping he could hear the word in my mind. *Please?*

It looked like he understood. He smiled at me, appreciatively. "I admire that you're putting in the practice on what we learned last time. I'll be extending what we talked about in a specific direction, with a specific end. One that may lead in short order to you giving instructions instead of taking them. In fact, on this topic, it may help if I am more forceful in my responses. I suggested last time that when you ask permission, you might try a plea. This time, that will be a requirement."

Requirement?

Wait.

My hand dropped. "You mean begging? I've never begged for anything in my entire life." Pride streaked through my body, but it faded and disappeared almost immediately. *I gave my word to obey, and my word means everything.*

Besides, he can certainly try.

"Hm." My eyes narrowed playfully, and I began to walk around Ramiren in a circle. "Begging entails desire. Desperate desire, along with depriving one of what they want. They are so frantic that they have no choice but to beg, which..." I stopped in front of him again, and looked up at his face, meeting his eyes. "...I'm not sure you're capable of."

There was no reaction to my taunt in his eyes or expression. "Since we'll be working through removing some element of active consent from you with the receiving of orders, we need to revisit the idea of a word to use if you want or need to stop or pause any activity." He stepped toward me suddenly, and I involuntarily took a step back.

My skin prickled in awareness. He wasn't being threatening, but he *was* giving me a gentle reminder to not be a brat.

Noted.

His smile returned, though I couldn't tell if it was from the subject matter, my reaction, or neither. "For example, my word is *orange*, as it is unlikely to be said in a sexual context, and also not to be mistaken for another word. The last time I used it was not because the act in question was more than I could handle, but due to an unexpected leg cramp. You should have a word, just in case. You ready your shield whether or not you are sure it will be needed."

I was admittedly impressed. Though my statement had been an honest one, as I truly doubted anyone could make me beg, even him, he handled it with grace and even diverted my attention to something else. *He would do well at the Camlite court.*

I replied softly, "My word is 'hummingbird.'"

He looked pleased. "Excellent. Two notes about this lesson. I want you to hear this, because it is very important. On the outside, it might appear that I have control. That is not at all the case. It is *you* who has the control. If you say 'hummingbird,' we stop. No questions. Never be afraid to use that word. I will never be angry. Or upset. Or frustrated. And I will never ever ignore it. Your safety and well-being are my top priority."

His reversal of my expectations surprised me. "Oh. I would have figured the control would be in your hands."

"An unfortunately common misconception that can lead to a great deal of damage. You control the narrative here, Nathalia, not I."

Accepting his clarification with a smile, trying to take in everything he was telling me, I nudged. "And the second note?"

He continued, "For this specific lesson, a *no* from me might mean *not yet* or *convince me*, hence a forcefulness that verges on domination. We practice this as a necessary step before you can proceed to giving the orders. It will be impossible for you to know for sure what some nameless future husband might prefer, so you must master both."

He stopped to think about his next words. "If you find the notion of begging distasteful, let this be your motivation. It is not whether I succeed, or fail, in *making* you beg. The question is do we move on to something new or do we repeat the lesson? Again, as before, be explicit, even vulgar. I will do the same. Specific names, what will be done to whom, using which parts. I may stop you with a command to reduce the risk of repeating this lesson. It will be: Silence. No, again. And unless I hear the word *hummingbird*, you will try again and do better."

A thrill shivered through me at his words, and I swallowed hard. Lifting the dress off my shoulders, I stood nude in front of him. Dropping the dress to the floor, I said, my voice now husky, "I understand. I want permission to undress you."

Ramiren shook his head, giving me a hard look. "No. I will not be nude, not just yet. Remember, a key part of asking for something is accepting a *no*, and we'll get some practice with that, as well."

I've already gotten a lot of practice with that.

"You will lay down on the bed, and you will spread your legs and rub your pussy with your fingers, especially where it feels best." He turned to the small chest on the table and opened it, taking out what appeared to be a pair of wands. One had a pink hue, and the other a larger one with a white tip. "These wands vibrate on command. You place it on your clit or inside you, depending on what brings you the most pleasure."

That's a new one. "Clit?"

The expression on his face immediately made me clarify, "I'm not being funny, I swear. I've never heard that word before."

"Oh." His smile returned. "It's short for clitoris. It's a particularly sensitive area. Here." He gently took my hand, turned it, and pushed my fingers through curls and slick skin to the *area* he referred to. When my fingertips brushed the firm bit of flesh I'd found before, a zap went up my spine. I sucked in a breath and groaned, then he released my hand.

Oh.

He handed the wands over, and I peered at them. "How do you have these? I've never heard of them."

He looked around with his eyes, then focused back onto me. "This room provides everything I could want for the implementation and follow-through for a pact. That is its purpose. You'll ask me to move from your fingers to using each of these wands, pink then white, a practice with begging. You will not stop using what you are using until I have given permission. Then, you will beg me to use my tongue on you. You will convince me, or I will refuse."

I went to lie on the bed and put the wands next to me before adjusting myself to get comfortable. After a deep breath, I cleared my throat and reached down to spread myself with searching fingers, again seeking out this clit he had mentioned.

There you are.

Intense tendrils of pleasure slithered through me at once. I allowed myself a moan as my fingers began to swirl around it. *Don't forget the wands.* "May I use the pink wand, please?"

"Yes," Ramiren replied, as he sat on the edge of the bed at my feet. "You activate it by saying the command word. For that one, it is *urdan.*"

Hovering the wand over my mouth, as though to speak into it, I whispered, "Urdan." Immediately, the wand began to gently vibrate in my hand. I looked at him, uncertain, then did as instructed. Putting it against my clit, I gasped with my toes immediately curling. Stars burst in my eyes. My pussy rhythmically pulsed in time with my rapid heartbeat.

Not yet. I want this to last. Not yet. Not yet.

But it was almost too much too soon. With a groan, my legs began to rub on the velvet cushions as I shuddered. "I'm going to-"

Ramiren interrupted me firmly, "No, you may not come yet."

With a soft whine, a sound I've never made, I lifted the wand from myself slightly so as to not accidentally disobey. The intensity lessened just enough, but the hard pulsing remained. Breathing became difficult, as though there wasn't enough air.

He watched me writhe using the wand, not touching me, with an imperceptible expression on his face. When I asked him to use his mouth, he declined once again. "Use the other one, the white one, first. The activation word for this one is *aurta*."

Grateful for the short break, I fumbled with the second wand and muttered the command word into it. When I pressed it to myself, my breath left me in a wheeze.

Shit, this one is stronger.

My muscles tightened, and every single ounce of skin on my body grew taut. A small smile that looked vaguely smug creased his face as he watched the greater intensity of the other implement take immediate effect. *He is enjoying this entirely too much.* "If you want me to devour you, Nathalia, you will need to earn it... and beg."

A glimmer of hope settled at the idea of his tongue on me, that he might actually agree to do that.

But I have to beg. I tried to see if I could avoid it with a more forceful request. "Can you please..."

I was interrupted immediately. "Silence. No, again."

A louder whine escaped me, but my mind was a jumble. Vulgar words I could barely register spilled out of me in Celestial. All I could feel was the wand and velvet covers. I desperately needed his touch. His tongue. The familiar feeling of a peak arose in my lower belly, but it did not summit. I knew, somehow, it wouldn't happen without him. I let out a frustrated growl, then threw my head back. "Fuck... me... "

I was vaguely aware of saying those words. Words that had never come out of me before. I didn't even know if I was blindly exclaiming my frustration or commanding him to...

No. Nope. Do not.

All I knew for sure is that I was pent up and absolutely going nowhere. I struggled against the feeling, knowing what I had to do but adamantly refusing. "I need you to lick me... please." He looked entirely unsympathetic, but he nodded. Relief flooded me, until he leaned in and flicked his tongue on my arm. He raised an eyebrow at me.

You. Asshole.

I whined again. Pathetically.

Eventually, after yet another peak but unsuccessful release, my pride broke, and it poured out of me in a sob, "*I need you to devour my pussy. Please. Pleasepleaseplease.*"

He grinned proudly, stretching out, and moved the white wand out of the way before spreading my legs even more with splayed fingers. I dropped the wand, still activated and entirely forgotten. He looked at me, over the rim of his glasses, before lowering his head to press his mouth to my clit.

The moment his mouth landed, I let out a shriek and bucked against him, as if trying to get as close to him as possible. He entered me with his fingers, curling them upwards, while working the surrounding skin in slow circles with his tongue. My hands went to his hair and tugged him closer.

I could not control anything as my body seemed to be solely focused on wringing as much as it could from him. The rush of needful pleasure dragged me down until I could barely breathe, and my limbs tingled from the tension. I peaked again, his tongue lashing against me. He made a sound, causing his mouth to vibrate against me, and there was a sensation of weightlessness, as though dropping from a great height.

I groaned, my breathing coming out in gasps. "*Please!* I can't..." Tears gathered in my eyes at the strain.

"You may come," he whispered, his lips brushing against my clit, and then flicked his tongue once firmly. My deep breath came out as a throaty scream as I finally submitted to it.

The mysterious voice screamed its word alongside me. ***CORDANI!***

Ramiren kissed my left inner thigh. "Good girl." The throbbing slowly subsided, as did my breathing, but did not seem to slake me. I wanted his pleasure now. He rose to sit up, smiling at me. "And now, what shall you ask for?"

"Remove your clothing. Now," I said, my throat hoarse and dry. Ramiren raised his eyebrows at my demanding tone, that hint of amusement sparking in his eyes. He seemed to evaluate the request and agreed, standing up to undress methodically, as though he had all the time in the world... or he was playing with me yet again. I crawled to the edge of the bed and reached for him when he had removed his last piece of clothing.

With correction, I built the intensity and desperation behind questions, asking to touch, to kiss where I had touched, but I was met with another hard *no* when I asked politely, if not enthusiastically, to put my mouth on his cock.

"More explicit, more vulgar." Looking over the rims of his glasses, he continued, "Would you say you *need* to suck my cock?"

"Please, yes... I need to suck your cock." I felt desperate. I needed to feel his cock against my tongue. Rubbing the roof of my mouth, my tongue *ached*. I felt relief, elation, when he moved to lie on the bed. As soon as he lay down, I lowered my head to his cock and ran the flat of my tongue from base to tip. As he entered my mouth, he adjusted his hips on the bed, causing him to thrust into my mouth. An intense pleasure flared between my legs, and I absolutely wanted a repeat. I lifted my head, my breath heavy. "Would you please do that again?"

"Do what?" He asked as though he already knew the answer, but he wanted me to say it. I let out an almost imperceptible growl.

"Thrust into my mouth."

He gripped my jaw and pulled me closer. His mouth crushed mine, his canines biting into my lower lip before his tongue soothed the sting. He broke the kiss, and his eyes, intense with the pupil almost enveloping the iris, stared me down. "More explicit, angel."

Searching those eyes for inspiration, I realized what he wanted to hear, what I needed to say. "I need you to fuck my mouth."

A slow grin formed, which I took as approval. When I resumed, he moved his grip to the sides of my head as he thrust upward with his hips, down, and up again, maintaining the ever-so-slightly rough motion. Relaxing my throat, the movement of him sliding along my tongue and touching the back of my throat made the throbbing and pressure return.

Then I wondered if it would feel like this, his cock sliding elsewhere, and my moan was answered with his grip in my hair tightening. His breath was audible. I wanted to see his face, so I let him drop from my mouth to raise my head. His jaw was bunched, and there was a light layer of sweat on his brow. He looked and sounded like he'd been running. When I asked him to please come in my mouth, he gritted, "We're past please. Tell me what you need. Again."

I gripped him in hand to stroke him firmly, base to tip, not saying anything. His hips stuttered for a split second, barely noticeable. But I did notice. *I really am in control here.*

Two more strokes of my hand had his eyes closing. He murmured a warning, "Nathalia."

Alright. Mercy, it is. "I need you to come in my mouth. Now."

He sucked in breath through his teeth and said roughly, "Yes, now earn it." I used my hands, one on his cock and the other cupping his balls. My mouth and tongue worked him, speed and intensity increasing until I began to moan from sheer wantonness. This was dirty, and I loved it. When I could feel him hardening, engorging, even further in my mouth, he said in a breathless whisper, "Tell me you need to taste my cum."

I didn't dare stop.

So, I hummed the answer.

He sucked in hard air and let out a hoarse yell that filled me with pride as he began to fill my mouth, spraying the taste of salted caramel to the back of my throat.

He relaxed his fingers in my hair and reached for me as he settled his breathing, and I crawled over to him on the bed without a word. He wrapped his arms around me, murmuring into my hair as puffs of warm breath hit my scalp. He grunted, "Good. That was... good."

I tucked my face into the crook of his neck to smirk, somehow knowing that *good* from him now was better than a *very good* from him previously. "I guess... you can make me beg." I closed my eyes to the sound of his soft laughter. I was relaxed, pressed against his incredible warmth.

I could hear the deep rumble in his chest as he replied, sounding very far away as I drifted off, "We'll be able to move to the next topic now, I think. Let's see what happens when you take charge."

Chapter Eleven
The Blue-Shrouded City

My Extended Pouch, capable of carrying many skins of water for our march through the Tanta Desert, had become a literal lifesaver. The sun beat down, heating my steel armor to the point it was painful to touch. Sweat trickled down my spine in uncomfortable drips. I'd let my silver hair down from its standard ponytail to shield my neck and the sides of my face from the burning sun.

Raewyn seemed to be faring fine for a change. Her silken robes and now silken cloak breathed, allowing her to stay cool and shaded. Georgina had to walk, as M.A.L.C.O.L.M.'s metal shoulders were as heated as my armor. Ramiren looked the least bothered. He wasn't even sweating.

Caravans became more spread out once the wildflowers disappeared to be replaced with sand. I made sure to keep watch for those coming from the desert, to see if anyone needed immediate water. Luckily, everyone appeared to have prepared for the trip. They were sweaty with their skin pink from the sun's rays, but no one was in distress.

"Ugh, I hate the heat. I hate it," Georgina muttered, wiping her sweaty brow on her sleeve. She took a long drink from the waterskin I had provided her.

"Quit your bellyaching," Raewyn said in a mocking tone, then laughed. The tables had turned, and Georgina looked none too happy about it.

The gnome cursed, "Oh, shut up. It's hot. You know it's hot. I can't help it that I'm sensitive to temperature."

Raewyn grinned. "Maybe, when we get to the capital, we'll get some cloth to stuff in *your-*"

"Raewyn. Not now, please." *Those two...*

Gone was the truce they had shared in Ghau. Now they were back at each other's throats like rabid dogs. To distract at least one of them, I asked Georgina to tell us about Elancia.

"Oh. Sure. Uh." She took a long swig of water. "I mean, I didn't spend much time in the city proper, so I can't really comment on that. Nice place with nice people, I suppose. The Workshop, though." She whistled appreciatively. "It is something else. It's not just one room or one floor. It's multiple levels. They have a level for gemology. One for blacksmithing. Another for armor. Whatever. You get the idea."

She took another drink, wiping her mouth on her sleeve again. "What boggles me is that there's no smoke *anywhere*. The air smells fresh as a daisy. It's like the reservoirs of Ghau. I don't know what sorcery the Feylands cooked up, but I swear the things here that should be filthy are clean as a whistle. We could use that magic in Tirvinir. You can't really stay more than a few hours without choking on fumes, unless you have a breather mask. It's why we developed automatons. Beasts of burden can't live there."

"Is that why you went to the carnival? For fresh air?" I asked, trying to keep my tone light.

I must have been successful, because she chuckled. "No. I went to the carnival because of the deep-fried pickles and the Technology Exhibit earlier that day. Did I tell you I was the guest of honor? I've been trying to bring the cleaner fey technology to Tirvinir." She peered up at the reddish sky. "I knew I should've left right after. But, Grand Tinkerer, those *pickles...*"

When she trailed off, probably daydreaming about those deep-fried carnival pickles, Ramiren picked up the slack. "That's a wonderful ambition, Mistress Georgina. I've been to Tirvinir, though I didn't stay long. You have much work ahead of you, but it is a worthwhile endeavor. If I can help in any way, please ask."

Georgina grinned at him. "You know, when most people say that, they're just saying it. They don't mean it. You, I think you actually mean it."

Ramiren replied with a gentle smile.

Raewyn looked back at me. "You know, I get that you and Georgina are uncomfortable. And I'm sorry for that, I really am. *But* I'm just happy to be the comfortable one, for once."

Georgina chuckled. "I thought something was different about you, Raewyn."

Raewyn beamed. "Yes, I-"

Georgina interrupted, "You haven't been yourself lately. I'm sure we all noticed the improvement."

Raewyn raised her waterskin to throw it at the back of Georgina's pink head but thought better of it. "Though maybe I'm not the *most* comfortable one." Her eyes turned toward Ramiren behind her.

Ramiren laughed. "Courtesy of my heritage, Mistress Raewyn. While gnomes are perhaps sensitive to heat, we broodlings embrace it."

"I envy you, Ramiren." Georgina sighed and took another drink of water.

"You'll not envy me when it gets cold, Mistress Georgina, and it gets cold at night in the desert. I'll stay tucked in my tent for the duration."

It made sense to me, as devils came from the scorching Gateway, the only means to enter the endless black void of the Dark Drop where the Lorindar pantheon resided. However, my tutors failed to mention temperature adaptation or sensitivity when discussing his kind.

What else did they fail to mention?

So, I asked. "Ramiren, what other abilities do broodlings have? I understand you can see in the dark. And now, I suppose, endure heat. What else?"

Ramiren glanced back at me, as though considering my question. After a long moment of quiet, he answered, "We are adept at magic, either innately or through study. For example, I can innately produce and flare fire, though I cannot exactly control it. With my pact training, I am able to understand a multitude of languages I don't currently know, after some intense concentration."

My face reddened as bright as the sun above. *Did he then understand my Celestial when it spilled out of me?* I hoped not. It felt invasive, like a private conversation had been eavesdropped on.

Not to mention what I had said...

"So, are you able to understand Celestial, then?" I said, then cleared my throat of the lump now poised there.

He looked back at me, a knowing smile on his lips. "As I said, only after concentrating. It's unmistakable when it happens."

My relief was palpable that he had indeed not understood what I had said in moments of no self-control. I still wasn't sure if he could hear thoughts. *And that word. Cordani. Had he heard it?* I still had no clue what it meant.

An idea popped into my head. *Of course! It has to mean something, not just meaningless syllables. Maybe I'll ask him to concentrate as I repeat the word...*

Oh, but what if you don't like the answer? Or he asks where I heard it?

Or, worse, he doesn't know.

"And what of celestials? I know some of you develop the ability to sprout wings for a short time, though I can't say I've ever seen it," Ramiren inquired.

I shuffled my doubting thoughts away to answer. "Yes, we can. If our ancestors had wings, there's a good chance we will, eventually, develop the ability to produce them on command. We can heal, cure diseases, or remove poisons. Celestials are able to care for their charges in a way that not many can. It's part of the reason celestials make excellent priests..." I said, indicating my sister, "... or protectors. So, we are quite formidable when we take our oath to a charge, and our shielding abilities develop too."

Georgina sputtered on her water. "*Shielding abilities?*"

It was the only real way to describe them. "Yes. If we're not next to our charge when they are attacked, we can... throw a shield?" I plucked a cloak from my pouch and placed it over my shoulders, hoping it'd keep me cooler than the molten armor I was wearing. "It's rather hard to explain without seeing it."

Ramiren tilted his head back toward me again. "And have you found a charge, then, Lady Nathalia?"

With a sigh, I shook my head. "No."

He's out there somewhere.

"No one worthy of your... ministrations, eh?" Georgina said over her shoulder with a pink brow cocked.

Though it was meant as a rib, I did not mind, especially because it was true. "That is exactly correct. Choosing a charge is the single most important decision a protector will ever make. We literally train to guard someone who we feel is more worthy of life than we are. We have to see it that way. Though there are some who take an oath to the Church of Horyn itself, I did not want to follow that route."

"She wants her *mysterious future husband* to be her charge." Raewyn chuckled.

A huff slipped out. "Yes. That is right, and I feel no shame for wanting that. A protector vows to one person in their lifetime. I will marry for life, so it makes sense. Besides, Father is a protector as well, and you know who he's sworn to, Raewyn. I'm just following his example."

Raewyn made an exasperated noise in response that sounded like a grunt combined with blowing a raspberry. "As though she needs the protection, Nat."

"So, like a bird mating for life?" Georgina asked. I listened for a mocking tone, but there was none. Mere curiosity.

I considered, then smiled slightly. "Yes, like a bird mating for life."

"What happens if your charge dies, then?" Georgina asked.

My smile faded, and my eyes drifted to the sand under my feet. "We are to join them into the afterlife. A dead charge means a failed protector, barring old age, of course. Our only hope of regaining honor is to follow."

Georgina goggled at me. "Whoa! That's rough."

Raewyn sighed. "I think it's romantic."

Beep. "IF GEORGINA DIED, I WOULD DIE TOO. DOES THAT MAKE ME A PROTECTOR?" Georgina patted her automaton on the leg as she walked next to him. She cursed in pain and shook her hand out, having forgotten how hot to the touch he was.

"In a sense, M.A.L. In a sense." Georgina poured water on her hand to help with the burn, then took a few gulps.

I continued, "It's why, when we swear to our charge, we say the phrase *my life for yours*. Because we mean that. Better one life is lost than two. It is our sacred duty to ensure the safety and survival of our charges."

"Then, you are right to be particular, Lady Nathalia. For that decision will dictate the rest of your life. And, perhaps, your death," Ramiren said quietly.

Pride straightened my spine. "Yes. It is not an oath to take lightly. It is a life of the ultimate service to another person."

"So, those that take this oath to the Church of Horyn itself. No one to protect, just an idea." Georgina frowned. "They'll live a long life?"

It was a point of contention within the church. Some feared factions were beginning to form, and gods knew what would happen then. Dogma against duty. I tried to answer her honestly, "Most assuredly, unless the church sends them to defend something. A person. A town. A nation. But their oath is still to the church itself, and they need not follow if who or what they're sent to protect dies."

Ramiren looked back at me and asked, "How often does that happen? How often are they sent out to defend something?"

I felt ashamed for some reason. "Rarely, I am sorry to say."

Raewyn spat out, "They're cowards. Dad thinks so, too. They want respect, but not the responsibility that goes with it."

It was difficult to disagree with my father and sister. I thought of counterpoints. Of reasons, but came up empty. So, I gave a warning, "Call a protector a coward, and you'll likely not enjoy their response."

We arrived a few rough days later in Elancia, the capital city of Tanta, with the buildings dressed in royal blue mourning shrouds. They were everywhere. Blue cloth was tied on the light poles lining the streets, feylight flickering inside the glass. Blue sheets decked the front of stores and inns. It was also extremely quiet, as though the entire city had been swallowed in a blanket of silence. Those who passed us averted their eyes. They, too, wore blue.

"Blue everywhere. Someone important must have died," Ramiren said pensively, a thought I had also considered.

"I wonder who?" Raewyn replied. "Let's ask."

With one last look at the blue cloth, I followed her into a nearby inn I didn't catch the name of. The common room was also quiet, disturbingly so. Though many were inside, drinking or eating, no one talked. A few turned their heads our way when we walked in, though their attention quickly went back to their food and drink.

A fey barkeep, an old man who looked older from acute exhaustion, stood behind the bar absently cleaning mugs in a small bucket. I couldn't determine what type of fey he was, and it seemed impolite to ask. Aside from the very pointed ears, he looked human. "Good afternoon, sir. If I might ask, what has happened here? The entire place is-"

"Death, young lady. Death happened. Our king's beloved general, Milon Tarq, died two days ago in his sleep." He shook his head. "He was only three hundred and fifty years old." His rich, deep timbre was gentle and soothing. *No doubt his singing is beau- Oh. A lusc fey. Nightingale.*

He shook out the water from the now-clean mug and set it down with the others. I wondered how long fey lived, but it was Raewyn who asked.

"Well, that's the thing. The general was an elf."

After drying his hands on a cloth hanging at his waist, he poured himself a glass of what looked to be strong spirits, lifted it in a salute, and downed it.

Ramiren frowned deeply, stepping forward. "An elf, you say? Strange. I've never heard of one dying in his sleep."

"Well, he did, according to the king's announcement." He poured another drink and raised it again. "To General Tarq. May his soul find its way to the Tarindar's Aerie." A few in the common room raised their mugs and glasses in kind, though the toast was a weary one. The barkeep downed the shot and eyed us. "You travelers from Laeth?"

He must have been well loved. "Yes, seeking rooms and information."

"Information about what, my lady?"

"Mischief hags. We believe one lives east of here, in the mountain pass."

The barkeep straightened. "Yes, one does. What would you want with the likes of them? Nothing but trouble."

His tone contained a warning, though I did not heed it. "They stole things from us we intend on getting back."

The barkeep raised his eyebrows. "Well, best of luck to you, then. Nasty creatures, they are."

Perhaps we came to the right place. "Have you encountered any?"

"Can't say I have, but I've heard plenty of stories. They steal your... essence. Your purpose. They don't use them, mind. They just like to cause misery."

I agreed with a nod. "Anything else you can tell us about them?"

He let out a sigh and refilled his glass a third time. "Aye, the one in Tanta likes to steal *people*, too. Some smaller, remote towns offer up their more unfortunate folk in exchange for being left alone. It's not known what she does with them. They're just never seen or heard from again. If you come across her, expect to see prisoners or... bones, I'd wager."

I made a disgruntled noise in my throat and decided to change the topic to a more immediate need. "Do you have four rooms available for us?"

The barkeep shook his head. "Sorry, but I don't. Many from all over have come for the funeral. I have one room available. Honestly, I doubt you'll find a place that has four, and the one I *do* have is tiny with a single bed only."

Great.

"Then, we will try another establishment."

The barkeep's lovely, tired voice followed in my wake. "Again, good luck."

As we walked outside to quiet streets, Raewyn laughed. It echoed oddly in the empty street, and she abruptly stopped. "Shame. I was looking forward to sharing a room with Georgina."

Georgina scoffed indignantly. "Well, I wasn't looking forward to sharing one with *you*, Raewyn."

Beep. "I WASN'T EITHER."

Georgina raised a hand toward M.A.L.C.O.L.M. "See? Even my automaton doesn't like you."

Beep. "IT'S BECAUSE YOU BECOME MEAN AROUND HER, GEORGINA. YOU USED TO BE NICE. TALK SOFTLY TO ME. NOW IT'S JUST RAEWYN THIS AND RAEWYN THAT. RAEWYN RAEWYN RAEWYN."

I rubbed my temples as a headache, that had nothing to do with the sun or my exhaustion, was starting to develop.

Georgina waved her arms in the air, as though making a point. "I mean... *c'mon*! How did you grow up with her, Nathalia?"

Don't answer that.

Beep. "SEE?"

Georgina huffed, her fists on her hips, and shook her head. "So, what now? Another inn?"

"If we can find one, yes," I said, though the barkeep's response made me think it was a hopeless task.

We spent the rest of the day scouting inns throughout the city. There were five others. Most had no vacancy. Some had one room, or even two, open. But none had four. My concern was we'd have to split up, which I did not want to do with a mischief hag so close. Perhaps this one could scry as well and take the opportunity when we were vulnerable and alone.

No. We have to stay together.

Raewyn groused as the sun was getting lower in the sky, and we were still without shelter for the evening.

A thought came to me. "Perhaps, as a visiting noble, we might petition the royalty for shelter."

Everyone stopped to look at me, but it was Georgina who started laughing. "Again, I ask you. Are you the Queen of Evraka?"

I raised an eyebrow at her. "No, I am not."

"Then, how do you expect to get us rooms at the fancy royal castle, hm? Smile and push your way in? Maybe sing for your supper? Fat lot of good that did us at the carnival."

Staring at Georgina, I pushed my annoyance down with a deep breath. "I was going to present myself as a noble of the Kingdom of Camlynn and simply ask."

Georgina started giggling. "Oh, you were just going to ask, eh? Just ask, simple as that?"

Beep. "AM I A NOBLE, GEORGINA?"

"No, M.A.L., you're not, and I'm starting to doubt that she is, too. Nobles are supposed to be smart, and that might be the dumbest idea I've ever heard."

Raewyn snorted. "Wanna bet on it, Georgina? My sister gets us rooms at the palace, and you gotta do something."

Georgina peered at Raewyn. "Oh yeah, like what?"

Raewyn pondered, hand tucked under her chin. "Oh, I don't know. Put a bowtie on M.A.L.C.O.L.M. here."

Beep. "WHY ARE YOU INVOLVING ME IN THIS?"

Raewyn's eyes took on an excited glint. "And I don't mean a standard-sized one. I mean a *big* bow. Maybe with pink dots on it."

Beep. "THAT SOUNDS PRETTY. I AGREE."

Georgina held up a hand to her automaton. "Hold on, it's for me to say if I agree to the terms, not you M.A.L."

Beep. "BUT I WANT A BOWTIE."

Georgina sighed, then frowned. "And what happens if I win?"

Raewyn smiled. "I won't complain a single syllable until we reach the hag here. Deal?"

Georgina narrowed her eyes, considering, and extended her hand to shake. "Deal. Now, do we just spit and shake on it or do we need to involve the pactmaker?"

Ramiren held up his hands, indicating he wanted nothing to do with it.

While Raewyn and Georgina were discussing terms, I looked at Ramiren and spoke quietly. "I might need the luck stone back for this endeavor."

Ramiren shook his head, replying under his breath, "I cannot, I'm afraid. It was given in payment for a pact. Returning it, even temporarily, would dissolve the pact. Unless you want that, of course?" He raised an eyebrow at me.

I didn't even consider it for a moment. "Never mind. I'll do it the old-fashioned way, then."

Ramiren smiled. "You do not need luck, Nathalia. You need only a kind word and a kind king."

We did not need directions to the palace district. The flag-topped spires and towers of Castle Tanta reached high into the sky, marking for us our destination. My lower lip was sore from chewing on it, wondering if my petition would even work. This seemed to be the only way for us to stay together, but my confidence was wavering.

None of us, especially me, enjoyed the idea of failure, since failure meant having to camp outside the city walls. We had left the desert behind us a day ago, the sands turning to lush greenery with the passing of several flooded rivers, and there was now a great deal of activity. And, possibly, bandits.

Do the Feylands even have bandits?

While M.A.L.C.O.L.M. did not require sleep, and made an able watchman when the rest of us slept, it was always a fitful rest worrying about him missing something. An approach of a band of miscreants, stealthy and quiet, could sneak past him and slit our throats in our slumber. It happened to another caravan two years ago on the way to Laswa in southern Camlynn, and the aftermath still haunted me.

Though I had not sworn a protector's oath to anyone in the party, I still felt responsible for their safety. Leaving that in another's hands, especially one who was getting worn down and banged up with every fight or hard march, left a sour taste in my mouth.

As we approached the castle, we went through several checkpoints. Their questions became more insistent, more direct, the closer we got to the castle. Who are you? What is your purpose here? Is the king aware of your presence? Are you here for the funeral?

I spoke for the group, informing them we were not here for the funeral, just passing through, and wanted to see if the castle could provide a visiting noble shelter. Some snickered at me for some reason, some frowned, but no one really commented before waving us on.

At the second to last checkpoint, we were made to peace-bond our weapons by the guards stationed there. They provided the cord, and I tied the hilt of my sword to the scabbard, making it impossible for me to draw it at a moment's notice. Though the practice was common for entering a castle district, in Laeth anyway, I felt naked without the ability to defend myself properly. Ramiren took the cord as well, tying his rapier down. Raewyn didn't carry any weapons, and neither did Georgina. They weren't sure what to do about M.A.L.C.O.L.M. Never having seen an automaton before, they asked where his weapons were.

"His fists are his weapons," Georgina replied simply.

The guards conversed for a few minutes and decided to tie his hands together, like manacles. Neither Georgina nor M.A.L.C.O.L.M. protested.

The automaton held out his hands, allowing the guards to tie them together. After inspecting our peace-bonds, ensuring they were indeed sound, they moved us along.

It was dusk before we made it to Castle Tanta. I was drained by the day's events, wanting nothing more than a scalding bath and a soft bed with some peace and quiet. Still, there was work to be done.

"I suppose I'll handle the talking," I murmured.

"Best of luck, my queen." Georgina smirked.

Raewyn peered down at Georgina next to her, "I hope you enjoy the taste of crow, Georgina."

Beep. "SHE LOVES EATING BIRDS."

Ramiren stayed silent, except for a gentle pat on my arm.

We approached the front gate. The royal sentries, dyna fey both, stood up straighter as we drew near. Those at the Puldoni gates had been dyna fey as well, though these looked far less friendly. These guards held tall halberds in their right hand, with a band of blue around their mail-covered left arm. For some reason, they did not wear helmets.

"Name and business, miss."

A kind word, Ramiren had said. I spoke gently, "Lady Nathalia Swordhand of Camlynn and her retinue to pay our respects to your king. We are weary and seek shelter."

There was a long pause where the guards looked at each other. My weight shifted from my right foot to my left, feeling more impatient the longer they remained silent. Then the guards started laughing. I furrowed my eyebrows and frowned. *This was not going according to plan.*

"Just like that, eh? Seek shelter? From the king? He's in *mourning*, girl. He ain't got time for the likes of you."

My temper flared, to be immediately tamped down. *They're just doing their job.*

"Sir, if you could just-"

The guard to my left barked, "I said, move on, girl!"

My headache returned in full force, the steady pulse beating like a drum behind my eyes. Still, I tried again. "Sir-"

The guard on my right hissed. "Are you deaf? Piss off!"

Oh, that does it.

I raised an eyebrow and stepped forward, causing the halberds in their hands to shift forward in defense. Stopping just short, I leveled them with my gaze.

"Am I to understand that simple palace guards keep the king's schedule and appointments? Is that part of your profession now?"

The guard to my left glared at me. "We protect the king's peace and person, girl. Now, don't start to go all-"

I snapped my head toward the one speaking. "You will address me as befits my station, guard. Or the steward will hear of-"

"Hear of what, *girl*? That we didn't let someone like you in? That we don't believe every story we hear?" One blew a raspberry while the other gave a chuckle. "Shall we bow, too?"

"Maybe you'd like a song and dance as well? Only the best for m'lady."

"Nat..."

I held a hand up to Raewyn just as their snickers turned into full laughter. My hackles rose. "Then tell your guard captain that we are here."

The guard to my left smiled smugly. "Here's an easy answer. No."

The urge to slap him was strong, but I pushed that feeling down, too. That would only lead to worse troubles. *And I can't fail.*

I decided to try another tactic.

"Perhaps, tonight, you are right. You'll not grant us passage. But tomorrow, I will send a message, informing the steward and your captain that you verbally abused a visiting noble and have reached above your station and duty. What will they think, hm? Can you stop every letter that comes into the castle, too?"

The guard to my left glowered. "We don't believe you, girl. Simple as that. You'll not get past us."

Praying for patience, I spoke through gritted teeth, "And what don't you believe?"

The guard to my right scoffed. "That you're a noble. You're dirty and on foot." He leaned in and sniffed twice. "And you smell like a-"

"Will the Swordhand sigil suffice?" My hand raised to show my signet ring, which displayed two feathered wings embracing a four-pointed star.

The guard to my right peered at it, and his eyes went wide. "Swordhand... wait, as in Maxlian Swordhand?"

Oh, for fuck's sake. "Yes, he's my father."

The guard who spoke turned toward the other. "Heard stories in my youth, I did. He beat down that one, with the Twin Spheres. What was the name...?"

Twin Spheres?

"Aw, rubbish. You can tell that by a picture on a ring she probably picked up in an antique store?" The guard to my left shook his head.

"I'm telling you! What was his wife's name? The one with the axe?"

I replied calmly, feeling a small measure of optimism for the first time today, "Resa Kett, now Lady Resa Swordhand."

"That's it. Wow. You're their daughter, then? My apologies, my lady. You and yours are free to pass. And, uh, please don't tell anyone about this encounter, right? Simple misunderstanding."

"But-" interjected the guard to my left.

"They'll pass, Morin." The right guard yelled over his shoulder, "Open the gates!"

It was mortifying that it took my parents' legends to get past two simple palace guards. I had to name drop in order to simply get some safe rest for myself and my companions, but if that's what it took...

Twin Spheres? I've never heard my parents tell that story before. And they love to tell stories.

When we walked through the gates, into an open-air stone courtyard filled with a few groups quietly talking among themselves, Georgina burst into giggles. "I thought your face was going to turn purple, Nathalia!"

My head tilted back to stare at the dusky magenta-colored sky. "I have *never*, in all of my years, had such trouble before."

Georgina went on, her head shaking in indignation as her voice took a mocking tone, "I'll send a strongly-worded letter!" She grinned and snapped her fingers, then pointed at me. "Admit it, you were reaching with that one. A message. Ha!"

My jaw clenched to the point of pain.

Beep. "YOU SHOULD HAVE JUST PUNCHED THEIR FACES IN. THAT SENDS A MESSAGE."

"Then, we would've been arrested and taken into the dungeons for assaulting a palace guard." Ramiren looked at M.A.L.C.O.L.M. "I don't think those are the kind of accommodations we are seeking. Lady Nathalia did everything right. It was the guards who were in the wrong, though perhaps that is how they were trained. Disbelieve everyone. If that's the case, the king must get many visitors. Or, at least, attempted visitors."

"Friends!"

We all turned our heads to see a man in fine garb approaching us. Tall and broad-shouldered, with sandy hair and brown eyes, he held his hands out wide to greet us jovially. He looked human, aside from his height and slightly pointed ears, but he was also not nearly as brawny as an elf. *A half-elf, perhaps?* Upon his shoulders sat a gilded chain, with a ruby centered over his heart. *His badge of office, no doubt.*

I faced him fully and let my upbringing take over. "Greetings, my lord. Apologies for the late hour."

"Nonsense! It is not yet fully dark, and the funeral feast is about to begin. I was just taking the air when I saw you. What is your name, my lady?"

"Lady Nathalia Swordhand of Camlynn in Laeth. This is my sister, Lady Raewyn Swordhand." I moved my hand to indicate Ramiren. "Ramiren, the pactmaker. And-"

The lord interrupted me, "Ramiren? Yes, of course. You are known to me. We struck a pact some years ago. I am not sure if you recall." He peered at Ramiren, then looked back at me. "I am Lord Remus Dalson, Earl of Longberry from Wistran." He bowed. "And your other companions?"

"This is Georgina, the tinkerer. And her automaton, M.A.L.C.O.L.M."

M.A.L.C.O.L.M. raised his bound hands to wave.

"Come. This way to the feasthall, where we celebrate the life of the general. Please." He stepped aside and motioned forward with his hand, indicating we should follow. He began to walk toward a set of tall double doors across a long courtyard. The low din of a raucous gathering could be heard, muffled by the thick doors in front of us.

He was cheerful, even bubbly, which was a welcome change from the grumpy guards I'd just been verbally assaulted by. "You shall sit at my table, of course. I brought only a small company with me, so there is plenty of room. All will be welcomed tonight."

Georgina snickered. "Not by the guards, though."

Lord Dalson hummed. "Ah, yes. They are on high alert. Rumor has it the general was poisoned. After all, how many elves die in their sleep, especially one so young?"

"Exactly my thoughts, Lord Dalson," Ramiren pondered. "I've never heard of such a thing."

"Quite right, Ramiren. Quite right." The earl led the way as we proceeded to the feasthall. He raised his voice above the noise to be heard as the double doors were opened by two guards at our approach. "But not a topic for the dinner table, I think. Swordhand, you said? Your family name is well-known in Wistran. I do believe your parents were successful in securing a mighty prize for the kingdom. I trust you followed in their footsteps?"

I replied, "In my father's footsteps, yes."

"Splendid. Perhaps you and I can discuss it, then. Strange things have been happening there of late."

"Oh? What strange things?" I decided to press, too tired to dance around the matter. "Perhaps something to do with a mischief hag residing in the middle of your capital? I would have figured her kind would not be welcomed in civilization."

He looked pleasantly surprised at my statement. "That's what I am referring to, aye. She came to live with the king and queen perhaps a few months ago now. No one can speak ill of her, even when she began stealing from people. She steals everything she can, beyond abilities. Wealth, gold mines, even land. No harsh word is allowed. A few tried to reason with the king and queen, but they were imprisoned for their talk. Now, she is simply tolerated. Strange! Strange goings-on. Some say she's bewitched the king and queen."

We were escorted to a half-empty table and seated ourselves. Servants brought over plates, utensils, and full carafes of wine, placing them in front of us.

The feasthall was brightly bedecked with banners of all sorts. Many had sigils, very few that were known to me, displayed to indicate those in attendance. The king sat at the head table at the front of the room. He was an older, possibly lusc, fey with wrinkles around the eyes and a careworn frown on his mouth. He looked even more tired than that innkeeper earlier.

I squinted. *Come to think of it, there's a resemblance between that innkeeper and the king.*

My attention was diverted when platters and bowls of steaming food were set in front of us, one at a time. Warm bread, butter-dressed peas with mint, an overly-decorated stuffed goose, pies, and boiled potatoes dredged in what smelled like a garlic sauce. My stomach rumbled in protest, though I side-eyed the gaudy goose.

"Oh, gods, I am *starving*," Raewyn exclaimed, and she began to dig into the pies first.

Calmly, I helped myself to the potatoes while a member of the staff sliced sections of goose for the table. It took all my resolve to not eat as Raewyn was, as I too was starving. Ramiren poured everyone wine. Georgina eyed Raewyn with disgust. "Aren't you supposed to be a lady?"

Raewyn merely shrugged, her mouth too full to respond.

"Because you look like a squirrel with a mouthful of nuts."

Raewyn swallowed her food before speaking. "And bolts. You really can't forget the bolts, Georgina."

Georgina bared her teeth at my grinning sister before resuming eating.

M.A.L.C.O.L.M. beeped, and for once he was not the loudest thing in the room. "CAN I HAVE SOME PIE, GEORGINA?"

"No," Georgina yelled back. "For the last time, you don't need to eat."

Beep. "WHEN DO I GET MY BOWTIE? CAN I PICK IT OUT MYSELF?"

Georgina stopped, a fork halfway to her mouth, and groaned. "I had forgotten." She eyed me, assessing. "But we haven't secured rooms yet, just a meal and a place to sit down."

I narrowed my eyes in challenge and rested my hand on the earl's sleeve to get his attention. I raised my voice enough to be heard. "Do you know of any vacant accommodations we could use for the evening? All of the inns are full."

The earl bowed his head. "The castle is quite as stuffed as that goose, my dear, but I still have some room in my own apartments. I'd be honored to house the children of Maxlian Swordhand and Resa Kett. And friends, of course." The earl raised his wine glass to Ramiren and Georgina.

"Most kind of you, Lord Dalson," I said, wondering what he was expecting in return.

Beep. "I WANT A PINK ONE WITH RED DOTS THAT MATCH MY EYES WHEN I'M ANGRY. SO PEOPLE KNOW I MEAN BUSINESS."

Georgina grimaced while Raewyn pressed a napkin to her mouth to hide her laughter. "I've suddenly lost my appetite," the gnome moaned as she dropped her fork onto her plate.

M.A.L.C.O.L.M. motioned with his bound hands toward the goose. Beep. "BUT I THOUGHT YOU LIKED CROW."

Chapter Twelve
A Protector's Command

I bathed, making extremely indecent sounds when my body finally hit the steaming hot water, and redressed in the last of my clean nightclothes.

Maybe I could get Ramiren to do my laundry. With a snort, I stuffed all of my dirty clothes in a cloth sack and left it outside my door for the castle staff, with a few coins as thanks.

As my door was closing, familiar voices approached. Raewyn and Ramiren rounded the corner and came into view, talking quietly. Though it was harder to tell with Raewyn, as she always wore the same thing, Ramiren had noticeably changed clothing. *He must have had the chance to bathe as well.* I wondered if that meant something.

Likely not, we're both tired.

Ramiren inclined his head in my direction with a smile. "Good night, Lady Nathalia." He headed to another room while my sister looked at me.

"Good night, Master Ramiren." My eyes followed him until his door shut behind him. I looked back at my sister, who was looking at me with a raised eyebrow.

"Need something, Nat?"

"Hm? Oh. No. Just leaving my laundry out. Good night, Raewyn," I replied.

"Good night," she smiled at me and turned toward her room.

"Raewyn...?"

My sister stopped short and looked at me expectantly.

"Did Mother or Father ever tell you a story about the Twin Spheres?"

Raewyn frowned, thinking. "No. Not that I can recall. I don't remember anything about any Twin Spheres."

My answering hum was more of a half-grunt. "Fair enough. Seems to be a well-known children's tale here, but not in Laeth."

"Fey love their stories. You know that. Good night." She gave a half-hearted wave and disappeared behind the door to her room.

My hand rested on the doorknob a beat, then I heard a whisper. Ramiren's whisper. ***"If you are not too exhausted, please come to my room."***

And suddenly, I wasn't tired anymore.

It had been days since our last lesson, though I'd barely had enough time to think about it, much less seek another one out.

Also, sweating across an entire desert did not exactly leave me with a sense of confidence in my hygiene. We had to conserve water for drinking. Bathing, normally a nightly necessity, had come second to the dangers of dehydration. Thankfully, no one seemed to care in the feasthall.

I stepped through the door, closing it behind me quietly, and crept ten paces to the door he disappeared behind. When Ramiren answered my gentle knock, he took one look at me and smiled. "Please, come in."

He inhaled deeply as I entered his room and turned to face him when he shut the door. He paused before speaking softly, "I had thought to simply chat, but based upon... the look in your eyes, it seems that won't be happening. If the topic is fixed in your thoughts, and you are ready to begin, we can depart at once."

My eyebrows raised, again wondering if he could read thoughts.

"I consent." I blinked to find myself in the bedroom. Instead of my eyes straying to this or that interesting item, my eyes stayed solely on Ramiren. Without a word, I began to undress, removing my long shirt. My head tilted, as he had not yet removed his clothing, or even moved to do so. The corners of my mouth tugged upward. *Right. His words from our last lesson.* "And I see you've made your mind up, as well. You're willing to let me be in charge, so to speak."

"You are aware of my safe word. This next lesson involves understanding basic roles from each side. You have my consent, and if you need to break the scene to ask questions, you have my permission and encouragement to do so. The agenda is yours."

"Your word is 'orange'. And mine is 'hummingbird.'" *I need to be firm. Like he was. Unyielding.*

"Very well, pl-" I caught myself and tightly pursed my lips to stop talking. *Well, this is starting off wonderfully.* Vague and unremarkable ideas of what he could be ordered to do filled my mind, each dismissed in turn. I thought about what he did with me. *He started slow last time, so I will as well. But how?*

My shoulders rolled to ease the tension, feeling the twinge from the past several days. It sparked an idea. *I am sore. Perhaps he is too.* Sometimes, we bribed the healers at the Horyn Academy to massage aching muscles when we became excessively sore from training.

I'll need to be more gentle than they were when I do this.

"Undo and remove your shirt. Lie on the bed, face down."

He complied, and I climbed onto the bed to straddle his hips. Placing my hands on his back, just below his shoulders, I began to knead the muscles there. Though never having practiced giving massages, I was well aware of basic anatomy and the tension one could carry, especially at the shoulders and along the spine.

The only way to learn was by paying attention to the healers when they worked on others, as I felt uncomfortable touching my fellow initiates that way. At the time, I thought my husband would enjoy that. But then the initiates would cry out in pain from having bruised tissue being worked on like clay by an angry sculptor, and the idea was promptly nixed.

Maybe my education would be useful tonight. Gentle, but firm.

I leaned into the massage, feeling knots in odd places. My hands worked deep into his shoulders, moving down his back, as my fingers found the stress his muscles betrayed, that he never showed on his face. *What secrets he must keep, all housed in these knots.* If I rubbed hard enough and in the right places, perhaps those muscles would yield them.

The wine at dinner must've gone to my head. What a ridiculous notion. Where is this obsession coming from?

Then, without warning, the answer hit.

He's the rich dessert I was denied. The hidden book I wasn't allowed to read. The words I couldn't say.

I want them because I can't have them.

A soft moan from Ramiren brought me back to the present.

Most of the tension had melted from his muscles. He stretched into a pillow, as if to sleep. He began to rumble a snore, making me snort in amusement. It was a small and innocent push against my authority that was met with a command to turn onto his back.

He turned, and my smile became a grin with my face hovering inches from his. When I began trailing light kisses down his neck, Ramiren tilted his head back, giving me full access.

"Take off your trousers."

I slid off him to allow the removal. When his trousers hit the floor, my eyebrow raised in question. Surprised to find him so... relaxed, I didn't quite understand.

Until I did.

Maybe I am *good at giving massages.*

Another idea popped into my head. *He had me use my hands on myself. Perhaps he could do the same.* "Use your hand on your cock. And don't stop until I tell you," I instructed. Authority, command, and control came easily to me, and I was used to giving orders. But with Ramiren, it felt like the control was somehow simultaneous, a gentle push and pull, even now. It was a thought that should have made me bristle, rebel, and demand complete deference, but it didn't. His type of control was safe.

I felt safe.

When he took the direction with his eyes on me, slowly running his hand up and down the rapidly hardening cock, I lowered my head to nuzzle my nose along his jawline. Breathing in deep, the familiar scent of honey was both comforting and incurably associated with my handsome broodling. "I'm going to kiss you." When Ramiren nodded his consent, I brushed my lips over his.

He continued to stroke as I kissed him as much and in any way I wished, until he used his other hand to tilt my head, deepening the kiss on his own terms. My lower lip brushed one of his canines, and the sharp sting made me inhale deeply. He nipped that same lip purposefully, and the pain shot a zap of pleasure straight to my clit. I groaned.

"Please put your mouth on-"

I smiled crookedly. "Silence. No, again."

He paused and beamed at me. "I *need* you to put your mouth on my cock."

Though it appeared I was contemplating his request, I knew it wasn't a request at all, merely a statement with no plea or hint of begging. "I'm sorry." I didn't sound sorry. "That must be frustrating for you."

He stopped, mid-stroke, and stared at me with an astonished expression. His warm breath puffed out between parted lips and ghosted over my own mouth. "What did you say?"

Fuck, this is fun.

The tip of my nose rubbed on his. "I said, the fact that I'm not tongue-fucking your cock right now must be so very frustrating."

His eyes widened, then somehow darkened. Hardened like the fully rigid cock now glistening in his hand. I reached down with the pad of my index finger and smoothed it through the slippery liquid at his tip. Without missing a beat, and without breaking eye contact, I brought my finger to my lips and sucked the salted caramel taste from it.

"Delicious," I whispered.

He muttered a very quiet, but very audible, "Fuck."

Got 'em.

My blood was on fire, not just from my own needs burning through me, but from the blatant desire on his face. He was trying to keep it in check and failing miserably. I wanted to wrap myself around him, take in his honey scent, and taste his skin to my heart's content. *Not yet.* I moved back, keeping my voice unbothered by the stark want on his face. "Not yet, I think. You've not earned it. Stand up and by the bed."

He did so after some hesitation and a harsh exhale.

Rolling over to my back and propping myself up by my elbows, I lifted my knees and parted them in turn. With the most imperious stare I could muster, I gave my next command. "I want you to approach me on the bed, put your face between my thighs, and lick my pussy and clit-t-t-t-t-t-t." He followed the orders precisely when given, as if expecting them, and took hold of my thighs before licking from my entrance up, then in swirls and slow circles. He took my clit between his lips and sucked.

A snaking, desperate need slithered through me, under my skin and in my very marrow. I exhaled a deep breath in a hiss and lay back, fully lounging into the velvet cushions beneath me. He gave a grunt in his throat, though if it was a noise of pleasure, or just a noise, I couldn't tell. Lowering my gaze to watch, I caught him staring up at me. Eyes locked, it became clear to me it wasn't his tongue I wanted. I wanted *him.* All of him.

Cordani.

Perhaps just a taste...

I whispered, "Stop." He did so without hesitation, rising slowly to catch his breath. I reached for him. "Come closer. Here..."

He furrowed his eyebrows in confusion, but he did as he was told. He crawled toward me, between my legs, and peered down at me. When he pressed his lower belly against my pussy, I groaned, wrapping my legs around his hips. Delirium spun my head. It was sensual. It was forbidden. It was everything.

And it still wasn't enough.

More. I want more! This stupid pact!

He almost seemed to hear me. He rolled his body like a snake, his lower belly grinding against me as he leaned into the act. He kissed my mouth, my neck, my breasts. His hands went into my hair, then down my curves to clutch at my hips.

A frantic and uncaring wish grabbed hold and wouldn't let go. My stomach seized, and my pussy felt needy. Ready. I grasped at him, his shoulders, his back, wanting him ever closer. But Ramiren kept a careful distance. The tension I'd so carefully massaged away had returned. He adjusted slightly mid-movement, and his hips pressed higher, his cock gliding against my clit. Pressure flared and suddenly radiated outward in a blinding flash, and I threw my head back with a scream.

After my breathing had calmed, I whispered, "You've earned it. Get on your back." He hesitated again for a few seconds, the muscle in his jaw jumping as though he was rhythmically clenching it. Finally, he complied, smoothly rolling onto his back next to me. I got up on my knees over him and leaned in to give him what he had given me.

He let me set the pace, depth, and speed, and I moved the hand I'd wrapped around his cock to flatten it across his stomach and chest, running fingers up and down over his textured skin.

He gasped when I rolled my tongue. He did not give corrections, only affirmation when I took initiative. My tongue began to ache with want. *I need to hear more from him. A moan, a whisper, praise, a scream even, like I had given him.*

If he won't give those sounds to me, then I'll take them.

I began plunging up and down with my entire head in a movement that was steady and quick, at the edge of sharp, building faster and faster.

He made a tortured sound in his throat. He whispered, deep and husky, "Angel..." He started to thread his shaking fingers into my hair but managed to stop himself. An unusual sound, not unlike a choke, escaped him. "I'm...I...need to...*please!*"

Elation rang through me, headier than the strongest wine. I felt in complete control for the first time. This man desperately needed something, and I was the only one who could provide it. I placed one of his hands in my hair, and Ramiren sucked in a breath through his teeth as his other joined in to grip my hair. He curled his fingers, tangling them with the silver strands. My muffled consent for him to finish, without removing him from my mouth, vibrated my tongue. The rough squeeze of my hair was my only warning. His hips lifted as he came with a growling yell, and I did not slow until he was done.

With a triumphant smile, my subsequent swallow was loud enough for him to hear. Following his direction from last time, I collapsed next to him on the bed and wrapped an arm around him, tucking my face into the crook of his shoulder. He did the same with his own arms, his chin resting on top of my head.

After a thought, I said quietly, "Still felt as though you were in charge. Perhaps that is my fault. I was having difficulty coming up with commands for you." I lifted my head to look at him. He studied my face and frowned.

"Orange," he said matter-of-factly. "I want to make certain you're all right, since that was new, and to get you used to hearing a safe word. If it is only ever used when something bad happens, it is associated with something bad happening, and you might hesitate to use it."

"I'm all right. Truly. It's just... I told you what the hags took from me. Giving commands on a field of battle is not really the same as giving them here. You study strategy and learn tactics. You follow them. If this, then that. Does that make sense?"

He kissed the top of my head, lingering longer than I thought he would with his lips pressed to my hair. "I understand. That might make this role challenging for you, though you can learn this, too. Giving pleasure is not so different from martial maneuvers." His smile brightened his face. "Besides, your creativity will be returned. I have faith."

He kissed my forehead. "And while I think I know the answer, I shouldn't assume. Do you favor the role of the dominated or the dominatrix?"

I considered his question for a moment. "I'd say I don't have a preference. Both have their merits. I enjoyed both for different reasons, but I suppose that might just be for you. For someone else, it might be different. Is that right?"

"That's certainly possible. For someone that does not have a strong or even complete aversion to one or the other role, the partner might change the mix of preferences. I think we're done for the moment with these specific roles, and we'll turn to another topic, maybe something different and playful in a way, next lesson. We may incorporate parts of these lessons again later. For now, what would you have me do?"

The previous few minutes played back in my mind. I had screamed in my lust-drunk thoughts to break the pact. I've been saving myself my whole life, and I almost threw it away on a whim.

"I think, right now, I need space. To be alone. Would you mind doing that now?"

Gods, I feel so bad for asking.

His smile returned, his voice soft. "If that's what you need, I don't mind in the slightest. I'll get dressed and give you that space now." He dressed himself, then stepped away. "If you need me, you need only call out. I won't be listening in on you, but if you call, I'll hear."

With my nod, he disappeared through some curtains to a side room.

Alone with my thoughts, a growing panic bloomed. I rubbed my eyes with the heels of my hands, silently cursing myself. *I had almost asked him to break the pact. Take my virtue. What was I thinking?*

I chewed on my lower lip and shook my head in disappointment.

Your husband is to be your lover, remember? Your only *lover. Just be careful. He did not try anything you didn't ask for. You can trust him.*

The thought calmed me. *Yes, this recent lesson showed I could trust him. Fully. Actions speak louder than words, and his actions showed that.*

Standing from the bed to put my longshirt back on, I poked my head through the curtains, finding him reading next to some lit candles. "Ramiren?"

He smiled at me as he stood from a plush chair, the small table beside him decked with books. I looked around, never having seen this room before. Bookshelves containing tomes of all kinds lined the walls. Two chairs at a table took up the center. *Where he had sat, waiting for me to calm myself. Patiently.* "Are you all right, Lady Nathalia?"

"Yes, thank you."

He went on, "Good. Once you've had enough time to compose yourself, we can return when you are prepared." To my eyes, he looked more relaxed than he was before we started, but only just.

My chest panged with a deep ache. "I wanted to thank you. For your patience. And gentleness. I feel, with anyone else, this would have been a horrible undertaking. Dangerous, even. But with you, it's something else."

He set the book in his hands down without bothering to mark the page. "You're welcome. I'm glad you're finding it useful and more pleasure than chore. I think that's the only way this works."

Should I tell him? Best to be honest. No one likes these kinds of surprises.

"The secret disclosed for this session. When you were on top of me... I almost asked to dissolve the pact. Or, at least, a specific stipulation," I said it simply, with as little emotion as I could muster, and took an inhale after finishing. *Please understand.*

Ramiren folded his hands in front of him in a pause, as though weighing my words. "Be reassured that, if you had, I would have refused and stopped the lessons entirely before returning your necklace with a dissolved pact. As I said at the beginning, difficulties could arise. This was one of them. I understand and applaud your restraint. It is hardest to hold to your boundaries when temptation tells you that you don't want to."

I stared at him, jaw clenched, for a good minute. *He understood. Thank the gods he understood.* I turned and walked back to the main bedroom without another word.

Chapter Thirteen
A King's Request

Beep. "AM I PRETTY?"

Georgina stared at M.A.L.C.O.L.M. with glazed eyes, then turned her eyes slowly to Raewyn, speaking with a mixture of awe and confusion, "Where in the Grand Tinkerer's swinging ballsack did you get a giant, pink bowtie at this hour of the morning?"

Raewyn grinned at Georgina, her good mood completely impervious to the gnome's glare. "I have my ways. What do you think? Doesn't he look splendid?"

I pinched the bridge of my nose while Ramiren chuckled.

Georgina boggled. "Splendid? He looks like a joke, dummy!"

A young clerk came out of the room behind the double doors in front of us and joined his hands together in front of him. "Ladies and gentlemen, His Majesty is ready to see you now."

Georgina poked her finger at Raewyn as she began to walk. "If this gets us in trouble, it's *your* fault."

Raewyn shrugged at the accusation. "Don't gamble if you can't afford to lose."

We entered the throne room behind the court clerk. It was a smaller room than I imagined it would be, perhaps fifteen feet from one end to the other. There was dark wood everywhere. Wooden panels on the walls. The floor was shiny hardwood. Wooden chairs, with mirrors behind them, lined the walls. With the mirrors everywhere, the room only needed a few lit sconces to make it bright. The king sat in a carved throne on a dais just big enough for his seat and a smaller, empty one beside him. We walked halfway, and I stopped to curtsy, glad I thought to wear my green dress instead of my traveling clothes.

The king was whispering to someone at his side. Based upon his clothing, I guessed an advisor. The advisor's eyes turned to us, and the king shifted in his chair to acknowledge our presence. "Ah, yes. Lord Dalson told me he met a group of fellows who were interested in the mischief hag in the area. You must be them."

Ramiren replied, "Yes, Your Majesty. We intend to face this mischief hag and retrieve that which was taken."

The king leaned forward in his chair. "And if you succeed, do you know what to do next?"

I replied this time, "Yes, break the vials."

The king leaned back again. "Yes, good. That is correct. There is a particular vial this mischief hag possesses. That of my girl, Sornya. My heir. My precious daughter." The king glanced at the small chair next to his and stood from his throne. "She had the most beautiful voice, and she loved to sing. But that was taken from her when the mischief hag came to our court and demanded tribute."

The king's face scrunched in pain, but he went on, "I would give you a great deal, a boon, your heart's greatest desire, if this vial were broken at your triumphant feet."

"I believe we can manage that, Your Majesty," Ramiren said behind me.

Raewyn agreed. "You have two singers in the group who would also mourn their voices. Consider it done, assuming we don't die, of course." She shifted on her feet. "What if it is impossible to receive our heart's greatest desire? What should we ask for then?"

The king pondered, then shrugged as though he cared not. "Then take money. Or a favor."

Raewyn grinned at me when I eyed her with furrowed eyebrows.

I murmured at her, "What's your heart's greatest desire?"

Raewyn looked mischievous. "Oh, that's kinda like revealing a birthday wish, isn't it? If I tell, it won't come true."

What a superstitious bit of fluff.

We curtsied and bowed after the king wished us good fortune and dismissed us.

Outside, we were greeted by a nervously pacing Lord Dalson. "So, you go after the mischief hag, then?"

I gave another curtsy because being in a pretty dress just made me want to. "We do, with the king's blessing. He had a special request for us to break a particular vial."

He blurted out, as though he could not contain himself, "Will you, after, go to Wistran to defeat the mischief hag there?"

Ah, that's what he wanted.

I replied, "That is our plan, Lord Dalson."

"Excellent. Most excellent. I fear the King and Queen of Wistran have both fallen prey to her spells, but there's no one who will take up the call. The prince himself has tried, to no avail. The army he brought to defeat her simply stood there until they dropped from exhaustion. Everyone is afraid."

If that's the case, this might take far more stealth than I'd like.

"Can you help us get into the castle?" Ramiren asked.

Lord Dalson fidgeted with his gold chain. "Oh, that would be quite impossible. You understand."

"What will *you* give if we do this?" Raewyn asked, ever the mercenary.

Dalson's hands stopped fidgeting. "I beg your pardon, Lady Raewyn?"

She shrugged with one shoulder. "What? It's a fair question. You obviously get something from this, and everyone's giving out prizes."

A look of outrage passed over the earl's face. "Why, I get the return of my sovereigns, of course! And I already gave y-"

Ramiren eyed the earl with a critical stare. "No, Raewyn is right. There *is* something else. I recall that pact we struck years ago, Lord Dalson. You paid me in raw gold. Freshly mined gold. Perhaps from mines that are now under the mischief hag's control, no?" He smiled placidly. "Speaking of pacts, you really should have thought about putting a better privacy clause in our contract, because, though I cannot speak a word of its contents, I can write about it."

Dalson sputtered. "You wouldn't dare, devil!"

Ramiren stepped forward slowly, and Lord Dalson reflexively backed up. When Ramiren spoke, I detected a hint of umbrage, "What did you call me?"

Lord Dalson's face turned dark pink. "You heard me! Devil! Fiend! Infernal!"

Ramiren fixed his hard stare on the earl and replied quietly, "Here's how this will work, Dalson. You will sneak us into the castle when the time comes. We will defeat the mischief hag. And then you will quietly retire into the countryside, never to be seen or heard from again. Is that clear?"

Dalson's mouth opened and closed, giving a wonderful impression of a red guppie.

Ramiren went on, "Clear, Dalson? Or the newly-freed king and queen, along with the entire Wistran court, will receive a very interesting letter about your... peculiar tastes, in excruciating detail."

Dalson blubbered, "Damned bastard you are, Ramiren! Fine, I'll get you in." The earl approached Ramiren with a raised finger in the broodling's face. "But, be warned. If you ever darken my doorstep again, you'll regret it."

After Dalson stalked off, Raewyn spun on Ramiren. Grinning madly, she took his arms in her hands to make him face her. "So, what were the terms? Because now I *have* to know."

Ramiren exhaled his anger and managed a chuckle. "He enjoys certain embarrassing sexual quirks. Nothing illegal or immoral. Merely embarrassing."

Raewyn hopped on her toes excitedly. "Oh, please. Please please please."

"Alas, I cannot speak of it, specifically. But if I must write down the details, you can read the letter. Agreed?"

Raewyn clapped her hands together like a child.

I was grateful I had stipulated a full privacy clause in our pact. *Not that he would tell.*

"Ugh! Not. This. Shit. Again!" Raewyn shrieked, shaking the mud off her new boots.

After finalizing supplies, including a new tent for me, we left Elancia. A day into our march, we found ourselves in a marshland as far as the eye could see. I consulted the map again, looking at the sun's path, and put the map back in my pouch. "We head due east."

The soft ground squelched underneath our feet but thankfully did not swallow them. I took my place at the back again while Georgina and M.A.L.C.O.L.M. took the front with Raewyn behind. Ramiren walked in front of me, and, as usual, my thoughts began to wander.

I still struggled with the idea that I had nearly demanded to dissolve the pact. All my discipline disappeared in his arms, it seemed, and that frightened me, despite Ramiren's reassurances.

He had said he would stop everything, and I wholeheartedly agreed with that. I was certainly stronger in my more lucid moments with him, so the sirenic temptation could be easily resisted when I was not heated from his touch or tongue.

His soft black hair came into view again, and I sighed.

Or just looking at him.

Would he even want me, anyway? He was a person too, with agency, and he could make his own decision regarding his desires. *My cravings are nothing if he does not have them, too.*

Something told me Ramiren would be proud of me at that thought.

My face warmed when my besotted brain reminded me, yet again, of his praise and pride in me. If he called me a good girl, my stomach flipped. If he whispered affirmations or told me how well I was doing, I throbbed. And now, a new praise had surfaced, invoking something deeper and almost primal in me, though he hadn't said it very often.

Angel.

It's what my father technically was but not me. I was merely a celestial, descended from an actual angel.

Ramiren had said it when he probably didn't even mean to, mere moments from release. No doubt simple passion had something to do with it, which meant I must've been doing something right.

When close to completion, I nearly cried out for him to take me. To dissolve our pact, and he understood, empathized even.

But it doesn't mean I meant it.

Does it?

A well-known Mineun saying stated *bliss shows our truth*, like imbibing too much wine.

Perhaps that's why so many of them drink to excess.

I never really understood that saying until Ramiren. *I suppose it's harder to hide things when you're naked and sweaty.*

Not that it meant anything. Despite a needling infatuation, that would go away eventually, we still had an agreement. *He is your instructor. He took your necklace as payment, and you are receiving lessons. He sees you as nothing more than that. A student. A novice.*

Oh? Why did he call me angel *then? And why in the Dark Drop am I arguing with myself? Isn't this a sign of madness?*

My mind went blank with no reply.

So, now you shut up? Put doubts in my head but not answers? Thanks. Appreciate the assistance.

Still, no reply.

Gods, my brain is an asshole.

"I hear yelling," Georgina cautioned. "Up ahead."

Doubling my pace to get in front of Georgina and M.A.L.C.O.L.M. as I slipped my shield from my back, I continued forward at the head of our group.

When we crested the hill, we saw a small village spread out into the distance. A loud commotion at the center in a clearing, like a town square, was muffled by our distance. The smoke from a large bonfire curled into the air, hazing the air with the acrid smell of half-rotted marshwood. Ramiren squinted. "Frogs. This is a frog village."

"Beware the frog and toad, for they are at war," Raewyn whispered, reminiscent of the jeweled seer snake who warned us when we first arrived, then giggled.

"Maybe we don't get involved? Skirt around?" Georgina asked from her perch on the automaton.

"They sound riled," I said. "If they're planning a warband, it could spell trouble for our travels through this area. We might want to go down there and see if we can quell the fighting, at least for a time. They have no quarrel with us."

"A wise idea, Lady Nathalia, though I would advise caution. We get involved in any capacity, and they may turn on us," Ramiren said, craning his neck to look around.

More praise. My expression did its best to stay neutral while my insides did a backflip.

We headed down into the village, walking by large grass huts and a few frogs who warily watched our passing but did not stop us. The yelling got louder as we approached. It sounded like an angry mob to my ears.

As we entered the clearing, there was no mistaking the violence in their clamor.

A toad had been lashed to a crude board. His coloring, a mottled gray and green rather than deep umber, and smaller size were different from everyone else present. He was crying in distress and squirming. And far too close to the bonfire for my liking.

Burns were both the most painful and the hardest to heal. *They'd better not...*

My fears were confirmed when the words hidden within the screams from the frogs became clear.

"Throw him in!"

"Burn him!"

"Crispy toad!"

A few frogs grabbed the toad's board to lift him up. The toad struggled fiercely, screaming in fear.

No! Nonono!

"Wait!" I yelled as loud as I could and held my hands up.

The frogs suddenly quieted. Even those holding the toad looked my way.

A large frog, walking upright with a large staff topped with antlers, stepped forward. "I am the Elder. What do you want, stranger?" Two others behind him held a trembling frog who wept with her whole body.

"For this to stop. This is horrific," I said, indicating the bonfire.

The Elder shook his head and croaked. "You do not know our ways, stranger. Move along." He turned away from me.

Think of something! Keep them talking!

I followed for a few steps, my voice earnest. "But. Really. Is this truly necessary? What did he do to deserve such punishment?"

The Elder wheeled around and screeched, "He tried to take my daughter!"

The immobilized toad cried out in reply, "I tried to wed his daughter!"

I blinked, looked back at my companions, then looked at the assembled. *Oh.* Motioning to the frog being held, I asked calmly, "Is that your daughter?"

The elder frog croaked again and bristled. "On your way, stranger. This is none of your concern."

"Because she is clearly upset about t-"

The Elder interrupted me angrily, "I said, on your way!"

"This is beyond us," Georgina said under her breath, still sitting on M.A.L.C.O.L.M.'s shoulders.

The Elder continued, "We are at war!"

"But I am not!" the daughter screamed. "I love him!"

A few in the mob cried out to burn her, too.

"Abomination!"

"Heretic!"

"Traitor!"

"Silence!" the Elder boomed over the din. The mob quieted again.

His word carries weight. If we can convince him, we can convince the rest of them.

A sentiment Ramiren seemed to understand as well, as he came to my side. "Why do you not wish for them to wed?"

"We fight, devilspawn, not marry our blood enemies." His gaze flicked to me, then back to Ramiren. "You travel with an angelspawn, by the look of her. The offspring of devils and angels do not belong together, either."

The daughter hung her head, wracked with sobbing and held up only by those holding her.

A strange look passed over Ramiren's face as he glanced my way. I wished I could interpret it.

Ramiren said, "Our blood does not determine who we are, Elder. I am no devil."

Just as I am no angel, Ramiren.

Ramiren continued, "Our ancestors' feuds do not define us or our... friendship. Our amity. Their war does not affect us, just as we wish war to not affect our children."

The frog struck his antlered staff against the dirt. I had a hope that the Elder was considering Ramiren's wise words because he paused for a moment before speaking again, "Frogs and toads cannot reproduce. It's an abomination for us to bind ourselves to toads."

Ramiren frowned. "Is that your only objection? But this could end the frog and toad war. This union."

"War is life!" someone in the mob shouted.

"Love is life!" Raewyn replied, equally as loud.

The Elder went on, "And the peace would end with their death, no children could carry on that legacy. We would be soft when the war started again. Unprepared."

Ramiren raised an eyebrow. "But it would last until then."

The elder frog scoffed, "And what then? More frogs and more toads join together? It'll lead to our extinction!"

Ramiren shook his head. "Doubtful. Most would stick with their own kind, I'm sure. But some... some frogs might decide to join with toads, and toads with frogs. Extending the peace with their affection. Nothing is so sweet as peace, when the bitterness of war is all you know."

The mob grumbled at Ramiren's words, but the mood was no longer murderous. Without consciously thinking about it, my hand had taken hold of my sword in a tight grip.

The Elder looked long and hard at Ramiren and finally raised his hand, "Let him go."

A frog holding the Elder's daughter protested, "But Elder..."

The Elder croaked, louder, "I said let him go!"

Immediately, the bonds holding the toad down to the board were cut. The toad tried to go to his love but was stopped by many hands.

Or was it feet?

They did not grapple him, but they did keep him from advancing toward her.

The toad looked at the Elder, his great dark eyes pleading to him.

The Elder matched his gaze and said quietly, "Take him back to his village. And take him out of my sight. I will see no more of him."

Those holding the toad pushed and pulled him toward us and tossed him to the ground at our feet. The toad let out a tired sob and was slow to rise.

The Elder's daughter collapsed. "Father, please..."

Her anguish hurt my heart. I wished I could do more.

But for the folly of fathers.

"Take him away. And do not return." The Elder's shoulders sagged as he waved his hand, as though wishing to be done with the whole affair.

When I picked the toad up from the ground, he sank into my hands, as though he had no bones in him.

"Come. Let's take you home," I said softly.

All he could do was nod.

"What is your name?" I asked, still calmly.

He whispered, as though he didn't have the strength to talk fully, "Jeffron."

Once we were out of earshot of the village, M.A.L.C.O.L.M., who had been thankfully quiet this entire time, beeped. "FROGS AND TOADS *DO* HAVE OPPOSABLE THUMBS."

Raewyn threw another stick into the water angrily. I carried Jeffron in my arms, as he had collapsed again after exiting the village, and watched her.

"Raewyn? Are you all right?" I asked, concerned.

She threw another stick. "No."

"What is wrong?"

She wheeled around at me. "They love each other, and they are not allowed to be together! Stupid people! Because of some stupid notion of racial purity? It's insane!"

Ramiren sighed, stopping because Raewyn stopped. "I agree with you, Raewyn, but there's nothing more we could have done. A years-long war is not ended with two peoples' love and a few words. This toad is alive and safe. I call that a victory."

"Well, why not ended? It should be!" Raewyn raised her voice at Ramiren, who quirked an eyebrow at her outburst.

Raewyn continued, riled up, "And what was it with him bringing you and Nat into it? You two are friends! You are a prime example of how it could work."

I adjusted Jeffron in my arms and prayed my face stayed its normal color.

Raewyn threw her hands up. "Abomination, indeed. Paqua's cock! You two should marry and flaunt it in front of that Elder. Broodlings and celestials can't produce children together either. Then he'd shut right up!"

Oh. Goodness. What an interesting, sludge-covered toadstool that is making me face away from absolutely everyone right now.

Chapter Fifteen
A Private Celebration

We didn't know what to anticipate when we first came to Jeffron's village, but I was certainly not expecting what we beheld. Homey cottages, stores, small farms, and even a school surrounded a large blue pond in the center. The air was damp and humid, though not uncomfortably so. Lily pads, colorful flowers, reeds, and cattails rimmed the water, which was being carefully tended to by other toads. Under the gently lapping waves, there were hundreds upon hundreds of tiny tadpoles. *Their birthing pond.* I chose to admire it at a distance.

We were welcomed with warmth, especially when Jeffron told the tale of how we saved his life from the frogs. He still appeared heartbroken. Though he lived, I felt like a failure.

We resolved to stay only for the night. When checking the date to see how many days of rations we had left, I realized with a moment's panic it was time. The toads provided me clean, hot water for bathing, which was another reason why they would feature in my prayers that night.

That evening, Ramiren was surprised to see my silent and sudden appearance at his tent without a whispered pretext, manufactured excuse, or any prearrangement whatsoever, but his ever-present smile widened. "Good evening, Lady Nathalia. Is there something I can do for you?"

"Well, actually, it's what I'd like to do for you." Lifting the lit candle I'd been palming, my smile turned to a grin. With a few notes of a familiar and far-reaching children's tune often sung at birthdays, I ducked into his tent. At its conclusion, I whispered, "Happy birthday, Ramiren. Make a wish."

"I'd nearly forgotten both the day, and that I'd revealed that information to you." He shook his head in disbelief with a small chuckle. "So many other things have happened. Thank you for remembering it for me."

"The date stuck with me. I did my best to keep track until then. Until now, I suppose." I lifted the candle higher. "After you make a wish, I'll tell you my present."

Ramiren exhaled, fluttering the small flame cupped in my hands but not extinguishing it. "My wish would be difficult to tell. I won't bore you with the technical wording required as part of a pact, but I can share with you its essence, the intended effect. In short, when appropriate, I'd like to have the opportunity to choose where I go, for once. Not any specific place, just anywhere at all. That sounds like a small thing, but I've never been able to make that call. Every home I've had, temporary or permanent, I have left due to the decision of another person or group. That's not as sad as it sounds, but it is something I would change, even at a price."

My face softened, feeling ashamed as I met Ramiren's eyes. "My present to you was to grant you whatever you wished for. Anything your heart desired, I would have seen it done. Of course, you may decide where you go. You could leave us tomorrow if you wanted."

Ramiren sighed and shook his head. "I know. Let's not get maudlin. I am, now, choosing to stay. I have no desire to leave." His face suddenly brightened with a crooked grin. "I should have chosen something simpler. I knew I should have just said *a pony*. A beginner's mistake, always choose the pony."

I let out a sudden laugh, shaking my head. "I understand. Sometimes circumstances dictate where we go, and nothing we do can change that."

"I appreciate the sentiment in any case. It was not just idle curiosity on your part, and something you intended to provide. I should have understood that. I am honored by your intent, even though I have no desire to depart any time soon." He inhaled sharply, turning his attention to the candle in my hands.

My smile nearly cracked my face in two while watching him blow out the flame. The only illumination now came from a lantern in the far corner. A quote from a favorite book came to mind. "'Fate is no more than a story of mistakes and triumphs, ever mysterious until the last page.'"

Ramiren's delighted eyes met mine. "You enjoy Quinta Lapro's work?"

I felt the sun in my chest, and I bit my lip to keep my smile from hurting my face. "You know her work?"

"She is a favorite of mine. 'Let men be gentle, and their fury saved for their own inadequacies.'"

My heart burst, and I could not form words for a long moment. "I am not naive enough to think all men are like you. In or outside the bedroom.

But I can hope the one I choose is half the man you are. I hope you know I mean every word."

His eyes took on a mischievous glint, his slow grin wide. "Oh, I think you mean everything you say, Nathalia. But you flatter me. I've learned what a combination of even completely sincere flattery and that expression means, but you still have to ask directly."

No longer surprised, or even ashamed, that he knew I was aroused, since I nearly always was around him. When walking behind him on a march. When watching him talk. When fighting deftly with his rapier. When watching him read. Laugh. Smile. Breathe. Exist.

Lifting a hand to his jaw, my fingers traced his trimmed beard with my thumb. "I didn't want to impose on your birthday."

"No imposition at all. It isn't labor or an inconvenience for me, and I enjoy each lesson as well. Do you wish to begin?"

"Actually, no."

Ramiren looked surprised, and he straightened.

I stuttered to clarify, "I mean, yes, but I don't want to do a lesson right now."

He showed mercy by inclining his head. "Then what would you have of me, Lady Nathalia?"

Just be honest. He could say no… but he could also say yes.

"I want to spend time with you. That's all. If it happens, it happens, but that is not my aim here. It's your birthday, Ramiren. You decide. I am at your service."

"Oh." He tilted his head. "I see."

I fidgeted with the spent candle in my hands. "Is that all right?"

Ramiren furrowed his eyebrows, as though confused. "Yes, it's all right. Of course, it's all right. It's just… I'm having a hard time thinking of the last time someone was at *my* service."

Fair play, Ramiren.

"Mm, let's not get maudlin."

Ramiren looked taken aback, and then laughed. "Well played."

Placing the melted candle down on the footboard of the bed, I went on, "We are not as unalike as I might have originally believed. We both seek to provide services to others. We are, at our core, giving people."

Ramiren crossed his arms. "Mm, though I'd wager our upbringing was vastly different."

"Quite possibly. You said you moved around often when you were younger. Why is that?" I sat on his bed and almost groaned at the softness under me.

Right. Feather bed. Lucky man.

"Oh. I probably should have expected that question." He puffed out his cheeks and blew out air, as though weighing the question. And his answer. Ramiren lowered himself beside me on the bed and ran his hands up and down his thighs. Finally, he spoke, "My parents were entertainers. They put on shows for the city's children during the day. For the adults at night. We played for thrown change. We were not wealthy by any means, but we survived. We had enough."

I sat up, intrigued. "Do you sing then, Ramiren?"

"Yes, though not nearly to your and your sister's caliber. My mother had the voice. My father played the fiddle. I played the pan flute. Accompanying her as she sang stories to an eager crowd."

Picturing Ramiren as a young boy entertaining a crowd made me grin. "Where are they now? Your parents? Still traveling Laeth, entertaining children?"

He pursed his lips and remained silent. I knew enough of him to understand what that meant, and there was pain in his red eyes. There was no way I could not bring myself to pry.

My hand moved to rest on his, giving it a squeeze in comfort. "I am sorry for asking."

He gave me a wan smile that didn't quite reach his eyes. "It's all right."

Change the gods-damned subject, Nathalia.

"Do you remember any songs from your youth? I'd love to hear you sing sometime."

Laughter burst from him. "No, you would not. I am quite out of practice."

"No, I would! Believe me, I would. Maybe someday, I will. After this business with the mischief hags is concluded, you'll feel the need to sing." I raised my eyebrows and muttered, "Gods above, I know I will."

He chuckled softly. "I will feel simple relief and gladness, I suspect. Bursting into song requires stronger emotions."

What would those stronger emotions look like on him? He was certainly intense. *What would true rage look like with him? Devastation? Happiness? Would he throw things? Quietly seethe? Would I see his shoulders shake if he were sad? Tears if he were happy?*

I resigned myself to never getting the answers to those questions. *Though I'd love to see him happy. A different sort of smile on his face. One of joy. Of pure, unadulterated joy. I'd like to see that someday.* "Anyway, back to my original question. What would you have of me on your birthday? We could do anything you wished. As I said, I am at your service."

He pondered a moment, until a sudden thought lit his eyes. "Do you consent to leave?"

As I nodded, he snapped his fingers, and we were back in the bedroom.

"I have an idea. Something I would like to try. It's, at its core, a lesson. But something fun, I think." He approached me, placing his rough hands on either side of my face. He lowered his mouth to mine in a gentle kiss, his forked tongue licking over mine.

For some reason, kisses seemed to be one of the more intimate things we did. With no complaints from me, my hands went to his shoulders as he deepened the embrace, moving one hand to my lower back to pull me in closer. His quick inhale mirrored my own. My stomach up-ended, and the warmth there spread from head to curled toes. I made a noise in my throat when his hand slid down my ass to cup it. His fingers were so close, and pressure and a gentle pulse began to build, centered on my pussy and radiating out.

Until, finally, he broke the kiss. He stared down at me, the red of his eyes nearly gone as the pupil devoured the iris. "It's something you're more familiar with than you might think." At my questioning look, he went on, "I will lie on the bed. You will lower yourself onto my mouth. And pleasure me at the same time with your own mouth. Chest to chest."

I stared at him for a good moment, then looked over my shoulder at the painting I had once admired. "Oh, I get it. Are you sure?"

"I am." He kissed me again, harder this time, and began to tug at my clothing. His slow and practiced hands dragged out the feelings of anticipation boiling within me. *The thought of riding his mouth, of controlling the pace with my hips...*

My pussy was disappointed as it clenched around nothing.

As he finished undressing me, it was my turn. My shaking hands, not so near as practiced as his, fumbled with ties and buttons.

He must have noticed, because grinned down at me. "Here, let me help you, Nathalia. You seem to be having trouble." His grin widened as he assisted me with the removal of his clothing.

I murmured, "I don't know why I'm shaking so much." Anxiety mixed with anticipation. It was as though I'd drunk far too much black tea. I was aroused. And needy. And a hundred other things I'd need a naughty dictionary to name.

He met my eyes, and I saw gentleness there. "The notion has affected you greatly. Channel that into action. Into enthusiasm. What excites you the most about it?"

"Giving and getting at the same time. Pressing myself into your mouth. Riding your tongue," I answered brazenly and without hesitation.

His smile turned crooked as the last of his clothing dropped to the ground. He commanded firmly, pointing behind me, "Bed. Now."

I obeyed.

As he laid down, I slowly began to crawl to him. Too slow for his liking. He gave me a heated look, sat up suddenly and grasped my hips. A gasp was startled out of me as he dragged me toward the head of the bed, moving my thighs to either side of his head.

Bracing myself against his chest, there was a teasing moment when he didn't move. But when I squirmed, he acted. He inclined his head slightly, placing the flat of his tongue on my clit and wiggling it. My eyes rolled back, and my head followed. I shook harder, almost as though I was cold. The pulse returned, then intensified until the throb echoed throughout my hips and almost into my chest.

He wrapped his arms around my thighs, pulling me to him and holding me still as he licked and sucked at tender flesh. I groaned in frustration at the fact I couldn't move except to lean forward. The desire, the sheer need, to buck against his mouth was overwhelming, but when I tried to do so, his grip tightened.

He is trying to control everything.

No.

"Ramiren?" I groaned.

"Mmm?" His mouth vibrated against me, almost making me forget what I was going to say. Almost.

My forehead fell to his thigh as I laughed. "I want to ride your mouth, and you are not letting me!"

I shuddered when his mouth broke contact with me. His chest rumbled against mine with a husky chuckle, and his voice sounded rough and deeper. "My deepest apologies, Lady Nathalia. By all means. Ride away."

His arms loosened their grip, his hands gentled, and his mouth moved again to my pussy, rapidly switching between laving me and sucking my clit. Rolling my hips against his mouth slowly, I gasped at the sudden sensations flooding me. The ability to control the pace, as my hips moved over an eager tongue, was just as heady as the lashing he was giving me. I realized my nails had dug into his hips when he jerked upwards with a sharp inhale.

My tongue pulsed with an ache, reminding me I too had a part to play in this dance. I licked my lips and lowered my mouth to his cock, slipping the tip farther and farther back, as far as it could go. Ramiren made a noise in his throat and bucked his hips upwards again in response. He began to grip my thighs again but stopped himself. He made another noise, one that almost made me forget my own damn name.

Was that a whine?

My tongue wiggled along his shaft, and I felt a little disappointed. There was no ridge for me to nuzzle. No vein for me to trace. I didn't care much for this angle. But he did, based upon his reactions, and that was enough for me.

For now, anyway.

My lips got softer, then harder, then rolled over the tip of his cock, almost savoring it. A strange moan escaped me then, and my legs and hips began to shake. He gave a warning moan, vibrating against me, and his arms wrapped fully around my lower back, then my thighs, then my ass as though he wasn't sure where he wanted to hold me. My belly flip-flopped. The near constant pressure there rose dramatically and peaked while my hips twitched in time to the throb. I gripped his hips with one hand, cupping his balls with the other, and swallowed him whole just as his hips surged up. We screamed into each other; sounds muffled by body parts.

Finally, I lifted my head, breathless, and moved to stretch out next to him. "That was..."

He cleared his throat, words tumbling out of him. "Good. You're progressing quickly."

Running my nose along his bearded jaw to hide a smirk, noting his rattled-off reply, I tried to catch my breath.

He planted a kiss on my forehead. "I can think of more than one elaborate birthday surprise that I did not enjoy half as much." He thought for a moment. "And the dress code is certainly much easier."

Beaming at him, I moved a lock of hair off of his forehead. My mouth curved into a wider grin. "Just think, I have to top it next year. I shouldn't have started the bar so high."

"Technically, you topped it this year." He gave a short laugh at my confused expression. "And when is your birthday? I fear I too have a high bar."

"Not for several months. I have time yet to think of my birthday wish."

He wrapped his arms around me, inhaling against my hair. "The heart of my wish..." he paused, and nodded to himself as if confirming his thoughts, "...is that home is not necessarily a place and things often end before I want them to."

I considered his words for a moment, then replied quietly, "Most things, for me, go on longer than they ought. But this... well, let's just say I hope it continues on as long as we want it to. Not necessarily as long as it needs to."

He hummed his agreement, then laughed. "...And this was much better than a pony."

Chapter Sixteen
Factoring in Memories

Leaving the marshlands behind us, we entered a forest, though this was no forest I'd ever seen before. The trees were bare and gnarled, twisting into the reddish sky. The dry, dusty wind whipped through the naked branches, causing them to creak and groan. It was disconcerting.

I checked the map and saw this area was labeled the Dead Forest.

Oh, wonderful. That's not ominous at all.

Ramiren asked Georgina, our resident tour guide, if she knew anything about this place. She confirmed, in no uncertain terms, she did not and said she would rather stick a pipe wrench into her sluice valve than be here.

I didn't quite understand what she was saying, but the context was clear.

We passed through small, remote villages in the Dead Forest on our way to the mountain pass, to the second mischief hag. We went into town for supplies, but, noting the hostile stares and the harsh whispers, we left without lingering. One village had a tiny inn that seemed to double as a local community building, but we did not give into the temptation to stay in town. Raewyn wanted to until Ramiren explained to her that, if the mischief hag was indeed stealing people, the townsfolk might be tempted to hand us over as an offering to leave their village alone.

Raewyn did not argue much after that.

As we walked, we saw steep hills to the north through the bare branches of the trees with the deep shadows of a mountain range beyond them. The map marked them as the Jenisaw Mountains, but we knew them as the Quilin Mountains in Laeth. *We're getting close.* Once we reached the mountain pass, we'd turn north. I prayed that Leraska's directions were accurate.

It was our last night here, at the edge of the forest, before we were to make our way across the plains toward the pass. Georgina set M.A.L.C.O.L.M. for guard duty, as usual, and everyone said goodnight. Wiggling out of my chain armor, I rolled my shoulders at the stiffness I always felt at its removal. My gambeson came next, the padded armor worn under my mail to keep the pinching to a minimum. Remembering the massage I had given Ramiren not long ago, I wouldn't complain if he reciprocated sometime.

A sudden wetness between my legs made me roll my eyes, continuing to undress. *Oh, for Celestia's sake, he's not even here.*

When I saw red splotches, I cursed under my breath. *Oh. Great. Well, no lessons for a while.* With everything going on, it had been the last thing on my mind.

After searching in my pouch for my rags, I poured one of the waterskins into a hammered copper bowl. I bathed with a bar of soap and cloth before changing into fresh clothing. The water was frigid, but I was too tired to warm it in our dying fire. A memory flickered, of Ramiren and his laundry. *Dark underclothes would be handy right about now. Perhaps I'll ask him where he got them.*

After cleaning everything up, and dumping the water behind my tent, I settled down into my bedroll. This time of the day was both my favorite and the absolute worst. It allowed me the chance to be alone, but my mind enjoyed tormenting me. The insects outside and the creaking of dead branches swaying in the breeze, at first unsettling, were now a lullaby. My lids drifted closed, and, or once, my thoughts were blessedly silent. I was just beginning to drift off when a whisper brushed past my ear.

Oh, no. Not now. I can't...

I turned my face to groan into my pillow. My foggy brain listened for the words of the whisper, but they did not come. My eyes opened as I lifted my head, straining my ears. *Strange.* It sounded more like a breath, a gasp, and then silence.

Ramiren?

Another whisper came, this time with muffled and incomplete words.

"...thalia... dang..."

When their meaning finally sank into my muddled consciousness, I sat bolt upright, at once wide awake.

Nathalia. Danger.

Not bothering with my armor, I instead reached for my shield and longsword, unsheathing the weapon in one smooth motion. After crawling to the opening of my tent. I listened again but did not hear anything out of the ordinary. Insects chirped, and dead branches croaked in the wind. My shield nudged a corner of the tent flap aside to look out. There was no one wandering around, except M.A.L.C.O.L.M., who was struggling against the vines now holding him down.

Exactly like the vines in the Hall of Mirrors.

Fuck, she's here.

Movement to my left caught my attention. A shadow at the opening of Ramiren's tent flickered, and a humanoid hand the color of soured milk closed the tent's door.

My veins flooded with ice water. *Was Ramiren the first or last she'd visited? Is my sister still alive? Georgina?* I ignored the questions piling up to concentrate on the present. And presently, Ramiren was in danger. Assuming he, too, was still living.

The false protector, the last one left alive... Fear gripped my heart like a clawed hand.

Her strength was unknown. Same with her weapons and abilities, aside from the vines and rifting away in a puff of smoke. All I knew was that Ramiren needed me. *Please, Horyn, let him still breathe.* That was all I needed.

I burst out of my tent into the eerily still camp and turned toward the enormous tent. When a soft, muffled cackle caught my attention, my mind went blank. Darkness clouded my vision. Running straight toward Ramiren's tent, anger and fear mixed into a heady cocktail. My lungs had a hard time taking in air. I was just outside the tent when I heard her speak. The barrier of the tent's walls couldn't fully deaden the words.

"Deals are your joy. Never again shall you bargain."

No!

I charged through the opening to see Ramiren, gagged with vines across his mouth. Those same vines bound his hands behind him as he knelt in front of her. His eyes met mine, and he started speaking, muffled yelling, though I could not make out what he was saying.

I rushed the mischief hag.

Not now. Not him!

"I steal from you your-"

I screamed a wordless battle cry, swinging my sword down, my terror fueling me. Instead of disappearing, she wailed in surprised agony as my sword bit deeply into her shoulder. I pulled my sword back, preparing for another strike. Green blood seeped out from the wound, covering my weapon with a viscous liquid that faintly hissed. Her spindly fingers went to stem the flow. I stabbed at her again, straight through her other shoulder.

She spat, wheeling on me, "You bitch of a girl! You ruined it!"

A third slice of my sword hit only the puff of green smoke she'd left behind. Spinning around, searching the tent for her, I sped toward the entrance of the tent and jerked it back to check our camp with my breath coming in winded puffs. But, still, there was no sign of her.

Releasing the tent flap, I hurried back to Ramiren's side. I fell to my knees, dropping my longsword and shield to remove the vines from Ramiren's mouth. They slipped down easily, and he graced me with a grateful, tremulous smile.

"Well done," he whispered.

With a short laugh, filled with fatigued relief, I threw my arms around his neck tightly. My eyes began to sting as tears flooded them, making me blink rapidly. "You're safe. You're safe. You're safe."

A few seconds later, the rest of the vines dropped and disappeared, and he returned the tight embrace around my waist. His hands rubbed up and down my back, then clutched my nightshirt in his grip, as he steadied his breath.

"How did you-" He stopped himself and just pressed his face firmly into the crook of my neck.

I heard movement outside the tent. Canvas shuffling. *So, at least someone else is still alive.*

And then a gnome's cry, "M.A.L.!"

I didn't care if anyone came in and saw. I pushed my face into the crook of his neck, my special place, and didn't want to let go.

Beep. "VINES... NOT F-F-FUN. DO NOT... R-R-RECOMMEND."

M.A.L.C.O.L.M.'s voice was scratchy and obviously damaged. After inspecting him, Georgina said the conjured vines must have wound themselves into his voice box in an attempt to quiet him. We all settled around the campfire to talk, but no one spoke for a while. We all just sat in stony silence, in shock over having been invaded.

Beep. "WHY D-D-DOES... HAG... KEEP PICKING... ON ME."

Georgina patted M.A.L. on the leg, eyeing me warily. "So, she was here? She tied up M.A.L. again? Why didn't you wake us, Nathalia?"

"I'm sorry, Georgina. There was no time. She was in Ramiren's tent. I had to act fast."

Georgina threw up her hands in disgust. Raewyn stared daggers at the gnome. "If my sister says there wasn't enough time, then there wasn't enough time."

Ramiren nodded in agreement. "I agree. I was seconds from losing a valuable ability, if not my life. She could've stolen me away at any time, and I'm not sure why she didn't."

"But we could've killed her here! Not in her home. Gods know how many traps and tricks she has there!" Georgina yelled.

I scoffed, taken aback. "I wasn't about to sacrifice-"

"We could've had her!" The gnome screamed in my direction, pointing an accusing finger. "But you failed! Again!"

My patience, already splintering, shattered like cheap glass. *If she thinks for one second I'd forfeit...*

"That. Is. Enough!" I bellowed, causing everyone to startle. Even M.A.L.C.O.L.M. quieted. My yell echoed among the dead trees, reverberating weirdly. Raewyn looked around, spooked. Georgina winced. Ramiren straightened, sucking in a short breath.

Staring Georgina down, my trembling hands balled into tight fists, I couldn't remember the last time I felt this much anger. No, this wasn't anger; this was rage. I could take her snide insults and harassment, but not this. This selfish disregard for another, a traveling companion even, all for the sake of a more convenient battlefield. My teeth clenched so hard they hurt. I saw redness at the edge of my vision when I looked at her.

My voice was calm, with an undercurrent of stark warning. "We will go to her home. And kill her there. None of us will be turned into fodder just so you can *maybe* get your tools back a little easier. Do you understand, Georgina?"

Georgina opened her mouth, but, based on her sneer, it wasn't to agree.

I interrupted her, bellowing even louder than before, "I said, do you understand?"

Georgina took a step back, and M.A.L.C.O.L.M.'s joints squeaked as he stood up in a defensive position for his mistress.

Georgina's mouth became a line. She uttered bitterly, muted, "Yes. I understand."

My indignant tone made it clear I would suffer no more arguments. "Good. Now, everyone go to bed. We have several days to go into the mountains. We leave when there's light enough to see." I turned heel to stalk back to my tent, leaving silence in my wake. It wasn't until my tent flaps were tied down that I let the tears go.

The next morning was subdued. No one spoke, not even M.A.L.C.O.L.M. or Raewyn. We packed up in utter silence and headed east, toward where we believed the mountain pass to be. No one mentioned the mischief hag. In fact, no one said anything all day except me giving directions or if someone needed to relieve themselves.

That night, we all agreed to sleep in Ramiren's large tent, privacy and anger be damned. She knew we were here, and as Ramiren had reminded everyone, she liked to steal people. The decision to sleep together, under the same roof, seemed wise.

Though we all had bedrolls, Ramiren insisted on giving me, Raewyn, and Georgina the bed while he took the floor. I protested, as this was Ramiren's tent, but Raewyn and Georgina overruled me. It was the first time they had actively cooperated, so I wasn't going to argue. Ramiren seemed grateful for the offer of the folding cot my sister had been using.

All three of us fit on the bed, thanks to Georgina's diminutive size. Raewyn took the side closest to the heated tent wall, as it was the warmest. Georgina the middle, as it was the most secure. Raewyn didn't seem to be happy sleeping next to the gnome, but exhaustion won out.

I slept closer to the open edge. Closer to Ramiren, I realized when settling on my left side into the soft feather mattress.

While dozing in and out of consciousness, my memories repeated themselves over and over in my head. *What if the hag had stolen Ramiren? Or my sister? Or Georgina? Gods know what she does with those taken.*

Would we find anyone alive there, in her cave? Or just piles of bones, as the barkeep had warned?

With a silent sigh, I dragged my stinging eyes open. Moonlight filtered through the tent's opening, silhouetting the damaged automaton who stood guard at the entrance. My vision adjusted to the darkness, and I tilted my head on the pillow to see Ramiren on his right side, wide awake and staring straight ahead. At me. He rarely removed his glasses, so I appreciated the new view. He looked almost innocent without them.

I whispered, "Can't sleep?"

"No, I'm afraid not," his whisper was even softer than mine. "You?"

"I can't seem to settle my mind."

"Oh? What troubles you?"

I shrugged the shoulder I wasn't lying on. "Anxieties. Fears. I am afraid."

His lips twitch downwards. "Of what?"

"Failure. Another person hurt, and I am too late to stop it."

He sounded gently instructive. "You can't save everyone. And if you try to, you'll set yourself up for failure before you've even begun. You'll save no one."

I exhaled loudly through my nose. "No, I know. I'm not a god, just a protector without a charge. I can only do so much, protect so many, just..."

There was silence between us as my words trailed off, though my eyes stayed on him.

My eyebrows rose. "Why can't *you* sleep?"

He licked his lips, and his tone turned serious, "When the mischief hag had me at her mercy, I tried to call for you."

Not enjoying the memory, my reflex was to be reassuring. "I know. I heard. One of your whispers."

He hesitated. The look in his eyes turned panicked. My head lifted slightly off the pillow. "What?"

His whisper softened. I almost couldn't hear it. "I didn't throw a whisper, Nathalia."

Blinking dumbly, I repeated myself. "What?"

He grimaced. "I tried to. However, I was disrupted, like you disrupted the hag's incantation. I couldn't finish it with my gag, but you heard it all the same. I am trying to figure out how. I've *been* trying to figure it out. I simply don't understand."

How could a thrown whisper work without magic? Who knows what kind of innate abilities broodlings have? "Perhaps your magic is more potent than you realized?"

Ramiren shook his head. "No. It has its limitations, like anything. I must be able to speak to throw a whisper."

My sister's loud, groggy voice startled me, "Minue's tits, would you two shut up?"

The tension vanished into smoke, like the mischief hag had. Ramiren and I both choked back embarrassed laughter, then grinned at each other. I extended my hand to him, into the small gulf between our two beds, and he took it without a word.

The sun rose and set twice more before we spotted it.

Oftentimes, Ramiren and I would find ourselves in each other's company, a comfort from the unfortunate but necessary situation we had found ourselves in. Usually we talked, but sometimes we'd just sit in a kind of companionable silence. I even lent him one of my books, which I'd never done for anyone besides Raewyn.

After several days of sharing stories, playing cards, or even the occasional game of chess, a whisper brushed past my ear. ***"Wine?"***

I had been sitting at the meager campfire, sharpening my sword with a whetstone when I heard it. Sheathing the weapon to silently approach Ramiren's tent, I tapped on the canvas. "Ramiren? It's me."

Ramiren's reply came from within, "Please, come in."

I stepped into the interior of his roomy tent and adjusted the flaps closed. He was lying on his feather bed, half-reclined, looking through the pouch next to him. "I'm not quite settled down for the evening. I'm afraid I'm running low on quality wineskins, but I likely have a few acceptable ones yet. If I can find them." His shirt hung open, unbuttoned to his mid-chest, revealing smooth tanned skin.

My eyes traveled up and down him as I walked over. The corner of my mouth tugged up in both amusement and enjoyment of the view. "Was this on purpose or do you always look like that when you lounge?" Sitting on the corner of the bed, I sank into the thick mattress and leaned against the footboard.

"I'm getting used to finding comfort when staying in places quite a bit more rough than I'm accustomed to." He smirked, peering at me over the rim of his glasses. "So, on purpose, but without specific intent. Ah, here it is." He plucked a small wineskin from his pouch.

I smiled fully, lifting my hand to catch the wineskin he tossed to me. "I trained at the Horyn Academy. Those might have been even more rough in manners than our current situation entails." Inhaling over the mouthpiece of the wineskin, my smile widened further. "Kibelan spiced red? I didn't know you could get this anymore." I tipped the wineskin to take a drink.

Damned orcs. Fomona wine just isn't the same.

"Yes, good enough, but not excellent. I should have stocked up on fey wine when we were in Elancia."

I sputtered, almost spraying the wine in a misty plume as the tawny port in Puldoni, and how giddy I felt after a few decent sips, came to mind. "Isn't fey wine dangerous?"

He laughed softly, shaking his head. "That's the rumor, but no, it's not dangerous. Just especially potent. Like our fortified wines."

"Mm. Maybe, after all of this is over, and we've gone our separate ways, we'll be able to share bottles over the years. I'd like to at least maintain a friendship between us." My smile fell.

Why does that make me feel sad?

His own smile did not waver. "We have as much time as we wish, as far as I'm concerned. Should we go our separate ways, no matter how far in the future, I know, for my part, I'd like that."

My smile returned as my eyebrow raised. "Should? Don't you mean *when*?"

Ramiren mirrored me, raising an eyebrow of his own. "Yes, of course. But my point still stands. We have all the time we need."

"And here I thought I was learning quickly." My full grin returned teasingly.

Flirting again?

Yes, I am flirting. What of it?

Careful you don't grow too attached. He is not for you. You two cannot have children. And despite his wealth, he is not a noble, which is the expectation for you.

I'm already too attached, you dumb harpy. I know. And most of the men who courted me in Camlynn were nobles and not worth the shit on a hog's backside...

Ramiren sat up, swinging his legs over the side of the bed. "I try to not assume anything and just let things play out. Though I believe you eventually *will*, who knows *when* you'll find the one you will eventually settle for. Deadlines, especially, can create pressure, which isn't really something I'd want introduced to our time together."

I looked at him after taking another sip straight from the wineskin and chuckled. "At least, not that kind of pressure."

He laughed softly, his shoulders shaking. "Fair enough. I suppose, sometimes, certain pressures are more or less required."

Something he'd said needled me. "Wait. Settle for? Don't you mean settle *with*?"

He looked back into his pouch. His expression was blank, schooled. "No, because while the one you marry would be lucky, you will always be settling."

My fingers fidgeted with the wineskin stopper. "Why's that?"

He finally looked up at me. His teasing grin did not match his eyes, and I wasn't sure which to believe. "Because I have my doubts that anyone is good enough for you."

I played off my rising awareness with a nervous chuckle, then stoppered the wineskin with gratitude that my monthly was over. "With that, I think I would like to break our half-week streak tonight if you'd allow. I'm afraid the moment I saw you lounging I was rather done. You are, unfortunately, quite beautiful."

"As are you." He snapped his fingers. The lanterns went out, save a small flame where his thumb and finger met, and then we were somewhere far more private. "I hope you'll forgive a bit of dramatic entrance. I think I said last time that we'll be breaking another streak, this lesson should be less intense than the others. More playful. As it has been a little while since our last lesson, I thought not jumping into the deep end was a wise course of action."

With a laugh, I looked around to see if there were any hints regarding what he had in mind and didn't see any. "I don't mind. You know, the theatrics used to scare me, but that was well before I knew you. Theatrics are for distracting others or to give a thrill. I think, for you, it's both."

"Both are usually most effective. I talked about exploring appetites. We'll be taking that literally." He moved to the large table, where a bowl of what looked like white fluff sat.

Damn, I missed that.

Wait...

"Whipped cream?"

"Yes. Do you like whipped cream?" He said as he made his way back over to me, bowl in hand.

"I do, on pies and pastries. I'm not sure why you have it, unless you've somehow installed a bakery between the library and bathing room. In which case, I should warn you that I hate rhubarb."

He dipped his finger into the cream and, with a speed I didn't know he was capable of, he put a tiny dollop on the tip of my nose. He grinned, and I couldn't help but return it.

He leaned in and licked the dollop away.

A half-hearted swat of my hand accompanied my laugh. "Why did you do that?"

Ramiren did not answer. He dipped his finger in the cream again and this time, when he raised his hand, he slowly spread it over my bottom lip. Something told me not to lick it off.

He leaned in to kiss me. His tongue flicked out, taking half the cream away, before sucking the rest off as though savoring it. He drew my lower lip in between his two, and I closed my eyes, lost in the sensation. His tongue brushed against mine with a tentativeness that seemed uncharacteristic of him. The sweetness of the cream mixed with his own taste, and I swallowed hard.

Oh.

My eyes opened to see him staring down at me. He reached up to take his glasses off, and my knees nearly gave out from the heat in his gaze, now revealed.

Ramiren rolled out of the bed, placing the empty cream bowl on the table. "Exceptional. Not everything playful needs to be passive or soft, and your instinct on when to switch to something more intense, nearly aggressive, was good. You show how much you want it, and we're both rewarded for the result." He turned back toward me. "I'll need to give some thought on the next lesson. I didn't assume we'd spend only one on this topic."

I stared up at the silk canopy above the bed, feeling dazed and sticky. "Take your time." My head rolled on the pillow to look at him. "And thank you."

"You're welcome. We can rest here for a time. We don't need to depart until we wish. Again, no time at all will have passed when we return. There is no hurry. We're free of that specific pressure here."

With a slight chuckle, I turned to look upwards again. "I mean for your compliment. Calling me beautiful earlier. I've been told that before, but I'd never really heard it until now."

His smile softened. "I meant it. I've been surrounded by enough beauty in my life to recognize it, especially when I know the person, and not feel hesitant to be honest about what I see. There may be secrets I keep, but that isn't one of them."

Speaking of. Time for bravery.

When I rose to sit on the edge of the bed, I met his eyes. "And my secret for the session. A small part of me is envious of every single woman you've ever touched." There was no feeling of shame, but I also didn't feel proud either. "It's not coming from a place of resentment. Merely regret that those touches weren't mine."

His jaw clenched as he remained silent for a long beat.

Is he angry with me?

But when he spoke, there was no anger, just understanding. "I think that being able to recognize that feeling and confront it, even to the point of saying it aloud, takes a rare kind of strength. I've been around for some time, but even I can find myself pleasantly surprised now and again. Factoring in memories, I may need to consider re-evaluation of the spiced red wines of Kibel, at least placing them as equals with those from Pouroe."

I tried to hide my relief in a deadpanned joke. "Do you, now? That's utter insanity, Ramiren. Practically sacrilege." I shook my head at him, tsking a few times.

Collapsing back onto the soft mattress with a bounce, my voice turned pensive. "No matter the subject, whether religion, politics, or the innate evil nature of orcs, anything can bring about differences of opinion. However, I think everyone can agree that Camlite wine is complete shit."

Ramiren let out a barking laugh. He climbed onto the bed next to me and reached over to brush hair out of my face. "Yes, I believe all can agree on that."

Chapter Seventeen
Cliff Runner

There was no trail. No markers of any kind to let us know we had made it to the right place to begin our ascent. Just a vague idea of direction and a prayer. The incline was not exactly treacherous, but our legs would be very tired by the end of the day and very sore tomorrow.

With the automaton's voice box having become even more damaged, it'd been quiet lately. Normally, I would've welcomed the peace, but not when that peace was brought about by injury or anger. After apologizing to Georgina for my tone, though not my words, the gnome simply nodded and walked away.

"Can M.A.L.C.O.L.M. track the mischief hag, like he tracked the bunyip?" I asked Georgina, who had spoken but a few words to me. She was barely speaking to anyone.

"No, that capability was damaged along with his voice box. The switch broke." Georgina looked up at M.A.L.C.O.L.M. Worry lines crossed her forehead as she stared at her life's work that'd developed a listing to one side.

Ramiren opened his mouth to speak but said nothing. He merely pursed his lips.

I couldn't blame him. *What do you say to someone when their proudest accomplishment withers away? When their friend is dying?*

I thought about what I'd want someone to say to me in that situation and came up empty.

If I had a charge, and they were dying in front of me while I could do nothing...

That snapped things into perspective for me. My oath and her tinkering were the same thing, equally important to us. But, at least with M.A.L.C.O.L.M., we could do something about it.

I replied finally, "We'll find her, Georgina, before it's too late."

The gnome did not reply. She just reached up and took M.A.L.C.O.L.M.'s metal hand in hers. His one good eye turned a soft green as he looked down at their joined hands, causing the horrific sound of metal grinding on metal. *He is far worse off than I thought.*

Beep. "LOVE... YOU... G-G-GEORGINA."

I turned to begin the graduated climb upward.

Our going was rough. The incline became even more pronounced the higher we got. Raewyn's whines were thankfully kept to a minimum. Every so often, I'd check on her, and every time she was smirking at Georgina huffing and puffing her way up the slope. She was having far too much fun watching the pink-haired gnome suffer, but I didn't want to draw attention to it and start another war.

M.A.L.C.O.L.M. was not in a fit state to carry the tinkerer, so she had to endure, but I kept an eye on her. When she inevitably tripped with a sharp yelp and began to slide down, I was ready.

Georgina flopped to a boneless rest about twenty feet down in a short dip. She slowly sat up and wiped her nose, sniffling.

I dropped to my hip and slid, causing pebbles and small rocks to tumble down the incline. With my legs and feet, I stopped next to her. "Are you all right?"

She looked up at me. Her enlarged eyes began to flood, and she turned her head. Her voice was steady, though only just, "Yes. Yes, I'm fine. It's just... I think I twisted my ankle. And I don't want to have to beg Raewyn again for healing."

Crawling closer to her, my hands hovered over her legs. "May I?"

When she whimpered and pointed to the one injured, I gently took her ankle in both hands. Though I was careful in removing her boot and sock, Georgina tensed and hissed.

The ankle was already bruised and swollen.

No. This is broken.

I'd occasionally healed myself when it was desperately needed, which didn't happen often, so I had very little practice with it. But as Georgina took her goggles off, her watery eyes were unable to hide her pain. I had to try.

"I'm going to try to mend your ankle myself. Give me a moment."

My warm hands wrapped around her warmer ankle as I closed my eyes, recalling the words my father had taught me, in Celestial.

"Vala ashalanore…" I felt something deep within me stir.

Behind me, Raewyn must have figured out what I was doing, because she yelled, "Why are you healing her? I can do that! Wait, Nat, is she actually hurt?"

Though I ignored her, I appreciated the question instead of a snide remark.

"…vasha torino…" The stirring rushed into my chest and out toward my hands.

Georgina gasped. "I feel it!"

"…balinde rodin Tarindar lema…" My hands began to warm, as though cupping the palms close to a candle's flame.

My eyes opened to see everyone standing around Georgina and me, though I had not heard their approach.

Raewyn looked annoyed. M.A.L.C.O.L.M.'s eye had gone a soft green. Ramiren smiled brightly, his elongated canines showing. He sounded relieved, "I am glad to see you weren't too injured, Mistress Georgina."

Georgina smiled shyly at Ramiren. "Thanks."

I removed my hands from her now pink ankle. "Stand, Georgina. It worked."

The gnome replaced her sock and boot, then stood, hopping up and down to test her ankle. She almost fell again from the rocky terrain, and I reached out to steady her. Georgina smiled. "Yep, that feels good!"

Looking down at Georgina, I asked, "Will you be all right?"

"I think so," she muttered. "But I'm not sure if I can walk this." She pointed up toward the mountain.

I hummed, thinking. "Permission to lift you?"

"What do you mean, lift me?" Georgina boggled at me and placed her goggles back over her eyes. "I guess, but- whoa!"

Georgina wheeled her arms as I picked her up, placing her on my shoulders like a parent might a toddler. Raewyn's jaw dropped in shock. "Nathalia Maxliana Swordhand! What are y-"

I gave my sister a sharp look, cutting off her words. Impatience leaked into my tone as I pointed a finger at the ground, my other hand holding the gnome's legs to my chest. "She is part of our group, Raewyn, and she's struggling. We need to look out for each other, and Ramiren and I cannot do it alone. No more requiring her to beg for healing. Act like petty rivals all you like, but when push comes to shove, I expect you to be there."

Raewyn frowned deeply but looked above me to where the tinkerer sat. "I wouldn't have withheld healing if it was really needed." She gave a long-suffering sigh. "Oh, all right. Fine. Georgina, I'm s-" Her eyes widened, and sudden outrage crossed my sister's face. She stumbled backwards, hand on chest, while Ramiren closed his eyes, shaking his head and smirking.

My eyes flickered between my sister and Ramiren, confused. "What happened?"

Raewyn pointed at Georgina accusingly. "She... she just flipped her middle finger at me!"

I slowly exhaled through my nose and muttered, "Glad to see things are back to normal."

A vicious storm blew in overnight. Though Ramiren's tent was sound and sturdy, and on the flattest ground we could find, our sleep was fitful due to the wind whipping and howling until daybreak. At least mine and Ramiren's was. Georgina passed out within moments, and Raewyn soon followed. Their gentle snoring was drowned out by the storm outside.

Though we mostly sat in silence, occasionally I or Ramiren would break the interior quiet with a whispered question or a statement about the day's events.

After discussing the possibility of reaching the hag the next day, Ramiren took a deep breath. "I wanted to tell you I'm proud of you."

My head shifted on the pillow, his words making me wonder what I had done to earn such praise. "For what?"

"Taking care of Georgina. She angered you greatly, and you still treat her with empathy."

I fidgeted with my thin blanket. "She needed help, and I could provide it. It'd be mean-spirited if I was able but not willing, though thank you for the compliment."

He extended a hand to touch my hair. He had moved his cot a little closer to the bed this time, close enough for us to touch without reaching. "Nathalia Maxliana Swordhand. Definitely the best of us."

That first night, where he'd said something similar, seemed so long ago, and I smiled. "I still can't believe she used my full name." But, undeniably, his words had filled me with a warm pleasant glow.

"Maxliana? After your father Maxlian, I presume?"

My cheek rubbed against the soft pillow under me as I nodded. "Yes."

He slid his hand down and curled a lock of my hair in his deft fingers. "And where did you get Nathalia? Ancestor? Family friend?"

"It was the name of the Valisetian priestess who married my parents. My mother said it was a good day, and she always wanted to be reminded of it. What about you? Where did your parents get Ramiren?"

"I honestly have no idea. I never asked them." Though his facial expression did not change, the sadness in his voice tugged at my heart and made me not want to pry.

But Ramiren what?

There had been a last name on his vial's tag, but I was so shocked that he had a vial at all I didn't remember it. *'O' something? Or was it 'A'?*

"And your last name?" I inquired finally.

The smile he gave me was a pained one, and he dropped his hand from my hair. "Good night, Nathalia."

Shit.

An apology hung on my tongue, but something held me back. Instead, I just returned his words, "Good night, Ramiren."

The second, and I hoped final, day was the worst one. I continued to carry Georgina on my shoulders, as there was no way for her to stay surefooted on the treacherous, steep and now slick, terrain. My feet almost slipped several times with the gnome's weight throwing off my balance. Raewyn fell twice but was not hurt. Ramiren tripped once, injuring his knee badly enough that Raewyn had to heal him with her prayers.

As we stopped for a midday meal of rations and the rest of the seasoned almonds, propping ourselves up on the sturdier-looking rocks and boulders, I spotted a deep shadow up ahead. *A cave entrance?*

Please, Horyn, let this be it.

I alerted everyone, as quietly as possible. The surge of energy, that we were perhaps finally at our destination, renewed our sore limbs and aching backs.

We approached cautiously, as we had with the first hag, and my head swiveled to catch any movement. But, as with the first hag, there was no sound. No small animals scurrying. And no hag. There was nothing but the dry wind and barren landscape.

I didn't like it then, and I don't like it now.

Pausing at the cave entrance, my nervous eyes darted around to look for traps. A trick. Anything. But, again, there was still nothing. Just the silent dark of the cave lay ahead, beckoning us closer in a mocking dare.

I looked back and whispered, "Everyone ready?"

Raewyn bobbed her head, looking nervous.

Georgina looked excited, clapping her hands together.

Ramiren confirmed with a firm nod. He unsheathed his rapier slowly. *No talking. No negotiation with this one. Good.*

Beep. "R-R-READY."

Everyone winced as M.A.L.C.O.L.M.'s voice echoed all around. Down the mountain. In the cave itself.

So much for the element of surprise.

I unsheathed my longsword, lifted my shield high, and walked in.

Everyone followed.

Georgina took out her heatless torch as we peered down into the cave, the flickering light causing shadows to flit along the floor and walls in a distracting dance. Again, there was nothing, just stone and rocks and sand. I glanced back, shrugged, and inched forward.

My doubts about this being our destination almost made me miss the sounds of dripping water and scared whimpering.

As we walked closer to the sound, a person came into view. He was tied down with vines, unable to move, and situated under a stalactite that was dripping water on his forehead. Based upon his clothing, he looked to be from one of the Dead Forest villages.

Intending to cut him loose, I moved forward until Ramiren whispered loudly, "Wait!"

There was a sharp click under my foot.

"Everyone, get back. Get back!" I yelled, not caring that it echoed. When I confirmed everyone had complied, though Ramiren was the slowest to obey, I slowly shifted my foot.

In a blur, a multitude of spiked vines shot out from the cave's walls. They wrapped around my wrists, making me drop my sword. Before I could blink, more vines appeared, wrapping around my waist, my ankles, and even my neck. The sharp spikes dug into my flesh until air was cut off. Completely immobilized, I couldn't even scream as pain shot up and down my spine, causing it to bow.

Georgina gasped in surprise. "Oh, shit!"

Raewyn shrieked. "Nat!"

Ramiren yelled with a tinge of panic. "Nathalia!"

Beep. "NOT-T-T-T FUN-N-N-N-N"

Ramiren dropped his rapier to unsheathe a dagger from his belt, then grabbed onto the vine around my neck. I looked at him, the pressure in my lungs and face increasing. He began to hurriedly carve through the vine.

Georgina took up a vine on my ankle, and Raewyn started on the binding around my waist.

Ramiren paused for a brief second when he heard it, then tried to cut even faster.

We all heard it.

Cackling.

The villager looked around wildly with his eyes and shrieked. "She comes! She comes!"

"M.A.L., defensive position around Nathalia," Georgina ordered.

Beep. "A-FIRM-A-T-T-TIVE"

My lungs burned and cried for breath as darkness began to cloud my sight. My limbs felt heavy, numbed from both my lack of oxygen and the vines stretching me almost beyond the limits of my joints. Thick tears streamed down my cheeks and temples when my eyes squeezed shut to clear them.

He'll never make it.

Ramiren sawed more and more frantically, with the tugging and pulling from his attempt choking me even more. He cursed under his breath, strained and frustrated.

Then, he suddenly stopped cutting and yelled incredulously, "Doesn't M.A.L.C.O.L.M. have scissors?"

Just as the world fell away, I heard the gnome's deadpanned reply, "Oh, yeah. I forgot."

I came to with a gasp and clawed at my raw neck, coughing and sucking in air. Raewyn hovered, tears in her eyes as her fingers clutched at me. Next to her, Ramiren looked down at me, his face unintelligible except for the muscle bunched at his jaw.

Raewyn hissed at Georgina, "You just *forgot*, huh?"

Georgina crossed her arms. "Hey, so did you. I have a lot of things on M.A.L. I can't remember them all. Besides, some aren't even *working*."

I snatched my sword up off the ground and made sure my shield was still strapped to my left arm.

As I stood on unsteady legs, my head swimming, Raewyn reached out to help. I fingered my sore neck and winced. There'd definitely be bruises there tomorrow. My throat was hoarse, strained, when I said, "I'm all right. Nothing too bad. Perhaps look at me when we're done here."

The cackles are getting closer.

"After all, we'd best not keep her waiting."

As we passed by the villager, heading further in, his eyes went wide when I lifted my sword to hack at his vines. The villager flinched away, or tried to, but couldn't move until my third slice. He threw the cut vines off and wobbled weakly. *Gods know how long he has been stuck here.*

"Can you walk?" I asked with a voice like gravel.

"Yes, I think so," he said, as though out of breath. He rubbed at his wet forehead with the heel of his hand roughly.

"Wait for us at the cave's entrance, and we'll take you back home after we're done with her," I instructed.

"No offense, lady, but I'm not waiting." And he stumbled back the way we came.

I can't blame him.

Up ahead, we saw an open cavern with strange blue lights emanating from it.

We marched forward together, my shield held high and my sword ready. Georgina told M.A.L.C.O.L.M. to keep his scissors out.

Ramiren raised his rapier and nodded to me.

Here we go.

M.A.L.C.O.L.M. cut a constricting vine off Ramiren, who dodged a thrown potion bottle that violently hissed when it shattered against the stone wall behind him.

Stumbling back, almost tripping over a snaking vine that had begun to wind its way up my leg, I gritted my teeth and charged the mischief hag again. As I ran, my shield raised, another bottle flew in my direction. It broke against the metal and smoke rose up from the splatter. I reached her and swiped downward with my sword, only for her to disappear in another puff of smoke and then reappear on the other side of the cavern.

She cackled with delight. "I don't care what Mistress said! *You're dead!*"

Mistress? Who?

I looked over at Raewyn again, who had been knocked unconscious by a black bolt from the mischief hag, to make sure she wasn't being hurt by the splatters. I had just enough time to ensure she still breathed before getting back into the fight. My healing would take too long, and Ramiren couldn't handle her on his own.

Georgina sat by Raewyn, looking through my sister's pouch and muttering, "I know you have potions, Rae. You took them from the first hag." She unstoppered one and gave it a sniff, then immediately recoiled.

"Ew, perfume." Georgina tossed it over her shoulder where it shattered behind her. She dug for another potion bottle.

M.A.L.C.O.L.M. snipped another vine off Ramiren and both came over to join me.

"We need to be clever. She must have a weakness," Ramiren said to me.

I agreed, thinking but coming up empty.

Georgina sniffed at another bottle and gagged. "More perfume." She, too, threw that behind her.

"I'm open to suggestions!" I rasped, moving off to the side to try to flank the hag.

"Hm, no idea what this is," Georgina shrugged, tossing that one over her shoulder as well.

Raewyn is going to be so mad when she wakes up.

Ramiren huffed, moving to the hag's opposite side. "What if we threw something at *her*? Or a ranged weapon?"

My shield instinctively went up as another bottle came flying at me. It too broke and hissed against the metal. "Good idea. Do you have one?" I croaked out.

Ramiren dodged his own thrown bottle as he looked at me. "No, do you?"

Georgina sniffed at another bottle from Raewyn's pouch and laughed. "Oh, boy. No." *Toss. Shatter.*

I coughed and called out to Georgina as loudly as possible while we maneuvered to the hag's side, "What are you looking for?"

The gnome shrugged, as though not a care in the world while we chased the mischief hag around the vine-covered, acid-covered, glass-covered cavern. "I dunno. I'll know it when I smell it." Georgina sniffed at another vial and wrinkled her nose. "No."

Beep. "DIS-TRACT HER AND I W-ILL GET-T-T HER-R-R." M.A.L.C.O.L.M. stuttered and teetered on his feet.

I coughed again. "Georgina, do you have any ranged weapons?" I swiped at the hag again while Ramiren feinted. But, unlike the first hag, this one merely disappeared again to reappear elsewhere and start her bottle barrage anew.

"Ranged? Oh, yeah, my crossbow, in my *toolkit*. Which I *can't use right now*, Nathalia." Georgina shook her head. "Dummy."

Ramiren halted midstride and boggled at her. "Then see if she has your vial in her cupboard and get your tools back!"

Georgina blinked at Ramiren and then stood, sauntering off toward the hag's cupboard. "Well, I guess I'll go do that, then!"

Ramiren yelled back, "Good!"

I guarded her as she moved to her destination, noticing the hag heard their conversation. She turned from cackling to raging. "No, my vials are precious to me!"

But when the hag got close to Georgina, Ramiren and I worked in tandem. He lunged while I struck, so she could never attack the gnome directly. She tried throwing more bottles, but I was able to block them with my shield, giving Georgina plenty of time to find her vial.

There was a happy gasp behind me. "Got it!"

This time, the shattering of glass wasn't from the hag's barrage.

I glanced back to see Georgina digging into her bag. "Now, where is it? Ah, there it is." She lifted her hand out of her satchel, a bag that looked far too large for the gnome to carry herself, and pulled out the oddest crossbow I'd ever seen in my life. Gears, switches, hitches, and levers covered the weapon.

Georgina loaded the bolt, still behind my shield, and then hoisted it, leveling the crossbow at the hag.

The gnome cried out, triumph written on her face, "Today is a good day!" When she pulled the trigger, an icy bolt came out of the crossbow and flew into the mischief hag's chest. She screamed as she flew back into the far wall, landing hard, and then crumpled to the ground.

Raewyn opened her eyes and groaned. I smiled down at her, grateful my middling healing could at least wake her up.

"How do you feel?" I whispered, helping her sit up.

Raewyn rubbed her raw chest, where the blackness had struck her. "Ugh, like the shit on your shoe. I guess throwing *and* healing are not your strong suits, Nat."

Ramiren stood at the cupboard, looking through the various vials. He stopped and lifted a vial, turning to us, "Found the princess's vial." He smashed it at his feet without another word.

"Is Leraska's in there, Ramiren?"

As I tended to Raewyn, my gaze flickered worriedly at Ramiren occasionally while he looked through the vials. When the last vial was shattered, he looked at me with a head shake. "No. It wasn't here."

"Hm. It must be in the last mischief hag's cupboard, then."

Ramiren didn't respond.

We spent the rest of the afternoon looking around the mischief hag's cavern. At the back of the cave, we found piles upon piles of bones. Raewyn looked in her potion pouch for holy water to bless those long dead and furrowed her eyebrows in confusion, peering within. "Wait. Why is my pouch so empty?"

I answered her, or tried to, "Because G-"

Georgina loudly interrupted "Well, one hag left, eh? About that..."

Beep. "WE WI-LL HE-LP-P-P YOU KILL THE LAST HAG-G-G-G AND R-R-REPLACE THE B-B-B-BOTTLES THAT G-G-GEOR-GINA B-B-BROKE."

Raewyn stared down into her pouch with a shocked expression, as M.A.L.C.O.L.M. looked down at Georgina when she exclaimed his name.

Beep. "OH, I AM SOR-RY G-G-GEORG-INA. WER-R-RE YOU GO-ING TO SAY S-SOME-THING?"

Georgina crossed her arms, staring at M.A.L.C.O.L.M. "Well, not now. I guess we'll help, or I'll look like a dick. Thanks, M.A.L.C.O.L.M."

Beep. "Y-Y-Y-YOU ARE WEL-COME, GEOR-G-G-INA. WHY ARE YOU THAN-KING ME?"

Georgina shook her head, her pink pigtails swaying, "It's sarcasm."

Beep. "OH. D-D-DOES SAR-CASM N-N-NOT MAKE YOU LOOK LIKE A D-D-DICK?"

Georgina glared at M.A.L.C.O.L.M.

Raewyn muttered, "I really liked that perfume, though."

Chapter Nineteen
Blessings and Damnation

We backtracked, using the map, to head due west toward Wistran. And the last mischief hag.

Georgina spent her time at night tweaking and repairing M.A.L.C.O.L.M. She looked like a completely different gnome. Happy. Even humming to herself as she worked.

It was when she opened her mouth that I realized she was still the same surly gnome.

It made me smile.

Every town or village we passed in the Dead Forest was told the news that the mischief hag was dead and would bother them no longer. Some didn't believe us, thinking we were talking for attention or even coin. Others did believe and welcomed our arrival with open arms. There the harsh whispers and hostile stares disappeared, to be replaced with gratitude, even adulation.

We spent another day at the toad village. I asked after Jeffron, but we received the unfortunate news that he had gone missing shortly after we left.

Avoiding the frogs, we arrived in Elancia a few days later with blue still draped across every available surface. We were told they would stay until the cloth was completely bleached by the sun's rays, to honor the beloved elven general. Going straight to Castle Tanta, we still had to peace-bond our weapons but were let inside without a fuss.

The king was listening to his daughter sing when we arrived. Her voice was lovely, a lyric soprano that felt far more mature than her youth should allow. After her song, she thanked us profusely and promised us a private concert in the future, as it was the only thing of true worth she felt she could give. Her father was grateful beyond words, granting us each a boon of our choice.

Georgia asked for a full day's time in the Workshop with M.A.L.C.O.L.M.

Raewyn asked for money.

M.A.L.C.O.L.M. asked for another bowtie, this one with green dots. His voice box had been repaired by Georgina, so he at least requested it at an acceptable volume.

Ramiren and I decided a favor would be owed in the future.

We passed through Puldoni again, staying at The Forever Inn for nostalgia's sake. The waitress recognized Ramiren but not the rest of us. I was not surprised.

It was a week before we reached Wistran, passing through smaller towns to take advantage of warmer beds and better food.

Raewyn asked a day after passing the kingdom's border, "Leraska's grove is near here, right? Should we stop in and say hello? Give a report or something?"

Georgina nodded at her. "That's not actually a bad idea. She might have more information for us."

I did not remark on this being the second time they had agreed on something. I didn't want to ruin the moment. The Ivory Grove was marked on the map, and we followed the trail.

Leraska looked delighted to see us, extending her arms out in welcome. "You have made it! One left to defeat!"

Ramiren's gait slowed in hesitation. "That's right. How did you know?"

"News has reached me, friends. Whispers of heroes from Laeth defeating the legendary mischief hags of the Feylands. Rumors of a beautiful woman with a gleaming shield..." She indicated me.

She said to Ramiren, "Gossip of a silver-tongued broodling..." Ramiren's face went stony.

"Reports of a masked priestess spreading... joy," she said haltingly, motioning to Raewyn.

"And, of course, talk of a capable tinkerer and her loyal automaton. I hear all these things."

Ramiren tried to keep his tone even, but I could hear the edge in it. "From who? We made good time."

Leraska laughed lightly, as though unbothered by his line of questions. "Why, the wind. The birds. The sunshine. They all speak to me, Ramiren."

Ramiren's mouth went into a line. "I see. We came to see if you have any information for us about the last remaining hag, since you appear to be so knowledgeable of them."

Leraska clapped her hands once. "Why, yes! I do, as a matter of fact. The specialty of the third mischief hag. While one liked traps and scrying, and the other enjoyed potions and strangling vines, the third loves illusions. She makes you see things that aren't there."

I recalled the mirrors and shuddered.

We were allowed to wander the grove to our heart's content. The fields of flowers, bushy colorful trees, and the gentle buzzing of bees and other insects reminded me of home, purple grass and red sky notwithstanding. I wandered the gardens, smelling every flower within reach. One made me sneeze, and a few of the flowers said in gentle voices, "Bless you!"

"Oh. Th-" I stopped myself from showing gratitude toward something that may or may not be fey, furrowed my eyebrow, and walked on.

It was getting dark before I realized I was lost. The garden turned from a simple hedgerow into a labyrinth. Though not particularly adept at mazes, I didn't think there'd be any harm in walking around. How complicated could it be?

More fool me.

Turning a corner I wasn't sure I hadn't just passed two minutes before, a dull blue light caught my attention. Caution and anxiety whipped through me, until I remembered this was a protected grove. *There is nothing dangerous here.*

I approached slowly, rounding the ivy trellises, to see, under a pink flowered arch, a fist-sized globe sitting on a stone base that looked like it was made to house the round object.

What is that...

"Lost, Nathalia?"

With a startled shriek, my skeleton nearly jumped out of my skin. Turning, I saw Leraska approach with an apologetic smile. "Sorry. I didn't mean to scare you."

"Oh, it's all right. I didn't mean to pry. I was lost and saw this." I indicated the blue globe beside me.

Leraska stepped forward, touching her fingertips to it. "Yes, it's for scrying. But, sadly, it doesn't work properly."

My curiosity got the best of me. "Oh? Why not?

She held out a hand toward me. "It's a long and rather painful story. Come."

Leraska began to lead me out of the maze. I knew that mischief hags were made by druids. Leraska might be a druid, though she never outright stated she was. *Perhaps she knows who this mysterious* mistress *the second mischief hag mentioned could be?*

"Leraska, if I may. There's something I hoped you could help me with. One of the mischief hags we defeated mentioned something about a mistress. I know mischief hags are created by evil druids. Have you heard of any causing trouble?"

Leraska stopped so abruptly, I almost ran into her. I backed away with an apology. She sighed grimly. "One, yes. She was known as K'sar. She was a powerful druid, some say the most powerful. She caused a lot of destruction, but no one has seen her face for, oh, over twenty years now, I believe. People say she died, but no one really knows. It's entirely possible she created the ones you've been facing." She smiled gently. "Thank you."

"Oh. You're welcome." I blinked. "What are you thanking me for?"

"For what you're going to accomplish. Not many people can say they helped change the world."

"Well, we agreed. They're a menace. I can only imagine how repugnant the one who created them is." We continued walking. Though I appreciated her acknowledgement, I made a conscious effort not to thank her in return.

Leraska and I bid each other good night after we exited the maze. Heading over to the clearing where Ramiren and I were camped, with Raewyn and Georgina having opted to stay in the grove's cottages, it was very quiet and serene. Normally, I would join them, but I wanted to be closer to Ramiren tonight. It was full-on dark by the time I tapped on the ornate tent. "Ramiren? Are you still awake?"

From within, I heard him. "Yes, please come in."

Stepping through, my eyes immediately went to the broodling. He was sitting at a table, with several papers and books in front of him.

He did not look up from the large parchment in his hands. "Evening, Nathalia. I was just finishing up some paperwork."

I came closer to sit in the chair beside him. "Oh? For what?"

He answered, still not looking up from the parchment, "A contract that needed to be reviewed, that's all. Now that I have my whistling back, I thought I'd re-acquaint myself with the particulars."

It took all that I had to not ask or peer over his shoulder at the tiny writing on the parchment.

He rotated his head to smile at me. "What can I do for you?"

"Nothing in particular. I just wanted to see my friend. See how he was," I replied. It was true. With no thoughts of a lesson tonight, I merely wanted to be around him.

Ramiren lowered the wrinkled parchment in his hands and turned slightly in his chair to look more fully at me, his eyes staring over the rim of his glasses. He raised an eyebrow.

His disbelief made me laugh. "Truly! That's why I came."

He lifted his head and gave a warm smile. "Your friend is fine. A bit tired, but fine. We've gone a long way in a very short period of time. I'm looking forward to a long rest after this business is concluded."

"As am I. I'm just not sure where. Perhaps Camlynn. Perhaps somewhere else."

He shifted in his chair, the parchment crinkling in his hands. "Camlynn sounds nice, actually. I've enjoyed Rowin every time I stayed there."

"You know my parents. You're friends with my father. You could visit them if you came with me." My eyes widened. "Us. I meant us."

He returned to his parchment. "True. I could. I haven't seen them in years."

"How do you and my father know each other, anyway? I don't believe I ever asked."

"I had the pleasure of overseeing a pact with your father five or so years ago. I cannot discuss the terms, I am forbidden." He grinned at my astonished expression. "I adore your mother, though I wasn't sure if she was going to kiss my forehead or put an axe through it. It's that assessing smile she has. Confident and vaguely menacing."

I chuckled softly, absently wrapping a stray thread from my shirt around my finger. "If my mother wanted to put an axe through your head, you would have an axe in your head. She tends to not balk. And my father?"

A twinkle in his eyes lit his face. "Oh, he puts on a good show, stoic and hard, but he's actually a complete pillow. Also, I see where you and your sister get your mannerisms. Though Raewyn is far more like your mother, you are the split image of your father."

Chuckling louder, my smirk mirrored his. "That sounds about right." My smirk faded. "Why did you not tell me how you knew them?"

He shook his head. "It distresses you when I cannot discuss things, and I cannot discuss this. It would be teasing you with information I could not elaborate on. They were business contacts."

"Am I not also a business contact?"

He grinned again, white canines almost piercing his lip. He hummed, bobbing his head back and forth as though weighing my question. "In a sense."

My smirk returned, and the impulse to kiss him was intense. I leaned in, but his grin vanished instantly as he emphatically shook his head.

Furrowing my eyebrows, confused, I stopped and straightened. Intense embarrassment filled me with shame. I shot up from the chair, looking anywhere but him. "I... I'd better go to bed."

"Nat!"

Already disoriented and flushed, I spun to see Raewyn behind me, standing at the tent's entrance. *Did she see that?*

"Evening, Raewyn. I thought I heard someone rustling around out there," Ramiren said, smiling at her.

Oh.

Wait, did he refuse because he heard her outside or because I crossed a line?

Raewyn chuckled at Ramiren, then stepped forward to nudge me with her elbow. "Going to bed? I looked in your tent, but you weren't there."

"Oh. Yes, I was just leaving. Did you need something?"

Raewyn pouted. "My pillows. The ones here are flat and awful."

"Oh, certainly, let me get them." When looking back at Ramiren, realizing what he just averted by refusing me, he had gone back to reading his contract, humming the melody to *Seasons Change* to himself.

Ramiren called out as we left the tent, "Good night, ladies."

The next morning, Raewyn walked up to me as I was folding my tent down to stuff back into my pouch. "Ready for me to take your pillows back, Raewyn?"

She seemed distracted. "Hm? Oh, yes, but that's not why I came over here."

Dropping the tent to give her my full attention, I asked, "What did you need?"

She crossed her arms over her chest, almost petulantly. "We need to get you bedded, Nathalia."

"Oh, for-" My head dropped forward with a frustrated growl. "Blessings and damnation, Raewyn," I snapped, exhaustion and frustration leaking into my voice. "Not this stupid business again."

She spoke with certainty, "The next town, we're finding someone for you."

"That will *not* be happening." I thought of Ramiren, and how important consent and permission was for him. Raewyn, it seemed, did not receive that same lesson in her own studies. *If I had said no to Ramiren, I never would've heard another word of it.* "Now, stop it with this incessant need to invade and control my life."

She scowled. "It's not control. It's concern. You're *wasting* your life waiting for something that might not ever happen. You're being *stubborn*."

The reasons for my stubborn refusal had been outright stated. Multiple times. "Yes, and well I should be. There's one man out there for me, Raewyn." I lifted my index finger toward her. "One. And I highly doubt he's in the next town."

"Maybe you've already met him, Nat, and you just don't realize it yet. No need to point him out if you're blind, though." She smirked, then waved a hand as though unconcerned. "The next town is the capital of Wistran. It's a big place. Anything is possible."

Deciding to ignore the first part of her argument, I redirected instead. "Remember what we were told from the earliest age we could understand? Safeguard your virtue, for it is a precious thing."

Raewyn narrowed her eyes. "I think you're forgetting that Dad never told me that." She suddenly smiled brightly. "How long have Mom and Dad been married again?"

My annoyed look clearly amused her. "Twenty-seven years. You know that."

Raewyn bit her lip, as though trying to not laugh. "And you're twenty-seven. Almost twenty-eight."

What does that have to do with anything?

"Yes, Raewyn, I can do the math. I was born five months after their wedding. Mother was pregnant with me before they got married."

She smirked. "So, Dad is a hypocrite. You're following the teachings of a hypocrite."

"No, not a hypocrite. They knew they were going to be wed." I shrugged, unconcerned.

"Still, if he expects you to wait until you are married or whatever before bedding another, then he is a *do as I say, not as I do* type."

I frowned deeply.

Wait.

"No. No, that's not it at-"

"Sorry, Nat, but this is why I preferred Mom's company. He put these silly ideas in your head about purity and waiting and blah blah blah. Maybe not even on purpose. Virtue means a lot of things. Besides, do you really think Dad waited until he met Mom to lose his virginity?"

Extremely inappropriate, sister. My tired eyes burned. My head hurt, and I was well past done with this conversation. "That is not something I care to think about."

She looked genuinely confused. "Why not? You seem to believe he thinks about your virginity."

I gawked at her. "Because he's our *father*, Raewyn. His sexual history is *none* of our business, and I'd prefer to not ponder it."

She rolled her eyes, as though my words were foolish. "Parents are sexual creatures too, Nat. Otherwise, we wouldn't be here." She turned to walk away, then spun around. "And the answer is no. He did not wait. Mom told me he was quite the ladies' man while they traveled together, before they realized their love and married. So, put that in your pipe and smoke it."

Chapter Twenty
The Fey Dragon Dealer

Just one more to go.

Anticipation, fear, and more than a little anxiety, made my steps heavy. It was plain the last mischief hag was the one who stole from Raewyn and me. The one who took my creativity and my sister's beauty like they were nothing.

Years ago, I asked Raewyn if her scars ever bothered her. She told me they didn't, but that my scars did. I was confused, as I didn't have scars. She said that the scars on her skin were much easier to deal with than the scars on my heart. What's outside can be covered, but what's inside always bleeds.

It's past time to stop the bleeding.

Would we be enough to defeat her? Unlike the others, this one was in the middle of a city, possibly surrounded by followers or supplicants. *Would we have to deal with more than just her?*

These thoughts, and more, bent my spirit and my shoulders.

We traveled on the dirt road, thankfully dry but no less dusty, with thick forest on either side. Heavy winds whipped through the red, gold, and orange trees, tossing the leaves and branches about wildly. Raewyn ended up pulling her long hair out of her mouth more than once, eventually having to borrow a length of leather to tie it back like I did. The birds were noticeably quiet. I looked overhead and spotted dark clouds on the horizon, in the direction we were traveling.

A storm is coming.

Above the howl of the wind, I heard humming ahead. And what sounded like animal cries.

We rounded the small bend to see a short fey standing next to a large cart pulled by two blue-colored mules. The fey's hairy goat-like legs ended in black hooves and his upper body was humanoid and bare, except for the multitude of bone and ivory necklaces tangling in unruly and copious amounts of chest hair. *Capra fey.*

Several elven soldiers, all dressed differently, milled about bored while they all hummed the same unfamiliar tune.

Mercenaries. Almost certainly.

Inside the cart were a dozen small wicker cages, stacked up three high and each filled with a strange and fantastical animal I'd never seen before. They all were crying and mewling pitifully. Suffering.

Halting, it took a moment for my brain to catch up to exactly what I was seeing. The shock of it blanked my thoughts. Until it didn't.

My hackles rose up like a swift tide, and my hand flew to the grip of my sword.

Fucking Dark Drop.

Red anger made me assess whether or not I could take the entire band myself. I counted ten mercenaries, all well-armed and very large, and the bastard fey who appeared to be the leader.

M.A.L.C.O.L.M. could take a few, same as me. Ramiren, maybe one or two. Raewyn, maybe one or two. Georgina? I'm not sure...

Then, a hand on my arm, Raewyn's hand, made me stop to really consider the situation. *Georgina is not a trained warrior. Ramiren has some training, but it's not his specialty. Raewyn is no shrinking violet, but that matters little against a practiced blade wielded by someone whose job is violence.*

That leaves me and the automaton.

I can't do that to them.

A deep breath allowed me to calm myself enough to think clearly. *We can't win by brute force, and even if we did win, we'd get hurt, possibly killed.*

"I said, get in there!" the capra fey yelled at the creature before him.

It looked like a tiny dragon, except for the vibrant pink and purple butterfly wings that sprouted from its back. Its white iridescent scales shimmered even in the dim light as though lit from within. Its tiny spiked head lowered at the harsh command, and its ears pulled down as though afraid. It mewed like a cat and slunk into the cage as the fey slammed the door shut.

No. We have to win in another way.

I shot Ramiren a hard look that hopefully conveyed my intentions and approached the cart, the others following behind. Raewyn squeezed my arm and whimpered, "We need to-"

"I know." I called out to the group, "Sir, what are you doing?"

It was supposed to come out as a simple, curious question, but my anger hadn't entirely receded. Even to my ears, it sounded more like an accusation than an inquiry.

The capra fey wheeled around and grabbed a pitchfork from the side of the cart, waving it at us. "No closer! These are mine!" The elven mercenaries woke up from their stupor and rushed over, forming a semicircle around the fey with their weapons half-drawn.

I stopped in the middle of a step at his threat. There wasn't enough coin on me to purchase them all. We couldn't take the mercenaries and steal the animals. And we couldn't just leave.

Instantly, it came to me.

Feint like Ramiren.

"I have a longsword. My broodling friend here has a rapier. My sister really likes animals, and this gnome has an angry automaton. Do you truly think a pitchfork and some hapless thugs would stop us if we had planned to take everything you owned?"

"Might be. Might be your weapons are for show, aye? Now, what can I do for you, whore?"

I channeled my mother with what was hopefully a menacing smile.

"If I may..." Ramiren stepped forward, and extended his arms to his sides, both as a greeting and to show he had no weapons. "Friend, perhaps we might come to an arrangement. I am guessing you capture and sell these animals?"

"Aye, and what's it to you?" He lowered the pitchfork slightly and eyed Ramiren with a squinty glare. "You mean to buy?"

"I have money! I have lots of money!" Raewyn exclaimed behind me.

The fey's eyes twitched Raewyn's way, and he grinned, his teeth showing more gold than white. "Yeah? Well, isn't that nice. I don't deal in money, bitch. I deal in favors."

"Then, how would the favor of the King of Tanta sound, hm?" Ramiren said, his tone enticing.

The fey's pointed ears perked up, and he fully lowered his pitchfork. "Might do. Might do. How would you go about giving that to me, hm?"

Ramiren replied smoothly. "I am a pactmaker, fey. I have a favor owed to me by that very same king. I would be willing to transfer that favor to you via a contract."

"Pactmaker, eh?" The fey looked around at his mercenaries. "No funny business, hear."

"Of course not. Now, the question remains. What would that favor be worth to you?" The magical scroll puffed into existence again, the one he used to jot down Leraska's directions and my own pact details, and began to record everything said with an invisible hand.

The fey looked back to his cart and hummed. "Your group may choose one."

Raewyn whispered, "One? Just one?" I looked back to see tears brimming in her eyes.

"I accept those terms." Ramiren stepped forward. "Though a pact requires payment to the pactmaker. Give me another, and I will deem it paid."

The fey gritted his teeth at Ramiren. For a moment, I thought he would back out and refuse, but he finally nodded. "Fine, but only if the red bitch and the dumb whore choose them."

Ramiren kept his face placid as he inclined his head in agreement. "The King of Tanta's favor for one of Raewyn's choice and one of Nathalia's choice. As we are giving a favor, an intangible item instead of something appreciable or a service, the pact cannot be dissolved. If you are agreeable, the pact is sealed."

The fey replied, as though he had been waiting to say the words, "Aye. The pact is sealed."

Ramiren's eyes flashed like a campfire. "I assume you are aware of the consequences of a broken pact?"

"Aye, I'm aware."

Ramiren looked back at Raewyn's teary face. His voice and eyes softened. "You choose one."

"The little white dragon. With the butterfly wings. Please," Raewyn said quietly.

"The white dragon is the first," Ramiren said, turning back around.

"Oh, the fey dragon?" The fey looked over his shoulder at the cart and seemed to consider a moment. "Good. That one gives me trouble anyway. And the second?"

Ramiren looked at me. "You choose."

I would sooner choose a favorite book. All deserve protection. Including animals.

My eyes washed over the animals. Some looked at me. Some looked at each other or their surroundings. Most kept their eyes on the fey, their tormentor. All of them were dirty and hunched, stuffed into too small cages for far too long.

The fey stomped his hoof into the dirt like a child. "Hurry up, whore."

I need all of them set free. But how?

Ramiren murmured to me, "You can choose anything in front of you, Nathalia. *Anything.*"

But the only thing in front of me is...

Oh.

I wondered if it would work. I prayed it would work.

My eyes dropped to the fey glaring at me. "I choose you, capra fey."

He straightened and screwed his face. "Eh? Are you simple, too? I said 'choose one *animal*.'"

"Mm. No, you said 'choose one'. You did not specify the animals. I choose you to take."

"Hmm, it seems she's right," Ramiren intoned in what I knew to be artificial surprise, looking over the hovering scroll as he tapped his bearded chin. "You did not specify an animal in the cart." Ramiren let that statement hang in the air as he turned his attention to the fey in front of me. "You simply said 'choose one' and failed to define what we were to choose."

The fey sputtered, "Well, that's silly! You knew what I meant!"

Ramiren hummed, still reading over the scroll. He spoke absently, "Perhaps you thought we, being not fey, were easy pickings. After all, if *we* failed to specify correctly, you could have handed us whatever animal you liked."

The fey looked at his mercenaries, who all shrugged. He turned back to us and shrieked in rage, "Double crossers!"

Time to pounce. "No more than you tried to do to us. I will, of course, take the rest of the animals in your stead." I smiled widely, hopefully not betraying my utter glee.

"Whore! Dumb, stupid whore!" The fey's face had turned a curious shade of purple.

Call me whatever you want. In fact, it's making this that much sweeter. "Rant and rave all you'd like, fey. The choice is now yours. You or the rest of your animals?"

"I dissolve the pact, then!"

Ramiren eyed the fey with a smirk. "You cannot. The only way to dissolve it is to break it, and you know what might happen then."

The look in the enraged fey's eyes as he measured us, to see if his mercenaries could maybe take us in a fight, had my hand creeping to my sword's grip. After a few seconds, he shook his head and huffed, throwing his pitchfork down. "Fine. Take them all, whore. Now, give me that contract with the king's favor."

A second scroll appeared in the air. It rolled up and lowered into Ramiren's upturned hand. "My favor is now yours." Ramiren smiled, elongated canines showing.

The fey snatched it out of Ramiren's hand. "Let's go. Fucking pactmakers..."

They unloaded the cart, putting cages on the ground by the side of the road. As they faded off into the distance, heading the way we came, Ramiren looked at me with pride in his eyes. "Excellent, Lady Nathalia. Though if he had accepted going with us, the pact would have invalidated itself. Non-binding, as though it never existed. I cannot enslave others with a pact. I refused to take that particular training."

My heart leapt at the look he gave me. "I recall you saying something to that effect." My smile turned crooked. "But he didn't know that."

"No, he did not know that." Ramiren beamed at me and walked toward the cages as Raewyn tackled me in a tight hug.

Georgina, having been silent this whole time, raised an eyebrow. "And just what are we gonna do with a dozen animals?"

Beep. "Play with the fluffies!"

Though no longer screaming since Georgina fixed his voice box, M.A.L.C.O.L.M. exclaimed so excitedly that a few of the caged birds squawked in fright.

Beep. "Oh. Sorry."

Ramiren's tent was the only one big enough to house all of the animals we had suddenly adopted. Raewyn spent her time there wrangling them while everyone else set up the camp to the side of the road. Georgina and M.A.L.C.O.L.M. found a small stream cutting through the forest to the south and fished for the animals' supper. Ramiren was kind enough to set up my and Raewyn's tents.

I started the fire, listening to Raewyn sing to the animals softly. After putting a pot of beans and rice on the fire and washing my hands, I looked in, seeing several animals playing on the feather bed. Some of them had ripped the stuffing loose from the mattress and were chasing the floating feathers around the interior.

A few huddled around Raewyn as she pet and cuddled them on the floor. Those animals that were too skittish were given space, food, and something soft to sleep on. A couple birds sat perched on M.A.L.C.O.L.M.'s shoulders as they cleaned their feathers. His eyes blinked a soft green, and he did not move or speak for fear of scaring the brightly-colored creatures again.

Even Georgina was playing with what looked to be a tiny orange bear cub who now seemed happy to have a full belly.

Sitting at his table, with a winged cat lay across his shoulders, Ramiren read a book quietly as though completely unbothered by the madness surrounding him. It purred and raised its head at my approach.

"Looks like you made a new friend," I said, smiling.

Ramiren grinned, but he did not move except to reach up a hand to scratch at the winged cat's ears.

Though not relishing this conversation, I knew it was needed. "We need to figure out what to do with these animals."

Raewyn looked up from the dark green miniature pony she was feeding clover to and pouted. "Can't we keep them?"

Without hesitation, I shook my head. "I don't think so, Raewyn. We still have a mischief hag to defeat. We'll need to release them."

Georgina frowned. "But they might die!"

"They almost certainly will die if they stay with us, Georgina. We are in no fit state to care for them."

"There might be another way," said Ramiren.

"Oh?" The fey dragon perched at the end of Ramiren's bed trilled at me, demanding attention.

Ramiren half-closed his book. "Perhaps this seems obvious, but what about the grove? Maybe they can be taken there. We're not that far away, and a druid's grove is a sanctuary. I saw many cared for animals there. I have some unconfirmed suspicions about her, but I believe she genuinely helps animals."

My hand extended to rub under the fey dragon's chin. It moved its chin forward and purred much like the cat still lounging on Ramiren. "The grove is an excellent idea. I wish I had thought of that." The entirety of what he'd said finally registered. "What suspicions?"

He reopened his book. "As I said, unconfirmed ones. I still don't know what she's getting out of the mischief hag's defeat, and that troubles me. Much like Lord Dalson, there might be a hidden agenda. Something to gain. I just can't see what." He turned a page in the book roughly.

There was nothing to say to that. Admitting I too had my doubts about her, at least in the beginning, would only muddy what we came here to do: kill the mischief hags and reclaim what was taken. If she indeed benefitted from their removal, beyond peace and safety, I couldn't see it either, and my commenting on it would only add opinions, not facts.

"Leraska will take care of you, precious," Raewyn scratched the ears of an especially fluffy wolf pup, who pawed at her hands playfully.

That night, the threatened storm arrived. Above the whistling of the wind, the pelting of the rain, and the thunder, I could hear a man's beautiful voice rising and falling in a lullaby, no doubt for the animals' benefit. It was an old song, melodic and soothing.

So, he can *sing.*

The next morning, we backtracked to the grove. Leraska was more than happy to take the creatures under her care, and when we told her how we acquired them, she burst into joyful laughter.

"Tricking fey is no small feat, Nathalia. I am glad I set you on this path."

I gave a small smile. "I'm afraid we will leave you with abused, skinny animals, Leraska, but you are the best person we know to care for them."

Leraska peered mournfully at the fey dragon fluttering at my side. "Don't worry. We'll love and fatten them up. These creatures will be well taken care of, I assure you."

Georgina, cuddling the tiny bear cub in her arms, gave it a final scratch on the head and murmured to it. She placed it on the ground, where it ran over to the waiting arms of another druid at the grove. The tinkerer sniffed, and Ramiren placed a hand on her shoulder. "The creature will be cared for, Georgina."

"I know." Georgina sniffled again. "But I named him Rufus."

"Rufus will be all right," Ramiren said softly.

Georgina's lower lip began to tremble, and she turned away.

After we gave our thanks, without actually saying thank you, we took to the road again, bound for the capital.

Chapter Twenty-One
Old Friends in New Places

"State your business," said the gate guard.

"We are travelers seeking rest and refuge, sir," I replied.

He eyed me with suspicion, noting my weapons and armor. At least, I thought he was. He was covered head to toe in bulky armor, including a full faceplate. I couldn't even tell what type of fey he was. He looked at the other guard with him, who shrugged.

My pleasant smile stayed in place.

We're here to save you, idiot.

The guard questioned again, "How long are you planning to stay, then?"

I hummed in thought. "Not long, a few days, then we'll go our merry way."

The guard grunted in his throat. "Alright. You may pass."

We started to enter, but I stopped just before going through. "One question, though. Do you know of a comfortable inn to stay at?"

That seemed to change the guard's demeanor, as though our story was more believable. "Aye. The Black Unicorn Inn should suit you fine. It's just up the main road on your right."

I nodded my thanks and looked back toward everyone. "Shall we?"

As we walked through the gates of Carpatha, the dinginess of the capital city of Wistran struck me. It was midday, but it looked dark, like a bleak miasma blanketed the entire capital. A vaguely smoky scent filled the air, as though there was a large fire filled with wet wood somewhere in the area.

"Gods, it feels like death in here. Even more than Elancia," my sister murmured.

As we sauntered past, only a handful of people met our eyes, and the ones who did narrowed their own in wariness. *This had to be the mischief hag's doing.*

The wide avenue leading through the city was quiet for a major capital at this time of day, at least I thought so. A creaky hanging blade sign, showing a black unicorn in full gallop, made us stop.

As we walked in, the dimness outside was mirrored by the stifling interior's atmosphere. The brightly painted walls, merry fire, and smell of fresh bread did little to encourage any positive reaction to the place.

Seeing no barkeep, we glanced around. Confused, I said aloud, "Hello?"

"What do you want?" boomed a nasally voice. A rotund, dark gray fey with a dirty apron came out from a back room, wiping his hands on a cloth . He threw the cloth across his shoulder and leaned in with his meaty hands spread on the dingy bartop. He glared at me, raising his eyebrows.

Ceta fey. Like Lord Leviathus.

"Rooms, please. Four."

He frowned. "You got coin?"

"We do." I reached into my pouch. "How much?"

His eyes ran over us and said smugly. "One gold a night. For each of you."

Raewyn sucked in a breath. "Awfully steep."

"Do you want rooms or not?" The barkeep tried to sound intimidating, but the sound was more clogged oboe than ruffian.

A handful of coins hitting the bartop pulled his attention away from my sister. I eyed the barkeep with what I hoped was a neutral expression. "The cost is fine."

He poked through the small pile of gold coins, counting them. "That metal thing too. It needs to pay."

"But he's sharing with me," Georgina protested.

"I said him too, girl," he said to Georgina, though his eyes stayed on me. "The charge is per occupant, not per room."

When I pulled out more coin, and plunked them down beside the others, I said shortly, "Fine."

The coins disappeared in his hand, and he gave a broad smile. "Welcome to the Black Unicorn Inn." He fished under the bar and pulled out four keys, each with a tag. "Here are your keys. Breakfast is at eight, sharp. Supper is at six, sharp. Miss it? Too bad."

I grunted as a reply. The barkeep turned to go back to his work as I started to dole out the keys to my companions.

"That much gold could buy us a decent stay at the Green Dragon Resort in Camlynn, Nat," my sister whispered.

Though I normally would have cared, my fatigue stopped my tongue from arguing and my feet from finding someplace else. "I know, but we won't be here for more than a few days, then we go home. It's possible we might have the same welcome in every other inn, and I'm tired."

We went upstairs to get settled. We would need time to send word to Lord Dalson that we were here and awaiting his assistance in getting access to the castle. And I had no idea how long that would take.

Ramiren's room was right across the hall from mine, as though it was planned.

It was late in the day by the time we managed to hire a messenger to take a message to Lord Dalson. The exorbitant price was not surprising. The city seemed to enjoy hustling strangers.

We barely made it to dinner on time. The barkeep was displeased with our tardiness, but he set out plates for us just the same. Overly-roasted meat that looked like the unknown animal had died years ago, tough bread, sour wine, and plainly dressed beans made up our fare. Raewyn choked the food down, but only just. Georgina stopped halfway through and pushed her plate away with a grimace. Ramiren chugged the wine. I took one bite of the beans and decided to have the rations from my pouch once I got back up to my room.

As we waited for Lord Dalson to reply, we kept quiet and to ourselves so as to not draw attention, except we went outside the inn for food. The innkeeper continued to receive five gold a day. On the third day, he had exchanged his dirty apron for an embroidered doublet that looked a size too small, no doubt affordable due to the sudden windfall of our presence and my dwindling coin reserve.

Finally, that night, an intricately folded piece of vellum, sealed with gold wax, slid under my door.

"*Meet at the castle gates tomorrow at noon.*"

It was not signed, and it didn't need to be. Knocking on doors to alert the others, we all gathered in Georgina's room with the message in hand.

"Trap?" Ramiren asked, passing the note to Raewyn to look at.

Georgina raised her goggles to the top of her head, leaving oily rings of residue around her eyes. "Could be, but if it is, then he's going to have some explaining to do about that letter you intend to send."

"I can't send it if I'm dead," Ramiren said grimly.

I took the vellum back from my sister and tapped it against my palm. "We will be wary and cautious, but he might be dealing right with us. He has much to gain from her demise, does he not?"

Ramiren's lips pressed into a thin line. "He does. Or perhaps he plans to bargain for his mines with our hides."

Raewyn narrowed her eyes playfully at Ramiren. "You have a cynical mind."

He placed his hands behind his back, standing tall, and cleared his throat. "You have to, in my line of work."

The way to Wistran's royal castle was far more open than in Elancia. No checkpoints, surprisingly, but that could have been due to the fact the Tanta general was possibly murdered.

The castle and spires were made of a glittery gray stone that would've shone beautifully in the sunlight had there been any. Many of the banners and flags waving from walls and parapets were ragged. Some were hanging by mere threads. The lawns were brown and dry, despite the deluge we'd received not long ago. No courtiers milled about.

This place looks abandoned.

We arrived at the wrought-iron castle gates precisely at noon to see Lord Dalson surrounded by and talking animatedly to a handful of guards. He smiled jovially at our approach. "Friends! You have come! I was just telling these fine gentlemen that you requested a tour of the castle, and that I was happy to oblige."

Ramiren gave a bright smile to Dalson in return. "That would be correct. We don't have many chances to tour the grand homes of royalty. It would be an honor to see it firsthand."

One of the guards, presumably the captain, stepped forward. "And *we* told him that was not possible. The king and queen are not accepting visitors."

Oh, not this again.

"Merely a tour. A taste, gentlemen! I have been here many times and can guide them myself." Lord Dalson fidgeted, his knuckles turning white as he clutched his gold badge of office. I could see sweat begin to coat his forehead, even at a distance.

"No can do, Lord Dalson. Our apologies, but it just isn't going to happen."

Lord Dalson gritted his teeth and muttered harshly to the guard captain, "We had an agreement!"

The guard captain smirked and made no attempt to whisper. "Oh yeah? And what agreement would that be?"

Dalson's face turned a shade of red. "You know damned well what it was. I paid good coin for-"

"Coin? I don't see any coin. Do you, boys?" The guard captain looked behind him at the others, who shook their heads innocently.

This is falling apart.

Ramiren huffed in annoyance, though it was so exaggerated I wasn't sure if it was real or just an act. "Very well. I told you this farce wouldn't work, Lord Dalson." The earl paled and began to sputter until Ramiren interrupted, addressing the captain. "The prince is expecting us."

It took all I had to not look at Ramiren in shock.

The guards all snapped their heads toward Ramiren. The captain balked. "What did you say?"

Ramiren raised an eyebrow. "I said, the prince is expecting us."

Lord Dalson stuttered. "He is, I'm afraid. Prince Jaylin is most anxious to-"

The guard captain held up his hand to silence Lord Dalson, without even looking at him. He kept his eyes on Ramiren. "And what does His Highness want with you?"

"This woman, specifically," he said, indicating Raewyn. "A priestess of Minue. We had thought to keep it quiet for Prince Jaylin's privacy, but you forced our hand."

Raewyn winked at the guards.

The captain flushed at Raewyn's attention, but he regained his bearings quickly. "Yeah? And why are the rest of you with her, then?"

"I am a pactmaker, brought in to ensure the pact that this priestess will have with him is legitimate. The woman in armor is my guard, as is the automaton. The gnome is my servant, wretched girl that she is."

Goodly gods of the Tarindar, please let Georgina play along.

Georgina made a noise in her throat but did not say anything.

Beep. "Georgina says I am a protector. So, I protect."

The guards looked at each other, nervously, before the captain spoke again, this time with a bit less skepticism, "A pact, you say?"

Ramiren nodded slowly. "Yes, that is correct."

The captain narrowed his eyes. "Show me proof that you're a pactmaker."

Ramiren waved his hand, and the scroll of parchment appeared next to him in a cloud of purple smoke. I scrunched my nose at the unexpected smell of sulfur in the air. A loud raven's cry echoed, and the guards looked around, spooked. Their eyes shifted nervously from Ramiren to the scroll, and all of them stepped back. "What is that?" one asked, pointing.

"My pact ledger. It records the exact wording of a pact to ensure fidelity and adherence."

As he spoke, his words appeared in letters on the scroll.

The guards inched forward slowly, mouths open in astonishment.

"Now." Ramiren waved his hand again, and the scroll disappeared, startling the guards. "Shall you open the gate or shall we inform the prince that you would not let his new lover pass?"

"Well, shit," the captain muttered. "Fine. But only you and the priestess. No one else."

"No. All or nothing, I insist," Ramiren glared at him in defiance. "I go nowhere without my guards and servant."

The captain rolled his eyes. "Oh, think you'll get jumped in the castle, eh?"

Ramiren hummed, as though unimpressed by his question. "My business is dangerous, and an assassin can hide in an alcove just as easily as an alleyway. I'm sure you and your guards are capable, but I can't be too careful. Allow my guards to take the brunt of the labor, captain."

The captain frowned deeply, then sighed. "Alright. Let them through."

The guards went to open the gates while Lord Dalson rushed to Ramiren, sweat now dripping down his face. "Our deal?"

"Still intact, Lord Dalson. No one will hear of your preferences from me, spoken or otherwise. You're as safe as a..." Ramiren smiled broadly, his sharp canines showing. "...diapered babe."

I looked at Ramiren curiously at his wording.

Lord Dalson turned a shade of purple but said nothing as we strolled past him through the now open gates.

As we entered the castle, the dank and dark of the city seemed to be magnified. Paintings, covered in a thick layer of dust and grime, hung crookedly on the walls on either side of the grand foyer. The largest painting depicted a family, presumably the royal family based upon the crowns they wore. The king stood, regal, his blond hair streaming behind him. *Leo fey.* The willowy queen posed in front of him, dignified and emotionless with her white hair curled over one shoulder. *Muste fey.* At their feet sat a young boy, the split image of the king, with a kitten in his arms.

"Where to?" Raewyn asked quietly.

I lifted my hand to point. "That looks like the Grand Hall ahead, with the doors ajar. Perhaps start there."

We moved toward the open doors, my hand on my hilt and my shield ready.

Chapter Twenty-Two
Voices in the Dark

We squeezed through the partially open doors of the Grand Hall. The doors wouldn't open the rest of the way due to their weight, but we also didn't try too hard. In this place, if the hinges protested, the squeal would certainly echo.

We passed between skewed broken long tables and chairs that had not been used in quite a while. Broken plates and crumbled bits of stone dotted the floor. Dust motes floated in the still air, dancing in the shafts of light that filtered in through the dirty, damaged windows above. The enormous hearths on either side were cold and caked in layers of soot. I held my longsword in front of me as I crept, careful of the shattered stone among the debris of the expansive room.

Slow footsteps at my back assured me my companions followed closely behind.

Up on the raised dais at the far side of the room sat an older fey man and woman on thrones. They wore dusty crowns covered in cobwebs and resembled older versions of those in the large portrait. I couldn't tell if they were alive or dead from here; they did not move at all.

"Your Majesties?" I called out and immediately regretted my decision, as the sound bounced off the bare walls. I closed my eyes, inwardly cursing myself.

"Yeeeees?" a high-pitched voice, like silverware scraping on a plate, replied.

The eyes flew open, and terror stiffened my limbs. *That voice. I remember that voice.*

A short creature with squinty eyes and a twisted mouth far too large for her face peeked out from behind the two thrones, as though playing. She had not changed even a scraggly hair on her bulbous head. "Boo!"

She giggled, and my stolen breath left me in a wheezing gasp.

Suddenly, I was a child again, screaming, demanding she leave us alone. I sucked in a shaky breath, and the mischief hag, my mischief hag, gave a rotten smile.

"I remember your scent, girl. Come to give me another gift?" She sniffed the air and groaned. "You have so many now, far more than you had when you were younger. Oh, you are ripe for plucking. Mmm, and your sweet sister too. What gifts you may give to me in tribute."

Ramiren snapped me out of my fog. "You've taken enough, hag. We've come to reclaim."

The hag chortled, clapping her spindly hands together. "Oh, you have gifts as well. Gifts aplenty!" She sniffed the air again. "Mmm, what a banquet you have put before me."

I blinked and then recoiled at the sudden brightness enveloping me, like stepping from a dark tunnel into overwhelming sunlight. I held my hand up against it. My eyes slowly adjusted, and I realized I was in the Hall of Mirrors again. And alone. Spinning this way and that, all I could see was myself reflected in the mirrors an infinite number of times. Panic rose. I swallowed hard through a nearly closed throat and shut my eyes, remembering Leraska's words.

I whispered, "She makes you see things. She makes you see things. I am not here."

There was an echoing cackle that seemed to come from all sides. Then, the scent of blood hit me as a coppery tang filled the air and coated my tongue. My eyes opened again, and a horrified scream erupted from me.

At my feet lay Ramiren, his red, lifeless eyes staring up at the ceiling, a hole in his chest where his heart should have been. Beside him was Raewyn, her twisted body laid out and bloody. Off to the side was Georgina, hanging from M.A.L.C.O.L.M.'s scissors, impaled, while M.A.L.C.O.L.M. twitched uncontrollably.

How long was I in the Hall of Mirrors? Long enough for her to kill them?

Stumbling backwards, turning my eyes away as bile rose in my throat, I couldn't tell if this was real or illusion. The trickle of gore from Georgina's corpse pooled under her, resonating in a loud, constant drip. My sister's delicate mask was broken with the shards scattered around as though it had burst. I could feel the anguish and fear on Ramiren's face, frozen in death, as though it were my own.

Clenching my teeth, I covered my ears when a voice that sounded like Ramiren's thrown whispers came from his still form, but my hands couldn't stop me from hearing it. "You failed."

"No... This isn't real. This can't be real. He needs to speak to whisper." I shook my head to clear it. "Wake up! Wake up! Wake up!"

But he didn't need to speak to call for you before, in the tent.

When the scene remained the same, a whimper, then a cry of pain broke from me as I crumpled to the ground next to Ramiren and pulled him into my lap. Rocking back and forth, I placed my lips to his forehead gently as a sob wracked me. "I'm sorry. I'm so sorry."

My creativity wasn't worth this. Nothing is.

My whole body felt numb except for the agony piercing my chest like a white-hot poker. Another sob had me gasping, and I held him tighter.

My fingers clutched at the jacket, at his breast, to cover the gruesome wound. I didn't want to see it. When my fingers touched something cold, I looked and saw the luck stone my mother gave to me, that I then gave to Ramiren.

He wore it.

Rubbing the jewel with my thumb to clean it of blood, something about it caught my eye.

Wait...

I leaned in closer and squinted, but the color did not change.

The stone was no longer a smoky gray with a plain setting, but pure onyx with gold filigree surrounding the gem.

The numbness I'd felt was immediately replaced with coldness, as though I'd been dunked in ice water. My jaw dropped as the chain jingled in my shaking hand.

The coldness evaporated, leaving the warmth of hope behind.

She got a detail wrong.

I carefully placed Ramiren's body down on the ground. In my heart, I knew it was an illusion but still couldn't bring myself to throw him off my lap. Picking up my sword and standing, my next words were spoken as a statement of fact and not a desperate plea. Not a question. "This isn't real. I deny it."

When nothing happened, I screamed, shrill and defiant, echoing my rage, "I deny it!"

The bodies disappeared. Even the smell of blood went away.

A battle in progress faded in. Panicked yells merged with amused cackles in the vast chamber. Ramiren was forced to continuously dance away from a barrage of green bolts shooting from the hag's hands, making a strike with his rapier almost impossible. M.A.L.C.O.L.M. swung his fists at something only he could see. Raewyn appeared to be in a trance of some sort. *The mischief hag must have bewitched her too.*

Georgina stared at me, wide-eyed as she loaded another bolt into her crossbow. "Oh. Good. You're awake now." She aimed and fired, but the icy shot went wide. It hit one of the crooked tables behind the hag, splintering the wood in a small explosion.

The hag dodged Ramiren's sudden lunge and tsked at Georgina. "Naughty, naughty! How the tables turn!"

Georgina shrieked and wheeled her arms when the table she was standing on tilted, sending her tumbling to the ground in a pink-haired heap.

Tightening my grip on my longsword, I stalked toward the hag, who was playfully twirling in a grotesque imitation of a dancer's spin.

I pushed M.A.L. out of the way firmly with my shield and bashed it into the back of the hag's skull. She stumbled and swung around to look at me. Her face lit up at the idea of a new toy to torment. "Oh, welcome back, sweetie!"

Without looking, she used one hand to continue her attack on Ramiren as black lightning danced along the yellowed fingertips of the other, but before her incantation could complete, I stepped closer and struck, slicing halfway through her wrist with my sword's well-honed edge. The lightning fizzled out as her amusement became screams. She gaped at her hand, now hanging limp and useless. Her face, already sallow, paled even further and a look of fear passed over her eyes. She cried out pitifully, "Mistress, you promised!"

There was no verbal reply. Nothing pithy or clever or even angry. No taunts or mocking comments. I merely raised my longsword and bore it down on her as hard as I could. The sound of a sharp crunch, of bones snapping under my blow, did not satisfy me.

My sword lifted again, and swung down again. Again. And again. And again. Green blood splattered across my face, though I felt no sting. My strikes quickened, lifting up then swinging down. Distant sounds of a feral scream, accompanied by the sound of wet cracking, harmonized with my assault as I drove my steel into her over and over.

This was no longer a fight but an exorcism. A purging of misery and loss. Eighteen years of living with half a heart channeled through me and fueled my blade now. Tears blurred my vision. I could only see the vague shape of her, but it was enough of a target to continue.

I heard my sister's voice, as though she were far away, "Nat? Nathalia!"

I felt strong hard hands, metal fingers scraping against the metal of my armor, on my shoulders, but I roughly shrugged them off.

She still hasn't paid for all she's done.

I heard Georgina yell, a little clearer than Raewyn's call, "Nathalia, she's dead! Gods, you can stop now!"

No, not enough. Not near enough.

Ramiren's gentle question finally broke through the cloud in my mind. "Angel?"

I halted my swing, sword raised above my head and primed for another downward strike, and realized I was out of breath. Feeling almost confused, I looked around but said nothing, and neither did anyone else.

I peered down to see the pile of bones, sinew, blood, and offal that had once been the mischief hag, now mutilated beyond all recognition. My sword finally lowered then dropped from my hand, clattering to the floor when Raewyn ran toward me.

My teary eyes shut as I collapsed to my knees and into Raewyn's enveloping arms. I leaned into her comfort. Though much smaller, she held me up without wavering as I clutched at her and wept.

"Ready?"

I smiled tiredly down at Raewyn and gave a single firm nod. "Ready."

We clinked our vials together, like wine glasses, and simultaneously threw them to the stone floor.

They shattered in a spray of tiny shards, the golden mist floating upwards. I watched as the mist curled around my legs then dissipated.

I waited.

And waited some more.

Nothing.

There was no change. I didn't feel any different.

I didn't know what to expect, but *nothing* wasn't it.

My disappointment almost swallowed me.

Raewyn gasped, and my head snapped up. She had taken off her mask and was touching her face, where her scars were. Or, rather, had been. They were gone, leaving unblemished, peachy skin behind.

"Ah! I am back!" Raewyn crowed. "Let's see them keep the high priesthood from me now!"

I turned away so Raewyn wouldn't see the unhappiness on my face. The Great Hall, which had reverted back to a clean, warm room immediately after the hag's death. Another illusion, we surmised. The king and queen, or what we thought were the king and queen, had disappeared along with the dust and the crooked tables. I was glad that wasn't another issue we'd have to deal with.

The clanging of heavy armored footsteps running just outside the hall caught my attention.

A group of soldiers, led by a tall fey with a regal bearing, entered the large room. His golden hair was pulled back from the sides of his face and reached past his shoulders. He held a thinner blade in his right hand tightly, with no shield in the other. His shaven square jaw was set firmly, as though preparing himself for what he would find. He was tall and broad-shouldered but wore no armor. Bright gray eyes searched the area before landing on us. He looked like a younger version of the king from the painting.

He must be the prince.

The prince approached us slowly, carefully, his sword tip lowered so as to not appear hostile. Instead, he looked curious. "She is dead, then?" he asked me.

I inclined my head in respect to his station. "She is, Your Highness."

A look of surprise crossed his features. "Have we met?"

"No, but a noble can recognize royalty easily enough." I tried to manage a smile, but my mouth barely twitched.

He stared at me, as though transfixed, until one of his footmen cleared his throat. "Prince Jaylin? Orders?"

"Hm? Oh, yes. These individuals have done what not even my army could. They will be treated with all due respect and decorum," he said in a commanding tone.

He faced me again as he stepped forward. "Your name, lady?"

"Lady Nathalia Swordhand, Your Highness. And this is my sis-"

He spoke softly, as though he were hypnotized, "Nathalia. A beautiful name for a beautiful woman."

My cheeks burned.

I rushed to a local bathhouse after slipping away from Prince Jaylin's heaping praise and the royal guard's scrutiny, desperate to get the day off of me with soap and scalding hot water. As soon as my room's door closed, I searched my pouch for parchment and a lead pencil. I plopped down at the desk, pencil tip ready and hovering over the blank sheet.

But nothing came to me.

I began to jot down whatever came to mind. I tried to craft a simple poem to ease into the process, but it was so awful I burned the parchment to remove the evidence of its existence.

No songs and no stories were born, not even ideas for future ones.

I hissed in frustration and threw the pencil across the room, then dropped my head into my hands. *The vial was broken. My curse is done. So, is this what writer's block feels like?* Writing used to be effortless, but I hadn't tried since I was nine.

Fuck it.

Grabbing a wineskin and the two ceramic goblets from my pouch, I left and locked my room before crossing the hall to Ramiren's door. "Ramiren? Are you there?" I knocked, then paused, pressing my fingertips to the wood of the door. "I'm sorry if I am intruding. I just-"

The doorknob clicked, and Ramiren quietly and slowly opened the door. "I'm here, and you don't need to worry about that. You're welcome here, and if there should ever be any reason I'd need privacy and not welcome a visit, you'd have ample warning." His ever-present smile faded, as his brows knit in concern. "Are you all right?"

He opened the door wider to let me in. As he closed it again, I replied, "I'm as all right as I can be. I don't feel any different though. I thought I would. Something, anyway. But, there's nothing. Seems now that I have my creativity back, I get to experience the privilege of writer's block."

Ramiren let out a breath. "That makes sense, actually."

My head snapped to him. "It does?"

"It does. Georgina's tools and the ability to use them, Raewyn's beauty, my whistling. All things that can be proven, shown, and do not rely on other factors, like inspiration. Creativity is not something that just happens. It comes and goes, like a visitor. And, right now, your creativity is simply away."

Creativity as a visitor. I like that.

"You may be right, but I already have friends I haven't seen in years. I don't need another." I would try again later, preferably with a pencil and paper at hand in case inspiration decided to knock on my door. With a wan smile, I decided to change the subject. "Are you all right? I didn't just come here to whine. I was concerned, too."

He stepped closer. "Things have been more dangerous than I am used to, but I think I'm handling that well. It helps that others do much of the actual violence, while I support and strike where and when I can."

I winced, recalling with startling clarity who did most of the violence in the previous fight. "I'm not sure I even wish to speak of earlier. More just... I managed to find a small skin of Evrakan white in my pouch. Enough for two glasses. I couldn't think of anyone I'd rather share it with." I lifted the small wineskin in one hand and two ceramic goblets in the other.

"I won't turn down the wine. I'd prefer we remove expectations entirely and simply enjoy each other's company." He motioned to a desk off to the side that I could use.

After putting the two goblets on it, I unstoppered the wineskin and poured. I turned, handing a goblet to him and raising mine in a toast, "To friends first and enemies last, a beautiful future and glorious past."

He laughed and tapped my goblet with his own. "I'll toast to all that, and be more than a little impressed with the rhyme."

I grinned broadly at him. "Thanks. It just came to me."

Then, my grin faded from my face.

"I made it up. Just now." My eyes widened and stung as they flooded with tears. "My creativity. It's truly back!" I exclaimed then sloshed the wine as I swooped in to kiss him full on the mouth.

He made a noise in his throat in surprise, which broke the kiss almost as soon as I'd started it.

My fingertips covered my lips in embarrassment. "Sorry."

He took a deep breath, in and out, and drank deep from his wine before replying, "It is... quite all right, Nathalia." He smiled ruefully. "If a woman like you wants to celebrate by kissing me, I'll not deny her."

My smile returned. I felt warm. Not from arousal, but from contentment.

This is where I needed to be tonight. Not huddled over paper, but with him.

The day had been filled with the highest highs and the lowest lows. Though I'd bathed, the grit of my disappointment and violent actions remained. Something else was needed now.

My eyes went to his mouth.

Well, maybe a little *from arousal.*

I sipped from the goblet and put it down. "I realize I've never asked. Do *you* want a lesson?"

He put his goblet down as well. "It isn't appropriate for me to ask, even though I enjoy the time we spend together. I can offer, suggest even, but asking, except in extreme circumstances, doesn't feel quite right."

I looked him dead in the eye. "I wish to amend the pact, please."

With a schooled expression, he gave a nod, and the hovering scroll appeared again, though this time I noticed the lack of a bird's cry or the smell of sulfur. "Of course. Please detail your requested amendment." The flames in the room flared violet, briefly.

"I, Nathalia, give permission, free and clear, for you, Ramiren, to ask for, request, or insinuate through body language that he would like to initiate a lesson, should he so wish."

"I concur. It is done." His eyes flashed campfire light. I felt no different, but I figured that was to be expected. "Now that drama is behind us, I want you to be comfortable with what you just amended, so I will use it immediately. I think we would both benefit from the practice, and I'll talk about one of the new elements for our next full lesson after."

I reached over, hooking my hand around his neck and bringing his head down in another kiss as he snapped his fingers.

He continued to hold me, rubbing my back in lazy brushes. When his breathing resumed to its normal rhythm, he whispered, "It's said that practice makes perfect, and that was quite close. You should be proud of yourself, and I'm glad that I anticipated this for what I hoped to introduce next." He gently kissed my hair and inhaled. "There is another kind of sexual activity that does not involve vaginal penetration, but it requires a little more preparation. It can be painful, instead of enjoyable, if not done properly."

"What's that?"

"Anal penetration."

Oh.

"And you said we could try this the next time we had a lesson?" I asked, intrigued.

"You will be ready, and soon, to try this activity. That isn't the only new thing. I would like to introduce pretending to be another, even resembling things you are not, as a part of sexual play."

I hummed. "I suppose that creates a safe area for you, pretending to be someone else. Allows you to explore without the inhibitions of your real self."

He grinned at me, as though happy I understood. "Yes, exactly. Though with my help, it is you who will be taking on the role. We'll come up with options together. Between your wardrobe, what items I can make here, and my own skills, we can make you look like the option you've chosen, no matter how fantastic." He tucked me into the crook of his neck, holding me closer.

There was something in his voice. A quickness of his breath. "Am I wrong to say this idea excites you?"

There was a moment of silence before he answered, sounding regretful. "You aren't wrong at all to ask. We've become close enough that I may even answer it one day. I've never shared something like that with another. I hope you'll understand if I reserve my option to hold my answer as a secret of my own."

My face pushed further into the crook of his neck so he couldn't see my smirk. "It's all right. I don't mind. I hope to earn your trust eventually."

I heard his smile in his words. "My trust, you have. In more than one way, in fact. There are certain secrets that contain within them the potential for complication or obligation, when one chooses to reveal them. With our.. arrangement, that's a serious decision to make."

My head tilted to look at him, then my lips brushed against his neck with a kiss. "I understand. But if you do decide to tell me secrets, I'll listen. Without judgment."

And with affection.

He nodded, his bearded chin rubbing on my forehead. "I do, actually, have a secret to tell you. I wasn't sure how to bring it up."

I almost sat upright in excitement but managed to tamp my reaction down to nothing more than a slight twitch of my stomach muscles. "Oh?"

His hand went into my hair, absently curling a lock. "Leraska's name wasn't on any vials in the cupboard."

This time, I did sit upright. "What?"

"I didn't know when to bring it up." He sat up, resting his arms on his bent knees. "I made sure to check in each cupboard. Her name wasn't in any of them."

What in the-

I scowled in utter confusion. "Maybe it was elsewhere, and we missed it?"

Ramiren slowly shook his head. "No. We didn't miss it. If M.A.L.C.O.L.M. had taken her vial in the first mischief hag's cupboard and broken it without having read it aloud, then she likely would have said her stolen thing had been returned when we visited her. Otherwise, we scoured all three places. There was nothing, Nathalia."

"Then, what in the Dark Drop was stolen from her? And by whom?"

I exited Ramiren's room to see the Crown Prince of Wistran patiently waiting in the hallway. He had been in the middle of a round of pacing when he spotted me. A few guards ambled around down the hall, giving us privacy.

Shutting the door harder than I needed to, I gave my best smile and a curtsy. "Your Highness! This is unexpected."

"But a pleasure, I do hope." His eyes flickered to the door behind me, and his smile wavered.

I cleared my throat, hoping to all the gods residing in Celestia I didn't have bed hair. *At least I know he's been waiting no more than a few minutes.* "Most certainly. Are you looking for someone?"

He leaned against the hallway wall, crossing his arms. "You, as a matter of fact."

"Me?" I pointed at myself in confusion, like an idiot.

His posture was casual, but there was tension in his shoulders. "Yes. I wished to have a moment to talk. I have heard reports of the mischief hag's henchmen gathering, and I was concerned for your safety. You are a hero of Wistran, and we cannot afford to lose you." His warm smile was gentle, as though simultaneously trying to put me at ease and emphasize my importance.

I had been concerned about that.

His earnest attention was making me self-conscious. "Most thoughtful, Your Highness, for you to care about my well-being."

"I aim to, Lady Nathalia. We owe you a great debt, and I intend to repay, however you'll let me." He stepped forward and took my hand in his warm one to kiss it. His eyes met mine, long enough for me to recognize desire in them. "I hope you will someday."

A thrill and flattered awareness rippled through me at his look. "We're to go back to Laeth soon, Your Highness."

A mixture of shock and sadness creeped into his gaze, and he gently placed his other hand on top of mine. "Then, I mustn't wait long to attempt recompense. I will see you tomorrow, I hope?"

My head bowed in deference. "Yes, your father requested us."

"I will allow you to rest, in that case. Until tomorrow, Lady Nathalia." He kissed my hand again, his lips lingering for a moment longer than necessary.

Chapter Twenty-Three
An Obligation

The next day, as we came out of the castle after being received by a grateful but distracted king, the dimness and despair of the city seemed to have completely vanished. The warm sun peeked out from the clouds, casting rays of golden light across the expanse of red-tiled roofs and glittering streets.

It was a physical manifestation of our work, our good work, that made me smile.

We saved this place. We really saved it.

"You'd think he'd cough up some coin for saving his ass. A favor. Anything. But no. Just *hey, great job* and a dismissal." Raewyn grumbled, crossing her arms over her chest.

I glanced at my sister, feeling amused, "He has a lot of rebuilding and diplomacy to do after what the mischief hag did. Perhaps he was tired?"

Raewyn tilted her head, considering. "You know, he did seem a bit out-"

A man called out behind me, "Wait!"

We all turned to see Prince Jaylin running toward us. He slowed to a stop, raising a hand. "I think my guards and I should accompany you back, with the mischief hag's henchmen about. They will be searching for you now to enact revenge on her behalf."

Kind, but why is he troubling himself? "It's all right. We're just going to our inn, Your Highness. Taking the main road. Surely, they would not-"

He interrupted me, "Oh, but they would, Lady Nathalia. They have no shame, I assure you."

Beep. "More beatings!"

Raewyn raised an eyebrow.

"Please, Lady Nathalia. I insist. If not for yourself, then for me. My peace of mind." Worry creased his brow.

Feeling as though I couldn't refuse, my manners won out. "Very well, Prince Jaylin. We accept your escort."

The prince's relief was palpable, and he nodded, then waved a small group of soldiers to his side. "Let's go."

The walk through the city was one of awe. Though I'd seen the city before, after the mischief hag's demise, it had been dark. Now, in full sunlight, the restored beauty of the city shone. People were smiling. Cheerful. Happy. Some bowed and greeted their prince as he passed, walking next to me. The prince, all smiles, waved in return.

When a little girl ran up to give him flowers and a curtsy, I finally commented. "They are quite happy to see you, Your Highness."

Prince Jaylin waved to another with a smile. "Thank you. I have not had much of a chance to interact with the folk here of late. People had grown suspicious. Even violent. I could not risk it."

I nodded. "Wise. I'm glad you are able to, now."

"As am I, Lady Nathalia. Thanks to you." He grinned charmingly at me and took up my hand to kiss it gently.

The last time someone kissed my hand like that was over five years ago. I miss court life, sometimes.

My sister cleared her throat then asked in a strange tone, "Why were you unable to do anything about the mischief hag yourself, Prince Jaylin? You had soldiers."

The prince looked back at my sister with a glare that morphed into sorrow. My glare stayed.

"She mesmerized and destroyed a hundred of those soldiers at once. She was far too powerful. I am an able warrior, but I was no match for her. Not like Lady Nathalia." He turned to me, and the sorrow faded.

My cheeks burned again at the unfair praise. "It was all of us, Your Highness, not just me."

The prince raised an eyebrow. "That is not what I hear."

"Oh?" Ramiren replied. "And where exactly would you have heard of our battle? You arrived after she was defeated."

The prince eyed Ramiren. A flicker of annoyance passed over his face, but it was quickly replaced with another smile that didn't quite reach his eyes. "I know it was all of you. I just choose to give compliments to not only a savior of my country, but a beautiful one. I am but a humble man. It's easy to heap compliments onto her, is it not?"

"Certainly, but she doesn't appreciate unearned ones," Ramiren replied with a frown in his voice.

To my left, a beggar hunched over a cane on the side of the street with a small child next to him. Both were dirty and disheveled. The girl, overly skinny, looked up at me with big eyes.

I walked over, pulling silver from my coin pouch. *I give him gold, and he's a target.* The man held out his hand. "Good lady, could you spare a coin for my daughter?"

"Yes, of course." I fished out two pieces.

"Nat," Raewyn spoke in warning.

"Hm? What? I have plenty of money-."

My eyes turned to see that we had been surrounded by a crowd of beggars. But they did not hold out their hands for coin. Their hands held weapons.

Ambush.

The beggar beside me straightened and pulled on the end of his cane to reveal a sword. The girl ran off as he cried, "Murderers! Kill them!"

"Fear not, Lady Nathalia. I shall protect you!" Prince Jaylin drew his own sword, brandishing it.

With no time to take the shield off my back, I pushed the false beggar beside me away, with the added distraction of two silver being thrown at his face, giving me the chance I needed to unsheathe the longsword on my hip.

The beggars all doffed their moth-eaten cloaks to reveal armor and more weapons at their sides. They were a strange mix of elves and lupa fey. Some sported daggers, others swords or handaxes. All of them looked ready and willing to use them.

Two lupa fey immediately felled an unfortunate footman and charged me like I'd personally insulted their mother. Dodging the club of one, while parrying the daggers of the other, immediately put me on the defensive. I did not enjoy taking two at a time, especially when they were as skilled as these two were.

These are not run-of-the-mill cutthroats.

The two footmen who were left surrounded the prince in a defensive formation with their halberds tilted forward, leaving the rest of us to fend for ourselves.

Ramiren moved forward with his own weapon, easily deflecting the sword of one with the tip of his blade. The broodling lunged, his rapier piercing the man's mail armor as though he wore none. The man cried out and stumbled backwards, clutching at his stomach.

Two went for Raewyn in a stalking fashion, leering smiles on their faces. She simply raised a mocking eyebrow, far more expressive now that she no longer needed her mask, "Not my type, I'm afraid." A prayer fell from her lips as searing flame erupted from her hands and shot out toward the ambushers, knocking them backwards. They rolled around, yelping, trying to extinguish the fire quickly enveloping their clothing.

Georgina climbed up onto M.A.L.C.O.L.M.'s shoulders, giggling. "Let's have some fun!" She leveled her crossbow at one, who took one look at either her or her metal automaton and ran away down the alley.

"Aw," the gnome moaned, disappointed.

Beep. "I was promised beatings!"

Keeping an eye on everyone else, they seemed to be fairing fine except for me. The two I faced off against were cunning and kept me on my toes. If one went high, the other slashed low. If I stepped, they stepped in kind. I could not gain ground, and all I had to show for my efforts was a sweat-covered brow.

The one with the daggers tapped each side of my sword with a blade, and then twisted in, knocking the sword out of my grip. It clattered away out of reach.

I'd never seen a maneuver like that before.

Shieldless and now weaponless, my hands went up, ready to face them with my fists if need be.

The one with the club stepped forward, swinging his weapon back to strike. When I put my hands up defensively to catch his hand, he stopped with the club held back and then jerked. A gurgling screaming was next as a thin sword point poked through from his back.

When he fell, I expected to see Ramiren there, but it was Prince Jaylin who was behind him. The one with the daggers saw his fellow fall, and he shuffled away slowly.

Prince Jaylin smiled at me brightly. "I told you I would protect you."

But I'm supposed to do the protecting! Feeling worse than useless that someone had to come to my rescue, that I couldn't even handle two cutthroats, I petulantly picked my sword back up with a huff.

Two unusually-skilled cutthroats.

The one with the daggers hesitated, as though not sure who to strike or if he should run.

"And now, ruffian, you will cease assaulting my lady." Prince Jaylin turned his sword point to him.

The man held his hands up with the daggers raised, to either strike or surrender, he opened his mouth to yell, "Tr-"

Prince Jaylin ran his blade through the man's throat, cutting him off.

The ambusher gurgled, dropping his daggers to hold his neck as redness seeped through his fingertips. His eyes rolled back as he collapsed to the ground.

A footman rushed to Prince Jaylin's side. "My prince, are you hurt?"

Prince Jaylin wiped his sword on the dead man's clothing and sheathed it. "No, and thanks to me, neither is Lady Nathalia."

"Yes. Sure. Thank you." Overwhelmed, annoyed, and distracted, the words fell meaninglessly from my lips.

Ramiren sucked in a breath.

Prince Jaylin flashed a dazzling smile. "You thanked me."

Oh, fuck.

Fuckfuckfuckfuck.

My eyes slammed shut. *Stupid! STUPID!*

The prince laughed. "Your only obligation is to come back to the castle tomorrow. I wish to discuss an important matter."

We had planned to leave the next morning for the grove. But I was caught like a rabbit in a snare. My jaw clenched then released. "Yes, of course."

He motioned to everyone else. "Your companions, of course, may come as well. We'll have lunch in the gardens and then talk."

The gory scene around us painted a strange juxtaposition to his words.

I replied quietly, "Yes, I will attend, but I cannot speak for everyone, though."

Everyone, who looked decidedly displeased with me.

"I'll stay, of course," Raewyn said, sighing softly. "What's one more day?"

Georgina somehow managed to stare me down, red-faced and holding her hands out in front like she was trying to throttle me from a distance. "*Fine.*"

Ramiren looked at Prince Jaylin instead of me. He seemed to be thinking when he said, "I'll not leave without Lady Nathalia."

"Splendid!" the prince exclaimed cheerfully. "The Black Unicorn Inn, I believe, was your destination?"

I stalked to my door with Ramiren hot on my tail. Before I could open it, he put his hands on the wood, caging me in with my back to him. With a groan, my forehead thumped the door twice. "I know. I know I messed up. I know I shouldn't have thanked him. I was..."

I wasn't sure what I was thinking at that moment.

He muttered between gritted teeth. "You *cannot* thank him again, Nathalia. Do you understand me? This goes beyond anything."

"I know. I'm sorry."

His voice softened. "You need not be sorry. Just please, I *beg* of you, don't ever do it again." Something, either his lips or his forehead, gently touched the back of my head, then was immediately removed when I heard Raewyn call out from the stairwell leading to our floor.

"At least we'll get a decent meal tomorrow. Gods' sakes."

Chapter Twenty-Four
A Different Kind of Oath

We were seated at a long table under a silk awning with formal place settings for each of us, which Georgina laughed at. My sister was seated to the right of me while Prince Jaylin took up my left. Ramiren and Georgina sat across, with M.A.L.C.O.L.M. standing at attention behind them.

The castle staff, in full livery, brought out a roasted suckling pig dressed in greens, and the sight made my skin crawl. I shifted in my chair but did not say anything. *We are guests, and it is not my place to criticize my host's table.*

But, of course, Prince Jaylin noticed. "Shall I have the servants carve a flank for you? It was prepared especially for you."

I cleared my throat and smiled at him. "No, Your Highness. I do not consume animals."

Prince Jaylin raised his eyebrows in surprise. "Truly? That's interesting. My sincerest apologies, Lady Nathalia. I shall have them take it away immediately." He raised his hand to a couple of staff standing by, who came forward to take the platter.

"No, Your Highness. It's fine. Everyone else can, but I will not eat it." The smell was making me nauseous, but I kept it down.

"Most kind of you. Thank you," he said with a smile. He reached over and kissed my hand again, bringing out a tight smile of my own. He looked up at me over our joined hands and gave a wink. My cheeks warmed, but I did not pull my hand away. It would be rude in this proximity.

Not as handsome as Ramiren, but only just.

I decided to change the subject. "You wished to talk, Your Highness?"

"Oh, yes, of course." He gently placed my hand into my lap. "I wanted to thank you properly for saving Wistran from that hag. These days have been dark, but *you* have brought us back into the light."

Again with this? It was not just me. "It was all of us, Your Highness. We work as a team."

His eyes glinted. "Are you always so modest?"

Yes. "No, your hi-"

"Because if I say it was you, then it was you, and nothing can convince me otherwise." He grinned teasingly, then picked up his glass of some sparkling wine to take a sip. My thoughts jumbled, unable to tell if he was joking or not. Either way, it was obvious he would brook no argument from me, so I let it go. He was, for the moment, a royal patron, and royal patrons liked to have their way. Looking across the table, my companions fidgeted with utensils, pushed food around, and shifted in their plush chairs.

"Now, I have a gift for you. I understand my father was thankful but did not compensate you properly. I intend to rectify that mistake." He waved over another staff member I had not seen until now, a human man, who came forward carrying a small box.

Prince Jaylin took it from the man and turned toward me. "This is for you, Lady Nathalia. With my best wishes."

He passed the small box to me, and I opened it to reveal a large opal necklace inset in gold. My fingers curled around the delicate chain as I picked it up to stare. "Your Highness, I-"

"I know. I know. But only the best for you, my dear lady."

Through the chain I could see Ramiren focusing on me, or rather the necklace, with a raised eyebrow. The broodling said, his voice emotionless, "A lovely gift, Prince Jaylin."

Prince Jaylin smiled at Ramiren, "As I said, only the best for her. That is only the beginning, of course. I have jewel makers ready and waiting to craft you whatever you desire, if this does not suffice."

"No, Your Highness, it is-"

He grinned happily, a contrast to the warning in his words, "I'd be quite upset with them if it did not meet your standards."

I cleared my throat and gave him a wan smile. "I love it."

"Wonderful! Let me put it on you." He took the necklace from me and unclasped it, then instructed me to turn in my chair. I did, lifting my hair out of the way. He closed the clasp, and the delicate chain immediately began to cut into the back of my neck with the large pendant anchoring it down. I turned back and smiled again while my clenched teeth held in a request to take it off immediately.

Prince Jaylin put his arm on the back of my chair. "I long to hear you thank me again. Such a sweet sound." He sighed. "But alas, you shouldn't, if you are to leave me."

The urge to say something, anything, that would convey my appreciation while those two dreaded words weighed on me more than the necklace. "It's very beautiful, Your Highness. You are most thoughtful."

Please take this off.

Prince Jaylin sighed again, this time in disappointment, and I sank into my chair. My eyes turned to Ramiren, but he was not looking at me. He was staring daggers at Prince Jaylin.

"Are you all right, Ramiren?"

Ramiren's eyes flicked to me with a strained smile. "Just fine, Lady Nathalia."

After our lunch, Prince Jaylin offered to give us a tour of the expansive gardens. They were even more impressive than Leraska's grove or the fields on the way to Tanta. Flowers of every imaginable color lined the paths and walkways. Trees the color of autumn's glory swayed in the gentle breeze, though it felt far too warm for the trees to have changed. He led us to a particular tree where he told us tales of climbing it in his youth, proudly stating he had never fallen from it.

It was at that tree where Prince Jaylin took my hand in both of his. "My dearest Lady Nathalia, it seems you have beguiled me, and I fear this is my only chance. Royals, no matter if they're in the Feylands or Laeth, rarely get to choose who they wed. But the Feylands have what's called an eluva. Do you know what that is?"

I shook off my shock long enough to say I did not.

"It's a once in a lifetime boon, if you will. It means a Feylands royal can claim eluva if they've found their elu. The *crack* in their armor, if you will. Prince or pauper, it does not matter. I know you are my other, Nathalia. I knew it when I first laid eyes on you. It might not be as intense for you as it is for me right now, as you are not fey. But I assure you, the eluva bond is without equal in love and fidelity once sealed by marriage. So, with that said..." He let out a long, cleansing exhale. "Will you become my wife? My elu?"

My jaw slowly dropped. I should've expected the question, the way he was talking. My hand in his. The almost desperate look in his eyes. But the suddenness of it, the abruptness, startled me down to my core.

Though...

Wife. Marriage. Family. Everything I'd ever wanted. He was offering me that. An eluva bond, whatever that was. I'd never heard of it, but I didn't know Feylands marriage customs that well. I'd have a husband. A loving, devoted princely husband.

But the pact would be done, and Ramiren would leave.

He'd want me to be happy. I could be happy with Jaylin. Here in Wistran. And I know I could make him happy. I learned how. He's not yet my friend, but we have things in common. We're both protective and thoughtful. We enjoy a challenging fight. He is attentive. Affectionate, even. He desires me. And it sounds like this bond would bind us even beyond a marriage vow.

Maybe this is my best chance. Besides, as Ramiren said, I'm settling no matter what. Might as well settle for a rich, handsome, fey husband who adores me.

I searched his earnest face, then looked over at my companions, who watched from afar but could likely surmise what was happening by context. My sister frowned, talking to Ramiren while he paced back and forth. Georgina looked bored. M.A.L.C.O.L.M. looked like M.A.L.C.O.L.M.

I said, loud enough for them to hear, "Your Highness, I would be glad to accept." I waited for the joy that would surely come, like I had waited for my creativity to return. And waited.

Nothing. Again.

But my creativity had eventually come. Perhaps this would take time as well.

My heart felt hollow. There was no joyfulness I thought I would feel at such a moment. *This is what I always wanted. Isn't it? This is what I dreamed of happening. So, why do I feel so empty?*

"Great. Wonderful. Can we go now?" Georgina yawned. "I have a journey to prepare for tomorrow."

Raewyn turned heel and stomped away, cursing just loud enough for me to tell the choice phrases she knew. Confused, I called after her, "Raewyn? Raewyn!"

She broke into a run, but I easily caught up to her with a gentle hand hooked into her elbow. "Raewyn, what's wrong?"

She spun and glared at me, tears flooding her eyes. "Oh, nothing. Nothing at all. I'm happy you're finally getting what you always wanted. Your *one*, right?" Her tone was sarcastic and biting.

My hand dropped from her arm as I flinched back.

What is this? I thought she'd be pleased.

I shook my head, my confusion becoming more and more acute the longer her eyes bored into me. "Raewyn, tell me, *please*. What's wrong?"

Her voice changed to a harsh whisper so as to not be overheard, "You want to know what's wrong? Sure, I'll tell you, Nathalia." She licked her lips and looked up, like she was trying to both think of the right words and stop tears from falling. She enunciated each word as they spilled out of her. "I can't stand here and watch you accept a proposal from him. Which, by the way, looked like the most awkward proposal in history. He didn't even kneel!"

Taking a step back as my eyes widened, I fully registered what she was saying. My lips opened slightly and stayed frozen, as I also tried to find the right words. "Wha... Where is this coming from?"

She threw her hands up in keen frustration. "You don't love him! There's no possible *way* you can. You're barely even acquaintances. This is a *blind marriage*, Nat. The Church of Minue and the Church of Valiset work together to ensure those don't happen, *especially* royal ones. The stability of *your marriage* affects the stability of the kingdom. You don't know each other. Our parents don't even know his. I can't stand by and watch while you marry someone you don't know, much less don't love, Nat." She shook her head vehemently. "I can't, and I won't."

The tenets of Valiset, the Goddess of Health, while not outright forbidding blind marriages, certainly discouraged them. They often ended in divorce. Heartache. Ruin. Hurting the body as well as the mind. *Is she saying this marriage is destined for failure?* I wanted to reassure her.

"Look, he told me about a special fey bond we have. Or will have, called an eluva bond. Apparently, the reason he's doing this is because he said he believes I'm his elu. Or something to that effect. Does that help you?"

"An eluva bond." She rolled her eyes. "What, pray tell, is that?" She held up a finger as I started to explain it. "Wait, don't tell me. Let me guess. A special, super powerful connection where you magically fall in love, have twenty fat babies, and call each other cringy pet names?"

I twisted my mouth as I muttered. "He wasn't very detailed on the specifics."

"Gods above, Nat. This isn't one of your *stories*! This is real life! That kind of thing hasn't existed since the pantheon split. And, even then, it wasn't called that. It was called c-something or whatever. He's making shit up."

I shrugged with raised hands, shaking my head and getting even more flustered. "I don't know, Raewyn. He just said it was a fey bond."

"Well, even if it is a *fey thing*, it won't work. You're still going to be two strangers who have the daunting task of being attached at the hip for life. Both of you are going to be miserable. But, hey! At least you get a nice hat and wardrobe to go along with it."

Miserable? No, not after all I've learned to keep him happy. And this offered bond? He's everything I asked for when setting out four years ago, when I came up with the idea of devoting my life to another's happiness. Checks all the boxes.

Where there had been hesitation, a void of joy, there was now resolve.

I just wanted to prove her wrong.

Heat rose in my chest. Anger, white hot, crawled its way from the churning pit of my stomach to my face. I spat, "Typical, Raewyn. Just typical of you. Only you know best for my life, right?"

My sister stepped closer to me, her harsh whisper continuing, "You know, maybe I don't know everything. But I know for damn sure you're not happy about this. You couldn't possibly be happy, so stop pretending like you are. You're latching onto the first proposal from a *worthy man* who sees you for more than just a nice name and a piece of ass."

My exasperation flared. "You wanted me to find someone, Raewyn! In the next town, no less, remember? I did that! I actually did that!"

Raewyn threw her hands up. "To fuck, Nat. Not marry! They're two separate things!"

"Not to me!" I snapped, and Raewyn was startled into silence. I instantly felt guilty, but it was pushed down by my rage. This was Raewyn's standard mode of operation. What I needed was decided by her, because I couldn't be trusted to determine it, and they somehow always came second to her wants. My life was a waste, filled with boredom and predictability.

If that's how she truly felt, fine.

Before I could continue, Raewyn spoke. Her eyes refilled with tears, with hurt. "I'm going with Georgina and M.A.L.C.O.L.M. to the grove, then I'm going home. I love you, Nat. May Minue and Valiset bless your *happy union.*"

I watched as my sister stalked off back toward the group, who were all staring at us. Except for Georgina, who was tinkering with the hinge on M.A.L.C.O.L.M.'s right elbow.

Prince Jaylin ran to me, hands extended. "Is everything all right?" Taking my hands in his, he looked concerned. "Are you still saying yes?" His eyes wide, it seemed like he was almost afraid.

My rage began to dissipate. My throat was hoarse when I spoke, but at least the anger within it was gone, leaving guilt in its place. "My answer is still yes, Your Highness. Of course. She just... my sister is stubborn and doesn't agree with my decision to marry you."

Prince Jaylin looked nonplussed. "I see. I am sorry she could not be more supportive of her sister. If I may say so, she sounds envious. Most are of an eluva bond. They're not common and are widely-celebrated."

"No." My eyes followed Raewyn. She wiped her eyes and approached Ramiren with bowed shoulders. They exchanged words, and I wondered what they were saying. "She may be the envious type. But for all her faults, she is not envious now."

"I understand, Lady Nathalia." He suddenly smiled brightly. "My mother and father will be overjoyed. I finally found my elu."

"Yes, I'm sure. Excuse me, please."

I slowly walked toward Raewyn and Ramiren, who were still talking. My ears strained to make out what she was saying.

"...but, why don't you just...?"

Raewyn abruptly stopped as she spotted me standing within earshot. She sniffled and stomped away. I stared at her back before turning to Ramiren. "Are you going to the grove with them?" My stomach knotted again to a sickening degree.

Raewyn is just having a tantrum, but she won't leave. She'll come to her senses and attend.

Georgina could go, her automaton too. But I couldn't bear Ramiren's departure. Only that was not feasible. I would be a married woman, and I could not find an excuse for him to stay. It would be selfish of me to even try.

Ramiren kept his eyes on me. "I will stay, at least until after the wedding." His eyes flitted above my head, and I could see them almost imperceptibly narrow.

Prince Jaylin, coming to stand behind me, placed his hands on my shoulders and gave them a gentle squeeze. I could hear the exaggerated cheerfulness in my future husband's voice, like he was trying to keep up appearances for my sake, "Certainly. You are most welcome."

I kept my eyes on Ramiren and thought back to what I had told Raewyn.

You can choose to be happy. Happiness is a choice.

Right?

Chapter Twenty-Five
The Water Nymph's Shawl

We walked back to the Black Unicorn Inn in silence. Later that night, we kept to ourselves as no one was hungry enough for supper. The stifling solitude and pacing eventually made me tired enough to exit my room and approach Ramiren's door.

At my gentle knock, Ramiren opened it and smiled tiredly. He said nothing, merely stepped aside so I could come in.

"Thank you." I entered his room, twisting my fingers together.

He closed the door. "I'm sure that proposal came as a surprise."

"Yes. It was a surprise, as was my sister's reaction to it."

"Agreed, most unusual. Still, when you finally do marry, I wish you nothing but peace, love, and plenty." His smile seemed to falter, but I took it as me imagining things.

And now the first reason I'm here. "Thank you. If I may ask, what do you think of Prince Jaylin? You're more practiced at reading people than I am. I would like your opinion."

"My opinion isn't important. Only yours is."

My smile felt strained trying to hide the frustration I felt. "Still, I would have your thoughts."

Ramiren let out a sigh and shook his head. "No, Nathalia. I won't. Please don't ask again."

Fuck.

"It's all right. I know you well enough to understand what that means." *He doesn't like him. He thinks my sister is right, and I won't be happy.*

Ramiren looked at me sideways. "Do you, now?"

I nodded once in reply.

"Please elaborate," he replied.

Oh no, Ramiren. You don't get to deny me and then pry.

"Hummingbird."

Ramiren blinked, then let out a rueful laugh. "That's not really the purpose of a safe word, Nathalia. But I'll give it to you. You're uncomfortable sharing your thoughts, and I have pushed too far." His smile returned. "I suppose you do have your limits."

The return of his smile set me at ease faster than an answer likely would have. "Don't we all?"

He nodded slowly. "Yes. Yes, we do. Now, what can I do for you?"

And the second reason. I replied immediately, "I wanted to talk to you about our next lesson."

He tilted his head, eyebrows furrowed. "But you are engaged."

With a shrug, I let the reminder of my impending marriage slide off my back. "Correct, I am, but I still have more to learn. If I were married, we would not be having this conversation. Thankfully, the ring is not yet on my finger."

"That is fair, but..." He pursed his lips. "We must decide when to dissolve the pact."

My stomach twisted into an even tighter knot. "Yes, but not today."

"True. Not today. But soon, I'm sure. I had a plan for the next lesson. A game of pretend. If you are sure you want to continue?"

Gods, yes.

"I am. And I'm all ears."

He snapped his fingers, and I found myself in the bedroom. A vanity filled with pots and powders took up a portion of the left wall, along with a full-length mirror.

The preparation before the start of the lesson passed in a blur. When I explained what I had in mind, a water nymph I had seen on the beach long ago, he raised an eyebrow. "We can work with that. It is more exotic than I expected for you for a first foray into a role, not that I mind in the slightest."

We worked together on effects, both cosmetic and magical, to transform my hair into a bright shade of light blue, and my skin glistened with a hue to match. The subtle illusions woven about me changed the appearance of my proportions, making my frame willowy and somewhat otherworldly.

He removed his glasses, placing them on a side table. "I think that the costuming for your first choice is especially easy this time, as you only need a shawl or water-caul."

I looked down at myself, at my shimmering hands, and finally back up to Ramiren. "Oh. Yes, I remember. She carried a white shawl about her shoulders. Do you have one I can use? Or a scarf, perhaps?"

He searched through a clothing trunk and handed me a gauze-like piece of pale cloth, almost but not quite transparent. He made a motion with his hands, with a short incantation, and the sound of gently lapping waves filled the room. "I'll look away. I won't spoil your moment of unveiling the last part of the effect."

As he turned around, I draped the shawl around my shoulders, as the water nymph had done all those years ago. "Alright, Ramiren. I'm ready."

He turned, and his smile got slightly wider. "You are... breathtaking."

I rolled my eyes with a reluctantly amused smirk, which he returned.

"Pun intended. Now, tell me about yourself, Nathalia. Tell me your story. It will both help you understand the role you are playing and let me know what is expected for my part. It is best practice to assume the other person in this sort of play might not know exactly the version of the character you hold in your mind, and it is always preferable to be on the same page."

"A story. I can do that." Taking a few steps to the side, deep in thought, inspiration visited me, and a full, new narrative immediately came to mind. "The legend of the water nymph is one of tragedy. Her one possession, her white shawl, was stolen from her by a man sitting on the beach. She had removed it to swim, and it lay on the rocks. He picked it up, not knowing what it was, and she cried out, 'Give me my shawl. I beg you. I will do anything.' Seeing a chance to have a beautiful wife, he asked her to marry him. She agreed, all to get her shawl."

This is what I love about stories. The simplest elements, combined with the empathy of the listener, could produce the most amazing effects.

"After three years, she cried again, 'Give me my shawl. I beg you. I will do anything.' So, he asked her to bear his children. She agreed, all to get her shawl. A son and daughter, she bore him, but his guilt had started to weigh him down. After three more years, she cried again, 'Give me my shawl. I beg you. I will do anything.' This time, he gave not a demand, but a confession, 'You gave me a home. You gave me children, asking for nothing save for what I wrongfully took. This is to settle the debt.' And he handed her the shawl. She took it, sprinting away as the man wept.

"She ran back into the ocean but stopped just before diving in. She realized she had given him more than a home. More than children. What he'd done was wrong, cruel even, but she'd given him her heart, regardless. She hurried back, but the man was gone along with the children. To this day, she leaves her shawl out at dawn, noon, and dusk, waiting for the man to come pick it up again and bind himself to her once again."

With a sad smile, I finished the story. "Opportunity isn't always something to be seized. Neither of them realized what they'd had until it was too late."

He was silent long enough for me to wonder if I'd said something wrong. When he finally spoke, his voice was oddly scratchy. "You remember our safe words. Use yours if at any time you feel discomfort, or pain, or unsafe. Knowing how your role responds when certain things happen, we can start with a simple example, one from your tale itself." Suddenly, and playfully, he snatched away the shawl from me and went to sit down at the chair along the far wall. "And now, what will you do?'

A sudden and strange feeling of instant loss gutted me. It wasn't even my shawl, but at that moment, I desperately wanted it back.

My eyes widened, and I moved to his side. My hands gripped his shoulders as I whispered, "I beg you. Please. I'll do anything."

My hand reached for my shawl, hesitantly, afraid it would be pulled away. When it was, my belly clenched, and I groaned. *I will tempt it from him.* Slipping into his lap, I looked down at him with begging eyes, my words coming out as a soft plea, "I will do anything. Please. Anything." My hands moved from his shoulders to the sides of his neck where my thumbs traced his increasing pulse.

To emphasize what I meant by *anything*, my lips moved close to his, then over his even before his first request. Being this close to Ramiren was always intoxicating, but now it was more than that. I was spellbound. I crushed myself against his chest, and my hips shifted closer until the rigid length of his cock pressed firmly along my clit.

He sucked in a breath, and the change in his demeanor was sudden. His face turned into a vicious mask. The hard look in his eyes startled and excited me. It was at once hungry and malicious. He dangled the shawl over his left hand while his right gripped my chin.

When he spoke, my lips ghosting against mine, it was harsh. Cruel. Demanding. "You will lie back, with your legs spread wide, and I will gorge myself until you either give me a pretty scream or beg for my cock. Then, you will swallow me down until I am spent. Only after will you have what you desire."

My entire body lit up like a bonfire, and he let my chin go with a slight push.

Sliding off his lap, I moved to lie on the bed with my knees raised and spread shoulder-width apart, staring up at this new Ramiren. He stood from the chair and approached with an assessing gaze roaming over me. I must have been found wanting, as he raised an eyebrow and shook his head, displeased. His hands shot out, and he grasped me under my knees to wrench them apart and away from him until they were pressed into my shoulders. The suddenness of his movement startled me, but I clutched the blanket under me to keep myself from jolting.

Now fully exposed, I stared wide-eyed and was already half-way to coming. The digging grip of his hands pushing my knees down, trapping my arms and nearly immobilizing me, gave me a sense of relinquishing control unlike any lesson before now. Being in his hands, both literally and figuratively, was somehow freeing. Despite the play we were doing now, there was no pretending about my spiking lust and the desperate need to be consumed by this man.

The air, a slight breeze from somewhere, hit my wet pussy, and the temperature difference, as well as the sensation of the draft itself against sensitive skin, made me shiver. He leaned down, still holding my legs, and licked from my entrance to just above my clit with the flat of his forked tongue. He dipped into my entrance, wiggling the tip of his tongue.

I groaned, "Oh, fuck."

Without warning, familiar pressure built with a heavy throbbing, but I still craved more. When his lips wrapped around my clit and squeezed it between them with rhythmic pulses, I sucked in a sharp breath. It felt decadent and filthy.

I tried to reach up to run my fingers through his hair, intending to press him into me when his hand slid from my legs to my wrist and turned it, pinning it down against the bed. I tried with the other hand and my other wrist received the same treatment. With my legs free, my feet rested on his back, which I used as leverage to slowly buck into his mouth.

My pussy throbbed in time with the insistent strokes of his tongue and his lips' rhythm. My chest constricted as breathing became difficult, each exhale coming out as a moan. I feebly struggled against his hands, but he gripped firmly. I felt his true strength then, what he'd been hiding.

If he truly wanted to keep me pinned, he could.

The thought alone, of being at his mercy, threw me before I was ready. I saw stars as the delicious pressure and intense throbbing peaked and released.

As demanded, I gave him a pretty scream.

But it wasn't nearly enough. I wanted to feel him caught. I needed his weight on me, pressing me into the bed as he had done with my wrists.

I whispered, "Stop."

Immediately, he raised his head to look at me. I noticed his breathing was erratic, fast. His eyes looked almost black, and I finally saw it. Recognized it.

Pure lust.

I did that. Me.

"Up here."

"What do you mean by that?" Ramiren whispered, looking at me over the rims of his glasses.

"I want you on top of me. Please."

Not part of the play. You don't make demands here.

Not demanding. Begging.

When he moved up between my legs and lowered his head, he touched his nose to mine before kissing me. I tasted myself on him, tangy and tart. I thought he was going to agree to my plea. Then, he smiled like he enjoyed my torment.

With a whisper, he answered, "No."

For some reason. For some gods-damned reason, hearing him deny me made me even more needy. I *wanted,* but not for me. *I want to hear* him *scream. I want him to lose control.*

"I want your cock in my mouth."

"And?" he replied.

"Please," I murmured. When he still looked unmoved, my frustration mixed with my arousal. "*Please*! I need your cock in my mouth. Please. *Please.*

I'll do anything." My tongue began to ache again as it rubbed the roof of my mouth as a reflex.

He looked at me with a satisfied expression. He reached down without looking and circled my clit with two fingers before dipping them into my overly sensitive pussy, pumping them twice. When I groaned and could feel myself clench around them, he lifted the hand to his mouth and sucked on his wet fingers one at a time, staring me down.

I couldn't look away and nearly came again from the sight alone.

"Now, be a good girl and show me. Keep your promise." He moved past me to recline on the bed, still fully clothed.

I hate clothes.

I rose and began to scoot his trousers down his hips, almost frantically. I was desperate to see him. Feel and taste him. When his cock was uncovered, erect with a glistening drop on the head, I almost went right for it. But at the last moment, I instead removed his trousers entirely, tossing them to the side of the bed. Taking one last look at his heated, dilated eyes, I devoured him.

He sucked in a harsh breath, putting his hands on either side of my head. Then, he raised my head off him and quickly climbed off the bed. "Kneel and let me see what that beautiful mouth can do."

It was not a request. *Bossy Ramiren is my favorite Ramiren.*

I obeyed without question, kneeling before him on the soft rug and meeting his eyes while taking him into my mouth again. My left hand wrapped around his cock and my right dropped to my drenched pussy, alternating between my clit and plunging fingers into myself, with my now confident fingers creating friction where I needed them most. I thrummed my clit like the string on a harp and hot lightning shot up my spine. I felt woefully empty and incomplete, my fingers barely helping.

I worked both of us into a frenzy, and a muffled cry quaked somewhere deep in my throat. My hips stuttered against my hand, and the need was almost painful. The desperation to come again was matched only by my tongue's attention on that vein and the little ridge I loved.

So close. So fucking close.

My grip on him tightened ever so slightly. His moans started out soft, but constant, then got louder. His hands went into my hair while his hips moved of their own accord, thrusting into my slick mouth.

Angel. Say it. Fucking say it.

I gave a half-moan, half-whine against him as the word rolled through my lust-addled brain.

I opened my eyes, risking a glance, to see an expression I'd never seen before. At once lustful and affectionate. His gaze met mine, and his eyes widened as he took a shaky breath. "Ang-" He shuddered and threw his head back to let out a moaning cry that was noticeably louder than any other time before.

Dimly, I thought I heard him call my name, and it became too much. I dipped my fingers into my pussy again, and the muscles clenched around them. A muffled scream from me accompanied him as I pressed his cock against my tongue and the back of my throat, forcing me to drink him down. I let go only when he let out his last sound.

We each took a moment to catch our breath, both of us staring at each other.

A thought occurred to me, and I grinned like an idiot. "Can I have my shawl back now?"

He blinked dumbly then let out a chortle. "Gods, I'd forgotten about the shawl."

He helped me stand on shaky, sore legs. I moved to walk past him when he pulled me to him to kiss me gently. I gasped and leaned back, startled and wide-eyed.

His eyes focused on the lower part of my face, though I wasn't sure which part specifically.

Do I have cum on me?

When I rubbed my chin, where I surmised his attention was, he kissed my forehead. "If nothing else, a surprise like that helps you remember something important. When we play like this, we are both the roles we are playing and... ourselves. We don't stop being us, but the rules shift somewhat with the play. Your choice of role both encouraged you to try things you might not have thought of and put certain restrictions on your behavior. I play along so as to not shatter the illusion, and what options make sense are also both freed and set within other new boundaries. How did it feel?"

I hummed. "I suppose I felt beholden to you. As though I truly would have done anything you asked. It felt freeing and confining at the same time.

I realize, now, that's how it normally feels with you. But intensified. Primal, almost. Like I belonged to you. If that makes any sense."

He smiled then looked down as he laced his fingers with mine. "This is one reason why these lessons are not held until after many of the basics are well on their way to mastery. Without a complete understanding of pleasure, desire, permission, consent, and self, this kind of lesson might be misinterpreted as *have sexual contact while wearing a funny hat*, but it seems as though you understand. Did you enjoy this kind of play?"

I bobbed my head with a happy grin. "I did. I very much did. Did you?"

"Of course. I enjoy both the activity and that you comprehend its purpose. This kind of play is exceedingly familiar to me, as it is a lot like, well, everything I do. I change myself to how others see me or wish to. I change the environment to match the one that everyone seems to want. I change the roles and the rules to everyone's satisfaction, and ideally, everyone is happy with the outcome, myself included. Play, rules, and roles are central to every pact, every fair one anyway."

He is being unusually open. "Do you ever get to change things to what you want?"

"If I have a stake in it, and enough time to shift the rules around..." he paused and grinned. "Nearly every time."

I felt as though I was seeing him with fresh eyes. "And did you change yourself to suit me?"

His smile did not falter, but he shook his head in a faint *no*. He only said one word in reply, "Orange."

Chapter Twenty-Six
The Queen on the Chessboard

The next day, I awoke to a knock at my door. My eyes opened and immediately squinted against the brightness that filled the room. Rubbing them, I groaned. *I must have overslept.* My pen had kept me up all night writing for the first time in years and could not stop the ideas coming to mind.

Ramiren was right. I just needed to wait for my visitor.

The knock came again, and I flopped out of bed to answer it.

A page, his green tunic emblazoned with the Wistran royal coat of arms, bowed, and handed me a folded letter. I took it, and he bowed again before promptly departing. After closing the door, I carefully unfolded the message. The lettering was neat and cursive but obviously hastily written.

• • • •

Lady Nathalia,

I hope this letter finds you well. I am overjoyed that you are to become my new daughter. Please meet me in the Great Hall this morning to discuss preparations for your wedding to my son. The omens are good, and this time of year is auspicious. We will hold the ceremony in one week's time.

I will be waiting.

Milanda Loranaskan

Queen of Wistran

• • • •

Preparations? A week?

Bathing as best I could in the provided basin, I dressed in my green silk gown. *I need to look my best for this.* The first time I wore it came to mind, and my stomach lurched. *We don't have much time left.* Thinking back on all the lessons Ramiren and I have had, my only conclusion was that there was still a great deal to learn.

With my creativity restored, ideas of all sorts came brimming to mind, and not just songs and stories. Things I wanted to try. Things I could do to make him gasp, or groan, or even whine again.

I shouldn't keep her waiting.

Heading downstairs, everyone was sitting at breakfast and chatting quietly. Even Raewyn was present, emphasizing just how much I overslept.

Ramiren spotted me first with his narrowed, assessing eyes looking me up and down. "Good morning, Lady Nathalia. You look lovely this morning. Sleep well?" He moved so I could sit on the bench.

"Yes, thank you, but I can't stay." I held up the letter in my hand. "The queen summoned me."

Raewyn muttered into her teacup, but I ignored it.

"Oh, is everything all right?" Over his shoulder, Ramiren peered at the letter in my hand, like it was a snake about to strike, before meeting my eyes.

With a shrug, I responded, "I think so. She wants to discuss wedding preparations."

"Oh, yeah? How long you got before you're chained to him?" Georgina asked.

I looked down at the letter, as though to read it. "A week, she says."

Ramiren choked on his food.

M.A.L.C.O.L.M. beeped. "You're supposed to chew first."

Ramiren ignored the automaton and turned around on the bench to look at me fully with a raised eyebrow. "*So soon*? Though I am not exactly an expert on royal engagements, they are typically not that short, Nathalia. The preparations alone can last for years."

"Apparently, they want to take advantage of auspicious omens, or something of that nature." I sighed, already exhausted. "I need to go. I will see you all later."

When I stepped onto the streets of the capital, most who passed me ignored my presence. Some inclined their head, given my dress, but most simply averted their eyes to get on with their work.

No one seemed to know I was to become their future queen.

My walk to the castle in the center of the city was pleasant. The summer air was warm. The sun shone and glinted off of the red-tiled roofs. Birds chirped.

After being escorted in by two footmen, I was taken to the Grand Hall when I gave my name. The heavy double doors of the hall were open to let the breeze in, and my breath hitched when I saw inside.

Massive long pews had been set up on either side of a green-carpeted aisle. Banners depicting the royal sigil, a tree with deep, winding roots, were being unfurled and cleaned in preparation for hanging.

All the bustle was centered around an older muste fey woman, handsome and finely dressed. Her green brocade dress caught the light and a silk veil, held up by a small crown, covered her white hair and fell to her ankles. She was tall, almost as tall as I. Based on her bearing, it was obvious, even from a distance, she was used to giving orders.

I'd forgotten the kingdom's color was green, like Camlynn's, though not as dark a hue. *Was there meaning behind that?* Silently applauding my choice of dress, I approached and gave a slight smile. "Your Majesty, I am here." I curtsied low.

She looked over her shoulder at me and huffed after quickly looking me up and down. "Do stand up straight, my dear. You're with the royal court now. Your posture must be better."

I froze.

No one has ever complained about my posture.

She directed a staff member to put a set of vases on a side table before speaking as she surveyed the hall, "And we'll need to get you better clothing. Perhaps that gown was good enough for Camlynn, but we have different standards here. And don't frown, you'll wrinkle."

Instantly, my anxiety peaked. There were few things worse than bad first impressions and having one with my future mother-in-law was a worry I'd had more than once. My face relaxed, and the queen smiled as she looked at me again.

"Better. Now, most of the preparations have already been done, so really there's nothing for you to do."

What?

"Nothing? Then, if I may ask, why summon me?"

She turned to me fully. "To meet you properly, of course! My son speaks very highly of you, and I wanted to see my boy's elu for myself."

I gave a small smile that didn't quite touch my eyes. "He does, does he?"

"Yes. He mentioned you were trained as a protector. Is that right?"

"Yes, Your Maje-"

"Well, you can put all that nonsense behind you." She approached me, arms wide, and took my hands in hers. "We have plenty of warriors here for protection. All you need to do is make my son happy. Show up, say your vows, *put that ring on your finger*, and live a blissful life. Perhaps give me a few grandchildren, if you'd be so kind, because I quite miss having babies around, and the Queen of Feawar won't stop taunting me with her daughter's boys." Her smile brightened. "How does that sound? Not a care in the world!"

My mouth opened but nothing came out.

She patted my arm. "Close your mouth, dear. You look like a fish."

I immediately shut my mouth with a click of my teeth. An invisible weight began to press down on my shoulders. I felt small. Ridiculous. *You can still salvage this.* "One week until, you said?"

"Yes, one week. We have a seer snake who told us the sooner the better, and a week is the soonest we can manage. And you are staying at the Black Unicorn Inn, correct?"

"Yes, Your M-"

She lightly slapped my arm. "Well, I *insist* you spend the next week in the castle. You will need to get used to the comforts this kind of life can provide. I can't have you being shy with the servants or meekly skulking about. You will be a Princess of Wistran." She paused and narrowed her eyes, "No romantic attachments? You're a virgin, yes? "

My eyes darted around, embarrassed that someone might've overheard, but no one paid us any heed. "I am a virgin, yes." I thought of answering her first question, but I had no idea how to quantify my complicated relationship with Ramiren. *Oh, no, Your Majesty. Sure, I contracted with a broodling to teach me how to give and receive sexual pleasure, and I fantasize about him bending me over a table and ramming his-*

"Good, never know with you traveling, heroic types." She raised an eyebrow. "You're slouching again, dear."

I actually was slouching that time.

My walk back from the castle was more of a trudge, certainly different from the pleasant journey there. My body felt beaten and bruised, as though having just been in a fight. My muscles ached. My stomach was in tight knots.

I wish my mother was here.

I went up the stairs to my room, put the key into the lock, and turned it when there was a soft voice behind me. "You're back."

I turned to see Ramiren leaning against the door frame of his room, arms crossed. My exhaustion reared its ugly head, making me wish for the peace and quiet of my room.

"Yes. I'm back."

He frowned. "What happened?"

Everything. "Nothing. She's just... very ..."

Ramiren finished for me. "Demanding?"

"Yes, that's one way of saying it. I am to leave the inn and move into the castle." There was a flicker of emotion behind his red eyes again for some reason. *I'm sure he's just worried. Stop imagining things.* "And I am to take nothing with me."

Ramiren dropped his arms and straightened. He slowly began to come closer, his footsteps heavy on the wood floor. "What do you mean *nothing*?"

I tried to shrug away his concern, but my shoulder muscles twitched in protest. "I am to get rid of all possessions. They will provide everything I need or want."

Ramiren stared. "That's quite extreme."

"She insisted. And if I am to please my new family-"

He never interrupted or chastised me. So, when he did this time, with his voice sounding unusually rough, my back went rod-straight. "They need to give you grace, Nathalia. This is all incredibly sudden, worryingly so. What of pleasing yourself? Making yourself happy? Is that not something you ever intend to do?"

This unexpected quest. The hard, dirty, uncomfortable traveling. Mindless caravan routes. The endless searching. The childhood loss and adulthood reclamation of my creativity. The battles with hags. This all-consuming pact. Fighting with and upsetting Raewyn. And, now, fighting with and displeasing Ramiren.

No control. No rudder. And doomed to fail everyone, even myself.

Something broke in me.

My legs turned to jelly and gave out as a great pressure settled on my chest, like a giant boulder rested there. I collapsed with my back against my door, sliding down and feeling the planks pull and catch the fabric of my gown. The rough wood was no doubt ruining my favorite silk dress, but I couldn't bring myself to care. *Not as though I'll be able to wear this again anyway.*

Ramiren was immediately at my side, taking my hands in his.

I inhaled, or tried to. My lungs forced out air in a wheeze and would not take breath in.

"I ca-... can't breathe..." I gasped, squeezing his hands. My chest *hurt*. Darkness crept up at the edge of my vision.

Panic.

"Look at me. Look at me, Nathalia," he commanded.

My eyes, watery and stinging, met his. There was concern there. And something like fear.

"Good. Now, take a deep br- don't shake your head at me. Take a deep breath. In and out."

Tears ran rivers down my cheeks as I tried to force the air out as he'd demanded.

"Now out, angel. In."

I inhaled, focusing on his face and calming voice. My shaking hands gripped his steady, rougher ones while he gently rubbed my palms with his thumbs.

"Out."

I breathed out slowly through my mouth, puffing my cheeks. My chest pain lessened. The stone slowly lifted, and my vision began to clear. My eyes closed for a moment, prompting more tears to fall down my cheeks. They were quickly swept away with a brush of his fingers.

With a sniffle, I whispered, "Sorry."

"You need never apologize for that." He moved errant strands of hair out of my face then bent my head down to press his lips to my forehead. I closed my eyes again at the embrace, grateful to have something solid to hang on to as I clutched his shirt sleeves in my hands.

"Now, what brought that on?"

"I felt out of control. Like I was on the brink of failure, and I could do nothing."

He helped me stand, taking almost all of my weight, and opened the door to allow me to enter my room.

He followed me in, closing the door, and sat me on the bed before crouching down silently in front of me. The warmth of his hands soaked through the silk fabric covering my thighs as his fingers slipped into mine.

More tears prickled at the back of my eyes and blinking them away did nothing except make them fall. I sniffed again and peered down at my lap. Trying for pragmatic, my voice sounded a little like M.A.L.C.O.L.M. when I finally spoke, "Raewyn wants my Extended Pouch, but she's not speaking to me. Could you give it to her for me, please?"

Ramiren sighed, rubbing his fingers on mine soothingly, and replied, "She left, angel."

My head shot up. "What?"

"Her, Georgina, and M.A.L.C.O.L.M. left shortly after you did for the Ivory Grove. I'm sorry to be the one to tell you."

With Georgina? But she didn't even say goodbye.

I straightened, taken aback, and tried to comprehend what he was saying. "She left with Georgina? But they hate each other."

"It seems they agreed on this. That it was best to go now before..." He trailed off. He closed his mouth, lips thinned in regret and sympathy.

She really wasn't going to be here.

Biting back a sob and shutting my eyes, I just wished the tears would just go away.

I hate crying.

It made me feel drained. Empty. I craved balance, not too emotional, not too cold. It was just so very difficult to do. Heartache threatened to overwhelm me again, like a too-full teacup, and I couldn't stop the overflow. A whimper escaped when my hands covered my face. I immediately felt warm arms wrap around me in a tight embrace.

There was no holding it in any longer. I just let go in a surge of racking sobs as my entire body shook, like taking a long bath in ice water. The dam burst, and all my fears, frustrations, and bitterness rushed out in a torrential flood of despair. Wave after wave of grief battered me and would not stop.

She left. She left. She left.

Ramiren did not try to shush me. He did not try to tell me everything would be all right. He simply held me and let me cry.

Please don't leave me, too.

Chapter Twenty-Seven
The Last Lesson

Almost a week later, there was a knock on my chamber door, gentle but insistent.

At this hour? Gods, I hope it's not the queen grumbling about my choice of gowns again.

I opened it to see Ramiren standing there, and I choked on my heart as it flew into my throat. It took everything I had to not crush him in an embrace, even if wriggling doubt nagged me

So, I kept the giddiness at bay. I had not seen him in the last week. Not since the day I had broken down, and he'd been forced to calm me. There was no indication he'd thought less of me, but our parting was filled with numb goodbyes.

I kept my mind busy as best I could with dress measurements, learning my place here, what my duties would be, and being introduced to important staff, namely the housekeeper and the head butler, and countless courtiers who'd come out of the woodwork now that the mischief hag was gone. They all had their opinions on me and my presence, but at least the staff were subtle about their more negative comments. *Some things never change, no matter where you are. They'd all accept me in time.*

I was strongly discouraged from going outside the castle, for my safety. Though they never specified exactly what they were keeping me safe from, I assumed more of the mischief hag's henchmen were still roaming about and very few guards could be provided for an escort with the increase of present nobility for the wedding. And I wanted to make them happy, after all, not worried for my well-being. If the henchmen were as skilled as the two I faced in the street, I couldn't exactly blame them.

I was told Ramiren, my one remaining friend in the city, had tried to see me, but the queen disapproved of the visit, saying it would spread unfair gossip. She said she didn't want to put me in that position.

Fast wagging tongues could destroy reputations, and I was just getting acquainted with everyone, so I didn't argue too vehemently there either.

But seeing him now, I realized just how badly I'd missed my friend. I missed his touch. His embrace. But, most of all, I missed talking to him. There'd been no whispers from him, and no messages received. I was completely alone here and knew no one. I'd tried to make a few friends, but those were among the staff. When the queen had learned of it, she'd chided me.

How is he here now? How'd he get in?

"Ramiren!" My heart hammered just seeing him again, and I couldn't help my smile. "How did you-," I said, stepping to the side to let him enter.

Ramiren walked in and immediately turned to face me, interrupting my question, "So, tomorrow is the day, yes?"

I poked my head out to see if the guards were there, but the corridor was entirely empty. *They're usually right outside my room.* I closed the door quietly. "It is, yes. Preparations are done. Guests are settled. Now, I just need to put on a dress and walk."

"Good, though it seems odd. Almost as though they were expecting you and the preparations began well before he proposed. I wonder if the prince gave his intentions to his parents before *courageously* coming to our rescue in the street. Which begs the question, why prepare for something that might not actually happen? If you had said no, I mean." He lowered his head to peer over his glasses at me.

I considered his words and shook my head. "He may not know me well enough to read my mind, but any single woman, I think, would enjoy being a prince's consort. Especially a handsome one."

He asked quietly. "And have you? Enjoyed being a prince's consort?"

My eyebrows furrowed at his question. "I'm not his consort yet."

It felt like he was trying to make a firm point, but I couldn't see it.

He stuck his hands in his pockets. I looked and saw the fists ball there. "I see. And what of his heart? His mind? Are those handsome as well?"

Where was this coming from? "I do not know them well enough to ascertain that yet."

His voice had a strange edge to it. "Well, I'm sure you'll find out soon enough. Nevertheless, I'm happy for you, if you are happy."

"Thank you," I gave a relieved sigh. There was no strength in me to fight him on this. Or anyone. Not anymore.

Ramiren approached me. "Tomorrow is an important day for you, and it'll be a long one, no doubt. So, if you want to dissolve the pact now, we can."

My heart went into my throat again with my pulse pounding my skull. *No. Not now. Please.*

The pact was the last remaining connection we had. In my quiet moments, I could feel it buzzing at the back of my mind. That link was the only reason my sanity hadn't frayed like an old rug.

I stumbled over words in my head to keep him there. *I am not yet married. A lesson. Please. A lesson.* "We have one night left. One lesson, if you agree."

Ramiren's chest brushed mine as he looked down at me. He seemed to consider my request, then took his glasses off to clean them on his shirt. "A last lesson, yes. Part of me hoped *you* would initiate one. I had a plan, if you consent." He put his glasses back on, sliding them up his nose with his index finger.

Why not just initiate one yourself, Ramiren? I gave you express permission to.

"Yes. I consent."

He snapped his fingers. At once, we found ourselves in comfortable surroundings. The pink and white wands sat on the bedside table.

While I undressed, something felt off. Disconnected. I couldn't put my finger on it, but there was certainly a difference between the previous lesson and this one.

He motioned toward the large canopy bed as he removed his glasses to set them on a table. "Climb onto the bed, stay by the edge, and bend over at the waist to get onto all fours, facing away from me. Use the wands as you see fit. You remember the command words?"

With a nod, I did as bidden, crawling onto the soft velvet cover with my rear toward him, but I did not reach for the wands yet. It was a new position. Vulnerable. Unable to see anything except the covers under me, I could only hear his breathing and a hard swallow. He placed a hand on my left hip, and I inhaled and shifted on the bed at the unexpected touch.

He spoke, and I looked over my right shoulder at him to listen. "I need to prepare you, first, so this causes as little pain as possible. To be transparent, I'm going to use my fingers in your ass, and in order for this to not be painful, you'll need to relax as best you can. Trust me. I won't hurt you." He lifted an ornate bottle from the table and put what looked like oil on his fingers.

Whispering my reply, I turned back around, lowering my head to my arms on the mattress with my ass raised toward him, "I trust you."

He set the bottle down and walked to my side again, running a gentle hand along my spine. I sucked in a breath as my back arched. Tracing fingertips along the curves of my hips and thighs, I heard him take a deep breath.

"You're not using the wands," he said. It was not a question, merely a statement.

"No, not yet. I have them within reach, but I didn't want to spoil this. If that's the right word."

He let out a low chuckle. "Understood."

He did what he promised, using his fingers, preparing me for what was to come. At first, it was alien. Uncomfortable and invasive. But the discomfort soon melted away, replaced with the same delicious pressure and pulsing I'd come to expect during a lesson. I let out a moan, and he added another finger in response. Again, the discomfort, the slight sting, but I did my best to relax as he instructed. After a moment, the discomfort receded again and an agonizing need took its place.

When my hips began to move with his fingers, seeking more friction, he slowly removed them and placed more of the oil on me. When he went to a water basin to wash his hands, I watched him, his face, as a myriad of emotions played out across his body and features. Some were known to me: need, arousal. Some not. He looked to be nervously thinking. After drying his hands, he stepped toward me again then stopped abruptly. His eyes shuttered. "I'm sorry. I don't think this is a good idea."

Wait, no!

My heart withered. I *knew* something was off. I gazed at him, confused, and sat down on my haunches and turned to look at him fully. "What's wrong, Ramiren?"

Ramiren stared at me without a word for a long while. Then, he finally spoke, "I have excellent control, but there's too great a chance of me slipping and accidentally breaking the pact, bringing down consequences quite unfairly."

I looked at him sideways, unease slipping into my tone. "What do you mean *slipping*?"

He grimaced. "Entering one passage when I meant to enter another. It... can sometimes happen, even with experienced lovers. I really shouldn't have suggested it."

I stared at him for a beat, then inhaled sharply while scrambling away. The initial, knee-jerk emotion I felt was one of indignation, like he was trying to manipulate me.

"How d-"

Then, before a sentence I'd surely regret could complete, the emotion softened to acceptance.

And softened again, to understanding.

It's Ramiren. He wouldn't do that. Not with this.

It had been disappointment and surprise, not anger, that'd fueled my reaction. He wanted to protect me from a broken pact, and he was certainly within his rights to amend our agreement, to refuse me, to refuse anything. Just as I had the right to refuse.

I was not used to being the one protected. And with Ramiren, there would be no boasting that he did so.

My trust in him was as solid as ever, and I had poorly wrestled with the relentless need, denying myself something desperately yearned for but couldn't bring myself to surrender to.

All of this pretense. All of these precautions. Why? To assuage my husband's pride?

With Ramiren, it certainly wasn't to avoid accidental pregnancy.

So, what else was it? Just so that I could say I was a virgin truthfully?

Pbbbt.

I didn't care anymore.

I was tired of caring.

Tired of dancing around the ache in my chest. The throbbing between my legs. The emptiness I wanted only him to fill. And now, the night before my wedding to someone else, I *wanted*.

I'd reprimanded Raewyn for her stubbornness, but which of us was the most stubborn?

Had any of it ever mattered? I guarded my virginity like I guarded people, with selfless abandon. Everything about me, my body, my shield, had been saved for others. I never took anything for myself.

But why? Because my father said to? My hypocrite father? Why would he do that? Say that?

Raewyn's words about him, his past, echoed in my head like a persistent song. It was not like him, a fully-winged former servant of the Tarindar, to try to have it both ways.

I thought back to what my father had said, *safeguard your virtue*, and realized with startling clarity, like a flash of lightning in my mind, that Raewyn was right. Virtue could mean many things. Maybe it didn't mean my virginity. Perhaps instead he meant my fortitude. My self-sacrifice. My virtues as a protector, and not as a woman. That's what was truly important.

My honor, not some vague notion of purity.

Again, instead of anger, I felt disappointment.

My entire life, I might have denied myself on a misunderstanding. I'd never asked my father to specify because of embarrassment. Shame. I assumed. I always assumed and rarely asked. I did it with my father, and I did it with Ramiren.

And if not? If he meant my virginity? Well. Then, my father can go fuck himself.

I'm doing something for myself for a change.

"I would like to dissolve the pact, Ramiren."

Ramiren's eyes went wide, and his chest lifted and fell rapidly with his breathing. The lights in the room, every candle and even the lit fireplace, flared bright purple for a moment then went back to their usual orange glow. The sadness in his eyes shone like a sea beacon. His voice was rough and tinged with regret. "Yes, I think that is wise. Tomorrow, you wed and will no longer have a use for the pact. Tonight's lesson would have been helpful, but not strictly necessary." He swallowed hard.

Was I imagining pain in his eyes? Frustration? Wordlessly, I lifted my hand toward him, palm up, asking for his hand.

Ramiren let out an exhale and reached out to take my hand. He looked down at our entwined fingers. "I'm sorry. It was not my intention in the slightest to cause you pain. Quite the opposite. I am so very sorry, Nathalia."

Either he refuses and leaves... or he accepts.

And luck favors the brave.

"No, Ramiren. You don't understand. I would like to make a *new* pact," I said calmly.

His eyes shot up, and he blinked a few times in surprise. "You're right. I *don't* understand. The hags are defeated. And after tomorrow, you will have a husband. You will no longer require my instruction."

It was true. I would have a husband. But that was tomorrow's problem. Tonight, I required more. More of him. And we needed a fresh start. A fresh pact. "Yes, even if the instruction is only for one night, I would like a new pact. And we would lose access to this place if we don't, I think. Would you like to?"

He stared at me for a long time before answering. "I would, yes," he said softly. "What are your terms?"

My eyes swept over his face, especially his mouth. I placed my fingertips there, not quite to silence him or any protest he might have. Merely to touch. My eyes met his. There was another pause, though there were no feelings of nervousness or hesitation, simply a respect due to the gravity of my words.

You want explicit, Ramiren? Fine.

Finally, I replied, "I want you to fuck me, Ramiren."

He stood like a pillar. Ramiren's lips parted, his jaw dropping just enough for me to see his canines. His eyes, however, softened with emotions I didn't recognize on him. He breathed out, "Why?"

I knew he was asking *why now*, the night before I was to wed Jaylin. When I was so close to my goal, why do this?

Words began pouring out of me. Words I didn't realize I'd kept inside until now. "Because my whole life, I thought I'd been told by my father, 'Safeguard your virtue, for it is a precious thing.' I always took that to mean my virginity. That my entire worth was tied up living for another's benefit and happiness. But that idea of worth came from my own expectations for myself, and now I understand what my father meant. He meant my heart, my oaths, my resolve, and my word. You've helped to show me what I was missing, Ramiren. My worth is in my friends, those I love, and the courage I feel when protecting them. It's in my songs, my smile." I smiled in a pause and felt the sting of tears gathering.

"My joy. It's in the small moments. You've made me see I was wrong. You've made me want more. You've made me feel like I deserve to be completely happy, for myself and not on another's behalf. You've shown me how life can be, in such a short amount of time. How it should be, with difficulties and dirt, yes, but also with laughter and warmth. You've shown what I was missing. In short, I want it to be you not because I think you deserve it, in so much as one can deserve such a thing, or that I feel obligated. It is my selfish choice, and my choice is you."

His eyes bored into mine, as if thinking before he spoke. "The answer is yes."

I give the monologue of my life, and that's how he responds?

"Yes, what?"

"Your question last week, after our previous lesson. The one I refused to answer. I did change myself for you. Or, at least, I tried to. It's a difficult habit to break with what I do, to adjust your behavior based upon what you feel others might need. I am a chameleon, my color blending into my surroundings. But more than I'd care to admit slipped through with you. It was not something I could help, though I damn well tried." He smiled ruefully before going on. "What you see now... is me. It's important to me that you do. Not the instructor, or the pactmaker. Simply me."

I hoped I managed to keep myself from grinning too smugly. "I know. You have more tells than you think, Ramiren."

He produced an amused smile I'd never seen before. It was open and honest, and so very unburdened. He moved to sit on the side of the bed near me and reached out a hand to graze my jawline with his thumb. His gaze moved to meet mine. "You are sure?"

Appreciating the question, I ran my fingers along his wrist. "I've never been so sure of anything in my entire life." I felt relaxed and at ease. That was when I knew for sure I'd made the right decision.

A warm glow settled in my chest when I looked at him naked and vulnerable before me. I lowered my hand, and he did the same. "For speed and efficiency, let's just say this new pact can be identical to the old one, with the exception of keeping my virginity intact. Agreed?"

He nodded solemnly, his smile gone. In its place was a set jaw. "I accept those terms."

My eyes shut firmly. "Oh, shit. Payment. I owe you payment, but you have everything that I once owned now. I have nothing to give."

He stared at me and narrowed his eyes as though thinking. "A kiss, then. A kiss should suffice for payment."

With a crooked smile, I rested my forehead on his shoulder. "So little?"

His fingers brushed my hair out of my face. "It's not little to me, Nathalia."

My hands went to either side of his face to pull him closer, bringing my lips to his. He inhaled, drawing his tongue across mine slowly. Breaking the kiss, he grinned, "The pact is sealed."

"The pact is sealed," I repeated.

Ramiren's eyes glowed like a campfire, and the candles in the room flickered. "Lie back now. I have plans for you."

Excitement thrummed in my blood. I didn't know what all to expect, but with my creativity restored, I'd at least have a better guess. "I hope those plans involve filling me full with your cock and cum."

He laughed under his breath. "*Gods above*, Nathalia. What have I created?" His sheepish grin married beautifully with the slight color on his cheeks.

No matter what happened in my life, I would always cherish the night I made Ramiren blush.

He gently maneuvered between my knees on the bed, moving legs that were already moving of their own accord. Lying down himself, he wrapped his hands around my thighs, tugged me closer, and took a long lick through my pussy, from entrance to clit. The pressure and throbbing resumed in full force, now mixed with the contentment stemming from the warm glow still living in my chest.

I gasped, throwing my head back, and inched a hand to his hairline. Instead of running my fingers through his hair, I gently touched the pitch-black horn on his left temple. He gripped my thighs harder and let out a rough moan against me. I felt trapped, but the inability to move, the necessity of having to take the lashing of his tongue, increased the sensations he was giving me. My hand moved to his hair, running my fingers through its softness.

I felt him move his right hand and open me with his fingers. Long, slow motions that heightened the building euphoria. He continued with his tongue, focusing mostly on my clit, and occasionally licked lower to lap at the arousal that would ease the later event. The pressure in my belly increased and dipped then began to slowly rise to hit a peak.

"Come here. *Please*," I begged.

Ramiren gave a throaty growl in reply and only lapped harder with the flat of his tongue. I murmured, begged, pleaded for him to fuck me, but he refused. I told him I needed him, and still he would not relent. The warmth and throbbing in my pussy was a torturous ache. I started to peak again, and Ramiren slowed, as though he knew I was close to release.

I whimpered, my thighs scraping against the tips of his horns as his head moved between them. My hand went into his hair, this time to grip it. His lips wrapped around my clit. Just as he started sucking, the pressure released like a valve. My back arched hard as I screamed, which continued long after I had run out of air in my lungs. I bucked so hard against his face that the rasp of his beard sent a fresh wave of need through me.

I shuddered as his licks turned soft and let out a breathy, ragged moan. I could barely speak, the words coming out as more of a whisper, "*Please. I need you.*"

I've always needed you. Please don't make me wait anymore.

Ramiren made a low, rough sound in his throat, vibrating his tongue, and my eyes rolled back.

Without warning, he grabbed my hips to pull me toward him on the bed. His breathing was quiet but fast, and he looked down with an intensity that shot through me. He swallowed, then lifted my hips to his. The tip of his cock pressed into my entrance and stopped, his hands somehow supporting my weight. I sucked in a breath then held it and waited.

I waited as patiently as I could. It might've been two seconds or two centuries. I couldn't tell.

When he still didn't move, I squirmed, trying to finish the job he'd started. He hissed, and I looked him full in the face. He was staring down at me, eyes wide and wild. I had no idea what he was doing. My held breath left me in a huff. "What are you-"

"*Don't. Fucking. Move.*"

His forehead had a sheen to it, finger-touseled waves falling over it and sticking. His muscles were flexed and strained, though I didn't think it was from holding me up. It was from holding himself back.

Fuck it.

I growled. "Ramiren, I swear, if you don't fuck me right-"

He bit off a curse and surged forward, entering me, cutting off my words with my own scream. The sting of stretching was manageable, easily overshadowed by the blissful feeling of fullness. He whispered in a strained exhale, "Holy fuck," as his fingers bit into my hips. He leaned forward, lowering me back on the bed.

When he put his weight on me, the glow in my chest radiated from my neck to my thighs. I wrapped myself around his warm body as he gently began to thrust in and out of me, kissing and nipping at my shoulder. When his cock delved even deeper, the stretching and fullness intensified until his hips were flush with mine, and I almost swallowed my tongue when I clenched around him.

He rolled his hips, grinding against my clit while running his right hand down my flank and under my ass. I wanted to cry. I felt like crying. Instead, I moaned softly, incapable of proper language.

My face turned to nuzzle his jaw and saw his own contorting with both strained arousal and tenderness. My hands moved to either side of his face, and I crushed my mouth to his. The snap of his hips quickened when his hand moved from under my ass to entangled in my hair and tilt my head just the way he wanted.

A soft whine escaped him, muffled in my mouth. *Gods, that whine again...*

He broke the kiss with a hoarse groan, planting his face firmly against my neck. I could feel his canines grazing the skin, and something dark within me wanted him to bite down. His hand released my hair and traveled down, ending at my breasts to cup and massage with kneading fingers. He plucked the hardened nipple, and it felt like he'd plucked my clit. I let out a shriek. Without warning, his movements became frantic and nearly uncontrolled while he murmured in a harsh language I didn't understand. The pressure began to build again, and when the first real throb hit, it combined with the stretch and delicious fullness into something divine, and somehow also profane. My fingers roamed from his jaw to his hair, tugging and messing the dark waves.

CORDANI!

The voice screamed the word. I didn't care if it was a hallucination. A word without context or definition, it was mine alone. Like Ramiren was now. Both precious to me.

I lifted his head by his hair, and my eyes bore into his as I rolled my hips in time with his grinding. He said something else in that harsh language, and though I didn't know the words, I understood the meaning.

Joy and pain. Exhilaration and loss. Capturing something, then having to let it go.

He reared up to his knees, pulling me with him. He lifted my ass off the bed again and held my hips as he drove into me. He gulped in air, letting out a tortured groan. His red eyes glowed faintly. Smoke curled off of his horns. His canines lengthened. For a moment, I didn't see a man staring down at me. I saw a devil.

But it didn't frighten me. It was still Ramiren.

I shuddered, as though suddenly cold, then choked out a sobbing scream at what was happening. There was a peak, but also a feeling of something intense and all-consuming unleashing itself, like it was leaving my body with a gentle but unstoppable force. It was emotional and desperate, and I was experiencing too much. I felt him everywhere.

In the haze of my orgasm, I heard the voice again. But now, it was in my head. And had gained more words.

Cordani tro acta.

He fell back over me, hand tangling my hair again. "Gods, angel," he whispered next to my ear, as though tormented and pained.

When I wrapped my arms around him fully. It occurred to me my hands had never been on his back when he finished. His muscles hardened under my palms, undulating with his body's movements. Ramiren let out a low growl, almost a warning. He buried his face in the crook of my neck again and gripped my hair hard as he gave a keening scream. His whole body shook over me. There was no pride or triumph, like I thought I would feel, at such a reaction from him. Merely a sense of deep satisfaction.

He continued to thrust into me long after, though noticeably slower and softer, as though he wanted to prolong the encounter. His rapid, heavy breathing began to ease.

Eventually, he slowed to a stop and silently lifted his head to look down at me. He was hoarse when he finally spoke with choked words. "Are you all right?" He frowned deeply, lifting his head higher. "You're crying." He released my hair, brushing his thumb across my damp temple.

I hadn't even realized.

My only response was a crooked grin, and his frown vanished with a look of relief. The throb in my pussy morphed into an ache, and I knew deep down I would be very sore for my wedding.

I do not fucking care.

I bent his head down to kiss his forehead softly, then his cheek, then lips. Wispy kisses. I ran my fingertips over the shells of his ears and smiled. Wonderful contentment filled me, just as surely as he had.

I guess the poets were right.

There were a few long moments of silence, broken only by the sounds of breathing. Then, he rolled over to my side, sliding out of me, and immediately took me into his arms. I rested my head on his shoulder and felt his heart still beating erratically when I placed my hand on his chest.

Finally, I broke the silence, "When are you leaving for the grove?"

He held me tighter. "Don't do that. Not now," he said quietly into my hair.

I pursed my lips. "Are you attending the wedding?"

He let out a harsh breath. "No. I will not, but I'll not leave until I hear bells ringing."

Unsurprising, but the idea made my chest ache so much I had trouble breathing. My hand went there and rubbed to ease the pain.

"Are you all right?" He lifted his head slightly to look down at me with stark concern.

"Hm? Yes, I'm all right." I put my hand back on his chest, splaying my fingers. I breathed with him, and the ache went away after a few moments.

There was a quiet pause, before it was broken by a whisper, "Why are you marrying him, Nathalia?"

I hid my face in the crook of his neck, my words muffled, "Because I gave my word."

Ramiren's hand went into my hair. "Is he worth your word?"

I replied coldly, "He has to be."

I could feel myself drifting off to sleep. Tomorrow, I would marry, but tonight I had what I wanted.

The next morning, I awoke alone in a cold bed. I curled up and began to weep, and I didn't know exactly why.

Chapter Twenty-Eight
Lavender is for Luck

"There, Lady Nathalia. All ready and quite beautiful, I must say." My older mus fey attendant fluffed my long-sleeved lavender dress then twitched her nose as she scrutinized me from head to toe for any necessary last minute alterations. While humans typically married in white and elves in gold, fey married in lavender. I was told the color gave good luck, and I needed all the luck I could get today.

Deep breath.

My heart beat like a drum in my ribcage, and my pulse throbbed in my ears. *I can do this. This is what I always wanted. I can do this.*

Raewyn's words suddenly popped into my mind, and I scoffed to myself. *Can't possibly be happy. Of course, I'm happy. This is what happiness looks like.*

A clawed hand burrowed into my chest and squeezed everything it could reach.

Isn't it?

"It's time," said the attendant, straightening as the broad mouse-like ears on her head opened fully. "I can hear the music."

"Hm? Oh, yes. Of course." My voice sounded far away. Everything sounded far away.

I stepped down off the pedestal, taking one last look in the mirror at myself. I did look beautiful. My silver hair was curled and plaited, running rivers down my back. A small tiara perched on top of my head glistened in diamonds and gray pearls.

The only problem was my haunted eyes staring back at me.

I looked away and moved toward the door.

"Wait!"

She pushed a bouquet of lavender roses into my hands with a smile. "You can't forget these!"

The woman opened the door for me, and I floated through, feeling as though my feet were barely touching the ground. Vaguely registering the hallway to the wide and winding stairs, I startled as, the next thing I knew,

I stood before the closed double doors that led to the Great Hall. Hundreds could fit inside its walls, and every available seat would be filled.

Hundreds I didn't know.

Important dignitaries, nobles, and the like were invited out of want or obligation by Her Majesty. I had no say in the guest list, which made sense as I barely knew anyone here. Tapestries and banners were displayed without my opinion, however the queen said tradition dictated which ones were to be used as this was an eluva match. Flowers were arranged without my approval, but I wasn't very familiar with Feylands florals.

Just the ones I saw in the meadows west of the Tanta Desert.

There would be no one to give me away. I wished my mother and father could be here with me. The queen said she sent a message to Camlynn, through magical means even, but there was no reply. I wished Raewyn could be here, too. And Ramiren. Even Georgina and M.A.L.C.O.L.M. Everyone in the Great Hall would be a stranger to me. No family. No friends. I was alone.

I swallowed, my anxiety palpable to the older elven footman standing next to me. He smiled kindly. "Don't be nervous, my lady. You'll do well."

I nodded, bouncing my head quickly in agreement, not trusting myself to speak.

He bowed, then the trumpets sounded from inside the hall. *My cue.*

He smiled at me again and went to open the doors with his partner on the other side. The heavy doors groaned in protest, and the footmen had to plant their feet in the floor to move them at all.

That was the moment I realized I'd never actually dissolved the new pact. And neither had Ramiren. *Why was I thinking of that?*

Plastering a pleasant, unbothered smile on my face as the doors opened, the music hit me full in the face. As did the sheer number of people present. As expected, the hall was packed to the brim with all sorts, fey and others, and I again wished my parents could be here to see this. I searched for Ramiren, even though he said he would not attend.

He was nowhere in sight.

For some reason, that made me glad.

I stepped across the marble floor and onto the green carpet runner between the pews of guests and witnesses, heading toward the altar. My future. Gripping my bouquet like a lifeline, the thorns from the roses bit into my skin and made me focus. Forward I went, upright and stiff. Some might call it good posture, but composed and rigid were not the same.

I stopped next to Jaylin, who smiled as he gently took my hand. We faced the priest together, with my eyes shifting from Jaylin to the fey priest of Valiset as he began to speak.

"The union of two souls into one is a holy event, symbolizing the meeting of heaven and earth. It is this..."

A buzzing began in my ears, drowning out the priest who was droning on about the religious importance of marriage. Normally, I would be interested in his words, but my stomach lurched.

"...Love and fidelity, being the cornerstones of marriage..."

Sweat began to bead at my temples and above my upper lip. My breathing increased.

"...forsaking the embrace of all others..."

Panic. Pure panic clutched at me. My heartbeat was pounding in my ears. Breathing became difficult as the boulder pressed down.

"...Do you, Jaylin Torik Lorenaskan, Prince of Wistran, Duke of Kopi..."

What the fuck are you doing?

"...swear to love and cherish your wife for all of your days..."

Wake up, Nathalia. Wake up. Wake up.

A wild thought occurred to me. *Maybe this is an illusion. Is the mischief hag still alive?*

My eyes darted around for any tells that it was an illusion, but there was nothing.

"...guide her, protect her, and honor her..."

Oh gods, this is real. I'm getting married. To him.

"And do you, Nathalia Maxliana Swordhand, Lady of Camlynn and Protector Initiate..."

My inner voice turned soft, familiar... and masculine. ***"Please don't."***

"...help him, submit to him, and honor him..."

The boulder evaporated from my chest, and the sudden relief made my next word come out as a gasp, "Stop."

Chapter Twenty-Nine
Princess Nathalia

The priest blinked rapidly, then he peered down at me in stark confusion. "I'm sorry, what did you say, child?"

Oh. I'd said it out loud.

But it felt so good, so freeing, that I said it again, this time louder. My heartbeat softened. The pain in my chest was gone. My mouth curved in a wide grin, and I must've looked like I was going mad.

"I said, stop."

Soft tittering sounded from the crowd at my simple words. The priest stuttered, "But, we're just starting, child, you're merely nervous and..."

"I said, *stop*!" I yelled so no one could be mistaken. It echoed throughout the Great Hall, over the chatter of those assembled.

Jaylin gripped my hand and whispered harshly into my ear, "Not now, Nathalia. We'll continue and sort this out later... Give me the ring." He turned toward the befuddled priest, squeezing my hand to the point of pain. Or it would have, if I was capable of feeling pain at that moment. I felt no pain. I felt alive.

"Nope. I'm done." I threw my sweaty hand back, away from him, to release it from his hard grasp. People in the pews gasped.

Jaylin's mouth twisted in anger. "Done? You gave me your word, you bi-"

"You can *politely* go fuck yourself, *Jaylin*." I raised the middle finger of my right hand at him. I'd never done it before, but it seemed appropriate.

Based upon everyone's reaction, it was also effective.

People stood from the pews in shocked cries and stifled laughter as I turned heel to run for the double doors at the back of the Great Hall. Toward my freedom.

Behind me, Jaylin yelled, "Footmen! Close the doors!"

You think you can trap me in here? Force me?

An amused snort escaped me as I leaned forward, running as fast as my legs could carry me. People continued rising from their pews in either outrage or surprise. The footmen sprang into action, straining to close the doors in time. *Almost there.*

When my slippered feet left the green carpet and hit the marble floor, I did the only thing I could think of.

Dropping to the ground as I ran, my silk dress provided no traction on the polished stone, and I slid right through the narrow passage between the doors just as they were closing.

Jaylin's yells continued, albeit muffled. "Footmen! Gods-damn it! Open the doors!"

With a smug grin, I stood and took note of my surroundings. There was no one else in the area. All guards and guests were trapped on the other side of the doors. *Free. I am free. But where to now?*

Immediately, Ramiren came to mind. *Perhaps he was still at the Black Unicorn Inn. The bells hadn't rung yet.*

I picked up my skirts and ran out the castle's open front doors to see a carriage had been hitched and pulled up, with guards on either side. The one closest to me looked surprised. "Princess Nathalia, what-"

Princess Nathalia. He thought I was already married. With all due authority.

"Get off your mount. I need it." When he hesitated, I scowled. "That's an order!"

He quickly dismounted off the six-legged feyhorse and stumbled back as I hopped up to straddle the mount's back. The ornery beast whinnied at my weight and reared up once as I grabbed the reins with my one free hand, refusing to submit. *Temperamental beasts. I had nearly forgotten.*

"Yah!" I yelled, snapping the reins while digging my heels into his flanks. The beast bucked once then took off like a bow shot through the open portcullis of the front gates of the castle.

"Guards! What are you doing? Stop her!"

Jaylin screamed angry commands, and the hoofbeats of several guards still mounted followed in my wake. The chase was on, and I welcomed them to try to drag me back. Though now hunted, my elation was almost equal to what I felt in Ramiren's arms the night before. Almost.

I also didn't realize how sore I was until now.

The feyhorse galloped through cobbled streets, dodging deftly between wheelbarrows, carts, and people. The mount's maneuverability was impressive. *Better than horses in Laeth. They'd better be, with how stubborn they are.* I chanced a glance over my shoulder and could see the other guards hot on my trail. Blood pumping and nerves spiked, I urged the feyhorse on faster. He whinnied again, but thankfully did as bidden.

Pedestrians screamed, throwing themselves to the side at my fast approach. I ducked under shop signs. Wagons overturned when the feyhorses and blue mules that were pulling them got spooked as my feyhorse ran past. A pang of guilt hit at the trouble I was causing, until I looked back again to see the guards having to stop when a particularly large cart had flipped in the middle of the avenue, blocking their path. One guard had been flung from his mount and was attempting to get back on him. My guilt vanished.

I guess lavender really is lucky.

Following the wide road as it curved to the left, heading in the direction that would lead to the inn, I did not slow my pace. My mount showed no signs of exhaustion, despite putting him through his paces.

Please be there. Please be there.

The shops and stalls on either side went by in an unfocused blur. Shouts behind me signaled that the guards had gotten through the block and would be closing in. There wasn't much time.

Eventually, the sign with a painted black unicorn came into view, and I pulled on the reins to stop in front of it. Suddenly grateful Ramiren had my Extended Pouch instead of my sister, I slid off the animal and ran into the inn with the sound of shouts and calls echoing behind me.

Charging through the large common room and bounding up the stairs, taking two at a time, I turned the corner around the bannister and collided with a chest covered in a black jacket with red trim. "Oof!"

A surprised and confused Ramiren didn't even stumble, though I did. His hand shot out to catch me from falling back down the stairs. "Nathalia? Wha-" He carried both pouches on his belt, looking ready to set out. *He was just leaving.*

"I couldn't do it. We need to get out of here. We need to go. *Now!*"

The sound of a dozen people crashing into the common room downstairs made his eyes go wide.

"Princess Nathalia!" they yelled.

"She ran up there!" a nasally man's voice barked, presumably the damnable barkeep. Taking a few steps away from him, I looked to see how close the guards were and if there was another exit.

He wasted no time. There was no hesitation. "I'll whistle, but we'll need a pact for it. Payment! Quickly!" He extended a trembling hand to me.

My hands still somehow held my bouquet. It was all I had. "Here!" I threw the flowers to his waiting hand.

Or would have, if I was good at throwing.

In my panic, I'd tossed it too hard, and it sailed past his snapping fingers to the far side of the hallway where it hit with a dull thud against the wall. A pained and panicked expression crossed his face as the clamoring of footsteps on the stairs got louder. "A kiss won't work for this!"

"Oh, my tiara!" I untangled it from my unruly hair and held it out to him. He took it from my hand this time.

"I will take you to safety. No addendums or stipulations. The pact is sealed." He snaked a hand around my waist. "Say it, Nathalia."

"The pact is sealed." My face was mere inches from his. I stared into his campfire eyes and saw determination. Relief.

He whistled just as the first guard reached for me, and I felt myself tumbling. Weightless. Falling. My eyes closed tightly against the hellish red light surrounding me, and the sudden oppressive heat and heavy smell of sulfur stole my breath. My arms reached out, as a reflex, for something to grab onto. Or someone. My hands found lean shoulders, the muscles underneath flexed and hard.

It is straining him.

Ramiren's arms tightened around my back as he crushed his face into my neck. Then, I heard it. Screaming. We were surrounded by tortured screams and cruel laughter, coming from every direction. The sensation of overwhelming malevolence made me not dare to open my eyes.

Then, the relief of cooler fresh air hit my cheeks, and I was prone, staring down at short purple grass. Birds chirped in a tree to my right. The chittering of squirrels and the trilling of insects replaced the horrible screams.

Ramiren groaned at my side. "I hate that part."

Chapter Thirty
Marked for the Hunt

"Where were we?" I asked. We stood, dusting ourselves off and getting an idea of our new surroundings. "And where are we now?"

We were right next to a road, just a small distance from a fork to our left. A bright city was just ahead, perhaps a mile or two away. The tell-tale red roofs of the buildings, and the silver spires of the castle in the center, told us it was Carpatha.

Ramiren answered, "Looks like we're still in Wistran. We need to head east, toward the grove. And get back to Laeth."

A dull horn blew in the distance.

"But now, we need to hide. We're still not in the clear," Ramiren warned. He took my hand in his warmer one and squeezed once. "Come."

I followed, my lavender skirts hampering my movement. He led me to the treeline off to the right. "Well, I'm glad I gave you my pouch."

He glanced at me over his shoulder as we hurried into the forest. "As am I. Are your armor and weapons in there?"

"Yes, they should be."

"Good. As soon as we can, you'll need to change." He grinned at me, helping me over a fallen log in front of the brightly-colored trees. "Unless you feel like wearing your wedding dress a while longer."

"Um. No, thank you."

We hunched down behind some orange brush, and I prayed it was enough to cover my contrasting lavender gown when the hoofbeats got louder.

The riders slowly came into view. Jaylin, still dressed in his wedding finery, led the pack of guards that was hot on his tail. He stopped at the fork and called out, "You and you, take the road to the south. You, take the road north. You will follow me east toward the Ivory Grove. If you find her, bring her back to the castle."

"My prince, she was with someone when she disappeared. Tanner saw him. A broodling, by the looks of him. What if they resist?"

The look on Jaylin's face turned from angry to practically raging.

He spat out, "You will kill the bastard with her and bring my bride back, in *manacles* if need be! If she fights you, it will be with her fists only. She carries no arms. He is of no concern. Words are his weapons. No matter what, no harm is to come to her. Now! *Go!*"

All three groups took off simultaneously, going their designated directions. After the sounds of their horses had faded, we stood up. My jaw dropped, I peered at Ramiren. "Kill you? Manacles? Did I hear him right?"

"You did, my dear," he said with derision. He silently handed me my pouch, dropping the tiara under a bush to hide it. That pact concluded; he did not need to keep it anymore. "Best get changed. We cannot take the roads, so through the woods we must go. They'll get there first, but hopefully they'll search the grove, see we're not there, and double back. After they leave, we'll talk to Leraska and go home to Laeth."

What would happen once we got to Laeth? Would we stay together? Part ways? Our new pact from last night was still in place; it had not yet been dissolved. Would he end it and go along his merry way, leaving me in...

The right word eluded me.

I took the pouch, stuffing my whole arm into it to retrieve my armor, clothing, and weapons. Taking them out one-by-one to lay them out on the forest floor, I began to slip out of my wedding dress. The sharp brambles and dirt had wrecked it entirely, but it made me glad to see it so destroyed. *What a ridiculous man I almost bonded myself to. Manacles? Threatening to kill Ramiren? This is not the man who proposed to me.* I felt like an idiot, finally seeing the real him. And him trying to lock me into the Great Hall as I ran from the altar?

He showed me what he was. I owe Raewyn an enormous apology. Probably on my knees. With a chocolate offering.

Ramiren had turned his back toward me as I changed clothing. It made me smile. "You know, it's not like you haven't seen me naked before."

There was amusement in his voice, but he still did not turn around, "I am watching for the riders."

I smirked, pulling my trousers on. "I see."

"Besides," he finally looked at me over his shoulder, a wry grin on his face. "I found you just as beautiful in your gown as I do out of it. Lavender suits you, even if the groom did not."

The compliment washed over me like a balm applied to a painful wound. "Well. In hindsight, it is a good thing you did not come to the wedding. I'm not sure we could have escaped."

"That is almost certainly correct."

"Why *did* you not come to the wedding?" I tried to keep my tone neutral, but the question had been burning inside of me ever since he said he wouldn't attend.

There was silence from him for a long moment before he spoke softly, without turning around again, "Orange."

I sighed in reply and continued to lace and button my trousers. *Orange. That damned word.* But I did not want to pry. This somehow went beyond simple secrets. He had his reasons. He would tell me when he was ready, and not a moment before.

After all, I had asked him if he had changed himself for me. That question initially received a reply of 'orange,' only to be answered a scant week later. Patience was necessary, not prodding.

As I adjusted mail armor in my arms, noting it needed to be re-oiled, an errant thought occurred to me. "Ramiren, how did you change yourself for me, anyway?"

More silence, until a sigh from him broke it, and he finally faced me. Before he could reply, I interjected, "I just wanted to know, because Jaylin apparently also changed himself for me. He put up a false front to lure me into... whatever game he is playing. I trust you, truly, but I need to know."

That seemed to mollify him, as his eyes softened from impatience to understanding. "I seduced you. Seduction requires one to slightly change, adjusting your behaviors to what you believe the other person finds most attractive."

I raised my eyebrows. A nervous laugh bubbled out of me. "What?"

Ramiren sighed again. "Not to push you to dissolve the pact and bed you. Or anything of that nature. But to show you what desire was, truly was, so you could recognize it when it happened. At least, that was my intention. I could've taught you techniques until you were blue in the face, but desire?

Passion? That comes from somewhere else and is not something that can be taught. Simply understood. Desire is a choice. I seduced you purposefully so you could make that distinction."

I eyed him, my smile slowly widening, until a different laugh came out. Ramiren furrowed his eyebrows, looking confused. "What is so amusing?"

"Oh my, oh..." I continued to laugh, dropping my mail armor to hold my stomach. My laugh slowly petered out as Ramiren appeared more and more annoyed. I wiped the tears from my eyes. "Ramiren, you didn't teach me desire. I desired you well before we started the pact."

Ramiren looked taken aback, surprised. "Oh?"

"During the singing contest, do you remember? I found you in the crowd."

"Yes, I remember. And?"

"Aaaand, I wanted you from then on. You mesmerized me. I'm half-surprised I was able to keep singing. And every time we had a lesson, the want increased. I wanted you so much I hallucinated this *voice* when we were-"

"Wait," Ramiren's hand lifted at my words to interrupt me. He stepped forward slowly, speaking low and eyes narrowed. "You heard voices?"

I corrected him. "*A* voice. But it only ever said one word. Well, until last night."

He leaned back, and his jaw went slack. "What were the words?"

I briefly considered using my safe word. *This is so private.* I wanted to be open with him. To share. "It said..." Taking a breath, my head dipped in intense embarrassment.

Oh, just tell him.

But he spoke first, "*Cordani.* The voice said *cordani*, didn't it? And last night, it was *cordani tro acta.*"

My head shot up. Eyes wide, it was my turn for my jaw to go slack. "Yes. Yes, that's right. How did you know?" I stepped forward with my question, twisting my hands together.

Ramiren pursed his lips. He let in a long inhale then exhaled slowly, as though weighing his words. "Because I heard it, too."

Moving toward him quickly, my hands gripped his arms. "Wait. Do you know what it means?"

He shook his head as he looked at me, dumbfounded. "I have no idea. I've never heard that before. I tried to use my abilities to understand the word *cordani*, and it's not one that the magic allows for. I can't even tell you what the language is."

In his eyes, there was no lie. Only confusion and a touch of fear.

My lips pursed. "When did it start for you?"

His face became a mask as he continued to stare down at me. "At The Forever Inn, in Puldoni. The first night of the pact. Ever since, every time we had a lesson, I heard that voice."

I tilted my head down. "And you've no idea what it means."

"None, do you?" There was a glimpse of his stony expression dropping. He searched my eyes with an intensity I had only seen during our lessons.

But I had no answer to give him, only a shrug and a shake of my head. "No. None."

"Damn," he cursed quietly.

"Why didn't you tell me?" I asked, placing my hands on the sides of his face.

He raised an eyebrow. "Why didn't *you* tell *me*?"

Because I didn't want you to think I was crazy and delusional.

We stared at each other for a long time before I dropped my hands to my sides. "Fair point."

Ramiren frowned and looked behind him, into the woods. "If you're finished dressing, we should leave for the grove. We need to get back to Laeth as soon as possible."

"Yes. Yes, I think you're actually right. Let's go." I plucked my mail armor from the ground, shook out the leaves and twigs that had attached themselves, and pulled it on over my head, careful of my hair. The leather thong I usually used to tie my hair back was nowhere to be found. *Somewhere in the Dark Drop that is my pouch.* I'd no doubt spend a year pulling strands of hair out from the chain links. "If it's all right, I'd like to travel with you for a while after we get back. To ensure your safety."

Armor settled and sword belt buckled, I secured my shield on my back, attached my pouch to my belt, and began to walk through the dense underbrush. Ramiren muttered under his breath behind me, but I couldn't make out what he said.

We trekked through the woods, barely keeping the road in sight to make sure we were going the right way. Occasionally, we would see a rider on the road moving at breakneck speeds. Messengers, no doubt. We paid none of them any mind. So long as they did not see us, and it was doubtful they could with the thick foliage, we didn't care if there were two or twenty on the wide road leading to the grove's path. Our destination.

As long as they weren't there when we arrived.

The sun already had a hard time breaking through the canopy above our heads, so when the light faded even more, we decided to make camp. Forgoing our tents, we found a small cave inset into a stony cliff. The night turned chilly, but we did not dare risk a fire.

Ramiren began to shiver. Broodlings liked heat well enough, but he had not been exaggerating about his sensitivity to colder temperatures.

I pulled out wool blankets from my pouch, putting a few under us to protect us from the chill of the rock. The rest I put around Ramiren's shoulders.

"I'm sorry. I have no more blankets, Ramiren. This will have to do."

In the dim light, his white smile strained to show as his teeth chattered. "It's all right. But what about you?"

I scratched at an itch on my neck then shook my head. "My gambeson is thick. I will be fine."

"Please..." He said, as he lifted the blankets with his left arm, clearly inviting me to sit beside him under them. "We can share warmth."

Though not particularly cold, if my body heat could help Ramiren, I would be remiss to refuse. After removing my weapons, pouch, and armor, leaving the gambeson on as a layer, I crawled in, putting my head on his shoulder and wrapping my hands around his left arm. We sat in silence for a long while, soaking in the events of the day and each other's warmth. It was pitch black out by the time he stopped shivering. Just as the sun had trouble during the day, the moonlight could not pierce the trees. I trusted Ramiren's sight now.

Eventually, I broke the silence. "I never thanked you. I'm not used to being the one protected, and it usually bothers me when people try."

His smile could be heard in his tone. "You are very welcome, Nathalia. I'm glad I was able to be of assistance."

"No, it's more than that. You saved me, Ramiren. I'm not used to that, either." I frowned. "Did you know?"

He hesitated in responding. "Know what?"

"What *he* was like? That he would go to this trouble to salvage his pride? Threaten you? Bring me back in chains, no less."

He whispered, as though it pained him to admit. "I had my suspicions about him, yes, but vocalizing them would do worse than nothing. You wanted what you wanted, at the time, and speaking against him might lead to you doubling-down. Look at what happened with Raewyn. And what if I was wrong, and you left a good man on my word? No, you needed to make your own decision, without my influence."

I smiled. "You know me."

The rumble of a low chuckle preceded his words. "I do. Though I can read others to varying degrees, you are, for me, easy to understand."

"Am I so transparent to you?" I scratched my neck again. *Damned bug must have bitten me.*

He shrugged. "Again, to me, yes."

Disappointment weighed on me. Not that I wanted to be an enigma to my friends, but a *little* mystique wouldn't go amiss. His beard brushed my forehead as he turned his head toward me. He must have been reading my face, or my thoughts even, because he put my hand in his gently. *Damn broodlings and their vision.*

He spoke firmly, "I want you to pay attention to me now, and understand what I am saying. Listen close, Nathalia, because it is very important you hear me. I am *grateful* I can see you so clearly. You are a remarkable person.

Kind, good-hearted, gentle... except in a fight, patient, selfless." He curled his fingers around mine, entangling them, almost playing. "But you have your faults, like any other. Your self-esteem is not what it should be. Your fear of failure holds you back. Your desperate need to please and not be a burden makes you vulnerable to another's manipulations. You look for approval from others, even those whose opinion should not matter. When you want something, you are bullheaded when it comes to getting it. And by all the gods above, you have no gift for throwing." His last sentence was said with a hint of amusement. "So, if *I* may ask, why did you run from your prince?"

That's a lot of faults, Ramiren. But there were none I disagreed with.

My reasons, ever since doing it, had hogged my thoughts with an unsurprising relentlessness. "Raewyn was right. I did not love him. It used to be that it wasn't necessarily important to me, for marriage. Love would come in time, especially with that eluva bond he mentioned, I was sure. But after spending time with you, I came to realize that..."

Don't say it. No good could come of it.

I searched for the words that would convey my meaning without actually saying it. "...friendship is a needed component, at least initially. He was not my friend yet."

I heard a frown when he said, "I see."

I went on, deadpanned. "Also, I ran because he *really* did not appreciate me raising my middle finger and telling him to go fuck himself."

Ramiren's shoulders shook in silent laughter.

We crouched down as we peered through the foliage of the ample brush, searching the gardens and cottages of the Ivory Grove. We had made it here shortly after daybreak but waited to ensure neither guards nor Jaylin were around. We saw a few six-legged feyhorses but didn't know if they belonged to Jaylin or the druids. Sure enough, after roughly an hour or so, Jaylin came out of one of the small cottages, obviously having slept there that night.

We sat, watching, but he just would not leave. He milled about endlessly. Occasionally, he'd get so impatient that he'd take out his sword and hack at a fallen log with it. Or bark orders at one of the grove's druids to bring him food or drink. Or merely sit with his forehead in his hands, rubbing it as though it pained him.

His frustration made me happier than wearing his ring ever would have.

Now, though, we could see Jaylin talking with Leraska. They seemed to be arguing.

"Interesting." Ramiren whispered.

I whispered back, "What?"

"They know each other. Their body language is familiar."

I hummed. "Perhaps he visits the grove often? Regardless, it's obvious he suspects she's hiding us, and she's telling him we're not there."

Ramiren made a noise in his throat.

My head tilted to get a good look at his doubting expression. "You disagree?"

Ramiren replied, his tone skeptical, "I don't outright disagree, but I'm not sure if I agree either." He shook his head. "Either way, neither of them knows where we are, and that's a good thing."

It took the rest of the morning and well into the afternoon before Jaylin finally gave up and left, riding away in the failing light. We waited a few more minutes, just in case, then stepped out of our hiding spot.

Leraska saw us immediately. Her demeanor went from annoyed to seething as she stalked over to us. "Where have you two been?"

Ramiren and I stopped and looked at each other. *The prince must've given her a very hard time.* Ramiren's face was enigmatic as he answered her. "Hiding in the woods."

Leraska's eyebrows shot up, putting both of her hands on her staff and thumping it into the ground. She responded incredulously, "For two days?"

Ramiren replied coolly, "Yes, and we'd like to leave before he returns."

Leraska frowned deeper, hesitating, but nodded. "Very well. Come forward."

As we did, the light from her gnarled staff brightened.

Leraska leveled us with a stare. "Farewell for now."

I opened my mouth to reply, but the light from her staff exploded, and I was sent tumbling again with no breath for words.

When my whole body hit something solid, I was prone yet again, gasping as my lungs finally flooded with air and the scent of warm earth. My fingers curled into the grass under me. Green grass.

Green. Green!

With a toss of my head to get my hair out of my face, I saw green, bushy trees swaying in the soft breeze. The blue sky above me held fluffy, white clouds.

"Yes! We're safe!" We both stood and stepped together into a tight embrace.

He leaned back slightly and nodded with a strained smile. "We are home, at any rate."

Home.

My spirits lifted, I asked while still in his arms, "So, what now? Camlynn?"

He finally broke the embrace by taking a step back with an almost apologetic expression. "I think it's perhaps best if we go our separate ways."

There was a sharp snapping sound from somewhere, and my chest filled with a pressing pain. *Did I break a rib somehow? And did he hear it, too?* It sounded like a thick twig breaking inside my chest, and my body went numb all over. "Wait. Really?"

He bowed his head to look away, rubbing his neck. He murmured an apology.

Searching his face, I tried to speak past the lump in my throat, but the words came out guttural and breathless. "But why?"

So much for having all the time in the world.

Ramiren replied, "Remember what I said of circumstance choosing the end instead of us? This would be a circumstance."

After everything, he leaves me?

My stinging eyes muddled my voice even more. "Well, I hope you got that luck stone's worth." The words came out far more bitter than I intended. I immediately spun to apologize and saw him glaring at me with his features twisted in anger.

"No, Nathalia." He snarled and reached into the breast of his jacket, pulling out my mother's necklace. "Besides, this isn't a luck stone." He shook the chain in his hands, as though emphasizing his point.

Am I hallucinating words again?

"Excuse me, what?"

He tucked the necklace back, under his shirt, and motioned toward me with a raised palm before dropping his hand. "It's just a mundane necklace. It has no magical properties."

Mother lied to me? She said it brought her luck...

I opened my mouth but only a strained squeak came out. Completely unmoored, my thoughts were in disarray. Then, finally, they pinpointed on one detail, and I found my voice. "Did you know? When we started this pact, did you know it was just a plain necklace?"

Ramiren simply nodded, his face unreadable.

My head tilted back as I gave a growling grunt, and my hair fell off my shoulders. I threw my hands up weakly. Confusion and annoyance mixed in my gut and churned it like bad food. "Why? Huh, Ramiren? It's not even pretty! If it's just a plain, little trinket, why did you accept it for the lessons? Why do you wear it if it's *not magical*?" I didn't know how to feel. How I *should* feel.

He opened his mouth to answer, and then his eyes flitted to my neck, now exposed with the tilting of my head. Ramiren's eyes squinted a brief second before widening. "Oh fuck..."

I straightened immediately, my hands immediately moving to my neck. "What? What's wrong?" I moved my hair out of the way fully to allow him to look closer.

"You have a mark on your neck. A sigil." My eyes strayed to Ramiren's neck as a reflex, where he had been rubbing, and I saw a burning glyph there, partially hidden by his black hair. It barely showed against his tanned skin.

Chapter Thirty-One
My Life For Yours

"I... wait, what? Let me see. You have something, too." I stumbled over to a pool of water in a fallen tree's trunk, and kneeled to peer at my reflection. On my neck blazed a strange symbol, red and flaming against my skin. *I thought it was a bug bite.*

"It's the same one you have." I spun on my knees to look at him. "Did the prince do this? What is this? I don't recognize the symbol." A rising panic began to swallow me. *Could the prince catch me with this? It's obviously magical in origin. What does it mean?*

Ramiren rubbed his throat. "No. Your prince did not do this. But I know who did."

I stood up, mouth agape. "Who?"

Ramiren looked down, almost ashamed, and rubbed his forehead then ran a hand through his hair. "That's the sigil of the archdevil Vrakus. The one I bargained with for the ability to whistle myself out of danger. Though I do not know why you are marked with it. Perhaps, because... ah, fuck!"

"What? What, Ramiren?" I stood, taking a few steps toward him. *Oh, don't hold back on me now.* The impatience in my raised voice couldn't be tamped down. "What were the terms of your pact with him?"

His furious expression suddenly shuttered. "That's not something I can disclose-"

My hands balled into tight fists at my sides, and my jaw clenched so hard my teeth hurt. My patience, once again, shattered. "Damn it to the Dark Drop, Ramiren! Enough with your secrets! Tell me!"

Ramiren almost imperceptibly winced at my outburst. For once, he was not smiling. "I cannot disclose the terms, else I break it."

My anger at his reticence mixed with my panic over the sigil and my heartache over his leaving as I spat out, "I have a mark on my neck. You know what it means, and you are not telling me. Whatever happened to *your secrets will never harm me*?" My eyes suddenly burned with unshed tears.

Ramiren's voice, normally even and calm, raised in volume to match my own. "It's not that, Nathalia. *Please*! If I tell you, it is not dissolved. It is *broken*. There is a difference! Remember what I told you about the consequences of breaking a pact?" Fear and frustration twisted his face as he steepled both hands together in front of him, as though praying to me that I'd understand.

I asked quietly, "Who bears the cost?"

His shoulders deflated. "Me. *I* would bear the cost. It would be I who broke it."

Unless...

"Unless you have another pact allowing another to take the burden."

"*Gods-damn it*, Nathalia!" Ramiren turned away from me, throwing up his hands in frustration.

"I *must* know, Ramiren. *I must know.* If I am to die anyway, because gods know what this sigil means, I would rather know the reason why." I didn't care that I was begging.

"I can't let you-"

My hands stretched toward him. "Ramiren, taking the burdens of another, that is something I trained my whole life for. Please let me do this."

Ramiren turned back to stare at me, his face a mask. He swallowed hard. "That is not something that is going to happen, Nathalia." He bowed his head and closed his eyes tightly. "But you're right. Because your life is in danger, I have to tell you. The terms with Vrakus were my fault, so I'll bear the burden myself."

My heart went into my throat. *Would he be flayed for telling me? Killed? I can't let that happen.* But before I could stop him, he threw my world into chaos.

"The pact between myself and Vrakus had addendums, written with a special ink that is invisible but still binding on the parchment. I didn't know of the ink's existence until it was too late. *That* is why I never deal with devils. Not anymore, anyway." He tugged his hands through his hair again, the strands beginning to stand up.

"The addendums stated if I used the ability to whistle myself out of danger, I would be brought to him. Hunted. Out of the frying pan and into the fire, as it were. He'd leave me alone unless I used the ability, believing if I used it then I obviously wanted his company. *That's* why I wasn't in a hurry to get my ability to whistle back from the mischief hag. She had that vial of mine for *twenty years*." He let out a derisive laugh. "Frankly, I was *glad* to no longer have the temptation." He paused, and his eyes darted around, as though waiting for something. When nothing happened, he seemed to relax.

My question came out as a whisper. "And what will this Vrakus do if he catches you?"

Ramiren's mouth became a thin line. The haunted look he gave me was all I needed to know.

He did that? For me?

Realization hit me like a ton of bricks. "I have the sigil as well because we both, in essence, used it."

Ramiren sighed. "Vrakus has been waiting very patiently for me to use the boon. He will come for me, for us, for whistling away from danger and now for disclosing the pact's details. I don't seem to have suffered any immediate effects, but that doesn't mean I won't."

I frowned. "Let him try."

"Oh, he will try. Have no doubt about that, Nathalia. He will try and most likely succeed."

My hands went to the top of my head as I reeled at the gravity of the situation. Then, it struck me. "Wait. Hold on. Did you want to go separate ways because you knew you were going to be hunted by this Vrakus?"

Ramiren tongued his cheek. "That was my plan, yes. I didn't realize you too had the mark."

My hands fell limp at my side. "You were going to run off without me so I wouldn't be in the fire with you?"

His response was almost too soft to hear. "Yes."

"Oh, for the love of Horyn, Ramiren!" I kicked a branch and leaned forward with my hands on my knees and huffed with a frustrated growl.

He needed me, now more than ever. The desperate compulsion to protect him, shield him, defend him from this Vrakus was almost too much to bear. *He is my charge. Always has been, I just didn't see it. Until now.*

I straightened and unsheathed my sword. Ramiren watched me, confusion marring his face, as I approached and stuck the point down into the ground to kneel in front of him. The cold, sodden ground soaked into my trousers, but I can't care.

"I, Nathalia Maxliana Swordhand-"

"Nathalia, what are you-"

My eyes shot up to his. "Shh! I've waited *decades* for this. Don't interrupt."

Ramiren's teeth clicked closed as he stared down at me.

I closed my eyes, remembering the words I'd repeated in my head a thousand times before. "I, Nathalia Maxliana Swordhand, Lady of Camlynn, Protector Initiate for the Church of Horyn, do swear and abide by the terms of this oath for all the rest of my days, be they many or few. This oath I take in the service of Ramiren..." I frowned and looked up at him. "What's your last name?"

Ramiren swallowed hard. His answer came out as a strained whisper, "Orasti."

"...This oath I take in the service of Ramiren Orasti. I swear to guard you from all dangers. I swear to guide you toward all good ends. I swear to be a sword at your front, and a shield at your back. Your light when it is darkest. Your hope when there is none. My life for yours. Do you accept me as a Protector Advocate, Ramiren Orasti, or do you decline?"

When he remained silent, I spoke again, "You have to actually say *I accept your service.*" The juxtaposition made me smile, remembering a similar conversation, flip-flopped, had happened what felt like eons ago when I initially accepted our pact.

His jaw bunched. At this height, I could clearly see his tightly-fisted hands, the knuckles nearly white. Slowly, those hands relaxed, and I looked back up at his face as he said, "I accept your service."

I felt something unfurl from my back. It was a strange sensation, like air twisting and rolling over me. I glanced over my shoulder to see two golden spectral wings, feathered but incorporeal, jutting out. *My wings. They manifested.*

More, different sensations budded as my oath took hold: the bond between us locking into place. My senses sharpened. I inhaled deeply and could smell the damp of the ground beneath my soaked trousers, decaying leaves, and other forest detritus. The near-soundless scurrying of a small animal off to my right caught my ears. Colors became more vivid. Taste and touch seemed the same, but I hoped wine tasted better, at least.

When I finally looked back at my new charge, he was not smiling. His eyes had welled up. His gaze brushed over my newly-sprouted wings before finally locking his eyes with mine. He said quietly, "You said your charge was going to be your husband, angel."

I smiled sadly at him. "You need me more."

And I need you alive.

Prince Jaylin tore open the folded envelope that had just been delivered by a messenger falcon and read the two words on it.

They left.

He crumpled the envelope and viciously cursed under his breath, throwing the parchment across the room. The messenger falcon screeched and flew back out the open window.

Jaylin approached the Ivory Grove on foot, looking around the sacred space with a perpetual frown on his face.

He jumped at the soft, feminine voice behind him. "You're too late. They watched until you had left the area before she and that broodling came out of the forest. I'm not sure why you bothered to pursue them. The damage had already been done."

Jaylin turned to face the fey woman, the twisted, gnarled staff in her hands. "If your orb worked without its mate, I could've known where she was hiding." His frown deepened. "Why did you let her go?"

Leraska's frown mirrored his, and she hissed. "Because we cannot force the ring on her finger. She had to willingly take it with an open heart, or the magic does not work properly. I told you! You knew this! You trying to trap her in the Great Hall would have had severe consequences." She huffed a long-suffering sigh, shaking her head in resignation. "It's no matter. We'll find another way." Leraska walked into the cottage. Jaylin followed close behind.

"I should've just given her the ring instead of that necklace. Or when I proposed."

Leraska frowned in disappointment. "Laethi don't give engagement rings, Jaylin. Something about it being bad luck. She likely would have refused it."

He scoffed. "Then, this is your fault. You said she would stay, Mother. But no, she ran."

Leraska threw a pointed stare toward her son. "That was the point of isolating her, Jaylin. That's exactly what I was trying to avoid! Besides, you're the one who let her off the hook when she thanked you."

Jaylin spoke through gritted teeth, "I was *trying* to create a rapport. Warm, fuzzy feelings. All of that bullshit women like."

Leraska rolled her eyes. "Yet, she still ran, despite all those *warm and fuzzy feelings*. It's no matter now, as I said. The ring did not work. We'll have to adjust our plans to get the other sphere from her thieving parents." She tossed a hand in the air and headed over to the purring fey dragon perched in the corner. She smiled and rubbed under its chin, then slowly turned to face her son. "Perhaps it's time we went on the offensive. An idea has come. Marshal the garrisons."

Acknowledgements

It takes a village to raise a child, and this book was a big, bawling baby with colic and no gas drops in sight.

Kinda.

Whatever. You get the idea.

First, to my husband Josh, who read this book to check for grammar, spelling, and where the hands were at all times. I love you!

To my father, who instilled a love of literature and fantasy in me.

To my mother, who taught me to always go out and get what I want.

I love you both, and I hope neither of you buy this book.

To Jenna, see: Dedication.

To my ARC readers, Amanda, Gabby, Courtney, Ellee, Bee, Rosemary, Hannah, Ilia, Tiffany, Erin, Jamie, Meranie, Melissa, Ariel, Hillary, Quarla, Robert, and Lindsay. You are very much appreciated.

To the writers and content creators on Facebook and TikTok. I am as technologically savvy as a medieval peasant, so your help, guidance, and suggestions were invaluable.

To those who picked up this book and decided to give it a shot. If I gave you even a moment of joy, amusement, titillation, or heartache, then fighting with said technology will have been worth it.

And, finally, to Inspiration. May you always feel welcome in my home. Just ignore the dogs. They bark a lot, but they don't bite.

www.ingramcontent.com/pod-product-compliance
Lightning Source LLC
Chambersburg PA
CBHW071751110726
47908CB00006B/1766